The Kollwitz Calamities

THE KOLLWITZ CALAMITIES

A MEGAN CRESPI MYSTERY SERIES NOVEL

ALESSANDRA COMINI

SUNSTONE
PRESS

SANTA FE

This book is a work of fiction.
Names, characters, places, and incidents are either the product of the author's
imagination or used fictionally. Any resemblance to actual events or
locales or persons, living or dead, is entirely coincidental.

Sunstone books may be purchased for educational, business, or sales promotional use.
For information please write: Special Markets Department, Sunstone Press,
P.O. Box 2321, Santa Fe, New Mexico 87504-2321.

Book and cover design › Vicki Ahl
Body typeface › Minion Pro
Printed on acid-free paper
∞
eBook 978-1-61139-497-9

Library of Congress Cataloging-in-Publication Data

Names: Comini, Alessandra, author.
Title: The Kollwitz calamities : a Megan Crespi mystery series novel / by
    Alessandra Comini.
Description: Santa Fe : Sunstone Press, 2017.
Identifiers: LCCN 2016046714 (print) | LCCN 2016056002 (ebook) | ISBN
    9781632931573 (softcover : alk. paper) | ISBN 9781611394979
Subjects: LCSH: Women art historians--Fiction. | Art
    thefts--Investigation--Fiction. | Murder--Investigation--Fiction. | GSAFD:
    Mystery fiction.
Classification: LCC PS3603.O477 K66 2017 (print) | LCC PS3603.O477 (ebook) |
    DDC 813/.6--dc23
LC record available at https://lccn.loc.gov/2016046714

SUNSTONE PRESS IS COMMITTED TO MINIMIZING OUR ENVIRONMENTAL IMPACT ON THE PLANET. THE PAPER USED IN THIS BOOK IS FROM
RESPONSIBLY MANAGED FORESTS. OUR PRINTER HAS RECEIVED CHAIN OF CUSTODY (COC) CERTIFICATION FROM: THE FOREST STEWARDSHIP
COUNCIL™ (FSC®), PROGRAMME FOR THE ENDORSEMENT OF FOREST CERTIFICATION™ (PEFC™), AND THE SUSTAINABLE FORESTRY INITIATIVE® (SFI®).
THE FSC® COUNCIL IS A NON-PROFIT ORGANIZATION, PROMOTING THE ENVIRONMENTALLY APPROPRIATE, SOCIALLY BENEFICIAL AND
ECONOMICALLY VIABLE MANAGEMENT OF THE WORLD'S FORESTS. FSC® CERTIFICATION IS RECOGNIZED INTERNATIONALLY AS A
RIGOROUS ENVIRONMENTAL AND SOCIAL STANDARD FOR RESPONSIBLE FOREST MANAGEMENT.

WWW.SUNSTONEPRESS.COM

SUNSTONE PRESS / POST OFFICE BOX 2321 / SANTA FE, NM 87504-2321 /USA
(505) 988-4418 / ORDERS ONLY (800) 243-5644 / FAX (505) 988-1025

To Horst Uhr,
beloved former student,
wiser and older than I by eleven months

List of Major Characters

Megan Crespi: retired art history professor, specializes in solving international art crimes

Dee Whally: Crespi's friend, in Germany to research her maiden name, Totebusch

Dr. Laura Forelle: director of the Käthe Kollwitz Museum in Cologne

Detective Herbert Schauen: Cologne arts crime investigator

Dr. Grete Bulliet: new director of the Käthe Kollwitz Museum in Berlin

Dr. Abraham Rückgabe: founder of a specialty clinic in Berlin's Wedding district and possessor of a trove of old journals

Reinhold Fromm: unscrupulous CEO and founder of the Dorotek factory on the German island of Rügen

Dr. Iliana Frankel: consulting physician at Dorotek, lives in Berlin's Prenzlauer Berg district

Wilhelm Schlau: Dorotek's company lawyer

Ferdinand Fehler: Dorotek's chief engineer

Mahdi Kartal: Dorotek factory worker

Yusri Pahlavi: youngest son of the late Shah of Iran

Farah Pahlavi: third wife of the late Shah of Iran and mother of Yusri Pahlavi

Wafiyy: employee of Yusri Pahlavi

Akram al-Aljamie: only son of famous Iraqi archaeologist Dief al-Aljamie, studying sculpture in Berlin

Monika von Putbus: descendant of the Putbus family of Rügen, also a sculpture student in Berlin

Dr. Slootmaekers: Vladslo Cemetery administrator

Kadeem Tawfeek: Muslim Turk living in Berlin's Wedding district

Jarir Uthman: Muslim Turk employed by Kadeem Tawfeek

Marie Schmidt: mysterious fanatical collector of Kollwitz graphics, lives in Moritzburg

Lukas Zamann: owner of Galerie Zamann in Berlin

Rolf von Putbus: estranged cousin of Monika von Putbus

Siegfried Schocken: major collector of Kollwitz, lives in Weimar

Aisha Saqqaf: hijab-wearing Iraqi, posted to Berlin by Dief al-Aljamie

Officer Anton Reininger: investigator with the Berlin-Wedding police

Hamzah el-Hashem: agent of Dief al-Aljamie, posted to Berlin

Karl Schneider: Nordhausen police chief

1

The two monumental statues by Käthe Kollwitz were gone.

"But this can't be! It's impossible!"

Stunned cemetery gravediggers stood where the larger-than-life statues had been just the night before. Even the granite pedestals were gone. Only wear stains on the cement support tiles remained of the German sculptor's powerful *Grieving Mother* and *Grieving Father*.

Silent stone mourners for those fallen in World War I, the two kneeling figures had had an intensely personal meaning for the artist. Her eighteen-year-old son Peter was killed on Flanders fields in the third month of the senseless war that devastated Europe for four years.

It took Kollwitz almost two decades to visualize and bring to final fruition the figures carved in Belgian granite that bore the abstracted features of her husband Karl and herself. The two kneeling parents had overlooked the mass graves of some 25,644 soldiers buried in the German Soldiers Cemetery by Vladslo near the small town of Diksmuide in Belgium.

The tall, dense hedge behind the statues had been knocked down and run over. Deep ruts in the ground showed that two large and very heavy vehicles had approached within a few feet of the artworks. What must have been an hydraulically powered crane on a boom truck had raised the two heavy loads up and onto the lift gate of some sort of cargo van and carted inside. The telltale double sets of tracks led away from the cemetery and out to the main road that backed it. It was impossible to tell which direction the vehicles had taken.

On the scene within minutes of being called, the local police fanned out over the carefully tended cemetery grounds looking for anything that might figure in the baffling theft. None of the mass graves had been disturbed. Nor had their flat markers, each bearing twenty names, ranks, and dates of death. The name Peter Kollwitz was on one of those markers. All cemetery personnel were questioned, repeatedly, but to no avail. Those off duty were summoned to the site. There had never been the need for a night watchman or for video camera surveillance. There were simply no clues.

What could the motive have been for such an unlikely theft?

2

Retired professor of art history Megan Crespi was sitting in the office of her colleague and friend Dr. Laura Forelle, director of the Käthe Kollwitz Museum in Cologne. The two women were similar in appearance. Crespi was five-foot-four, with short brown hair and inquisitive, sparkling brown eyes. Forelle was of about the same height but slimmer and much younger than Megan. Her brown hair fell in thick tight curls about her face, framing intelligent blue eyes which often had a thoughtful expression.

The two women had been discussing Megan's planned itinerary across northern Germany, beginning in Berlin, where she was scheduled to give a lecture on Kollwitz. After that she would be heading toward the famed island of Rügen off the Pomeranian Coast in the Baltic Sea.

"You are going there because of Caspar David Friedrich, I presume, Megan?"

"Exactly, Laura. Friedrich was such a compelling artist. I used to devote a whole lecture to him when I was teaching Romanticism in early nineteenth-century German art. The students adored his somber land-and-seascapes. I've gone to Rügen just once, decades ago, to photograph his favorite view of the island's spectacular chalk cliffs. Can't wait to go back there, though I may not be as athletic a climber as I once was," smiled Megan wanly.

Still sprightly and active at the age of eighty, due to the strenuous daily exercise routine she maintained, Megan and her fellow American traveler, Dee Whally, were in Germany to follow the itinerary of Dee's brother Bun who, as a soldier during World War II, had been assigned graves registration duty. His stories concerning unexpected finds and bitter family feuds had fascinated Dee for decades, and now that he had passed away, this was a way to feel close to him again.

Megan had agreed to the itinerary as long as they could end up visiting both Rügen island and the nearby city of Greifswald, Friedrich's hometown. This had pleased Dee because she also wished to research her maiden name, Totebusch. She knew that it was North German, and hoped to explore some cemeteries in Greifswald. Dee, with white hair and wise blue eyes, was a few years older than Megan and, after hip replacement surgery, was not an enthusiastic walker, so she was doubly grateful that Megan had volunteered to do the cemetery rounds with her.

They had planned to begin with the quiet Central Cemetery in Berlin's borough of Friedrichfelde, of additional interest to Megan because Käthe Kollwitz was buried there. Megan loved to show her classes the photograph she had taken of the somber family tombstone. The gravesite was marked by a poignant bronze relief the artist had designed a decade before her death, in 1945. It showed her face in peaceful sleep, framed within two large hands. In closing her class lecture on Kollwitz, Megan always showed that tombstone next to the artist's lithograph of a defiant man with raised right hand titled *Nie wieder Krieg—Never again War.*

Once, as students poured out of the auditorium where Megan had taught for so many years, a former student came up to her and said, smiling triumphantly, "I know who you taught about today—Kollwitz."

"Yes, I did, but how did you know?" Megan had replied, mystified.

"Because everybody's wiping away tears."

The abrupt sound of the director's phone ringing brought Megan back to the present. She saw Laura Forelle's face grow pale.

"What? Impossible! Can you repeat that?"

Megan looked concernedly at her friend who had become so agitated she had begun pacing the room.

"Yes, yes, I understand. I shall notify the police and the press immediately. Yes. You were right to call me."

Laura turned on her heel, hung up, and looked at Megan who was seated in the chair facing her, a quizzical expression on her face.

"*The Kollwitz statues in Belgium have been stolen!*"

Now it was Megan's turn to maintain that such a thing was impossible.

"Well, that's what I thought too," Laura said in frustration. "But it has happened. *Both* statues. Gone. Even their plinths."

"Good lord! Who called you about this, the Belgian police?"

"No, it was the cemetery administrator, Slootmaekers. He knew about the Kollwitz Museum here in Cologne and wanted to let us know. Hoped we might be able to help somehow. He asked if we knew of anyone who would covet the two statues. What could I say? Any serious collector of Kollwitz would not mind having her two most famous sculptures in their possession, but of course no one we know about is so crazy—and there are definitely some crazies out there—as to *steal* such famous objects."

"And such *heavy* objects." Megan added.

Laura called Cologne's central police office and was immediately put in touch with the arts crime investigator, a Detective Herbert Schauen. He asked if he could visit Laura in her office to obtain some idea of the art involved in the theft. They made an appointment for later that afternoon.

"How can he *not* know what the two statues look like? My god, we have copies of them right here in our own Cologne war memorial!"

"The ones in the ruins of the church that was destroyed by bombs in World War II? Where only pillars and the vestibule remain?"

"Yes. The Ruine Alt St. Alban."

"Oh, of course, that's the name. I know just where it is here in the city. But the only way I was able to see and photograph the statues was through the bars of an iron grill that completely spans an open archway. I guess if you're on a tour they let you inside from somewhere."

Laura was already online looking up the contact numbers for local television channels and newspapers. She phoned the television channels first and found herself immediately barraged with demands to be interviewed in her museum against a background of Kollwitz works.

"*Ach, Gott,* what am I letting myself in for?" she sighed.

"But it's really important that you do so; spread the word and fast."

"You're right, of course. I'd better call *Der Spiegel* and the *Berliner Morgenpost* as well."

"While you do that, I'll call my friend Dee and explain why I'm late meeting her at our hotel." Megan pulled out her iPhone and discreetly walked to the far end of Laura's office, where she dialed her Altera Pars Hotel room and updated her friend. Dee was glad to have the extra time before lunch and told Megan there was no need to hurry on her account.

"Now I better call the directors of the two other Kollwitz museums." Laura picked up her phone. Megan listened, nodding her head, as Laura phoned the Berlin Kollwitz Museum and spoke to its new director Grete Bulliet, who was as astonished as they were.

"I better notify the police," she said.

"That would be wise. Although it's hard to imagine any of your Kollwitz sculptures being stolen from off the fourth floor there," Laura almost laughed.

"*Ja*, it was hard enough getting them up there in the first place. Listen. Would you like me to inform the Moritzburg people?" Grete was referring to Kollwitz's last residence, now a "Kollwitz Memorial House," with a few works lent to it from the Cologne Kollwitz Museum.

"The Kollwitz House there has such a small staff, you never know who is filling in for whom," she added. "It would be good for the director, Celine Gränisch, to know."

"Oh, yes, I'd be grateful if you would do that. And you might let the local Moritzburg police know as well, just in case the thief has his eye on all three Kollwitz sites."

After another minute Laura hung up and collapsed into the chair behind her desk, her fingers clasped behind her head. Then she looked keenly at Megan. A thought was forming in her mind.

"Megan. How would you and your friend like to make a little side excursion to Belgium before heading off to Berlin?"

"To *Belgium*? You mean, I think, to the German Soldiers Cemetery by Vladslo?"

"Yes, the Vladslo Cemetery."

"But you told me the local police have searched it and found nothing."

"That's just why I think it's important that *you* go there. Look what happened when you went to Vienna to help solve that curious Gustav Klimt theft, and the strange Egon Schiele happenings that led to the discovery of unknown portraits by him. And your solution of the crazy Oskar Kokoschka capers concerning his self-portrait with Alma Mahler."

"Yes, good things happened, but most of them were by simple stubbornness and chance," said Megan modestly, although in her inner soul of souls she was proud of the fact that an art historian who lived in Dallas, Texas had been able help solve three distinct sets of crimes concerning artists on whom she had published. And her expertise on Edvard Munch had recently taken her to Norway where again, mostly by chance, she had been instrumental in solving several crimes related to the artist.

"So?" Laura looked meaningfully at Megan.

"So what?"

"So you have a certain knack where art thefts and hidden troves are concerned. Maybe it's because you are American and *see* things differently from our police and art experts over here, but you have had phenomenal success. And to think. You're from Texas!"

"Now, wait a minute, hold on, Laura. I live there now, and taught there too for thirty-one years, but I also taught at Columbia University for ten years and lived in New York for a number of years after I graduated from Barnard College there. My father was Italian, so after the war we often went to Italy to see my grandparents in Milan when I was growing up. I lived in Vienna during the Hungarian Revolution, back in nineteen-fifty-six, and for a number of years I lived in San Francisco where I was a folk singer and while I was getting my master's at Berkeley. So I've had a rather full life outside the boundaries of the state of Texas." Surprised by her own sudden outburst, Megan came to an abrupt halt.

"Of course, of course," soothed Laura. "From your accent one would never know where exactly you come from in America. And in German, after all, you sound Viennese. Or possibly Italian."

Megan discontinued her rant and smiled. She considered that a compliment. And she was beginning to warm to the idea of a Belgian detour. It had been years since she had communed with that eccentric contemporary of Kollwitz, the Belgian artist James Ensor. The small four-story building he had inherited, where he lived alone above a souvenir shop, was preserved as a house/museum.

Megan consulted Google on her iPhone while Laura was busy with another phone call. She found that Ensor's town, Ostend on the coast, was not far at all from inland Diksmuide, the city nearest the Vladslo Cemetery. In fact Ostend was directly north of the cemetery from which the Kollwitz statues had been stolen. So the side trip to Belgium would make sense. And it would be fascinating to visit Vladslo Cemetery, where she had never been, and attempt to assess what had happened there. Now all she had to do was convince Dee about taking a slight detour west before heading east for Berlin.

Laura had hung up and was eyeing Megan with amusement. She could almost see her mind at work balancing pros and cons.

"Well?"

"All right, yes. I think I can manage a trip to Vladslo Cemetery before returning to Germany and points east."

"That's wonderful, Megan. I have no doubt that you will find or think of something significant."

"Hm. That's for you to know then and me to find out?"

"You could put it that way, I suppose."

Megan smiled and turned to go.

"Oh, one last thing, Megan." Curiosity animated Laura's features.

"Yes?"

"Was your mother Italian also?"

"No. She was a Laird, of Scotch-Irish descent, and grew up in Minnesota. And she also went to Barnard College."

"Well, then how did she meet your father?"

"On the island of Ibiza."

"Ibiza off Spain?"

"Yes. Back in the thirties it was quite the meeting place for ex-patriots."

"So you were born there?"

"No. A few weeks before I was due they went to my mother's hometown, Winona, Minnesota, so I would be an American citizen."

"And that's where you grew up then. No wonder you don't have a Texas accent."

"No, that's still not the reason," Megan said, smiling. "My parents went right back to Spain after I was born, only this time to Barcelona, not Ibiza. That's where I began growing up, but then Franco came when I was two and we fled to Milan. But then Mussolini burst upon the scene and we fled, once again, this time to America. My father hated the cold of Minnesota, however, so when a copy of *The New Yorker* magazine featured an ad saying: 'Tired of the cold? Come to Dallas,' we did. End of long story."

"Not long enough!"

"Well, if you truly want to know more I'll send you a copy of my memoir, *In Passionate Pursuit*. It begins with my discovery of Schiele's prison cell back in nineteen-sixty-three—something, oddly enough, no Austrian scholar had ever thought of looking for."

"But don't you see, Megan, that's *exactly* why I urge you to go to the Kollwitz cemetery. You Americans tend to see and approach things differently."

"Ha! Perhaps. It's quite a long shot, but I'll certainly give it a try."

Laura's blue eyes sparkled with pleasure as she saw her interesting colleague to the door.

3

Famed Berlin-born surgeon Dr. Abraham Rückgabe had two passions. One was his clinic, perhaps the most successful clinic in private hands in the city. The other was the intriguing collection of diaries he had inherited from his grandmother.

The clinic was known by its initials only, WGI, but all Berlin knew what those initials stood for: *Wiederherstellung Genitaler Integrität*—Restoration of Genital Integrity. Dr. Rückgabe had been circumcised within hours of being born: his family had not questioned the centuries-old custom for Jews. Nor had he as an adolescent. It was only after he began the study of medicine that he started to wonder about the practice of infant circumcision.

Wondered about the possible diminution of sexual pleasure without a foreskin. Wondered about the importance of the foreskin in providing the slack tissue needed to accommodate an erection.

At some point he read the Jewish psychiatrist Wilhelm Reich on the subject and *felt* his outrage:

> Take that poor penis. Take a knife—right? And start cutting. And everybody says, it doesn't hurt. They say that the sheaths of the nerve are not yet developed. Therefore, the child doesn't feel a thing. Now, that's murder!

When Rückgabe became aware of the fact that circumcision was also part of the Muslim faith, and that Shiites and Sunnis considered it a duty, he was spurred to action. He would open a clinic to reconstruct the foreskin in those who had undergone neonatal circumcision and wished to reverse what had been done to them. And he would locate his clinic in one of the Berlin districts most heavily populated by the city's tens of thousands of Turkish immigrants, Wedding.

Almost overnight the clinic had been a success. Rückgabe was surprised, then gratified. Word of the existence of his clinic spread quickly. Soon Muslims of Turkish origin were coming to the WGI. And other Muslim immigrants as well: men and boys from Bosnia-Herzegovina, Libya, Syria, Kuwait, and Lebanon. And of course Jewish clients. Rückgabe's humane approach and success in treating patients made him something of a local hero.

The bearded physician's other passion was reading and rereading the poignant diaries his grandmother Lina had preserved from the ruins of an apartment house at Weissenburger Strasse 25 during the World War II bombing of Berlin on November 23 of 1943. Lina had been for a number of decades the live-in housekeeper for a doctor's family who lived in the third-floor, four-room apartment of a corner building facing the busy square then known as Wörther Platz. The elderly widow, who continued to live there after her husband passed away in 1940, had finally fled the bombings only four months before her home was destroyed and Lina did not know how to contact her. But she recognized her employer's handwriting in the thirty-six black oilcloth journals she found in an undamaged metal trunk and took them home with her. She gave the diaries to her favorite grandson Abraham on the occasion of his graduation from medical school. The journals covered the years of 1908 to August of 1943 and were those of Käthe Kollwitz.

4

On Caspar David Friedrich's favorite island of Rügen off the Pomeranian coast on the Baltic Sea an urgent meeting was taking place. Reinhold Fromm, CEO and founder of Dorotek, Germany's largest manufacturer of thermoformed components made of plastic, was in heated discussion with his company's physician, Dr. Iliana Frankel, his company lawyer, Wilhelm Schlau, and his chief engineer, Ferdinand Fehler.

"*But what you tell me is all wrong. I do not accept this!*" Fromm, a short, grossly overweight man in his early sixties with unruly black hair and black eyes, stared at the tall, slender brunette in front of him who emanated such authority and calm.

"I thought so too," she said, her beautiful face serious and without expression. Originally from Vienna, her musical intonation with its long vowels had been one of the peripheral reasons Fromm had hired her. Another reason was that, with her willowy figure, dark hair and stern eyes, she reminded him of one of the dominatrix figures in his private art collection of erotica.

"But now," Dr. Frankel continued, "all the evidence has been evaluated and it corroborates what we at first treated as anecdotal evidence in cases of lung cancer at your factory. The truth is your workers here at Prora have been exposed to occupational, life-threatening asbestos."

They were talking about the colossal beachfront complex Adolf Hitler had built on Rügen in 1936 to house some 20,000 vacationing workers. This was the Führer's reward to those who joined his organization *Kraft durch*

Freude—Strength Through Joy. The stark row of literally one continuous cream-colored building stretched for some three miles along the island's east coast, and during 1944 refugees from the bombing of Hamburg had lived there. Under Communist rule Prora was used off and on by the East German army, but by 1993 the austere, deserted complex was put up for sale and Reinhold Fromm had been quick to acquire it. Away from big city inspection routines, Prora was ideal for the kind of plastic component production that had built his fortune. Soon he was able to expand to rubber suspension, hose technology, and metal reclamation. Ten years later he had doubled his workforce and in the second decade of the new century he increased it once again. Now he had 3,000 employees working for him, all at minimum wages, as many of the workers were Turkish migrants and their offspring. Business could not be better. And profits were enormous.

But now, from out of nowhere, Fromm's corporate lawyer had informed him that Dorotek was named in twelve lawsuits claiming asbestos poisoning by men who had worked at Prora years ago. Four of them had actually died from asbestosis. And a thirteenth lawsuit had just been filed by the widow of one of Fromm's former employees. She maintained that during his final years at the factory her husband suffered from asbestosis. Last year he developed signs of malignant mesothelioma and died two months ago of cancer of the pleura.

"Exactly what the hell *is* mesothelioma anyway?" Fromm asked Dr. Frankel in exasperation.

"It is a cancer brought on by exposure to asbestos. It attacks the thin membranes lining the abdomen and chest. This is known as the pleural type, but the cancer can also form around the lining of the abdomen or heart."

"But why *now*? Why are we only getting complaints *now*?"

"Because first symptoms of the disease don't necessarily appear until as long as twenty, thirty, even forty years after asbestos exposure."

"What exposure? I was told when I converted the Prora complex into a factory that any asbestos presence was at a safe level and..."

"There *is* no 'safe level' of exposure to asbestos," interrupted Dr. Frankel adamantly.

"Asbestos is a very friable material. And according to the degree of binding and disturbance, microscopic fibers are released into the air which, when they are breathed in, can get into the lungs. The fibers are not soluble so they can remain there for many years and cause scarring. Also inflammation. Both can affect breathing. And smokers are fifty times more likely to develop lung cancer than nonsmokers."

"Ah ha! So maybe we can prove all thirteen cases involve men who were heavy smokers? That they had lung cancer from smoking, not from asbestos?" Fromm looked at his tall, thin lawyer hopefully.

"Yes, perhaps. That is a possible avenue of pursuit, Herr Fromm. But I have to be blunt: unless we can demonstrate that there was and is *no* asbestos in your building complex our chances of beating these lawsuits are pretty slight. Grim, in fact."

Fromm looked at his engineer accusingly. "*You* were in charge when we converted the buildings."

Ferdinand Fehler held his employer's gaze: "And *you* are the one who instructed me to keep costs down and proceed with all possible haste."

"Yes, and you did both. But you did not inform me that there was *asbestos* to deal with."

"Well, there was. In the cement foundations, lining the heating pipes, the electrical wiring..."

"*I don't want to hear this!*" Fromm interrupted. He looked helplessly over at Dr. Frankel.

Fehler continued. "Do you remember when we first took over I asked you if we could refit with fiberglass. You said that was out of the question, to keep all costs down."

"Ha! Of course! And I also remember that the first thing you wanted to do was to tear the buildings down. You told me they would have to be deconstructed piece by piece."

"Yes, that would have been the correct procedure for asbestos-fitted buildings erected in the nineteen-thirties, as yours were."

"I thought they stopped using asbestos in construction early in the last century," Fromm blustered.

"Listen," Dr. Frankel said earnestly. "Asbestos was in use during most of the twentieth century. Most dramatic example of that? They say more than one thousand tons of asbestos were released into the air during the destruction of New York's World Trade Center on nine-eleven."

"Well, who knows *what* stuff the *Americans* have been using for building materials. It can't be that bad over here," Fromm said.

"I'm afraid it has been," Fehler caught his employer's gaze and held it.

"Now let's see here, Doctor Frankel," said Fromm finally, turning to the serious woman who was looking at him with what he sensed was disapproval. He continued unfazed.

"You have been with Dorotek for what is it now, fifteen years?"

"Twelve," corrected Frankel, sensing what might be coming next.

"So you have not been in direct contact with any of the men who are suing me now, I don't suppose?"

"No, I don't believe so."

"But, nevertheless, I think Dorotek has the right to our own medical examination of the surviving men involved. And you could do that now, Doktor Frankel. Prove that they were all heavy smokers."

"I could not do that even if I wanted to, Herr Fromm, as my professional connection with Dorotek means recusing myself as regards medical examination of any of your past workers who are now in litigation against Dorotek."

"In other words you might be accused as being prejudiced in favor of my company?"

"I would not be, personally, but the law would justifiably see it that way," Frankel said, astonished at the man's bluster and apparent lack of legal savvy.

"Quite so," nodded the lawyer in the room.

"Okay," said Fromm, slowly placing a cigar into his thick pursed lips. It was a Gurkha Signature 1887. "Okay, so I will find some other way to *prove* these men were all heavy smokers. I have my means and I'll get right on it."

All three employees in the room raised their eyebrows. They also realized, as a sour oaky smell filled the room, they had just been dismissed.

As she walked toward the nearby Prora train station that gave onto the Dorotek factory grounds, Iliana Frankel was picturing to herself one of the patients she had examined just last week in her role of onsite physician to the company's employees. Although she lived in the Prenslauer Berg section of Berlin, Iliana commuted five days a week to Rügen. She loved her job there and was devoted to her patients. They in turn adored the gentle doctor who showed such interest and concern for them and their families. The three-hour train ride there and back gave her precious time to unwind and read biographies of great musicians as she listened to their music on her discreet Bose earphones.

Frankel's favorite composer was Johannes Brahms and it appealed to her that during the year 1876 he had spent a long time in Rügen's famous old port town of Sassnitz working on the fourth movement of his C minor First Symphony. Music was Iliana's life companion, much more important to her than art, about which she knew very little.

The patient she was thinking of now, Mahdi Kartal, had presented chest pains, shortness of breath, fatigue, and night sweats. He had come in to see her, however, because he was having uncontrollable fits of coughing at work.

"I almost fainted in front of my fellow workers," he admitted, looking at her shyly.

Iliana had tried to put him at ease, but what concerned her, especially after the company engineer's confirmation that the Dorotek factory infrastructure did indeed contain asbestos, was the probability that Mahdi might have asbestosis, rather than the more easily treatable beryllium toxicity she had first suspected. He was Iliana's first patient to show the telltale symptoms of asbestos poisoning. Chest X-rays had confirmed her suspicions: large areas of the lung tissue appeared as very white. This had ignited Iliana's massive research over the weekend on asbestos-related diseases. She was going to have to tell poor Mahdi Kartal. And soon.

As she thought about implications for the future concerning the health of Fromm's hard-worked employees, she stopped dead in her tracks. The sight of tired workers shuffling into and out of the Prora train station looked just like a poignant image she had recently seen in the window of a small Berlin antique shop in her Prenzlauer Berg neighborhood in Berlin. The picture was a rectangular composition in depressing browns and blacks that showed people exiting from a train station into their working-class neighborhood from a shift that has lasted until after dark. The lights in a factory at the left were still burning and in addition to a lone laundress with her heavy load, two other women could be seen emerging with the men from the station door. To the far left a frail, shabbily dressed man was raising his hand to greet one of the workers coming home. How the picture echoed the humble people she saw five days a week.

Iliana felt indignation rise in her as she thought of her employer's willful neglect of safety measures in his factory. She would like to wave that poignant picture in his face.

I really must drop in at that shop this weekend and see if the drawing is still there, Iliana told herself. Three hours later as her train pulled into the majestic Berlin Hauptbahnhof with its stunning multi-glass panels and arches, she thought of the image again as she mingled with the crowds of other tired people returning to Berlin from distant locations. *Yes, I'd really like to own that picture.*

5

In the summer of 1943, finally persuaded by her anxious family to flee the intensified bombing raids over Berlin, seventy-five year-old Käthe Kollwitz reluctantly abandoned her Wörther Platz home of over fifty years. A four-hour trip in a Red Cross truck brought her down south to the small town of Nordhausen on the Zorge River in Thuringia. There Kollwitz stayed in the large country farmhouse generously offered by a fellow sculptor. But when Nordhausen also became the target of air raids, Prince Ernst Heinrich of Saxony offered Germany's venerable artist lodgings at his estate in Moritz-burg near Dresden.

Also at Nordhausen in the summer of 1943 an extermination camp—*Vernichtungslager*—was created by the SS for prisoners too ill or too weak to work on the fabrication of German V2 rockets at nearby Mittelbau-Dora. They were permitted to die, not in a gas chamber, but simply from starvation.

Some three quarters of a century later, the fourth son of the late Shah of Iran, Yusri Pahlavi, completed his three-year construction of an intricate complex on the site of the ruins of Nordhausen's Benedictine monastery. He called it *Jamshad*—shining river—and it was situated on one of the southern slopes of the Harz Mountains, looking down on the Zorge River from a height of some five thousand feet. One of its interconnecting courtyards was open; the other two were roofed over preventing full aerial cognizance of the vast compound and adding to the mystery of why Pahlavi had expended so much time and money on what World War II bomber pilots correctly suspected had been turned into a storage for rockets being produced in the tunnels below. Why indeed had an Arab prince elected to construct a royal residence atop the ruins of a monastery-turned-rocket factory near an extermination camp in the heart of ancient Thuringia?

6

"Which would you rather do first, Dee?" Megan asked early the next morning as she pulled their rented blue Volkswagen Tiguan SUV away from the curb of their cozy Altera Pars Hotel. "Ensor's house in Ostend or Vladslo Cemetery?"

"I have to confess that I'm not all that excited about what, to me at least, is James Ensor's weird work, so my preference would be to go directly to the Kollwitz cemetery. Especially, while the trail is still hot, as they say."

"That's fine with me," Megan said amiably. They were at the top of a narrow street that framed Cologne's imposing cathedral façade and she slowed down to take a farewell look at the immense Gothic structure, once the tallest building in the world. And yet for four centuries after the nave and choir had been built, in 1473, further construction had gradually come to a halt. A giant crane was left in place for the next four hundred years. It was only within the vortex of romantic nationalism sweeping Germany in the nineteenth century that completion of the cathedral and its soaring twin towers took place. Franz Liszt had been involved at the triumphant opening ceremony in 1880.

Megan was familiar with the cathedral's stirring history because she used to devote an entire lecture to it when teaching her nineteenth-century art class at Southern Methodist University. In fact, she was scheduled to be giving it on the morning of the 9/11 attacks in 2001. She had wondered what to do—cancel class as many of her colleagues were electing to do, or hold it anyway.

She was voicing her memories about that difficult day to Dee as they drove out of Cologne's inner city and headed west toward Belgium.

"So what was your decision? Did you cancel class or go ahead and give it?"

"I decided to give it. But first I went to my slide collection—yes, we still used slides in those days—and added two opening images and two closing images to my carousels. So I began with, on the left, a drawing of uncompleted Cologne cathedral as it had looked for centuries with the forlorn crane poised over the nave, and, on the right, a photograph of Manhattan's twin towers standing tall and majestic over the city."

"Ooh, that gives me the shivers. What was your final pair of slides then?"

"Well, the final pair, after recounting the cathedral's building history, showed, on the left, the completed cathedral, and, again on the right, the twin towers as they had looked before the attack. My message was, of course, that the towers could be rebuilt, that we, as a country, could rise again."

"And did some students show up?"

"I'll say! The *entire* class of one hundred and eighty-six were already in their seats when I entered the auditorium, and even some docents from the Meadows Museum came. When I concluded with the first few measures of the 'cathedral' movement of Schumann's Rhenish Symphony not a soul stirred."

"I suppose it constituted the beginning of a healing process."

"Well, that's what I heard from some of the students afterward. Actually, I still hear about that class every now and then via e-mail or Facebook."

"I bet they went right out and bought a CD of the Schumann symphony."

"Perhaps. And one of my favorite students, Mark Craig, an Air Force band member on educational leave, brought my attention to the fact that the symphony's fourth movement, of five by the way, is scored for alto, tenor, and bass trombones. Imagine the resulting orchestral texture!"

Megan turned on the car radio wondering if, by serendipity, a major miracle might have Schumann's symphony playing. No such luck. A lesser miracle was taking place, however. An old-time electronic music band, *Kraftwerk*, was playing a song from the 1970s that was quite appropriate for the E 40 Autobahn they had just entered. The monotonous song was titled *Autobahn* and the words ran: "*Wir fahr'n fahr'n fahr'n auf der Autobahn*"— *We're drivin' drivin' drivin' on the highway.*"

Dee reached over and turned the radio off. "I hope you don't mind," she declared rather than asked.

"I was just about to do that myself," Megan laughed.

As they turned west and continued on E 314 in companionable silence, Dee studied the map she had pulled up on her iPad.

"Where is that *real* map I brought along? The paper one. Every time I try to enlarge this darn Google map of Belgium it either gets far too large or recedes into a tiny square."

"I know exactly what you mean. But with or without a map I figure we'll be reaching Brussels in about two hours. And I suggest we bypass that impossibly busy city which has become the object of such terrible terrorist attacks. We can take its northern ring road for a stretch and then pick up the E 40 again in the direction of Ghent. Unless—unless you'd like to drop down south about twelve miles and visit Waterloo. I once took photos of the reverse sloping there where Wellington so cleverly hid his troops."

"I don't think I'm in any condition to climb down or up any reverse sloping."

"Well, I guess it doesn't really appeal to me either. We'll just stop at Ghent for lunch then, although we could take a peek at the Ghent Altarpiece, if you like."

"I would like that. But I think we should just press on after lunch. You and I have both seen the van Eyck altarpiece in earlier lives, after all. No, I think we should best continue our Kollwitz pilgrimage."

"As usual, Dee, you are right. I always try to pack too much into a day."

As she drove, Megan began to think about the fifteenth-century masterpiece by the two van Eyck brothers, Hubert and Jan. It was a polyptych numbering twelve panels. In 1432 it was the first major European work to have been done in oil, with its capability for fine detail, rather than the customary opaque, egg-based tempera paint. Its more than one hundred particularized figures presented an intricate compendium of Catholic mysticism that over the centuries had inspired admiration, Calvinist indignation, and, unfortunately, greed.

She glanced at Dee then asked dramatically, "Did you know that the Ghent Altarpiece has been the object of *thirteen* thefts over the centuries? Some successful, others botched?"

"What? No. I never heard of that. Wouldn't it be too heavy and too large to steal?"

"You're absolutely right. It weighs over a ton. And it's well over eleven feet in both height and width. Nevertheless, partial *and* total thefts of the heavy oak panels have taken place. One of Napoleon's generals, for starters, brought the four central panels featuring the *Adoration of the Mystic Lamb* back to France as booty. The panels were put on display at the Louvre where they could be seen by an educated public and not by 'serfs.' And they weren't returned until Louis XVIII reclaimed his throne after Napoleon's final defeat."

"What other robberies were there?"

"Ha! The next one was, incredibly, very close to home and just a couple of years later. While the local bishop was out of town, the cathedral's vicar, claiming he was trying to raise money for the bishopric, sold the six wing panels to a dealer who sold them to an English merchant who was then in Berlin. Later the Prussian king acquired them for a museum he was building to outdo the Louvre."

"Golly. Complicated! Didn't the bishop complain?"

"Apparently the money-raising explanation satisfied him. Says something about his appreciation of art, though, doesn't it?"

They had just gotten back onto E 40 after completing the northern ring over Brussels and successfully avoiding city traffic.

"So how long did the panels remain in Germany?" Dee asked, now quite horrified by the idea of important parts of the Ghent Altarpiece languishing in Germany.

"Until the end of World War I. Thanks to the Treaty of Versailles, which made specific reference to them, not only the Ghent Altarpiece panels but thousands of artworks in Germany were returned to their mother countries."

"And that's the end of the story?"

"Not by a kilometer. In nineteen-thirty-four, thieves broke into the cathedral and stole two outer panels on the lower left and lower right, *The Just Judges* and *Saint John the Baptist. The Baptist* one was soon recovered but the *Judges* one seems to be irretrievably lost. They've looked for it everywhere, including X-raying the cathedral floor down to a depth of thirty-two feet. But the *Judges* just seems to have disappeared for keeps."

"What a sad history!"

"I haven't finished yet."

"You mean there's *more?*"

"You bet there is. Guess who coveted the 'Germanic' altarpiece during World War II? Hermann Göring *and* Adolf Hitler! Hermann for his private collection outside Berlin and Adolf for the massive *Führermuseum* of conquest masterpieces he was planning to build in his boyhood town of Linz. You can guess who won that competition."

"Gosh!"

"Then, as the Third Reich began to disintegrate in nineteen-forty-five, the altarpiece was sent to an abandoned Austrian salt mine that had been converted into a storage facility. There it was *salted* away, ha, ha, with several thousand other looted artworks. The SS then wired the mine with dynamite, intending to blow it up should the Allies start to close in."

"This is beginning to sound like something for the monuments men."

"Well, that is exactly what happened in the end. Some brave salt miners disabled the wiring in the nick of time and after the war ended, Allied monuments men were finally informed of the giant trove. The Ghent Altarpiece was returned to Belgium but, as you can imagine, in terrible condition."

"I'm thinking of when my brother was there during that time at the end of the war," said Dee, shaking her head. "He was in graves registration, as you know, so I guess his work didn't take him to looted art sites. But still. Just think of it. That terrible period in European history."

The two women were silent for some time, each with her own thoughts. The ring road over Brussels had proven to be a real time saver and they reached the heart of Ghent even sooner than they had calculated.

Megan headed for Saint Bavo's Cathedral with its tower facade, thinking that if they didn't take time to visit the van Eyck brothers' altarpiece there, they could at least have lunch as close as possible. She found a parking place on a nearby side street and a few minutes later they were seated in the Brasserie Agrea, just a few hundred steps from the cathedral.

"What are you in the mood for?" Dee asked Megan as they studied the menu.

"Well, Belgian waffles, what else?"

"Ha! They might not have them in a brasserie, you know."

"I bet they do."

It turned out that the cozy, informal restaurant did indeed serve waffles, even the slightly denser Liège ones. Both women ordered them without any toppings and ate them with their hands.

"Yummy!" was Dee's judgment.

"You know, all those years I lived in New York, I never drove through Queens to La Guardia without thinking of when Belgian waffles made such a success there at the nineteen-sixty-four World's Fair."

"Does that mean you got hungry for them every time you drove to the airport?"

"No, I just remembered about becoming aware of their existence because they were introduced at that fair."

"Fair enough."

Both women laughed and Dee confessed that she could eat yet another Liège waffle. And a cup of coffee would be welcome.

"I'll tell you what," said Megan, who did not feel like having either. "Why don't you go ahead and order them and I'll just zip over to Saint Bavo's and take a photo of the altarpiece with my Google Glass. That would be such fun for me."

"Of course, you go, honey, if that's what you want. I'll happily linger here," beamed the Texan at her energetic art historian friend.

Megan got up immediately and walked over to the cathedral, taking off her sunglasses and substituting her Google Glass. She had last used it to good avail when tracking down an unknown double portrait by Schiele in Russia. She also hung around her neck the trusty small monocular she used for scanning artworks from a distance—a necessity in some museums and churches.

When she entered the cathedral a few minutes later she was taken by surprise. There was a long line of people waiting to buy entrance tickets. *Pay to get in?* No thank you. Megan produced the press pass she had once been issued when reviewing exhibitions for *Arts Magazine* and flashed it at a guard who waved her on into the nave of the cathedral. A sign directed her to the chapel she remembered from her previous visit in the 1960s, and yet when she arrived there she saw something that was unthinkable. *Tourists were stepping up to the altarpiece opening and closing the wings*! Guides talking to small groups did nothing to stop them. Then Megan realized she was looking at an exact *copy* of the van Eyck brothers' masterpiece.

She asked one of the guides where the original was kept and he directed her to another side chapel. There individual panels from the altarpiece were on display behind a hermetic glass pane, probably bullet-proof, Megan surmised. A sign explained that the missing panels were at the Ghent Museum of Fine Arts being restored—a process that would take several years. Well, at least the major *Adoration of the Mystic Lamb* panel was still to be seen in the original. Megan stared at it long and lovingly. Around the fearless lamb which was standing on a distant altar were grouped martyrs, saints, pagan writers, and Jewish prophets.

Megan had forgotten how copious and green the grass was under the kneeling figures. She took her Google Glass off after taking several photos and lifted the mini scope to her eye. Yes, not only was the grass unusually verdant, the individual blades stood up like miniature pinched tubes. Talk about local color! She had noticed the same type of sturdy grass shooting up from the pavestones as she and Dee had walked to the brasserie. Too bad she couldn't photograph a close-up detail of the *Mystic Lamb* panel. She took one magnified shot with her beloved iPhone, but it hardly did justice to the lush grassy terrain.

Yikes! Megan glanced at her watch and realized it was really time to push on to the Kollwitz cemetery. She hurried back to the Brasserie Agrea where Dee had just finished her coffee. They paid the check and walked back to the car.

Once they were again on E 40 Dee checked her foldout map, then switched to her laptop for a calculation of the driving time.

"Google says it's only fifty-nine minutes from here to Diksmuide and then the Vladslo Cemetery is just a few miles further on."

"Not bad at all. I'll see if I can make it in exactly fifty-nine minutes," she teased, speeding up.

"Now please don't make me nervous."

"Not to worry," Megan said, slowing down and settling into a steady speed of seventy miles an hour. The Autobahn was not crowded and the road was straight and level.

"Now, Megan, tell me how come you know so much about Napoleon." Dee asked.

"Oh, I only know certain facts—those within the context of the artists and cultural figures I taught about. Like David, Ingres, Goya, Goethe, and Madame de Staël. We began with the French Revolution and every fall we re-enacted it. I would invite two students up to the stage to be Marie Antoinette and Louis XVI and then urged the rest of the students to stand up and slowly merge on the unfortunate couple as we all 'dadadumed' the *Marseillaise*. One semester a trumpet player from our university orchestra was in my class and we secretly arranged beforehand that he would stand at the back of the auditorium and sound the opening notes of the anthem. It was absolutely thrilling!"

"Have you ever been to Elba to see where Napoleon was exiled?"

"Yup, saw his winter and summer palaces there. Did you know he bottled the local mineral water and it's still sold under his moniker today?"

"No, I did not. But if you visited Elba, I suppose you also went to Corsica to see where he was born."

"Certainly did. That larger island had much higher mountain terrain. I saw the sizeable family house in Ajaccio and the town's main square has a very funny, very pretentious bronze tribute to Napoleon and his four brothers, all in *togas*."

"That's pretty funny. What about his last place of exile? Don't tell me you've flown all the way out to Saint Helena!"

"No, I drew the line there. The island is twelve hundred miles off the west coast of Africa, after all. But I did challenge my students to go, telling them they would get an automatic A if they went. The challenge went unanswered for decades but a few years ago, after I'd retired from teaching, I received a postcard from Saint Helena with an image of Napoleon looking out to sea and the droll message that I now needed 'retroactively' to change a B grade to an A. And the writer of the card was the trumpet player of long ago."

"That's a wonderful story," laughed Dee.

"Yes, and now Facebook has really changed things for me. It used to be postcards, then e-mails from former students; now it's Facebook. I have a pile to get through each morning."

Time went by quickly as Megan entertained Dee with anecdotes from her teaching days. Then Dee decided to pull up images of Kollwitz's *Grieving Parents* statues online and began studying them.

"Are they supposed to be actual portraits of Käthe and her husband Karl?"

"Well *abstracted* portraits certainly."

"It's interesting. They are both kneeling, but the father's body is upright, with arms crossed in front, his face looking straight ahead. The mother, on the other hand, leans forward, her arms folded under her great shawl and her head bent down. So different. The one stalwart, the other giving in to her grief."

"Yes. When Käthe and Karl made the trip to visit the installation, she wrote later, and I've always remembered her words: 'I stood before the woman, saw her—my own face—I cried and stroked her cheeks.' And Käthe did not realize Karl was behind her until she heard his voice quietly whispering, 'yes, yes.'"

"Oh, that is so touching."

A moment later Dee cried out suddenly, "Look! There's the sign for Diksmuide, so we can't be far now"

A quarter of an hour later and about a mile and a half northeast of the small town of Vladslo they pulled up at a road sign in three languages—Dutch, French, and German—identifying the spot as "German Soldiers Cemetery." They had made it there in an hour and fifteen minutes. It was 3:30 on a lovely July afternoon and the sun was high in the sky.

Megan parked the car in an area that fronted a small visitors house and a few minutes later she and Dee were inside paging through various guests books and reading the moving entries. One read: "God bless you Käthe Kollwitz." It was signed: "A former enemy."

Dee was so moved she began tearing up.

"I'm just going over to talk to the woman behind the desk there and see if the cemetery administrator is in," said Megan. A few minutes later she was led to a small office where a harassed looking young man was busily leafing through various ledgers on his desk.

"Doktor Slootmaekers, sorry to interrupt you, sir, but this lady says she comes to you direct from the Kollwitz Museum in Cologne." The woman was speaking in what sounded to Megan like Dutch, although the Belgians like to call it Flemish.

"Oh, yes," Slootmaekers turned to Megan, speaking English. "Do come in. The museum director called and told me to expect you today. That you are a Kollwitz expert from America. How was the drive over from Cologne?"

"Just fine, thank you. We had lunch in Ghent, then drove straight here. As you can imagine, I am eager to have a look at the site where the Kollwitz statues were stolen."

"But of course. Although, truthfully, there is nothing to see except the cement tiles that supported the statues. The thieves even took the pedestals."

"Terrible. Just terrible. Nevertheless, I really would like to go over the terrain, if I may."

"Our cemetery personnel have, the local police have, an inspector from Brussels has, we've all had a thorough look around. Gone over the area with a fine toothcomb. No one has come up with anything. The only thing to see is how the hedge behind the statues was totally run down by heavy vehicles, one most likely a large flat-bottom truck with a crane."

"Most distressing, most distressing. However, if you'll point me in the right direction I should like to go over the ground for myself."

Reluctantly, the young man put aside his ledgers, stood up, and led Megan to the far part of the cemetery where the Kollwitz statues had been. Dee joined them, walking at a slower pace behind. She was quite used to limping behind a galloping Megan.

"Have you not been here before?" Slootmaekers asked Megan.

"No, this is one Kollwitz site I have never had the opportunity to visit. And I'm only too sorry for the reason I'm visiting it now."

They were walking between rows of flat headstones flanked intermittently by tall narrow tree trunks. Their goal was a dense hedge on the far side of the graves that obviously marked the cemetery boundary. Slootmaekers stopped just in front of the damaged bordering hedge at a spot where a second, slightly taller, now mangled hedge stood. There on the ground were the large blocks of cement upon which the statues on their pedestals had so recently stood. The surfaces were stained; the weight they had once borne was evident.

"So this is where the trucks made their entry," Megan said, half to herself. "Right through both hedges."

"Correct. We hope to transfer new hedges for the area soon. They are on order."

"I didn't expect it to be so green here," remarked Dee, catching up with them.

"Nor did I," replied Megan. "I'd like to follow the tire tracks back to where they turned off onto the road that borders the cemetery."

Before either of her companions could speak, Megan struck off through the damaged hedge, her eyes glued to the ground. I've seen springy grass like this just today, she thought. In Ghent between the pavestones. And in the van Eyck altarpiece. Why was it holding such an attraction for her now? Was it because the deep tire tracks enhanced their plucky presence? She had reached the road. The grass looked even more verdant on the other side. She crossed over and stooped down to touch the tiny blades of grass that sprang up in thick, tough clusters.

Her hand touched something that was not grass. At first glance it looked like a rosary. But it was a string of identical beads, each evenly spaced from the next. They were made of amber, probably Baltic amber in this part of the world, and had an elongated marker at the end with a knitted silver tassel. Megan counted the beads. There were thirty-three of them. With the marker they constituted prayer beads.

What was a Muslim misbahah doing a few hundred steps from a Kollwitz site?

7

Back in Berlin from her long workweek Dr. Iliana Frankel decided to treat herself. She would visit the antique shop in her neighborhood where she had seen the interesting picture that invoked the scenes she witnessed so often of fatigued Dorotek employees leaving work. It was a sunny Saturday morning and her household chores were done. Making sure her cat Uli had enough water, Iliana picked up her extra large shopping bag that folded up so nicely and stepped out of her modern first-floor apartment on Pasteurstrasse in the Prenslauer Berg district and walked a few blocks over to the Akermann Antiquariat, which was tucked in between a fresh food market and an electronics store.

Super! The picture was still in the window. She asked the owner if he knew who the artist was but he shrugged his shoulders.

"You can have it for one hundred and seventy-five euros, if you like."

"That's a pretty hefty price for an unknown artist."

"Maybe. But it's nicely framed and matted and you can see it's an old drawing, maybe a hundred years or more. Look here, it's pen *and* watercolor, and some graphite too. See how it's heightened here and there with white. A sad scene but sort of dramatic in its own way."

"I don't like the dark mat very much, but I'll offer you a hundred and fifty euros for the picture."

"One hundred and sixty and it's yours."

"All right then, One hundred and sixty."

Iliana paid Herr Akermann, unfolded her shopping bag, and carefully inserted the artwork now encased in bubble wrap. Then, after stopping at the market next door and buying a couple of cucumbers, she walked back home in a jubilant mood.

She cleared the kitchen table, wiped it clean, and laid the picture on it. Perhaps just taking the mat off would make it look better. Cautiously she removed the artwork from the frame. Ah ha! The picture was a bit larger than the mat had indicated. On the bottom right was an illegible signature, a date—1897—and a title written in cursive script: *Arbeiter nach Hause gehend am Lehrter Bahnhof—Workers Going Home at the Lehrter Railroad Station.*

Lehrter Bahnhof? That was the site in Wedding where the enormous new Berlin *Hauptbahnhof* had been opened in 2006. She must show this new acquisition to her colleague who lived in Wedding, Dr. Abraham Rückgabe. They had gone to medical school together in Berlin and he had been her go-to friend while she was going through a difficult divorce. Two or three times a month they got together on Saturday evenings for dinner, sometimes with his mother as well. The two physicians' friendship was purely platonic, but they were good buddies, enjoyed teasing each other about their respective Berlin and Viennese accents, and loved talking about medicine. She had specialized in obstetrics and gynecology at med school and Abraham was forever teasing her for now working only with male patients at Dorotek.

Following up on her impulse, Iliana telephoned Abraham and said teasingly she had something interesting to show him, something from "his" neighborhood. They made a dinner date for that very evening.

8

While still living in Iraq, twenty-one-year-old Akram al-Aljamie, only son of the famous Iraqi archaeologist Dief al-Aljamie, had enjoyed the confidence and privileges of society's upper crust. He had a certain celebrity status as son of the man who, some years earlier, and with the active patronage of Saddam Hussein, had excavated secret chambers and discovered priceless carvings in Iraq's most famous ziggurat, Aqar-Quf, just outside Bagdad.

Fascinated by the processes involved in creating sculpture, especially the lost-wax method, Akram had persuaded his father to let him study abroad and he spent four years at the Universität der Künste in Berlin. As the only Arab studying sculpture techniques there, Akram, with his full black beard and pronounced black eyebrows, stood out from his fellow students. For the most part they avoided him.

It was at the beginning of Akram's final year, in a class visit to a bronze casting foundry, that he met the mysterious, head-turning beauty, Monika von Putbus. Both of them, tall, slim, with jet black hair and dark eyes, instantaneously sensed something magnetic. They gravitated toward each other and began speaking. Although they could feel the disapproving looks of their classmates, they continued talking and even laughing, rare for them both. It was she who suggested they meet that evening inside the Neue Wache, Berlin's war memorial on the north side of Unter den Linden.

It soon became their regular meeting place, as both lived nearby. They were fascinated by the Neue Wache's large bronze sculpture showing a mourning mother holding her dead adult son in her arms, But it was not only the Pietà aspect of the arresting ensemble that held their attention. It was also the fact that the sculpture had been placed directly underneath the building's huge oculus, thus exposing it to all the elements. The thinking behind this unusual setting, they read, was that it symbolized civilian suffering during World War II. The poignant statue was identified as an enlarged copy of *Mother with Her Dead Son*. The artist, unknown until then to either Monika or Akram, was Käthe Kollwitz.

Over the next months Monika took a tender interest in improving Akram's fluent but heavily accented German and he was a willing and excellent student. Although Monika was fascinated by Akram's family background, begging to learn Arabic designations and endearments, she volunteered little information about her own family. Nor did she explain to Akram why she was so particularly delighted when she learned that his name meant "noble" in Arabic.

At Christmas Monika left Berlin for an unspecified location, asking her new friend to trust her and not ask questions. For his part Akram returned to Iraq during the semester break. As usual, his parents were urging their only son to marry, but he had not met any woman in his circle of friends back home who measured up to beautiful, intelligent Monika. Instinct told him not to discuss her with his parents. Their prejudice against non-Muslims was ferocious.

It was only after a ten-month friendship, and they had become gentle lovers, that Monika revealed more about herself to Akram. She was the daughter of Malte von Putbus, descendant of the noble family who at one time owned a sixth of the island of Rügen. Famous Putbus Castle and the

Granitz hunting lodge, itself a castle, had once been host to some of the most prominent persons in German society, including Chancellor Bismarck himself. Recent attempts by Putbus heirs, including Monika's estranged cousin Rolf, to reclaim the hunting lodge had failed in court. It was now a museum open to thousands of enthusiastic tourists—a continuing spectacle that had left Monika wanting to avoid public attention.

In July, after both had completed their university studies, Monika invited Akram to travel to Rügen with her. She had decided to show her lover the sites that once belonged to her family. During the three-hour drive from Berlin to the island she spoke about colorful members of the ancient Putbus line. She also told Akram about the destruction in 1962 of the large family castle at the town of Putbus by the East German communist regime as a "symbol of Prussian imperialism." Only the stables and orangery survived.

Upon arrival at the island they first visited the park and buildings on the former palace grounds at the town of Putbus. They lightheartedly posed for selfies in front of the orangery's life-size *Wounded Gaul*—a fine replica in bronze of the famous Roman marble copy of a lost bronze Greek sculpture. After lunch in town they drove to the palatial Putbus hunting lodge, the *Jagdschloss*, that had been built on the highest hill in southeast Rügen.

Elbowing their way through hordes of noisy tourists, they walked around the large, two-story rectangular structure with its four corner towers and then made their way up a circular iron staircase in the building's fifth and center tower to an observation deck at the top. The view of sea, sand, and forest was spectacular. Speechless, they stood, hand in hand, taking in the panorama.

Monika decided this was the moment to tell her lover that she was pregnant with his child. Three-and-a-half months pregnant.

Akram turned to Monika and without hesitation declared his joy at the marvelous news. They were creating something wonderful together. Avowing his love for her and for her magical island, he asked her to marry him. Bracing themselves against the wind, they stood in a silent, protracted hug looking into each other's eyes.

"But Akram?" she murmured at last as they continued standing on the observation platform, the wind nipping at their clothes and hair.

"Yes, dear heart?"

"You know that I am Catholic."

"I do."

"If we were to marry, I should need—should want—to marry within the church. To have my husband of the same faith."

Akram gave her a keen glance.

"To marry you, my dearest darling, I would give up any faith and embrace yours in an instant."

"Are you serious?" Monika's delight sounded in her voice.

"Yes, I am completely serious. I may have been born a Muslim, but I have never observed any of the rituals, much to the regret of my parents."

"So if you converted to Catholicism it would not be in conflict with any of your own beliefs?"

"I have no beliefs, except my faith in destiny. The destiny that brought us together."

They continued to stand in a close embrace, smiling into each other's eyes and stroking one another's cheeks. Akram put his hand reverently on Monika's belly and held it there a long time. Finally he spoke.

"Under the skies of Rügen I pledge my everlasting love to you."

"And I to you."

"And to our child."

"And to our child."

It was then that Monika resolved to show Akram another Putbus hunting lodge—a private one unknown to the tourist trade. She had inherited it from her father. Hidden in the hills of the beech wood forest before Lauterbach, the *Trosthaus*—consolation house—as she called it, the lodge had become Monika's refuge after her parents' sudden death in an automobile collision a few years earlier. She loved the lodge as dearly as had her parents, and she strove to keep public knowledge of its existence limited.

And now she wanted to share *Trosthaus* with the man she knew providence had chosen to be her life companion.

At her request Akram cancelled their hotel reservation at Putbus, ran inside a nearby grocery store for provisions, then sat with mounting suspense as Monika drove them south of the city and into the winding hills and valleys of a dense forest. The sun was beginning to set.

Akram's first sight of *Trosthaus* gave him a jolt. Built on top of a rectangular, three-stepped base, with a peaked top, it reminded him, in miniature form, of the ziggurats of his homeland.

He expressed his surprise to Monika.

"Yes, my mother's father, and it was he who built the lodge, was an amateur astronomer. He wanted to situate his private sanctuary in the depth of the woods, so it wouldn't be visible from afar, but also high and clear of trees enough for observing the heavens. The three cement platforms you are looking at provided the solution. You'll see the observatory when we get inside. It's enormous, takes up a quarter of the house."

"Oh, Monika, darling, you can't know how excited I am by what you just told me."

"Why?"

"Because, like your grandfather, I am a fanatic starwatcher; have been all my life. Unfortunately I had to leave my collection of high-powered telescopes in Iraq."

"In that case you are going to love my grandfather's formidable Bresser scope."

"A *Bresser* did you say? Oh, you have brought me to paradise, Monika!"

They parked at the nearside of the lodge and climbed the low steps carved into the three cement rises that led to an entry door on the south side of the lodge. There was actually no front door as Akram soon discovered. Instead, after passing through a kitchen, a cold storage, and a prep room, the house opened up onto what, in any other lodge would have been the hunting salon, hung with antlers. But in this long, rectangular room the walls were bare and all focus was on a mighty Bresser telescope. It stood on its eighty-pound tripod in black mechanical splendor and, with an aperture of sixteen inches, was aimed at a matching oculus at the peak of the house. It was of glass and retractable.

"Oh, Monika. May I take a look through the scope right away?"

Amused, Monika nodded happy assent.

Akram ran to the Bresser, adjusted the focus, and looked out at the early evening sky.

"Oh, yes, there they are. All the planets visible during June. Mercury is just disappearing, but I can clearly see Venus, Saturn, Jupiter, and Mars. All shining bright. Wonderful!

"You can stargaze more later. Let me show you the rest of the house now."

"Oh, of course. Gladly."

On the back side of the room was a fireplace with some deep leather armchairs and side tables. And at the far corner a door opened onto a corridor leading to the bedrooms and bathrooms.

"Yes, I know what you're thinking," said Monika smiling. "That this is a strange family room?"

"No, dear heart. I am thinking that this would be a perfect place for a honeymoon."

A week later Akram and Monika returned to Berlin and combined their households, moving into a modern four-room apartment just off Fasanenstrasse and not far from their former university.

Akram still kept the large studio in Berlin's southwest district of Dahlem that he had furnished with an electric kiln for firing up his clay sculpture. He spent the weekdays there devotedly working on a facsimile of one of Syria's lost treasures, the 2,000-year-old arch of triumph at Palmyra that had been ruthlessly demolished by ISIS. Akram shared his archaeologist father's appreciation of ancient civilizations, and was heartsick at the ISIS looting of antiquities in its attempt to impose Islamic law. He knew that a dedicated group of local Syrians, dubbed "Syria's Monuments Men," had smuggled some of the precious artifacts out of Palmyra before it fell to ISIS. And he was also aware of the fact that the terrorist group itself had "spared" some of the less traceable objects in order to sell them on the black market. The most recent United Nations' report, he told Monika indignantly, estimated that ISIS had already earned somewhere in the neighborhood of $40 million in smuggled antiquities.

Monika had accepted employment as a translator for UNICEF, although with the vast fortune she had inherited, there was certainly no need for her to work. It was the focus and challenge of the job that engaged her, and she was equally at home in German, French, Italian, and English.

Her husband-to-be devotedly embarked upon a series of catechism classes and one month after their return from Rügen they were married in a side chapel of the Mater Dolorosa church in Berlin-Lankwitz. The couple returned to Rügen to spend their honeymoon at *Trosthaus*, just as Akram had envisioned.

Monika's wedding gift to Akram was a white Nissan compact cargo van for transporting artworks and material. His to her was a bronze shellacked, eleven-inch-high clay replica of the mother and son ensemble they had both been so taken by inside the Neue Wache, site of their many trysts. Monika burst into tears at this precious reminder of the silent witness to how their love had grown.

Akram had but one worry. How could he tell his father he had married a non-Muslim and converted to her faith? And that they were expecting a child?

9

Kadeem Tawfeek was not enjoying the good fortune of his surname's meaning. In fact, if anything, he was at present the most unfortunate man of his acquaintance. His precious misbahah was missing. The one made of thirty-three amber beads.

And yes, he had had a scuffle by the side of the cemetery road with Jarir Uthman, the driver of the boom truck he had rented for lifting and lowering two statues onto the lift gate of his cargo van. The idiot had lowered the second statue too close to the first one, causing a slight grinding sound. Then he had almost toppled one of the statues when he eased Kadeem's steel dolly under the kneeling female figure. The two men came to blows and each drove his respective vehicle back to Germany cursing silently.

It was not until the next morning at his private warehouse in the Wedding district of Berlin that Kadeem discovered his misbaha was missing. But Jarir swore he did not have the prayer beads. Kadeem had held his Kriegar stiletto to the bearded man's throat, just puncturing the skin below his prominent Adam's apple. Still no confession. He slid the Kriegar stiletto over onto Jarir's left carotid artery and held it there. All he needed to do was plunge and twist the blade.

But he wanted the trembling man alive. The boom truck had to be driven by someone. Such a complicated delivery could not be made without help. The great crane on that truck was still needed. They would start out immediately for the three-hour drive down south.

And Kadeem would simply have to hope for the best as far as that bit of surface damage to the statues was concerned.

10

It was Saturday evening and Iliana Frankel was running a little late. She could not decide where best to hang her picture of factory workers exiting the old Lehrter train station. She had reversed and cut the mat back to reveal the writing on the lower right before replacing it in its frame. Now it should be one of the first things Abraham Rückgabe saw when he arrived at her apartment before they went out for dinner. Finally she hung the drawing on the wall over the living room couch where it was nicely illuminated by a tall reading lamp. Yes. That was the perfect spot. Abraham would see it the moment she opened her front door to him.

Things worked out just as she had hoped. Her visitor stopped dead in his tracks after entering the living room.

"Where did you get this Kollwitz?"

"Oh? You *know* who made that drawing?"

"Of course I know. It's by Käthe Kollwitz. The woman after whom your Kollwitzplatz is named."

"*What*? Oh! Well, of course, I know the square—it's just a few blocks from here—but I never thought about whom it was named for. Sorry. My knowledge of art leaves much to be desired." Iliana felt very much the fool.

"Not to worry. You know about music; I know a bit about art. But where on earth did you find this extraordinary drawing?"

"I just picked it up at an antique shop this afternoon because the theme appealed to me. Seems so like what I see daily during the week when my Dorotek workers go off duty at the factory."

"And the shop owner didn't know who the artist was?"

"No. He didn't. Just said the drawing might be a hundred years old or more. When I took the frame and old mat off at home I did see a sort of signature, but I couldn't make it out. A title had been written underneath and I was able to read that. And the date, eighteen-ninety-seven. Look, I framed it so one could see the title. It refers to workers coming home at the Lehrter train station. That's why I wanted to show it to you. The locale is in *your* neighborhood."

"Oh, certainly. The historic old train station where our enormous Hauptbahnhof now stands."

"Right."

"And you say the man who sold it to you did not know who did it?"

"Correct."

"Iliana, dear. Do you realize that, had he known, he could have sold your work to a museum, it's of such high quality? Plus being signed, dated, and titled by the artist herself. And the fact that it's a pen and wash drawing rather than a print. This is an extremely valuable Kollwitz. Worth, I think at the minimum, thirty-five hundred euros."

"I think I have to sit down. This is news I wasn't prepared to hear." Iliana lowered herself down onto the couch, turning so she could look up at the picture.

"May I take it down off the wall?"

"Of course. Let's look at it more closely."

"I want to study what you call her signature."

In one practiced motion Abraham gingerly took the artwork off the wall and held it out in front of himself as he sat down next to Iliana.

"Hm. I guess what I thought was a scrawl is two "K"s woven together?" she queried.

"Not so. Look again carefully. The whole name is there, just conjoined."

"Oh, now I see. 'KätheKollwitz.'"

"Iliana, you really have something quite precious here. A very early Kollwitz drawing that is already focused on one of her favorite themes, the poor working class of Berlin."

"But I don't know anything about this artist. How do *you* know so much about her?"

Abraham looked at his close friend of many years with affection. He had never shared this information with anyone else. But Iliana was reliable and discreet.

"If I tell you, will you promise not to tell anyone else?"

"Well, of course. But why would your knowing who an artist is be a dark secret? Couldn't *anybody* be knowledgeable about an artist if they wanted to?"

"I need to be circumspect because my knowledge about Kollwitz comes from a *direct source.*"

Abraham took a deep breath.

" I am in possession of thirty-six of her diaries, her journals. And no one knows about this, no museum director, no private collector."

"For heavens sake! But how did you get them?"

"My grandmother Lina was a live-in housemaid for the Kollwitz family for several decades, right into the nineteen-forties. The building they resided in—a corner one on the old Wörther Platz—was bombed to smithereens during the war and afterward, among the ruins, my grandmother found an old undamaged metal trunk full of her employer's diaries."

"Did the family not survive?"

"Käthe did, yes, but she had evacuated somewhere to the countryside and Lina didn't know where. Karl Kollwitz, Käthe's husband, had passed away a few years earlier. And, as I learned later, *she* died down in Moritzburg just a few days before the end of the war. In the confused aftermath and rebuilding of Berlin, my grandmother completely forgot about the diaries. She remembered them only around the time you and I graduated from med school, and in fact she gave them to me as a sort of graduation present."

"And you knew she was a famous artist?"

"No, not then. I simply began reading the journals, chronologically, and that's when I fell in love with her. And her work."

"Why, this is an aspect of you I didn't know about, Abraham."

"Well, I haven't spoken of it because I did not want nosey people from the art world to find out about my trove. Right now I want to keep Käthe to myself."

"I suppose you have some of her artworks as well?"

"I do own a few prints." Abraham smiled with an expression of pride on his face. "I'll show you next time you're at my place."

"I'm still not clear as to why she is so famous. Based on her drawing here, her art looks so sad, and her figures so downtrodden. I thought real art was supposed to be elevating and beautiful."

"To Kollwitz beauty was in the figures of the working classes, burdened as they were by the repetition and hopelessness of their lives."

"Oh, I see. That's what appealed to me in this drawing—there was something so poignant about it. Reminded me so much of the workers I treat every day of the week."

"Well, there you are. Her art *spoke* to you. That's her great strength."

"Won't you tell me more about her at dinner?"

"Gladly, Iliana, gladly."

Over dessert and espresso at the quiet dining room of the Hilton Berlin hotel on Mohrenstrasse, Iliana reminded Abraham that he was going to tell her more about the artist who had made her Lehrter train station drawing. He beamed with pleasure at her request.

"Well, I might sum her up as an artist like this: with her arresting depictions of the working class she shook a mighty fist in the face of two rulers of Germany. First Kaiser Wilhelm II, then Hitler. The Nazis forbade her work from being displayed and her works were banished to a cellar of the Crown Prince's palace."

"So her themes were commentaries on the human condition?"

"Yes. And she did not do paintings. She preferred working in stark black and white. The graphic arts—etchings, lithographs, woodcuts. But she was also a powerful sculptor."

"A sculptor! Where can I see pieces by her?"

"Some very potent ones are right here in Berlin's own Kollwitz Museum; and the Kollwitz Museum in Cologne has fifteen bronzes, most of them early casts."

"Oh, dear. She must indeed be a famous artist to have not one but two museums of her work. And I've been totally unaware of them."

"You are not alone. But if you've ever gone inside the Neue Wache, you have seen a copy of her *Mother with Dying Son*."

"I certainly have been inside and I remember a riveting piece of sculpture right in the center of the building."

"Well, that's it. And next time you look at it, think about the fact that she lost a son in World War I and a grandson in World War II."

"Goodness! How terrible. So Kollwitz is one of Berlin's great twentieth-century artists."

"Yes. Most certainly. I would say one of the *world's* great twentieth-century artists. By the way, she was not a born *Berlinerin*, even though she lived here for over half a century."

"Oh? Where did she come from?"

"She was born in far eastern Prussia, at the Baltic seaport of Königsberg."

"Königsberg! Isn't that the city associated with Immanuel Kant?"

"Yes. The philosopher was born and died there. And Käthe's mother was the daughter of a kind of philosopher in his own right. Julius Rupp. He was founder and leader of the Free Congregation church there—a Protestant church at odds with the state-controlled Prussian church and a church that believed in improving the lot of the poor and establishing social equality."

"So she had an early example in him."

"Yes, and Käthe's father, who was a stone mason and built houses, also had strong socialist beliefs. Plus he believed in educating his *girls* as well as his boys."

"How wonderful!"

"Yes, I thought you'd like that. Anyway, when he discovered Käthe's talent for drawing he immediately sent her for art lessons locally, then for classes in Berlin and after that, Munich."

"And she went back to Berlin, right?"

"No, not at first. She didn't settle here until she married a friend of her brother's, a young physician just starting out, Karl Kollwitz. Like her brother he was a social democrat and wanted to improve the lot of the poor. So he accepted a post here for tailors and their families insured under public health. Opened a surgery in *your* Prenzlauer Berg. The couple lived in an apartment overlooking old Wörther Platz for the next fifty years. It was renamed for her after the war and now you know all about the person for whom Kollwitzplatz is named."

"Thank you. But now I want to learn more about her and I want to see her works."

"All right, and so you shall. Let's go over to my place, if you're not too tired, and I'll show you her first cycle of prints—completed in the same year as your drawing. It's called *A Weavers' Revolt*."

"Sounds interesting. Already concerned with social themes."

"Correct. And if we have time, Iliana, I might show you one of her journals. *If* you truly promise not to say a word about them."

"I truly promise. And I can't wait!" Iliana gulped down the last of her espresso, thrilled by the amazing turn events had taken.

11

For Megan and Dee the half-hour drive from the Vladslo Cemetery to the Ensor House in Ostend passed quickly. Dee, shaken by the sight of so many gravestones attesting to the horrible deaths of World War I trench warfare, was trying to recall the words that followed the initial two lines of the poem "In Flanders Fields." She recited as much as she could remember.

"In Flanders fields the poppies blow, between the crosses, row on row."

Megan tried her best to remember what came next but nothing came to her.

"Why don't you just Google it on your iPhone, Dee?"

Internet connectivity on the highway was good just then and in seconds Dee was reading the poem aloud:

In Flanders fields the poppies blow
Between the crosses, row on row
That mark our place; and in the sky
The larks, still bravely singing, fly
Scarce heard amid the guns below.

We are the Dead. Short days ago
We lived, felt dawn, saw sunset glow,
Loved and were loved, and now we lie
In Flanders fields.

Take up our quarrel with the foe:
To you from failing hands we throw
The torch; be yours to hold it high.
If ye break faith with us who die
We shall not sleep, though poppies grow
In Flanders fields.

"Oh, yes," nodded Megan. "And here we are driving through Flanders fields at this very moment. Golly! Gives me goose bumps. All those lives lost. Who wrote that poem anyhow?"

"Let's see. Okay, Wikipedia tells us it was written by a Canadian brigade doctor named John McCrae. He wrote it on the battlefield right after the death of one of his comrades."

"And did McCrae survive the war?"

"No. But not from enemy attack. It says here he died of pneumonia in nineteen-eighteen."

"Oh, just like Egon Schiele. The influenza pandemic of nineteen-eighteen killed more people than did World War I. Some twenty-five million worldwide, as I recall from writing my books on Schiele."

The two friends fell silent for awhile. Suddenly Megan thought of the prayer bead discovery she had made by the Vladslo Cemetery. She had stuffed the beads into her sling purse, not particularly wanting to show them to Slootmaekers.

"Dee. Reach into my bag and take out what you'll feel right on top."

"All right. Oh? What's this?" Dee slowly lifted up a long string of beads from Megan's purse and dangled it in front of her.

"A set of Muslim prayer beads. I found them in the grass on the other side of the road from where it borders the Vladslo Cemetery."

"Oh, so *that's* where you disappeared to. The cemetery manager and

I were both wondering why you took so long to come back. You actually crossed the road?"

"Yup. And in this case it really was a case of 'grass being greener on the other side.' I guess I'd been so sensitized to grassland from having just looked at the Ghent Altarpiece, that I crossed over to take a look at the unusually green grass on the other side of the road. It's that simple."

"And these prayer beads?"

"They're what I found when I stooped down to feel the grass. They were lying there under the blades. First I scooped up the beads, then lifted them up high. They were all on a string. Thought they were a rosary until I looked more closely and realized they were Muslim prayer beads. *Muslim prayer beads* near the site of a robbery?"

"Goodness! I see what you mean. Really odd. Let's say a devout Muslim could have been part of the Kollwitz robbery. And that he accidentally dropped his prayer beads. Then the big question is *why* would a Muslim be involved in stealing something that is *Western* art?"

"Right," Megan answered. "What would a Muslim, or Muslims, be doing with two pieces of Western *figural* art?"

"Isn't representation of persons banned in Islam?"

"Pretty much so. Of course there was Persian miniature painting— plenty of cavorting figures there—but on the whole, historically at least, the representation of living beings has been pretty much taboo in Islamic art. There was the belief that only God can create living images. And the fear of idolatry played a role."

"Well, that aside, at least you now seem to have established, on a theoretical plane at least, that whatever vehicles were used to lift and cart the Kollwitz sculptures away, they crossed over to the other side of the road afterward."

"Which means they were headed in the direction of Brussels."

"And perhaps even beyond that, on to Germany," Dee theorized.

The friends continued to discuss the possible hows and whys of the two stolen Kollwitz sculptures. Everything about the "case," as Dee was now referring to the event, was baffling.

Approaching Ostend's seaside esplanade, they spotted the tall hotel where they had made reservations to spend the night. Looking more like a modern, multi-floored apartment house than a hotel, it was a corner building and its floor-to-ceiling windows commanded an impressive view of the fine sand beach beyond. The hotel had a name and a seafood restaurant equal to its glitter: De Mangerie Guesthouse Promenade. Best of all for Megan and Dee, it was only five blocks from Ensor's house, which they planned to visit the next morning. After checking in and admiring both the view and their novel bathroom that sported bright red walls, they went down to the mangerie where they had a leisurely dinner of trout almandine, asparagus spears, and potato croquettes. Then they settled in for a deliberately slow consumption of chocolate mousse.

"Tell me a little bit about James Ensor and what we're going to see tomorrow," Dee requested.

"Oh, golly, where to begin? He was a contemporary of Kollwitz *and* of Munch for starters. They were all three born in the eighteen-sixties and lived into the nineteen-forties. In fact, of the three, Ensor even outlived World War II. But you couldn't find artists more *outwardly* different from one another than Kollwitz and Ensor. Or Munch, with his angstful images, for that matter. With Kollwitz, one sees her heartfelt social commentaries often whittled down to universal figures of exhausted men, anxious women, and hungry children."

Dee nodded in agreement.

"With Ensor," Megan continued, "one thinks immediately of his huge—something like eight by fourteen feet—sardonic critique of art, society, politics, and religion, *Christ's Entry into Brussels*."

"Oh, yes! I remember. We saw that crowded, colorful painting when we visited my brother in Los Angeles ten years ago. It was the first time I'd ever been in the Getty Museum. Didn't we have to take a sort of tram up from the parking garage?"

"I think that's right. Well, boy, was acquisition of that picture a coup for the museum. It's great that at last people can examine it close up, since the miniscule figure of Christ on a donkey in the center of the canvas is almost lost in the teeming chaos of grotesque carnival masks and blustering politicians. And it all takes place under a battery of slogan signs. Do you remember the long red banner on top that says *VIVE LA SOCIALE*?"

"'Long live the, um, social'?"

"Well, maybe better: 'Long live welfare.'"

"Oh, I see. So he was a social reformer?"

"Um, not in the sense that moniker usually means. Ensor, the recluse, was a sardonic critic of many things. One of the placards in his *Christ Entering Brussels* picture refers to vivisectionists, for example, while another sign inveighs against Wagner's 'noisy' music. That's pretty telling, I think, considering that Ensor was a musician himself. And then there's another banner that reads simply 'Colman's Mustard.'"

"What a mix!"

"The main thing, I guess, is that Ensor has Christ entering *Brussels* on Palm Sunday, not Jerusalem."

"So you could say it's a slam against the Brussels of his day and its competing factions."

"Yes, good way to express it. And that's why I said his and Kollwitz's art were outwardly different. Totally different. But inwardly the art was created by two powerfully *driven* personalities."

"How so?"

"Well, Ensor rarely traveled; he preferred to remain in his home and studio for all but three years of his long life—his student years in Brussels. And out of this voluntary *exile* from the world he developed a very personal mythology full of satire, grotesque caricatures, sea shells, and carnival masks like the ones sold in the souvenir shop below his living quarters.

"Kollwitz, on the other hand engaged with the world in her art. She balanced the duties of marriage and motherhood to become a tireless artist-advocate for *public* issues—hunger, unemployment, health. And remember her husband was a physician dedicated to treating the poor."

"Still and all, Megan, I somehow don't see the connection between their work as distinctly as you do. Her works are dark; his work is colorful."

"And I don't mean to push things, Dee How about if I say 'parallel in their intensity' instead?"

"Well, okay, that helps. Anyway, now I *am* looking forward to visiting Ensor's house tomorrow."

"And I don't think you'll be disappointed," smiled Megan, scooping up the last remnant of her chocolate mousse.

12

"*You are an apostate!*" Akram's father shrieked when his son telephoned with the news of his marriage to a German woman and his conversion to her Catholic faith.

"You must repent and return to Islam," the irate man continued, his voice rising to hysterical heights. "The punishment for apostasy is death!"

"But, Father, that's *old* Sharia law. Things are different now, especially in our modern Iraq."

"Not for *me* are they different. All my life I have striven to unearth and preserve our ancient culture. *You have broken my heart.*"

Dief al-Aljamie slammed down the phone on his infidel son.

13

Gazing out at Rügen's calm sea from his small island house, Reinhold Fromm realized he was anything but calm. In fact the Herr Direktor of Dorotek was frazzled. This was a new sensation for him. But the assault of lawsuits against Dorotek claiming death from asbestos poisoning had unnerved him. And yesterday, Schlau, his company lawyer, had informed him of yet another asbestos lawsuit, bringing the total to fourteen.

As he looked at the complainants' surnames he suddenly realized that four of them were Muslim Turks. Oh, yes, ever since its 1961 labor recruitment agreement with the, then West Germany, Turkey had taken advantage of the status of "guest worker" and over the decades had flooded and fooled his country. Always eager to save on wage expenditures, he himself had hired a number of them. But now there were about four million Turks in Germany.

And more Muslims were pouring in daily, no longer as guest workers but as refugees from Syria.

And it was all the fault of that damn woman Agata Merle! The nation had adoringly called her "Mutti," but the popular chancellor was no munificent Mommy in Fromm's eyes. She and the Christian Democrats were ruining the country with their open door policy. Actually *inviting* Muslim refugees to come to Germany.

How he hated the woman in her ubiquitous pant suits who had become famous for what newspapers and adoring students called the "Merle-Raute"—the Merle rhombus. This came from her constant hand gesture of connecting the tips of her fingers and thumbs over her stomach in what looked like a triangle or quadrangle. Comedians had mercilessly impersonated her "diamond" gesture on TV and youthful pro-Merle flash mobs would take over public places. It was all despicable.

Reinhold's lawyer was working to prove that all of the lawsuit instigators had been heavy smokers. What about those four Turks? Did their Muslim religion approve of the narcotic? Reinhold turned to his laptop and typed out the question in his search engine. From a bevy of URLs he chose one that informed him:

> One of the principles of Islamic jurisprudence is that all that is harmful and filthy is considered *haram* (forbidden). There is enough scientific evidence to prove that smoking is harmful to one's health. Islam teaches us to take care of our health and not to destroy it. By smoking we are causing our own destruction, and Allah's order in the Qur'an is clear: "Do not cause your own destruction."

Reinhold snorted in contempt as he read the words. He had *seen* young Muslim men smoking in the street. Well, not many. Well, maybe only one. It might be difficult to prove that the deaths of all four Turks in his employ were related to smoking. He'd have to find another way to handle the litigations haunting Dorotek.

He placed a call.

Then he opened up his bedroom safe and removed a portfolio of erotic drawings to divert his mind.

14

Abraham stepped back into the hall to allow Iliana to enter his apartment first. She had actually never seen the inside, as they usually met at one of their favorite restaurants or he picked her up at her place.

"Are all these pictures by Kollwitz?" she asked, reverently pointing to the artworks on three of the four walls of his living room.

"Yes. These six over here belong to her very first print cycle. She worked on it for *four* years in total and didn't show them publically until eighteen-ninety-eight."

"Stubborn perfectionist *she* must have been! What is the series called?"

"*A Weavers' Revolt*. It was inspired by a real event that happened half a century earlier in Silesia when home workers rebelled at their miserable conditions and low wages. They marched as a group to their employer's regal residence to protest. The playwright Gerhart Hauptmann had just written a play about the uprising which he titled simply *The Weavers*, and when Käthe saw it in a private, initial performance she was inspired to create a print cycle on the subject. It would be her way of bringing attention to contemporary social injustices by addressing past injustices."

"Tell me about it," Iliana implored, thinking about the dangerous working conditions at her Dorotek.

"Gladly. This one begins the series and is titled simply *Need*. We're looking inside one of the worker's dismal huts and there in front of the hand looms you see an anguished woman, her hands to her head, sitting helplessly before a tiny baby lying in the cottage's great bed. You see how the looks and stance of the other people in the room—the father and older child—convey their misery and helplessness. Poverty and starvation have condemned the infant to death."

"Oh, yes, I see. The image is riveting. The very lines transmit emotion. Is this an etching?"

"No, no, this first image is a lithograph. A pen and crayon drawing with scratch technique on a printing plate. And mine is just an unsigned trial proof made on her own hand press. Käthe made lithos *and* etchings for the cycle. She wanted to convey her theme in a condensed, commanding manner, and sometimes it worked better for her as a lithograph, sometimes as an etching."

"Oh, dear. Explain to me exactly what a lithograph is, please."

"Well, in Käthe's day, a lithographic print was made by drawing on a stone slab or plate—usually gray limestone—with wax crayons or pen or both. Then ink was applied on the stone surface and it was placed under a press. Once the image was fully inked, paper was laid over it—in this case imitation laid paper—the pressure of the press transferred the image onto the paper and, voilà, you had your print. Your original copy of an original work. Nowadays they use flexible aluminum plates rather than stone. The date of the stone used for *Need* is between eighteen-ninety-three and eighteen-ninety-seven. And my proof was pulled from it by a professional printer in nineteen-twenty-one."

"So it's a chemical process, then? The mutual repulsion of water and oil?"

"You could put it that way. Look at this second image. It's called *Death*. And it's also a lithograph. See how Käthe recreates the somber mood of the claustrophobic hut interior, but now in between the sorrowing mother and standing father with his back to us, the skull-faced figure of death is present. It reaches across a frightened child and touches the arm of the mother—'I call you next.'"

"Brrrr. Makes me shiver to look at it."

"I know. You can't forget it once you've seen it."

"And what about this third image?"

"She titled it *Conspirancy,* and as you can see the locale has changed. This rushing perspective takes us to the back corner table of a tavern where a man leans forward urging his avid listeners to take action against their oppressor. And this one is an etching not a litho."

"Oh, goodness. And an etching differs how?" Iliana was embarrassed by her ignorance in such matters. But Abraham smiled at her patiently.

"I had to learn about this too. You could explain the difference briefly by just thinking that with a lithograph you *draw* on a prepared surface; with an etching you *incise* the prepared surface. It's an intaglio method in which the parts of the plate that are to be printed are cut into. Etching involves coating a metal plate—usually copper—with a layer of acid-resistant wax or varnish. Then, as Käthe did here, you scratch through the ground with an etching needle to expose the metal beneath. After that, the plate is immersed in an acid bath—the longer you leave it, the wider and darker the lines. Under a heavy press the acid bites into the lines exposed by the needle. This results in slightly raised ink on the paper and in the plate mark showing the edges of the plate. See them here?"

"Oh, yes, I was just noticing them." Iliana resisted her impulse to touch the corners, even though they were under glass, and moved on to the next image.

"And this one showing angry people marching. It also looks like an etching."

"Yes, it's a line etching as well."

"You don't have to tell me the name of this one. It must be *Marching*."

"*Weavers March*, yes."

Iliana looked at the print a long time in silence.

"Hm" she finally said, "there must be eighteen people in this print! Each face is particularized. And I see how the heavy low horizon line oppresses and holds them down. At first glance they seem to be all men, some of them peasants, except for this prominent figure just right of center. She's a mother carrying her sleeping child on her back. And she is marching right along with them."

"Yes. And she looks just as determined as the men—see that angry one with a raised fist shouting, and this grimly determined one holding a scythe on his shoulder."

"It's a remarkable work of art. Oh, Abraham, I can't believe I didn't know about Kollwitz. She's such a powerful artist. And conveying it all only in black and white. Did she never ever paint?"

"No. She tried color at first, but turned it down as not being right for what she wanted to do. However, as I told you earlier, she did find another medium in which she felt comfortable. Sculpture.

"And you may have read in the paper or seen on TV that two sculptures were stolen recently from a soldiers cemetery in Belgium. Well, they were by her as well."

"Oh, dear, I have to confess I rarely take time for newspapers or TV when I'm home. And my three-hour commute to and from Rügen is devoted entirely to music and reading composers biographies.

"Well it's certainly true. In our profession one doesn't have much free time, and what we do have, we dedicate to our favorite activities. Mine is reading and rereading Käthe's journals and being on the lookout for prints by her."

"I don't know if I am worthy yet of seeing the journals," Iliana said with genuine humility in the presence of the extraordinary artist who was being revealed to her.

"We'll see, we'll see," soothed Abraham. He had not seen this side of Iliana before and loved her all the more for it.

"Now you talk about power," he said, moving to the next image on his wall. "Look at this next etching of the weavers demonstrating in front of their employer's palatial residence, with its fancy tall iron gates and high wall. See how the men are shouting and raising their fists, and banging on the gates. And see in the foreground how a woman and even a child dig up cobblestones to hurl at the house. And how effective the white wall is in framing the determined mother on the right with her frightened child. It's just amazing how this complicated scene is immediately readable."

"And its title?"

"Simply *Storm*, or if you like, *Attack*."

"And then this final one, this etching?"

"She entitled it simply *End*. No 'The' before it, just *End*. And as you see, we're back in the weaver's hut now. Look at the large hand loom on the left and below it, next to the corpses of two men, the huddled figure of a sobbing woman. And see how in the middle a tall woman in black stands with clenched fists and watches silently as men carry in yet another body through the door. Entering with them is a white waft of battle smoke, indicating that suppression and killing of the rebel weavers is not yet ended."

"What a revelation, Abraham. To experience these artworks under your caring tutelage."

"I am only too happy to share my Käthe with you." Once again he was charmed by Iliana's willingness to learn.

"And don't think I haven't noticed that the individual titles of the cycle all have the punch of a single word: '*Not, Tod, Beratung, Weberzug, Sturm,* and *Ende*.' Remarkable. As much power in the titles as in the images. My dear friend, you have converted me into a Kollwitz fan."

Abraham smiled and ran his hand over his beard. Another time he would show Iliana the journals. Her Kollwitz conversion was enough for now.

15

At his Nordhausen complex high above the Zorge River, Yusri Pahlavi sat in his living room alone looking at photographs. They were old photographs of his father, the late Shah of Iran, his mother—the Shah's beautiful third wife Farah—his sister Leila, and his brother Ali-Reza. Tremendous sorrow had been visited upon the family not only by the revolution that forced their flight from Iran in 1979, but also by the suicides of Leila in 2001 and Ali-Reza in 2011. Now his mother, who had actively helped shape so much of her country's cultural life, lived in Washington, DC and was still active in cultural and charitable causes. But Yusri knew her heart had been broken by the double suicides. And that, at heart, she was a very lonely woman.

A chance encounter with two unusual works of art three years earlier at a most unlikely spot in Belgium had given the peripatetic Yusri an extraordinary idea. He would settle down, find a remote site somewhere in Germany, much more to his taste than Belgium, build a compound with two independent residential areas connected by courtyards, acquire and install the two art works, and then invite his mother to come see them. Yusri knew that once she had seen the works in situ and examined the beautiful dwelling he had built for her, she would remain. He adored his mother and knew this gesture would mean the world to her.

The Nordhausen complex was completed. Now he awaited delivery of the artworks. He looked at his watch. It was eight-thirty in the morning. Within the hour.

16

Both Megan and Dee had gotten up early. Dee continued her rereading of Tolstoy's *War and Peace* on her iPad while Megan went through her daily set of hotel-room-adjusted morning exercises—Pilates, squats, bends, torso lifts, and vigorous running in place with plastic water bottles as weights followed by happy collapse on her bed until her heartbeat returned to normal.

Downstairs they lingered over breakfast in the hotel's elegant restaurant, now set up with a lavish buffet for guests. Then back up to their room for a few minutes to go to the bathroom and take their "senior" pills before going down to the lobby.

As they started to leave the hotel at nine o'clock Megan came to a full stop before a sign just inside the hotel entrance saying pets were allowed.

"Aw, just think. Little Button could be staying here with us. He would have loved trotting on the beach." She was referring to her thirteen-year-old Maltese dog who had accompanied her on her last art adventure—an exciting pursuit of stolen Edvard Munch paintings that took her throughout Scandinavia. In fact, even though he was now blind, Button had been instrumental in the final denouement of his mistress's investigation.

Megan paused and took her iPhone out of her purse to do what she had already done a number of times on the trip. Take a live look at Button via her Amcrest app. A connection was made and Megan raised and lowered the panorama camera at her sister Tina's house until she found Button in his guest playpen. He was sleeping soundly. After all, it was two in the morning in Dallas. Seeing the little dog in real time made her enormously happy.

They walked the brief distance to the Ensor House and arrived at exactly ten o'clock. It was a narrow, four-story building just one block from the beach promenade. But to their surprise and irritation a hand-scribbled sign affixed to the green entry door read "*Ensorhuis gesloten tot de middag vandaag.*"

"What the heck do you think *that* means?" Dee asked.

"I get the general drift: Ensor house—closed till noon. Somewhat close to German. Sounds more dramatic in Flemish though, doesn't it?"

"I don't know. It's Dutch to me. Ha!"

"Well that's it exactly. Flemish is actually a Dutch dialect, not that Belgians would ever admit that."

The two women could not even peek into the shop window as its green metal shutter had been pulled all the way down.

"Well, heck! That's not what the information online gave. It's supposed to be open at ten." Megan said.

"You even logged in again before we went down to breakfast."

"Well, it said the museum was run by volunteers, so maybe one of them had a crisis."

"So what would you like to do for the next two hours?"

"Um, if we were passionate walkers we could go out to Ostend's Atlantic Wall. It was fortified by the Germans during both World Wars. When I went out there, and I have to say, it was decades ago, it was extremely interesting because in addition to the guns and cannons, the bunkers and dugouts were maintained as they would have looked in the two wars."

"Ah, 'had we but world enough, and *energy*,'" Dee sighed, purposely misquoting Andrew Marvell.

Just then a short, baldheaded little man came running toward them. Out of breath, he wheezed: "*Toeristen*?"

"Is he calling us terrorists?" Dee whispered, half seriously.

Megan answered the man in English. "Yes. We want to visit the Museum."

"Ah!" The man answered in excellent English. "I will let you in and give you a tour. I am sorry for the delay. Had a false alarm issue with my family."

"*Issue* or *problem*?" Megan hissed to Dee while smiling graciously at the man as he caught up with them. Dee knew what a bête noire the word "issue" had become for her professor friend. No one had "problems" anymore she would rant; everything was an *issue*, such as "I had an issue starting my car this morning." And TV anchors were to blame, Megan maintained.

Still panting, the friendly man unlocked the museum door, took his sign down, and stood back to let the women in. What they encountered were glass cases stuffed with shells, toys, fans, and above all, carnival masks. A true early twentieth-century souvenir shop. The guide slipped behind a counter to the left and charged them two euros each, a remarkably modest price for a museum. No wonder it used volunteer help.

"Our famous artist James Ensor lived in this very house from nineteen-seventeen until the day he died in nineteen-forty-nine. If you like, there is a film about Ensor on the mezzanine. Or you can go right to the first floor with the three large windows giving onto the street. That was the artist's living room and dining room. Although the artworks you see up there by him are all reproductions, the furniture is from his time there. And you can see the artist's harmonium."

"*Harmonium*?" asked Dee.

"Yes," answered Megan before the guide had a chance to reply. "Ensor was an avid amateur musician and loved to play his own compositions for guests."

"Ah, I see you have your own knowledgeable guide. I do not need to accompany you upstairs then."

"It's not my being so knowledgeable, it's just I've never forgotten that in his later years Ensor practically gave up art as he concentrated on his other passion, music. You know, the way Rossini, after writing thirty-eight operas in thirty-eight years, stopped composing almost entirely in favor of being a gourmand—hence the stout images of him—and an enthusiastic, full-time chef. You can still order *tournados Rossini* in restaurants today."

The guide waved away this superfluous information and returned to the front of the shop. His visitors decided to take in the forty-five minute documentary on Ensor, since Dee wanted a fuller introduction to his work.

"Goodness!" she breathed after the film came to a close. "Imagine keeping a human skull on top of your easel all the time. And then all the *etchings* he made."

"Uh huh, I also hadn't realized he did so many etchings. Shall we go upstairs now?"

On their way up they peeked into a small room with reproductions of Ensor's early works on the walls. It was as though the maritime contents of the souvenir store below had been sucked up as motifs. Shells upon shells, all of odd shapes and colors. Other pictures were sarcastic caricatures or scatological, with defecating politicians interspersed between images of Jesus being persecuted.

"Perhaps all this makes sense after witnessing World War I firsthand here in Ostend," mused Dee, becoming more open to the aggrieved, unpredictable artist.

The women entered the cluttered, claustrophobic living room. A life-size costumed dummy with distorted, grinning head greeted them soundlessly from a chair. Everywhere, on all surfaces and walls, were grotesque carnival masks of various sizes and shapes. The harmonium was pushed up against a huge copy of *Christ's Entry into Brussels* that took up the entire wall. Its vast crowd seen up so close threatened to burst into the room. On the harmonium were small reproductions of works by other artists Ensor had admired. There were more on the entry wall.

Megan came to a stop before one of them, then looked urgently over to Dee.

"Come over here for a minute, please."

"What?"

"Do you recognize this artist?" Megan pointed triumphantly to a small, black-framed etching.

"Hmm. Looks like a procession of angry workers and farmers. All those wrathful faces. And here's a woman marching alongside them in front with a baby on her back. A lot of rage and defiance there."

"Yes?"

"Could it perhaps be by Kollwitz?"

"Right on! It's *March of the Weavers* from her *A Weavers Revolt* cycle. And this isn't a reproduction, it's an actual *print*. A first edition." Megan had her magnifying glass out and was scanning the raised edges of the image.

"I think you just won your 'parallel' of Ensor's and Kollwitz's work, my dear," acquiesced Dee.

"Well, thank you. I think it's nifty that he actually knew and liked her work enough to obtain one. The variety of contorted *faces* here must have appealed to him enormously."

"Wonder if *she* had one of Ensor's works?"

"I doubt that very much. But there is one more thing they did have in common, now that I think of it. Both produced dozens and dozens of self-portraits. His, usually quirky; hers, often with the weight of the world upon her features."

The two friends continued to digest the peculiar pictorial world of James Ensor as more visitors began to crowd in noisily. Finally they had their fill and went back downstairs.

"Is the artist's bedroom not open to the public?" Megan asked the helpful guide.

"No. That's closed to the public. But not much to see there."

"I was surprised to find that Ensor owned an original Kollwitz print."

"Ha!" The guide exuded insider excitement. "There's quite a story there." He hunched in toward the women conspiratorially and lowered his voice.

"Seems there is a *fanatic* Kollwitz print collector out there who for years has tried to buy that particular print from our museum. She wants it because it is a first edition signed print. It's crazy, really. Through an agent she's offered us a later print of the same thing if only we'll swap with her. Can't tell you how many times her representative has approached us. Of course our director has said no, it wouldn't be proper. Just last Tuesday the agent contacted us again. Offered us more than it was worth. Really bizarre."

Where does this collector live if she works through an agent?" Megan was curious.

"Well, we don't actually know her true identity or where she resides. She goes by the name of Marie Schmidt, ha! But her agent comes from Germany. So we're thinking she must live somewhere in Germany."

Megan made a mental note to ask her Kollwitz museum director friend in Cologne if she knew who the "fanatical" woman collector might be.

She thanked the guide and a moment later they were back on the street, walking to the beach promenade and shaking off the house-of-horrors dust of the Ensorhuis.

As they headed for the fine sand, Dee, for one brief second, took her eyes off the ground where she habitually looked to maintain her balance when walking, and gazed out at the ocean. The next second she stumbled and almost crumpled to the ground. But, fortunately, Megan, right next to her, wheeled, caught her under her armpits, and prevented her from falling all the way.

"Whew! That was a close one," Dee said, trembling and trying to compose herself.

"I didn't think I'd need my cane for the Ensor House."

"Let's sit down over there." Megan pointed to a nearby bench.

They remained seated for quite some time looking out at the water as Dee calmed down. Finally they decided to return to the hotel for a late lunch. They stood up. Dee uttered a yelp.

"My hip! My hip! It's out of whack."

"All right, all right, let's just stand here for a minute," Megan murmured, trying to sound calm. Although Dee had faithfully followed her therapy exercises she had not recovered as quickly as hoped.

Finally, with Dee hanging heavily on Megan's left arm, the two friends made their arduous way up the five blocks to the hotel. They collapsed on a couch in the lobby.

"Could we stay in Ostend one more night before returning to Germany?" Dee asked apologetically. "I think some time without any activity would be good for me. That almost falling was a scare and my hip is pretty sore now."

"*Of course* we can stay another night. I'll go tell the front desk right now and then we'll update our Cologne hotel reservation."

Megan was more than worried on behalf of her dear friend. She had not realized just how fragile the hip operation had left her and she faulted herself for pushing too hard. For talking Dee into adding Belgium to their travel itinerary, for visiting the Kollwitz cemetery, and then driving on to Ostend. Yes, a second night at their comfortable hotel before driving back to Germany would be good for them both. And she could bring up her PowerPoint illustrations on her laptop and practice her lecture on Kollwitz for the Berlin Kollwitz Museum.

17

"Give me twenty-four hours and I can rectify this."

Kadeem Tawfeek looked at his irate employer beseechingly. Delivery of the two Belgian statues to Nordhausen and then up the steep, curving road to *Jamshad* had been a disaster. True, there had been no problem unloading the heavy items. But when the protective packing blankets were pulled away for the impatient Yusri Pahlavi to see, the man had yelled his head off.

"But they are damaged! Look at the sides! You stupid, clumsy man!"

Kadeem saw the scarred sides of the statues but did not even look at his blundering helper Jarir, whose fault the damage was.

Instead he gave an instant explanation.

"I beg to inform you. It was your mountain road, Herr Pahlavi. We were not prepared for such steepness. You should have warned us."

Pahlavi was taken aback. He had not thought about the fact that the statues could shift because of the winding road's incline. Yes, he admitted bitterly, he ought to have thought of warning the men about the abruptness of the gradient. But how could the Arab fellow facing him so confidently rectify the situation?

"And how do you propose to do that?"

"We will reload these sculptures and drive back to Berlin immediately where I will store them in my warehouse. Then I will assemble an expert team for the six-hour trip to Cologne. We'll leave Berlin at eight this evening, which will get us into the Cologne at two in the morning when things are quiet. Then we'll go to the preserved ruins of Alt St. Alban where the..."

"...stone replicas of these damaged statues are," finished Pahlavi. Brilliant! He knew exactly what Kadeem was talking about. He had learned about their existence after his epiphany-like encounter with the originals in Belgium when a guide had pointed out to him that the gaze of the father figure's eyes came to rest on the ninth stone in front of him. The gravestone upon which his son's name was engraved.

Researching those heart-rending Vladslo statues, Pahlavi learned about the stone copies hewn after World War II, in 1954, for placement within the skeletal ruins of Alt St. Alban. They were to be part of the war memorial for which the remains of the old church were being preserved.

He also understood the enormity of Kadeem's brilliant plan.

"But even at two in the morning how could you ever gain entry to the ruins and remove the statues without somebody noticing?"

"We would create a diversion," was Kadeem's immediate answer. His agile mind was already hatching a bold plan and he was becoming surer of it every moment.

"I will bring you the statues by this time tomorrow. Nine in the morning."

A long silence ensued. Pahlavi finally spoke.

"All right. Do it."

"Consider it done."

18

The first weekend after returning to Berlin from their Rügen honeymoon, Akram and Monika made a visit to the city's Käthe Kollwitz Museum. Located in a restored neoclassical town house at Fasanenstrasse 24, it was, to their delighted astonishment, just a stone's throw from their apartment.

In front of the four-story villa stood a large black-and-white photograph of Kollwitz's serious, unsmiling face. On the ground a low red-brick pedestal supported a bronze version of the artist's *Woman with Two Children*. The patina, the protective wax coating, was greatly weathered, however. Obviously the statue had been outside a very long time.

Inside the museum, after asking directions to the various permanent exhibits, the couple bypassed the rather dimly-lit two floors devoted to the artist's graphic works and climbed up a narrow staircase to the top floor where the sculptures were. Here the light was much better since all sides of the large room were lit by a continuous clearstory of individual small windows. As they entered, glancing to the right, they gave a start at what was by far the largest sculpture in the room—more than six feet high. It was a bronze-colored effigy of an elderly, dignified, seated Kollwitz. An image executed in the artist's own simplified, yet epic style. A placard informed them the work was by Gustav Seitz and that a bronze version graced the grounds of the Kollwitzplatz.

"How is it that we never heard about Kollwitz in any of our sculpture classes at the university?" Akram asked, then answered his own question: "I suppose it's the old story; because she was a *woman* artist. And also our classes were about sculptural techniques, not individual sculptors."

"But I grew up right here in Berlin and I never heard of her. Never even wondered who the 'Kollwitz' of Kollwitzplatz was. It was just a name."

"Isn't that square out in the Prenzlauer Berg quarter?"

"Yes, and that's where we'll go sometime," promised Monika, looking in wonder at the huge, gaunt effigy.

Next to the Seitz figure, Kollwitz's six sculptures on tall white pedestals looked quite small, the largest perhaps no more than twenty inches or so high. One ceramic sculpture coated with bronze-colored shellac from the 1930s showed what they had seen as they entered the museum: a crouching mother cradling two small children in her arms. The accompanying label noted that the artist had also carved a limestone copy but that it was now lost.

"Perhaps *we* will be the ones to find that lost sculpture," Monika whispered, tugging at Akram's arm affectionately.

"And just where would you propose we begin looking?" he smiled down at her.

"Perhaps in a private collection that was looted by the Nazis and they left the 'ugly' Kollwitz?"

"Perhaps." Akram looked at Monika, then whispered in her ear: "Under the skies of Berlin that cover these Kollwitz sculptures, I pledge my love to you."

Monika blushed and whispered back to him: "And I to you, dear one."

They proceeded to the next sculpture, one much earlier, completed in 1915. It was a mother with a child in her lap. Both were monumental in feeling if not size. The two heads were simultaneously individualized and yet universal.

"Extraordinary," Akram murmured.

"I just love it," his wife confided.

They walked over to one of the largest Kollwitz sculptures in the room, possibly the plaster mold for "their" *Mother with Dead Son* at the Neue Wache. Painted over with a bronze varnish, the two figures melted into each other as the mourning mother's man-child lay bundled between her legs. Her right hand supported her chin, her left hand refused to release that of her son's. It was difficult to stop looking at the ensemble.

Other people began to enter the room, puffing from the long climb. As usual, disapproving glances were aimed in their direction—a bearded Arab with a German woman on his arm. *Entsetzlich*!

A tiny baby hoisted over its mother's shoulder constituted another sculpture and beyond it, created in 1943, was a poignant reminder of a familiar sight in World War II, *Two Soldiers Wives Waiting*. On the floor nearby was a version of *Mother with Two Children*.

Another visitor quietly entered the rapidly filling sculpture room. In appearance she was Muslim, a hijab covering her hair. Other visitors eyed the woman briefly, radiating disapproval.

Monika and Akram did not notice her. They were riveted by the final Kollwitz sculpture in the room: *Soldiers Wives Waving*. It was a tightly knit ensemble of some ten different figures, seven adults, two standing children, and one babe in arms. With one of the women holding her hands up to her face, the group sorrow was almost palpable.

After processing the full impact of the sculpture and their creator's great heart, Akram and Monika looked at each other, nodded silent agreement, and walked back down to the ground floor. At the gift counter they bought a recently published oeuvre catalogue of Kollwitz's sculptures, then left the museum and walked in the direction of Kurfürstendamm for a late lunch at Ho Lin Wah's.

Some twenty paces behind them a woman wearing a hijab also walked in the direction of Berlin's elegant Kürfurstendamm.

19

It was Sunday and Iliana had eagerly returned to Abraham's apartment in Wedding for a second installment in her education about Käthe Kollwitz. This time, instead of walking Iliana through the other cycle of prints on his wall, *Peasants War*, Abraham invited her to sit down on the living room couch with him. In his hands were a red Baedeker guide, a recent biography of the artist, and a black oilcloth journal.

"First let's look at a quick summary of her life," he said, setting the three items down on the coffee table in front of them. He opened the biography and turned to an illustrated chronology in the back.

They looked at the first photograph. It was labeled "Baltic Seaport Königsberg."

"That city was taken over by Russia at the end of World War II, wasn't it?" asked Iliana.

"Exactly. Although there wasn't much left of it after the bombing it endured. Now it's called Kaliningrad. At least they kept the 'K!'"

Abraham pointed to a photograph of twenty-three members of the extended Schmidt family and continued his narration.

"Here's Käthe, in her mid-teens, standing in the back row behind her father. She was the third of four surviving children her mother gave birth to. It's said she had a slight lisp and was a silent, high-strung little child. Well, quite early her father realized she had a remarkable talent for drawing and he was willing to send her to art schools, in Berlin and then in Munich, as I've told you. That's where she discovered painting was not for her. Her strength was in black and white."

"And her subject matter was already about injustice and social problems?"

"Not quite, but she would draw laborers in the street or down at the Königsberg docks because she thought their motions and the lines of their bodies were graceful. 'Beautiful,' in her estimation."

Iliana pointed to the photograph of a slim, bearded young man.

"That's Karl Kollwitz, her brother's school friend. He had the same social democrat convictions as Käthe and her family and was a medical student. They became engaged when she was seventeen and they married just a few weeks before her twentieth birthday.

"How old was he?"

"Twenty-eight. And a short time later he set up his practice in Berlin, in *your* Prenzlauer Berg. In those days it was one of the poorest sections of Berlin."

"How ironic. These days it's turning from hippie hot spot to elegant residential."

"Right. But at the turn of the last century it was just a repetitive grid of rental barracks—*Mietskasernen.* They were hastily and cheaply constructed to house the tremendous influx of workers looking for employment at the factories springing up there and in my Wedding district too."

Abraham pointed to a photograph on the next page.

"Just think. The housing complexes had four to seven stories and sometimes as many as *five* successive dark and damp inner courtyards—the only place for most children to play."

"Good lord! What perfect breeding grounds for tuberculosis."

"You're damn right they were. Look at this photo of Käthe's two darling boys, Hans and Peter. They were about twelve and eight here. And they both suffered lung infections. In fact Peter—the one who was killed in World War I—did come down with tuberculosis."

"That's terrible! Say, didn't Christopher Isherwood describe those huge housing units as 'human warrens'?"

"I don't know. Did he?"

"Yes, I forget where, probably in one of his *Berlin Diary* books. But I've seen a plaque marking the building where he lived out in Schöneberg during the early thirties."

"Uh-huh. Well that's what they were. Human warrens. Now look here. This is a photo of the corner building overlooking the Wörther Platz where Käthe lived for fifty-two years. Just imagine. From that small third-story corner balcony Käthe witnessed the change in traffic from horse-drawn carriages to electric streetcars."

"That's an enormous span."

"Yes, but even more important during that long time was Wörther Platz itself. It became a living stage for her, a theater with its teeming cast of characters, its daily human comedies and tragedies. This public square in an impoverished section of the city became her microcosm in the macrocosm that was Berlin."

Abraham reached for his cherished 1912 Baedeker guide to Berlin, opened it, and folded out a detailed map for Iliana.

"You can see here that the triangular park she looked out on was in fact one of the few open places in Prenzlauer Berg. Look how *seven* different streets converge on the square. But here's another open area right next to it, twice as large."

"I see. It's labeled 'Jewish Cemetery.'"

"Yes, one of the few Jewish cemeteries not totally destroyed by the Nazis. Since you love reading biographies of composers, I should tell you that Giacomo Meyerbeer is buried there. And this cemetery is where, in nineteen-thirty-five, with Hitler's hate campaign against Jews already in place, Käthe had the courage to attend the funeral of her renowned colleague Max Liebermann, Berlin's foremost portraitist. She was one of only thirty-eight mourners to sign the condolence book. That tells you something about the ominous shadow hovering over the heads of our city's Jewish population."

"Makes me shudder to think of those terrible times."

"Actually, Käthe had a number of Jewish acquaintances, collectors, and even patrons. In fact, for example, she was commissioned to create a gravestone by the widow of Franz Levy. He was a Cologne businessman who had died at the early age of forty-five in nineteen-thirty-seven. Käthe responded with a granite bas-relief slab showing four wrist-clasping hands. Very simple but very poignant. You can see it in Cologne's Bocklemünd Cemetery. The marble gravestone escaped Nazi desecration and Levy's wife and children were able to escape to England."

"Thank goodness. But aren't we getting ahead of our chronology a bit?"

"Sorry. There's just so much to tell you about Käthe. Okay. You recognize this picture from the eighteen-nineties, don't you?"

"Ah ha! I do. It's the third image from the *Weavers Revolt* cycle you showed me yesterday. *Conspiracy*. And I now know that it's an etching. Gosh, the individual rocketing lines of the shooting perspective. And the cross-hatchings are so dynamic."

"They are. Well, the year eighteen-ninety-eight was crucial for Käthe because she showed her print cycle at the Greater Berlin Art Exhibition and its jury recommended she receive a gold medal for it."

"How marvelous!"

"*But*, and here's the irony, Wilhelm II—that skittish emperor who led Germany into World War I—*nixed the jury's choice!* The idea of glorifying a people's revolt was considered pernicious and the Kaiser is also reported to have declared that a medal for a woman would be going too far, that such things belonged on the breasts of men, not those of women."

"Oh, dear. Sexism alive and kicking. I remember that Wilhelm also felt qualified to chastise Richard Strauss for what he considered his musical shortcomings."

"Ha! Well, in a sense, the denial of a medal to Käthe shot her to fame, and the next year, at the urging of Max Liebermann, she did receive a gold medal at a major exhibition in Dresden. She was also invited to teach drawing and engraving at Berlin's Women's Academy."

"And she was only thirty-one."

"Yes. She had successfully balanced being a wife, a mother, and an artist."

"Bully for her! And then?"

"She also managed some international travel. Studied in Paris for a couple of months, visited Rodin twice, and another year she got to spend some months in Florence."

"So meeting Rodin was a factor in eventually propelling her to sculpture?"

"Oh, you bet it was. Now look here at the poster she made in nineteen-six for a German Home Workers exhibition. See how few details she gives now; just essence. Not a figure, just a face. The fatigued, lamp-lit face of a woman whose bleary eyes say it all.

"Well, this poster got Käthe in deep trouble with empress Augusta Victoria. She was appalled at the dismal image it broadcast of Berlin's thousands of downtrodden women who worked for a living in their homes. So she, as 'mother' of her country, refused to attend the show until billboards with the poster were taken down."

"I think I understand what was happening in Käthe's art. First she wanted to comment on the present by showing incidents from the past, as with her *Weavers Revolt*. But now she was exposing present day injustices by showing contemporary, *real* people around her."

"Yes, yes, exactly. And she would do that for the rest of her life. But let's take a break for dinner now," Abraham suggested, gratified by Iliana's understanding and enthusiasm. "I've got smoked salmon, cream cheese, capers, lemon, and bagels, plus a salad already made."

"Wonderful! And I've brought the wine." Iliana open up her immense shopping bag and produced a bottle of pinot noir and one of pinot grigio. Take your pick." She was beginning to realize how much she was enjoying Abraham's company. This common pursuit of Kollwitz had brought them much closer together.

After dinner and a dessert of freshly-sliced peaches, they returned to the living room. This time Abraham picked up the black oilcloth journal he had laid on the coffee table.

"This, Iliana, is one of Käthe's diaries. She began keeping journals in September of nineteen-eight and wrote sporadically in them for thirty-five years. Let me read this entry aloud. It fits right in with what you said before dinner about her shift in subject matter from persons of the past to people right around her in the present. Especially the patients she encountered as they waited to see her husband. This is an entry from the first year."

Frau Pankopf was here. She had a black eye. Her husband had flown into a rage.... The more I see of it, the more I realize that this is the typical misfortune of workers' families. As soon as the man drinks or is sick and unemployed, it is always the same story. Either he hangs on his family like a dead weight...or he becomes melancholy, or he goes mad, or he takes his own life. For the woman the misery is always the same. She keeps the children whom she must feed, scolds and complains about her husband. She sees only what has become of him and not how he became that way.

"Whew! That really gives you a picture of how dismal the times were back then," Iliana said with emotion.

Abraham looked at her, a serious expression on his face. "With all the refugees pouring into Berlin these days, do you think it's much better now?"

"I surely see what you mean," Iliana nodded. "I think the huge unemployment they face is horrendous. But tell me, is that *all* Käthe wrote about? The pitiable patients waiting to see her husband?"

"Certainly not. There is much discussion of how her work is going. Many hurdles, some successes. How she aims for ever more abbreviated form. And as a mother watching her boys enter puberty, there are some truly marvelous observations."

"Read me an example, if you will."

"She began writing her observations on this when Hans turned eighteen. Listen to this, referring to both her sons. It's from May, nineteen-ten."

How soon now something very real and definite will emerge out of the boys' lovelorn enthusiasms. Sensuality is burgeoning in all these young people; it shows up in every one of their movements, everything, everything. It is only a matter of opening a door and then they will *understand* it too, then the veil will be gone and the struggle with the most powerful of instincts begin. Never thereafter will they be entirely free of sensuality; often they will feel it their enemy, and sometimes they will almost suffocate for the joy it brings.

"How unexpected!" Iliana burst out. "It's almost as though she were writing about *herself* as well."

"That's what I was hoping you might divine. The truth is that she had only recently ended her one and only extramarital affair."

"Oh! Did she and her husband have problems?"

"Yes and no. Karl loved her deeply, but he was totally devoted to his medical practice, put all his time and energy into what Käthe sometimes referred to as his *damned* practice.

"Here's a line about him from this same year written in September: 'I know no person who can love as he can, with his whole soul. Often this love has oppressed me; I wanted to be free.' But then she also immediately wrote that his love had made her terribly happy. It was more a case of their loving each other in different ways."

"That's something I can understand," Iliana murmured, thinking of the difficult divorce proceedings that had called her back to Vienna just as she had begun medical school in Berlin. Thank goodness for Abraham. He had seen her through a truly tough time.

Her friend closed the journal, reached for the biography, and turned to an illustration in the middle of the book. It showed a loving nude couple locked in a mutual embrace, the seated man with his legs and arm wrapped tightly around the arcing body of the woman, her eyes closed in ecstasy.

"This is one of the images Käthe kept hidden all her life. She called them her 'Secreta' drawings. She wasn't sure what would happen to them after her death, but she couldn't bear to destroy them. It dates from nineteen-nine and is the direct result of her brief, but passionate affair."

"Goodness! Somehow, because of the solemnity of the work by her you've shown me, it just doesn't seem possible that she had another side to her. A passionate side, as you say. And is it known with whom she had the affair?"

"Yes, indeed. He was an erudite, charismatic Hungarian Jew who started up an art gallery, a bookstore, and a publishing entity in Vienna. His social democrat interests brought him to Berlin for a few years and it was there that he met Käthe. Then he returned to Vienna and founded a Wednesday Evening Society which was regularly attended by Freud among other luminaries."

Iliana's face went white. She stared at Abraham, her mouth open.

"Was his name Hugo Heller?"

"Why, yes, it was."

"*Hugo Heller was my grandfather.*"

20

It was half past nine in the morning when Kadeem and his blundering helper Jarir pulled out of Nordhausen in their two vehicles—the rented boom truck and Kadeem's delivery truck—for the three-hour drive back to Berlin.

The rejected statues were immediately unloaded and hidden in the back of Kadeem's warehouse. Later, he thought, he would see about selling them on the black market. As for now, he would round up a team to drive to Cologne's Alt St. Alban church where the second set of large Kollwitz sculptures were. And Jarir would not be a part of that team. The miserable man was told to return the rented boom truck, and given his walking papers.

Everything worked out pretty much as Kadeem had planned. He was able to enlist three reliable helpers he knew from Berlin's Muslim Brotherhood meetings. One, Rashad, was a crane operator and had his own boom truck, the other two, Amin and Hashim had experience with explosives and picking locks. Amin was also a professional welder. The three men understood the mission and were more than agreeable once they heard the wages Kadeem was offering. All were to meet at his Berlin warehouse at eight-thirty that evening for the six-and-a-half hour drive to Cologne. Amin, the welder, would ride with Kadeem in his delivery van. The other two men, Rashad and Hashim, would follow in the boom truck with its thirty-foot rotating telescopic lift. The men were to tell their wives to swear they were home in Berlin that night, should anyone ask.

At nearby Possling's giant hardware store Kadeem picked up a large supply of bubble-pack sheets, packing blankets, FiberFix tape, and a water bucket. Calculating that each statue weighed around three and a half tons, he bought a supply of four-inch nylon straps as well as a twelve-foot reverse eye nylon sling. This time there would be no surface damage to the statues.

Back at his warehouse while waiting for the men to arrive, Kadeem did some Internet research on the creator of the statues that meant so much to his touchy employer at Nordhausen. Turned out the sculptor was a female! He noted that a third carved work by her was also located in Cologne. It was at the Jewish cemetery in the city's outlying district of Bocklemünd Mengenich, and the photo that popped up showed it had an image of hands clasping. Excellent. No face. Good for any religion. Kadeem decided to add that item to what he would be transporting back down to Nordhausen. *That* should appease his angry patron. Might even fetch an extra compensation. What an ingenious idea.

The two-vehicle caravan arrived at Cologne's Old Town at two-thirty in the morning and drove slowly past Alt St. Alban on Quartermarkt. The historic parish church's ruins were joined to newer buildings on either side. On the right stood the Gürzenich festival hall, and on the left the new cubic home of Cologne's great Wallraf-Richartz Museum.

As previously agreed, the men pulled up on Martinstrasse, the street behind the building complex. Four large apartment buildings lined the far side. Their attic roofs were tall and pitched. Ideal for what Kadeem had in mind. The men synchronized their watches, then Amin and Hashim, each carrying a bulging briefcase, walked quickly to opposite ends of the street. They were easily able to pick the front door locks of the corner apartment houses and they accessed the attics without being seen. Expertly they laid out a net of C-4 plastic explosives on the floors and window ledges. Almost simultaneously they ran their detonator lines back down the deserted stairs to the lobbies. They looked at their watches, then set them off.

The blasts were deafening. Both attics caught fire immediately and spectacularly. Flames moved toward the attics of the two inner buildings. Amin and Hashim ran back to their respective vehicles. Amid a growing crowd of panicked people exiting the burning buildings the vehicles returned to Alt St. Alban and came to a stop right alongside of the church. A soft orange spotlight, even at this late hour, illuminated the kneeling stone figures within.

The blaring sound of sirens and fire trucks grew louder and more frequent as the men began their work. Putting on eye-protection glasses, Amin picked up his acetylene torch and began melting bars of an iron grill over the small street entry that Kadeem had spotted in online photographs. Two remaining sections of the nave now formed a new façade and above it was nothing but air. No roof. A huge pointed arch window over the left entry had no panes of glass or bars. Twice as large as the street entry door, it was open to the elements. Open to the intrusion of Kadeem's telescoping crane.

Both vehicles were in place. The back of the boom truck faced the church. The delivery van's rear was alongside it, its lift gate lowered to receive the statues. The grill over the street entry was now melted away enough for Amin and Hashim to enter the old nave and begin their work. Rashad took control of the articulating crane. Expertly, he raised it, then extended the neck through the open arch. He had a perfect line of sight and, in addition, a camera system backup. Directing the crane head precisely above the statue of the woman on the right, he lowered the crane's cable.

Kadeem stood at the breached iron bars supervising the operation. A Luger automatic in his right hand, he watched and waited. The stone figures knelt directly on the ground. No heavy pedestals to contend with here, unlike the difficult grabs he had made at Vladslo.

After tightly securing bubble wrap around the figures with duct tape, Amin and Hashim dipped the FiberFix rolls into their water bucket, waited fifteen seconds, then swiftly wound the tape around the statues. Within five minutes the tape had hardened to steel strength. The men wrapped moving blankets around the statues as an added protection. The eyes of nylon straps on either side of the statues were secured over the blankets to the crane's cable. The statues were ready to be lifted and loaded. The mother figure would be first.

"*Hey*! *What's going on here*?" a man's high-pitched voice addressed Kadeem. The voice belonged to a policeman.

"Nothing you need know about," Kadeem answered, silencing his questioner with a single shot to the forehead. Sirens and shouts masked the sound as the flames on Martinstrasse continued to spread. All hell was breaking out one street over.

And now, with Amin and Hashim signaling to him that their hitching work was done, Kadeem in turn gave a thumbs up to Rashad at the crane controls. There was more than enough vertical clearance for the crane with its dangling load to retract slowly through the open arch. Delicately, it lifted up the precious load, and began its retraction. Then, just as delicately, it made a quarter turn to the left and slowly lowered the sculpture over the delivery van's lift and onto one of two four-wheeled steel hand carts by which Amin and Hashim were now waiting. They rolled it to the back of the van and tethered the cart and its load in place. The same procedure was repeated with the father figure, and it too was silently and safely installed. The whole operation had taken no more than an hour.

Now it was time to quit the agitated neighborhood. The two vehicles threaded their way through a dense labyrinth of police cars, ambulances, and fire trucks. Soon they lost sight of each other, but this, after all, was the plan.

They would make the trip back separately rather than attract attention as a convoy. Kadeem and Amin would take the slightly faster A 44 route, and the other two men would drive by way of A 7.

It was three-forty-five a.m. Not enough time to grab that Jewish headstone, but certainly plenty of time to make the four-hour trip west to Nordhausen by nine that morning—comfortably within the twenty-four hours granted Kadeem by his demanding patron Pahlavi.

21

A day's rest in Ostend lazily contemplating the ocean had completely rejuvenated Dee, as did a hearty early breakfast at the hotel's hot buffet. After Megan had packed up the luggage, including a small, slim portfolio she had brought over from the States, she gassed up the SUV for the drive back to Cologne. She and Dee were on the road by nine a.m. The sun was out, traffic was light, and they were both in a good mood. Dee volunteered to do the driving.

Megan was thinking about the amber Muslim prayer beads she had found on the road by the Vladslo Cemetery. She fervently hoped it might be a clue in solving the case of the stolen Kollwitz statues. Dee had called both her sons the night before and was now caught up on family news. Megan had texted with her sister Tina and all was well on the Dallas home front, including Button, on vacation with Tina's four dogs and two cats.

Dee and Megan were discussing their family updates when the phone began ringing. Megan had synchronized her iPhone with the SUV and the audio system announced the caller: Laura Forelle.

"Why, Laura. How nice to hear from you. We're just on our way back to Cologne."

"Megan! I have terrible news!" Laura's voice sounded tremulous.

"Oh, no! What?"

"*There has been another Kollwitz robbery.*"

"Another? From your museum?"

"No, thank god, not from our museum. The Kollwitz replicas have been stolen right out of Alt St. Alban's!"

"What? *Both* of them?"

"Yes. During a horrific fire last night that devastated the street just behind the church. Right next to the Wallraf-Richartz Museum. While all the city's resources were focused on the apartment block—imagine, *four* buildings in flames!—the thieves used the cover to remove both statues."

"You think the thieves started the fire as a diversion?"

"Absolutely. That's what the police say as well. Just too convenient not to be connected. And a policeman was found shot to death at the site."

"And do they have any idea at all who could have done it?"

"Not yet. They do have one witness, however. A man who lives further down Quartermarkt was walking his dog and he thought he saw a large delivery van and beyond it some sort of crane-bearing vehicle parked right in front of the church. He didn't give it much thought though, since he was more interested in taking a look at the fire one block over."

"Sounds like a pretty slim lead, but at least it's something."

"Let's hope so. Which reminds me, speaking of slim leads. I don't suppose you found anything of interest at the Vladslo Cemetery?"

"Well, yes, Laura. I actually *did* find something. And it might be of real importance. But I'll keep it a secret until we see each other in person."

"Oh, that's really mean of you. Tell me now."

"Sorry, not yet. What I'd like you to do is set up an appointment for the two of us with that arts crime inspector who wanted to meet with you after I left your office."

"Oh, you mean Detective Schauen. Yes, of course, I can do that. He's very nice and a quick learner. He'd already studied up about Kollwitz before I showed him around the museum. I think you'll like him."

"Good. We should get to Cologne about noon. We'd need to stop by our hotel and maybe grab a quick lunch, but do you think you could get Schauen to come by your office this afternoon?"

"I'll give it a try, and call you back with the time if we can set it up."

"Perfect."

"And you're really not going to tell me what you found at Vladslo, you cruel thing?"

"No. Sorry. In this case *seeing* is better than hearing."

The two friends hung up, Laura's curiosity reaching the boiling point.

Dee had been listening with bated breath to the conversation and now Megan filled her in with the details.

"It's the stuff of a movie, isn't it?" Dee asked. "The coordination of blazing buildings with the removal of the sculptures just one block over."

"I agree. It would make a great action film. If only the Kollwitz sculptures had not been stolen."

"I'm confused, Megan. *Are* the figures by Kollwitz or aren't they?"

"It can be a bit confusing. Sorry. They are replicas. In nineteen-fifty-three a professor at the Düsseldorf Academy received a commission from the city of Cologne to create *replicas* of Kollwitz's Vladslo Cemetery figures for the interior of the war memorial it was creating at Alt St. Alban. Two of the professor's master class students carried out the assignment: Erwin Heerich, later known for his cardboard creations, carved the mother figure, and a man who later became the bête noire of the art world, Joseph Beuys, carved the father figure. The statues were installed in nineteen-fifty-four."

"Oh, yes, that last name, Beuys, is certainly familiar to me. Didn't he do installations and weird performance art?"

"Yep. Usually with scorching social and political implications."

Just then the phone rang again.

"Laura?"

"Hallo! Everything is set for three o'clock this afternoon. Is that good for you?"

"Perfect. Look forward to seeing you."

"Me too. Till then."

"Oh, good. We can both sneak in a little nap if we want to," Dee pronounced with pleasure.

They arrived back at the Altera Pars Hotel on Cologne's Thieboldgasse a little after the noon hour and had a quick lunch. Megan skipped taking a nap in favor of doing some Internet research on the type of misbaha she had found by the side of the road at Vladslo. She learned that they usually came with ninety-nine beads, corresponding to the ninety-nine names of Allah to be uttered. If the misbaha had only thirty-three beads, like the one she had found, then the prayer cycle was repeated three times, adding up to ninety-nine. They could be made of precious material, as was the one she had discovered, but also of wood or even olive seeds. Megan looked at her amber find with greater appreciation. Certainly the person who lost it must be looking for it. Perhaps even asking about it on social media? She checked, but was defeated by the plethora of unrelated URLs that appeared.

She glanced at her Apple sport watch with its cheerful yellow strap. She'd better get cracking if she didn't want to be late for the museum meeting.

"I'll be back in plenty of time for dinner," she said as she left the room. Dee was busy with e-mail and hardly looked up, except to voice a pleasant affirmative.

It was a short walk from Megan's hotel to the Kollwitz Museum in the heart of the Neumarktpassage. Adorning the building, two red, gray, and white banners advertised its presence inside the shopping center. Megan took the glass-walled elevator up to the fourth floor and turned to her left. The museum's host was the Kreissparkasse bank, which in 1985 had founded the first Kollwitz museum, initially from its own collection of the artist's works. It was a collection that included some sixty drawings bought from heirs of the artist to prevent their disbursement at auction. In the nineteenth century, German savings banks had served those same poor workers who figured in the artist's work, and the union between bank and museum seemed highly appropriate. Nowadays it was the world's largest holder of Kollwitz drawings, prints, posters, and sculptures. It was also the largest venue for her work: almost thirty-three-hundred feet in exhibition dimension.

Megan headed for the museum entrance and saw a very serious Laura approaching her with a tall, baldheaded man in tow. She was introduced to Detective Herbert Schauen, who grasped her proffered hand warmly. Minutes later they were seated around the small conference table in Laura's outer office. They spoke in German.

Detective Schauen showed Megan photographs of the Cologne crime scene and explained how the hoist, literally, had been accomplished. He told the women that the only witness to have seen anything unusual on Quartermarkt was a man walking his dog who had noticed two large vehicles, one of them with a raised crane, parked in front of the church. But he was hurrying to see the spectacular fire one block over and did not stop to gawk at the sight.

"And the dog wasn't any more helpful," quipped Schauen, spreading his hands out.

"No indications of which direction the vehicles headed off to?" Megan asked, thinking of her discovery at Vladslo.

"None. Only at the church front is there any evidence of heavy machine presence—a short section of sidewalk curb there has been crushed."

"So now we have both sets of *Grieving Parents* stolen—Vladslo and Cologne," Laura pronounced sadly.

"Which brings me to the question," she continued, "what did you discover in Belgium, Megan? You teased me on the phone saying you had found something but that it was better to *see* it than hear about it. Detective Schauen and I are chomping at the bit to know what it is."

Megan smiled obligingly, pulled the misbahah out of her shoulder bag, and laid it on the table.

"This is what I found on the grass by the far side of the road bordering the bottom of the cemetery and just opposite the telltale tire tracks of the vehicles involved in the theft. The beads are of amber and must be quite valuable. I believe it was dropped by one of the thieves."

"An expensive misbahah by the side of the road," murmured Schauen. "Now that's a first, I must say."

"So at least one of the robbers was Muslim," Laura mused. "That probably means his helper, or helpers, were also Muslim. Hm. Detective Schauen, do you know whether there are any Muslim criminals in Belgium who have been arrested for stealing large or precious objects?"

"I haven't heard of any. But there is one gang of young Muslim men we rounded up right here in Cologne recently for theft. In this case it was all about stealing a valuable Torah from the Roonstrasse Jewish synagogue. I don't see them graduating to heavy duty robbery at a war cemetery in Belgium."

"Yes, that's highly unlikely," Megan agreed. "However, I should think that because the misbahah lay on the far side of the road it might suggest that the vehicles were headed east in the direction of Cologne. Therefore it's possible, I think, that the stolen statues were headed for Germany."

Laura and Detective Schauen nodded their agreement. Megan continued her line of thought.

"It's not so much how—obviously a truck-mounted crane of some sort was involved in both instances—but who, and why. Who would want to remove those two Vladslo statues? Why would they want to have them? To own, or to sell on the black market? And the same questions apply to the second robbery. Who were the culprits and why take the replicas? Was it a copycat crime? Were the thieves inspired by the first theft or were they possibly the same thieves? That just doesn't make sense. Again, in either case, who and why?"

"Frau Doktor Forelle," said Schauen, "could you give me a list of the major collectors of Kollwitz art in Europe, starting with Germany and Belgium?"

"I thought you might be interested in that. Here, I've prepared a list for both you and Professor Crespi." Laura handed them each a list printed out on a single sheet of paper.

"As you can see, it is a very short list. It's comprised only of those few passionate Kollwitz collectors who could actually *afford* such a complicated heist operation as we've seen in Vladslo and Cologne. I've searched international auction results for big European, American, and Chinese buyers."

"For Chinese buyers?" Schauen asked.

"Oh yes, her woodcuts were extremely popular in China in the early nineteen-thirties. Anyway, despite scrutiny for important Kollwitz buyers over the past forty years and more, the results have led only to Germany."

Megan studied the list in silence. Only one of the names was familiar to her. The great grandson of Kollwitz's art school comrade Beate Bonus-Jeep. The women's close friendship spanned sixty years. And in spite of the fact that many of the letters from Kollwitz to Jeep, as well as drawings by her in Jeep's possession had gone to Cologne's Kollwitz Museum, it was common knowledge that this great grandson—Julius Bonus—had held a large part of the collection back, especially the artist's early drawings. A succession of them had regularly appeared in auction catalogues, particularly after major exhibitions of the artist's work when interest was heightened.

And now Julius Bonus was indulging in an expensive style of life with homes in three different countries, a penthouse in Hamburg, and a luxury yacht at anchor in the city's harbor. He could have afforded the heist, yes, but why? The statues could never be put up for sale, and it was clear the man did not truly treasure Kollwitz's work. No, Bonus was probably out as a serious candidate.

"Who is Ernst Nehmen?" asked detective Schauen, looking at the next name on the list.

Laura answered. "Ernst Nehmen inherited his father's important Kollwitz collection and has sought to expand it over the years. He inherited a lucrative plumbing business and could very well have financed a statue theft or two. Lives in a big house right here in Cologne. In the upmarket Friesenviertel."

"So Nehmen is someone who might relish owning Kollwitz sculptures for his own edification, rather than trying to sell them on the black market," Schauen conjectured.

"We can certainly check to see if there have been any unusual movements around his home," Schauen continued.

"What's *this* name?" giggled Megan, pointing at the next one on her list. "Come on, Laura, there can't be just a plain old 'Marie Schmidt'! Surely that's a pseudonym."

"Oh, of course it is. It's the pseudonym of a mysterious woman who is notorious for her single-minded greed in acquiring Kollwitz graphics. Her agent is Lukas Zamann, of the Galerie Zamann, well known for ferreting out works of art from private collections. And he's based in Berlin, so she could be too."

"Well, I'm not going to get very far hunting down all the Marie Schmidts in Germany, that's for sure. I shall, however, have the Berlin police check out this Zamann character," Schauen assured them.

"You know," contributed Megan, "when I was at the Ensor House day before yesterday I spotted an unlikely original print on the wall. It was Kollwitz's *March of the Weavers*. And when I remarked on it to the guide, he said that an insistent, anonymous collector had tried to buy it from them for years because it was a first edition, signed print. In fact he said that just last Tuesday a German agent had tried once again to wrest the print from them. So that agent could very well have been your Lukas Zamann, and the employer, your mysterious Marie Schmidt."

"Now that is *most* interesting," Laura acknowledged with raised eyebrows.

Detective Schauen agreed. He returned to the list.

"Well, now, *everybody* knows who Reinhold Fromm is," he said.

"I don't," confessed Megan.

" He's the founder of a huge manufacturing company, Dorotek, out at Prora. They manufacture building components," Laura answered.

"And where's Prora?"

"On Rügen."

Megan looked interested. She was, after all, about to visit the island with Dee. But she had certainly never heard of Prora. *Her* Rügen was the Rügen of Caspar David Friedrich.

"And in the art world," Laura continued, "we know Fromm as the owner of what we call 'the one that got away,' meaning that a specifically sexual drawing by Kollwitz was stolen from the last place she lived—Moritzburg—before her son Hans could arrive to supervise things."

"Moritzburg? Now it's my turn to ask. Where's Moritzburg?" Schauen asked.

"Oh, it's in Saxony, about thirteen kilometers northwest of Dresden. That's eight miles for you, Megan. Have you never heard of Moritzburg Castle, Detective Schauen?"

"Can't say I have."

"All right," Laura changed topics. "Here's the final candidate," she continued, pointing to her copy of the list.

"Siegfried Schocken, originally of Israel, and grandnephew of the Zionist publisher Salman Schocken, who fled Germany when Hitler came into power. Now granduncle Salman owned one of the largest and best private collections of Kollwitz—very famous. After leaving Israel, grandnephew Siegfried settled in Germany, at Weimar, and created his own small, private museum of Kollwitz art, calls it the Schocken Kollwitz Museum."

"All right," Schauen summed up. "We've got a Julius Bonus, an Ernst Beck, a mysterious 'Marie Schmidt,' a Reinhold Fromm, and a Siegfried Schocken—a Wagnerian Jew, I take it. I'll start researching and follow wherever the leads take me. And we won't neglect the Muslim prayer beads aspect."

He paused, then said: "And let's remember this. The men who stole Kollwitz's sculptures are not only criminals, they are *murderers*. A policeman was shot at the site of the crime here."

"Do you think that policeman saw what was going on and tried to stop it?" Laura asked.

"I think, rather, he was probably leaving the fire site and simply chanced upon what was going on at the church."

Schauen's cellphone rang. He answered it immediately, listened, then turned to the women.

"Ladies. Another Kollwitz theft has just been reported. The tombstone for the grave of a Franz Levy at Bocklemünd Cemetery disappeared during the night."

Megan and Laura looked at each other in disbelief.

Five Kollwitz sculptures stolen in five days?

22

The train time from Prora on the east coast of Rügen island to the port city of Stralsund on the mainland took forty minutes. Most of Dorotek's Turkish workers lived there, albeit not in the picturesque Old Town. They lived in hastily constructed, bleak apartment housing in the outer district of Knieper Nord, an area of poverty and neglect known as "Muslim Town" by the locals. The influx of Turkish guest workers into Germany from the 1960s onward had reached even this northeastern outpost. Now a new generation inhabited the teeming quarter and formed a pool from which Dorotek took its workers at the lowest wages possible.

All four of the Muslim families suing Dorotek lived in Knieper Nord. On this mild summer evening in Knieper Nord the apartments of two of the four families were blown apart. Preliminary police reports attributed the incidents to gas leaks.

23

"I want to show you something I've made," Akram told Monika after he picked her up from work at UNICEF.

"Ah ha! Have you finished the Palmyra facsimile?"

"No, not yet. Still working on it."

"All right. Oh, I know. You've made another Kollwitz plaster."

"Not this time. You'll see."

They were leaving central Berlin and driving out to Akram's Dahlem sculpture studio. When they pulled up there were several children in front of his building playing *Himmel und Hölle,* jumping from one chalked square to another.

"Oh, it's Akram, it's Akram!" shouted one of the children. They all stopped their hopscotching and ran to the Nissan van.

"Can we go to the studio, can we go to the studio?" they begged.

"Not now, but next time for sure." Akram patted the nearest child on the head.

In the well-lit studio were several large tables across from the kiln. On one of them was Akram's facsimile of Palmyra's ISIS-destroyed main building of the Temple of Bel, with its rows of columns. Another table was covered by a lightweight green blanket and there was something large and bulky underneath.

"Well, now I am completely mystified," said Monika, her eyes dancing with delight.

"Be mystified no longer, my darling." Akram whipped the blanket off to reveal a model of the Iraqi hill of Aqar Quf outside Baghdad, with its famous ziggurat and surrounding temple complexes. Also replicated in precise detail was the palace area of Tell al-Abyad, with its architectural layers. Stratigraphic evidence showed the palace to have been constructed in three-room modules around large courts. Akram had also indicated the treasury and ceremonial chambers of the royal residence. As for the eroded ziggurat remnant, he had lovingly duplicated in miniature the sun-dried square bricks held together in groups of seven by reed mats, as well as the fired bricks of the ziggurat's outer layers. The ensemble was extraordinary.

"My family used to picnic there on Fridays when I was a child."

"This is simply marvelous! But what made you shift your attention from recreating Syria's Palmyra to this Iraqi historical site?"

"I have made it as a peace offering to my father," Akram replied simply. "After all, it was he who, under Saddam Hussein, excavated its secret chambers. And now the ziggurat is in terrible shape—no government support. That was the only good thing about Saddam. But now the ziggurat is in danger of collapsing. So I thought my father might cherish this replica. It has been made with love."

"What a wonderful idea. Perhaps the gift will move him to forgive you."

"That is my fervent hope. I shall have it crated and sent tomorrow."

Neither the children playing outside nor the man and woman in the studio were aware of the gray Volkswagen Jetta parked down the opposite side of the street. The driver was a woman and she was wearing a hijab.

24

"*Hugo Heller was your grandfather?*" Abraham was looking at Iliana in shock.

"Yes, he was. I thought you *knew* my maiden name is Heller. Didn't I discuss with you at the time of my horrible divorce that, if it weren't for the fuss involved, it might be time for me to revert to it?"

"I do remember your telling me that you didn't want to go to the trouble of doing that, but you never mentioned what your maiden name was."

"Then let me clear things up for you now. Hugo Heller had two sons, Wolf and Samuel, both born in Vienna. Wolf was my father. His interests were very different from those of my grandfather. He became a banker and rarely visited his father."

"Did your father never tell you about *his* father's affair with Käthe?"

"No, definitely not. Not a word. He rarely told stories about his father. I think it is probable he didn't know."

"Well, that's certainly possible. You do know Hugo's wife—that would be your grandmother, Hermine—was an artist, don't you?"

"Oh, yes, *that* I'd heard about."

"Good. Her work, like Käthe's, was also involved with social injustices. And when she died of TB in nineteen-nine, Hugo asked Käthe to come to Vienna and marry him, or at least live with him. But she could not bring herself to leave Karl and the sons."

"*What*? But how do you *know* this?" Iliana had become quite agitated.

"From certain entries, dear, most of them coded in a sense, in her journals. She quotes, remembers, refers to dreams, examines, and even questions her relationship with Karl. Another day I'll show you some of the entries, especially for the year nineteen-ten, when the affair was over but still fresh in her mind. One thing she wrote about was that she simply did not know what to do with the Secreta drawings. She kept them hidden away and, of course, never ever considered exhibiting them."

"And when were they found?"

"Right after her death. At her little house in Moritzburg. Her son Hans found them. But some unknown person had gotten to them first and took several of the Secretas, as we know now from two of them having shown up on the art market."

"Do you know how my grandfather and Käthe met in the first place?"

"They met in Berlin, as you now know. It was soon after he'd moved there with your grandmother and the boys in nineteen-two. As a dedicated and articulate social democrat, he was invited to contribute to a couple of the local party's newspapers, and in his role as an art critic he met Käthe and reviewed her work. Favorably, I might add."

"And she was thirty-five or so?"

"Yes, thirty-five. Hugo, by the way, was three years younger than she."

"Well, he died in nineteen-twenty-three. So my grandfather missed Hitler's extermination."

"Yes, thank god for that."

Abraham thought for a minute, then expressed what was on his mind.

"Iliana, I want to show you another of my prized works by Käthe. It's a lithograph, done a good thirty years after her *Weavers Revolt*."

Iliana followed Abraham into his bedroom, which she had never seen. It was full of bookshelves and comfortably furnished. But she gasped at what she saw hanging on the wall above his bed. With only ten broad strokes of black, Kollwitz had summoned an unforgettable scene: the skeletal figure of death snatching a screaming mother away from the small baby in her arms. Like a powerful C minor chord, the three interconnected heads sounded their melancholy triad diagonally down the stark white paper from right to left.

"I've seen depictions of death before," Iliana said finally, "but this image makes it..." she searched for words, "so *real*. So powerful. How does she do it?"

"Years and years of honing her talent. She continuously worked for brevity of form while imbuing it with instant meaning. And by nineteen-thirty-four, when she drew this, she was master of both form and content."

"This print is every bit as trenchant as her *Pietà* statue in the Neue Wache."

"It really is remarkable, isn't it? Käthe was so potent in two such very different mediums."

Iliana glanced at her watch. It was past eleven o'clock and she had to be up at five the next morning for the start of her work week and the three-hour train commute to Prora. She felt so at home with Abraham, she could have stayed another two hours.

"I can't believe how quickly the time has flown by."

"And I didn't realize it was so late or I never would have kept you Kollwitzing with me so long," smiled Abraham.

Iliana paused and turned to him just before leaving his apartment. Wordlessly, she gave him a light kiss and a courageous smile. She had come to a major decision. One that might imperil her job at Dorotek, but one that was the only right thing to do.

25

Kadeem and his three-man crew had regrouped at Nordhausen with their precious cargo well before nine in the morning. At a cautious pace they began the 5000-foot climb to the complex Yusri Pahlavi had built overlooking the Zorge River. Would the exacting prince be pleased this time?

26

Megan and Dee agreed. It was high time to leave Cologne and drive on to Berlin. They had already had to move back by a day their reservation at Megan's favorite hotel there, the Kempinski just off the Kurfürstendamm—the Ku'Damm, as the Berliners referred to their great avenue.

Megan loved the fact that the hotel had a heated indoor pool. Her favorite exercise was swimming laps for thirty minutes, outfitted with a snorkel so she would not have to lift her head out of water. Some of her best scholarly ideas had come to her while swimming. For that very reason she had built an indoor "Endless Pool" at her lake house in Bonham—some seventy miles northeast of her Dallas home—and she tried to get there every other weekend at least. The last time she had swum in a hotel pool was when she was pursuing a lost panel by Gustav Klimt in Girdwood, Alaska. Perhaps this time luck would lead her to discovering the whereabouts of a lost Kollwitz sculpture or two, or four, or five. Ha! Small chance of that. But one never knew. Megan's antennae were up.

And her hands were on the wheel. After an animated dinner with Laura Forelle the evening before, the two comrades had left Cologne at seven in the morning. Their northeast route via the A 2 would put them into Berlin in about six hours. Conversation was focused on the five mysterious Kollwitz robberies.

"But why *two* sets of the same statues?" Dee asked for the third time.

"Right," Megan also said for the third time, adding: "I certainly don't see it as being a copycat robbery. Just think of the mechanics involved. It's hard to think of two different gangs, if we want to call them that, both conveniently in possession of hydraulic cranes and moving vans."

"Yes. That does challenge the imagination."

"And then there's the speedy follow-up of the second heist to consider. As though the instigator wasn't satisfied with the first pair."

"Well, let's think about that for a minute," Dee mused. "What if, in taking the first pair of kneeling figures, the gangsters *damaged* them somehow. You told me they were made of granite, not bronze. So they might have gotten chipped in the moving. And that would be why the thieves took the second set."

"You could really be on to something there, Dee. I had been vaguely wondering about that too, but hadn't yet really articulated it in my mind. Yes, let's say for now that the motive in taking the second pair was because of some sort of damage to the first pair."

"Okay. We've established a possible motive for the follow-up robbery. Now all we have to do is figure out the motive for the *first* set," Dee smiled, holding up her hands helplessly.

"I think the *title* and original intention of the figures might play a key role here. *Grieving Parents.* You know, Dee, Kollwitz created them in prolonged reaction to her son's death. Let's say a knowledgeable Kollwitz collector is involved. One who obviously knows about the sculptures. Let's say that he or she has recently undergone the loss of a child or a spouse. And let's say the loss caused that person to become deranged. He or she would have to be extremely wealthy to initiate such a 'transfer.' The figures—all four of them, because of theoretical damage to the first pair—would have to be secreted away to some remote setting. Perhaps a small cemetery on private grounds. Say of a large estate. Doesn't even have to be in Germany."

"Oh, I like that. Stealing the Kollwitz pieces in order to have a private memorial."

"And," Megan continued, suddenly inspired, "possibly someone who is Jewish, considering that the fifth theft—the tombstone with its wrist-clasping hands—is a sculpture for the grave of a Jew."

"Didn't Detective Schauen characterize one name on the list of possible suspects as that of a 'Wagnerian Jew'?"

"Yeah. Although I didn't care for his witticism, it *was* an interesting pairing of opposites."

"What do you mean opposites?"

"Well, Wagner was an anti-Semite, as was his second wife Cosima, who carried his prejudice into the twentieth century. So the coupling of 'Siegfried,'—hero of *The Ring*'s third music drama—with a Jewish surname does present a contradiction."

"Good grief! I didn't know Wagner was anti-Semitic."

"Oh, was he ever," exclaimed Megan, warming to the topic. "A malevolent one. When he was in his mid-thirties he published an anonymous essay titled 'Jewishness in Music'—'*Das Judenthum in der Musik*.' And almost twenty years later he published it again, under his own name this time, with an addendum that was almost as long as the original essay. Sound like his operas? He maintained that one could always *tell* when a Jew was speaking because of a certain sing song in tone—he called it a jumbled blabber—especially prominent in the 'commoner class,' as he put it. His conclusion was that Jews were therefore incapable of composing true music."

"Ridiculous! What about Mendelssohn? What about Meyerbeer?"

"Both were the objects of his jealous attacks. And Meyerbeer had even helped him, given him financial support."

"Was he jealous of Meyerbeer?"

"You bet. Of his operatic success in Paris. And after Mendelssohn died, Wagner described his music as 'sweet and tinkling,' without any depth. He maintained that Jews could not speak German or any other European language correctly. For him, Jews were outside the German *Volk*."

"Yikes! No wonder Hitler adored him."

"Yes, and Hitler was thrilled to meet the wife of Wagner's son Siegfried, Winifred Wagner. There's a famous photo of them together at a Bayreuth performance. I used to show it to my classes."

"And here I thought you were teaching *art* history," Dee teased, knowing full well the scope her friend's lectures covered.

"True, but it was important to place the art *in context*. After all, most of the artists we had learned about up to then, Jews and non-Jews, were in Hitler's *Degenerate Art* exhibition of nineteen-thirty-seven. Franz Marc, Wassily Kandinsky, Paul Klee, Ernst Ludwig Kirchner, Emil Nolde, and Jewish artists like Marc Chagall and Ludwig Meidner—they were all in the show."

"Well, perhaps we should concentrate on this Siegfried Schocken first."

They were approaching the entry to the A 2 and Megan took her eyes off the road for a split second to look at her passenger challengingly.

"If you felt you were up to it, Dee, we could take the southern route to Berlin via Weimar and look up this Siegfried fellow."

"Oh, sure! Just drive right up to his residence and knock on his door."

"No," said Megan turning onto a side street and pulling up to the curb.

"What I mean is that we could Google him and possibly find his phone number, then call him for an appointment."

"*Today?*"

"Why not? We'd still get to Berlin this evening and we'd have run down one of the likely suspects."

"You are a dreamer, Megan, a dreamer."

"Reach into the back and pull the laptop out of my sling bag, would you?"

With a look of disbelief on her face, and shaking her head, Dee withdrew Megan's treasured MacBook Air from the bag and handed it to her friend.

Megan immediately went online, typing into her Firefox search machine the words "Siegfried Schocken, Kollwitz, Weimar, Germany." A cluster of URLs appeared, one of the texts indicating Kollwitz's granddaughter Jutta Bohnke-Kollwitz as author of a study on German Jews in the Weimar Republic. Megan knew she had been director of the Jewish Library in Frankfurt for many years.

"Well, that's interesting. But let's keep looking," Megan said as she clicked on the second page of URLs.

"Ah! Here's a reference."

"Come on. I don't believe it."

"Well, it's a roundabout reference."

Megan began reading aloud. "Siegfried Schocken Landgut und

Kollwitz Museum: Nussweg 3, Weimar. Open afternoons, Sunday through Friday, alternate weeks. For information call 49-3643- 45300."

"Hm," ruminated Dee, "it's an *estate*. Just what we're looking for."

"I'm gonna call it," Megan uttered excitedly. She dialed the number on her iPhone and waited for a pickup. It came. A man's rasping voice announced slowly: "Schocken Landgut und Kollwitz Museum."

"Hallo. This is Professor Megan Crespi from America. Might I speak to Herr Schocken?"

The raspy voice said with deliberate slowness: "You are speaking to him and I know who you are. I have read your excellent essay on Kollwitz for the Washington National Gallery exhibition of her work. And I have read about you on Wikipedia."

"Oh, well, thank you for the compliment. Goodness! How did I have the good luck to reach you in person?"

Again the answer came slowly and wheezingly: "It is only because I happened to stop in at the museum this morning. But how can I be of service?"

"Well, I am in Cologne right now and shall be driving through Weimar in a few hours on my way to Berlin. So I was hoping to stop by your Kollwitz Museum, see it, and possibly meet you in person."

"I should like that. Let me talk to my staff for a moment."

There was a pause.

Megan held on, signaling to Dee that things were looking upbeat.

"Yes, the Museum will be open this afternoon and I can arrange to have a staff member call me at the big house once you have arrived."

"Prima," Megan said, knowing Germans favored that optimistic word.

They hung up and Megan looked at her friend triumphantly.

"See the wonders of the Internet?"

"I see the wonder of your persistence, that's what I see."

"Okay. Now we have to look at our paper roadmap; I don't trust the online maps." Megan folded out the map.

"Looks as if we have to go southeast from here and take the A 4 into Weimar. Now let's check that out online. Yes, same information. God bless the Internet after all."

"How long do you think our drive will take? Weimar looks quite a bit south of Berlin."

"It says right here: for this route, four hours and twenty-three minutes. What specificity."

Dee was still shaking her head in wonderment.

"Oh, I'm sorry. Do you not feel up to such a detour?" Megan suddenly remembered how the side trip to Ostend had challenged her friend's energy.

"It's all right. I do feel up to it. At least now while I'm sitting down. Especially as I've never been to Weimar. Perhaps we can even tour Goethe's house there. It's now a museum. I know that much at least."

"Great! That's the ticket. We'll give it a try if we have time. After all we don't have any set time for arriving in Berlin. And it's only three hours from Weimar. In the meantime, once we get to the manor at Nussweg 3, we're going to have to figure out how to get a look around for something like a cemetery on the premises. Perhaps we can split up? I'll meet with Schocken while you check the lay of the land."

"Oh, sure. At my age." Her striking blue eyes rolled up heavenward.

"Just a short reconnoiter?"

"All right. I'm gammy but game," conceded Dee merrily.

27

"It's done."

This was the call for which Fromm had been waiting.

"Target extermination?"

"Yes, both targets plus wives and a couple of kids."

"And delivery of the notes to the others?"

"Done."

28

"It's been *vandalized!*"

"Calm down, darling. What are you talking about?" Monika was at her UNICEF office, cellphone to her ear, and pacing the floor in frustration.

"I'm telling you everything has been destroyed," continued an agonized Akram. My Palmyra reproduction, the Aqar Quf ziggurat, everything smashed to pieces."

"No! But that's terrible, darling. Are the police there with you?"

"Yes, they came immediately, but they have no idea who could have done this. What they did discover was that one of the small basement windows on the street side had been pried open."

"You don't think it could have been one of the children who play outside your studio? A kid just up to mischief?"

"This is *no* mischief, Monika! This is purposeful *vandalism*. Some malevolent person was armed with a hammer and he literally pulverized my work."

"Awful, my darling, just awful. I could come out right after work."

"No, no, Monika. I don't want you to see the studio this way. I'll be waiting for you at home."

After a few more anguished exchanges they hung up. Akram sat with his head in his hands. Monika was unable to concentrate on her work. Two frightening scenarios had flashed across her mind. The first concerned Akram's father, Dief al-Aljamie. Could the man who had cursed his son as an infidel because he had married her and converted to Catholicism be behind this? Akram wept every time he spoke of his irreconcilable father.

The second scene plaguing her mind was the vehement condemnation of her "Arab marriage" expressed by her estranged cousin Rolf von Putbus. Although they had briefly joined forces with other family members in their failed lawsuit attempt to regain ownership of the Granitz hunting lodge in Rügen, they had no love for one another. Rolf had, in fact, sent her a nasty note after hearing of her wedding. He declared that she had "brought shame to the Putbus line" and that he would fight in court for possession of her *Trosthaus* lodge. This had been enough for Monika to have her lawyer immediately draw up a document naming Akram as joint owner of her beloved hideaway as well as the fortune she had inherited.

Dare she voice these two worries to her already devastated husband?

29

Iliana's Monday morning commute to Prora seemed to pass quickly as she rehearsed to herself the lines she would use to her patient Mahdi Kartal. She had diagnosed him as having asbestos poisoning and now she was going to encourage him to initiate a lawsuit against their mutual employer, Dorotek.

It occurred to her that in her new role as instigator of action against injustice she was imitating the extraordinary woman whose works Abraham had introduced her to. A happy smile came to her face. Yes, I too will be a fighter for the poor, for the dispossessed, for the helpless.

In fact, Iliana had already been such a fighter for the poor, often stretching the hours of her medical practice to accommodate night workers, frequently visiting patients in their own squalid homes, and often bearing the expense of vital medications herself.

Oh, Käthe, she thought, I feel so close to you right now. If you could be an artist-advocate, I can be a physician-advocate. Give me your strength.

She returned to the Kollwitz biography Abraham had lent her. She had almost finished it when she came across the fervid words confided by the artist to her journal: "How my life was rich in passion, in pain, in joy, in life force."

Iliana repeated to herself: 'Life force'! Yes, that's what I feel so often. A surge to do good, to help others. And knowing that I have the means to do so. At least medically.

She would visit the Dorotek employee Mahdi Kartal at his Stralsund home after work that very evening. Gently break the news to him that he had asbestosis and that he should sue the company. The address on his file showed he lived in the apartment complex of Knieper Nord. She knew that a number of the Turks who worked for Dorotek lived in that impoverished district of the city on the mainland.

As Iliana exited the train at the Prora station a headline in the local paper at a newsstand caught her eye.

"GAS LEAKS AT KNIEPER NORD LEAVE SEVEN DEAD." She bought a copy of the paper and stuffed it into her bag. After settling in her office and seeing the first patients of the day, she began reading the newspaper article over her lunch break. The tragedy was horrendous: two entire families wiped out. Police credited the tragedy to gas line leaks, but the unexplainable thing was that the two demolished apartments were in separate buildings. Two gas leaks in two buildings at almost exactly the same time? Not likely. The only thing police could find that connected the two explosions at all was that both heads of household were Turkish migrants and worked for the same firm, Dorotek at Prora on Rügen. But that was not unusual. A number of Turks living in Knieper Nord worked for the vast manufacturing company. A coincidence, the police had decided.

Iliana's eyebrows raised at that last line. She knew the Muslim families of at least four former employees at Dorotek had filed suit against Reinhold Fromm and his company. And last week the widow of a thirteenth employee had joined the barrage of lawsuits. Could other complainants be Turks?

She would contact Dorotek's lawyer, Wilhelm Schlau. He should be in his office. He would know if any of the other lawsuit initiators happened to be Turkish Muslims.

Locking her purse away in the bottom drawer of her desk, Iliana walked briskly up the three flights of stairs to the glassed-in connective bridge that led from her modern annex to the old factory building where Schlau had his office. It was next to the company's chief engineer, Ferdinand Fehler. She remembered with some bitterness how all three of them had tried to explain to their irascible employer the asbestos danger inherent in his factory.

Schlau's door was open and his secretary waved her on into his large office with windows overlooking the company parking lots.

"Well! What brings me such a welcome sight?" he asked, giving her a broad smile.

Iliana gently closed the door behind her and sat down in the chair opposite Schlau's desk.

"I don't mean to be mysterious, Willi, but might you tell me if any of the families suing Dorotek are Turkish migrants?"

"Ah, ha. You are not being mysterious at all, my friend. You ask because of the terrible double 'accidents' at Knieper Nord that killed two Muslim Turkish families, don't you?"

"I do."

"The answer is a double yes. First, the two families who perished in the explosion yesterday were indeed suing Dorotek. And secondly, there are two more Muslim Turkish families with lawsuits pending against Dorotek." Schlau paused as Iliana took in the information. Then he spoke again, very softly.

"What are you thinking, Iliana?"

"That I am very worried for them."

"You echo my thoughts, dear. But consider carefully. Would our drama queen CEO actually go that far? You remember he enjoined me to prove that all the men concerned in the lawsuits were heavy smokers. Which would then account for the reason they contracted the lung condition that killed them. No small task. I actually did find one former litigious employee who was known to be a heavy smoker. But he was Polish. As for the rest..."

"As for the rest, there are still two Turkish families who might be in danger."

"Oh, come on now, Iliana. There are other means to 'dissuade' the complainants from persevering with their lawsuits. You don't have to blow everybody up."

"I wish I could believe you."

"Do you think I would continue to work here if I thought there were any chance that what you imply could possibly be true?"

"Let me tell you, Willi, I am having second thoughts about staying on here myself. Something *has* to be done about the continued presence of asbestos at Dorotek. Now, more than ever, I feel the workers need me."

"Yes. Well, all right. I am going to tell you something in confidence, Iliana. But it must remain absolutely confidential. You cannot tell anyone about it."

"Of course, Willi. I promise."

"I have just returned from conferring with a senior official at the Department of Labor. There is going to be an unannounced visit to Dorotek from a government inspector within the next few days. At that time, I've been promised, there will be an assessment of residual traces of asbestos and any other dangerous materials present in the factory. Our director will either have to start getting rid of the asbestos immediately or close down."

"Oh! That is marvelous, just marvelous. Thank you, Willi, for taking me into your confidence. I shall not abuse it."

A few minutes later Iliana was heading back toward her office. She felt relieved by Schlau's words, but now a new question nagged at her. Should she go ahead with her plan to visit her patient Mahdi Kartal that evening? She had to let him know he had asbestosis. But should she encourage him to sue Dorotek as she had planned to?

"*Doktor Frankel? What are you doing over here?*"

Recognizing the voice, she turned on her heel and faced her employer. A perspiring, obese Reinhold Fromm was dressed in gray sweats and had obviously just come from the gym.

She started to reply but was cut off by him.

"You should come over here more often. Plenty of sunshine. Must be gloomy over there down in your little clinic." His inviting smile and penetrating black eyes took in her whole figure.

Was the man actually *leering* at her?

"I have patients waiting." Iliana turned away and resumed her brisk walk toward the bridge way back to the annex. She walked down the hall at an even faster pace.

Fromm, perspiring even more now, stood staring in the direction she had taken. *God, what a cool, unreadable woman that bitch is! Someday...*"

30

Dee was the first to spot the sign as they neared the outskirts of Weimar: Siegfried Schocken Landgut und Kollwitz Museum: Nussweg 3.

"Oh, good. We're not far from Nussweg now," she commented, studying

Megan's open laptop. Their drive from Cologne to Weimar had taken around four-and-a-half hours and their stomachs were letting them know that it was time for lunch.

"If we get off the A 4 and take Highway eighty-five into the city there's a McDonald's right on it."

"Oh, gwad!" Megan's nose wrinkled in disapproval.

"It's convenient."

"Okay. Maybe they are better in Europe. Never been to one over here."

"Have you ever been to one in *America*?" Dee was testing her disdaining friend.

"Of course I have. Just can't remember when."

The teasing continued until they saw the unmistakable McDonald's sign ahead. Megan had to admit that the cheeseburger she ordered "wasn't bad." The bun was even warm.

They had been discussing what awaited them at the Goethe House Museum, should they have time to visit it. Megan had been there when Weimar was still under Communist rule but her recall of the house was vivid as she described the seven main rooms to Dee.

"They are all connected in a straight line across the front of a long yellow building that overlooks a small square. A large living room, two smaller reception rooms, two workrooms, and Goethe's bedroom where, on his deathbed, his last words were: 'Light! More light!' Scholars have been arguing ever since whether that was a demand for the curtains to be opened, or a great philosophical pronouncement."

Dee laughed appreciatively. "That's like Steve Jobs saying on his deathbed: 'Oh wow, oh wow, oh wow!' I love that. Gives me a ray of hope that there is more after death."

"Maybe. My mother used to say she didn't believe in the hereafter but if she woke up there it would be fine with her."

"Fair enough. But you mentioned *seven* major rooms at the Goethe House."

"Right, and for me the seventh is the most interesting. It's called the Juno room because of a colossal marble bust supposedly of Juno at one end. But I would rather call it the music room because there is a fortepiano along the wall there at which guess who played?"

"Oh, gosh. Beethoven?

"Oh, no! Beethoven adored Goethe's writings but Goethe did not care for Beethoven's music."

"Yikes! Well, who then?"

"Felix Mendelssohn, several times. And an eleven-year-old prodigy of the opposite sex...can you guess?"

"Maybe Clara Schumann?"

"You got it! She was Clara Wieck then, of course. And guess how Goethe complimented her? He said she played 'like a man.'"

"Oh, dear."

"I'll give you a more positive insight into Goethe and his way of thinking. Most people know him for his early blockbuster, *The Sorrows of Young Werther*, or his major opus, *Faust*, but he was also extremely interested in science. From color theory to anatomy. He actually discovered the intermaxillary bone in humans.

"What's *that*?"

"I think it's part of the upper jaw bone. The point is that in Goethe's time, scientific dogma held that what differentiated humans from animals was that humans did not have an intermaxillary bone. Goethe proved that theory wrong."

"I'm just impressed that you can remember the word 'intermaxillary.'"

Megan laughed. "That's because I used to throw that medical tidbit out to those students in my classes who were planning to go on to medical school. And I would hear from some of them years later about that intermaxillary moment in class. Delicious fun. In fact one former student, Ralph Broadwater, who became a famous surgical oncologist, even *sent* me the bone once. I never asked how he came by it."

She glanced at her watch and realized it was time to proceed to their goal, the Schocken Museum. It should be open by now.

Nussweg proved a little more difficult to locate than anticipated, but finally with online help they found the road. Slowing down to a crawl, they scanned the low wall surrounding the estate for any site that might look like a cemetery. Nothing. A majestic entrance gate announced in no uncertain terms that they were at the museum. Theirs was the first car in the small parking lot. A short distance from the one-story museum structure stood the neoclassical villa of the owner. It rose three stories and was fronted at the attic story by a lively marble frieze featuring battling or drunken centaurs. So different from Kollwitz's sober frieze of life.

As they entered the building a dark-featured man broke off conversation with the museum guard and began walking toward them, an inquiring smile on his face. He was short with graying hair and had a tracheal tube in his throat. Prominent on the right sleeve of his jacket was a black mourning band. Megan and Dee exchanged meaningful glances.

Putting a finger to his throat as he approached them, the man asked in a raspy voice: "Frau Professor Crespi?" He looked from one woman to the other.

"I am Megan Crespi. And you must be Herr Schocken." She recognized the hoarse voice she had heard on her iPhone.

The man nodded in vigorous agreement.

"May I present my dear friend Dee Whalley."

"It is an honor to meet you both." They shook hands all around.

"Please pardon my tracheostomy tube. It is punishment for the sins of my youth: too much smoking."

"I'm so sorry," Dee said sincerely.

"My mother died of double lung cancer from smoking," Megan volunteered. "She smoked one package of Camels, one of Chesterfields, and one of Phillip Morris every day."

"What a powerful dose. Smoking is a terrible habit, almost impossible to break. But please do not feel sorry for me. I am quite adjusted to this damnable trach. And I am still alive. That is what counts."

Megan nodded her head vigorously, then looked beyond the man to the works on the walls.

"Ah, yes. But of course you want to view the Kollwitz works. Why do you not take your time and when you are ready you ask my guard here to phone up to the big house for me. My wife would like to serve you both afternoon tea, if that is agreeable."

"That would be lovely," said Megan hypocritically, realizing that Dee would not be able to stay behind now to ferret out a possible family graveyard. And Dee was already thinking: there goes the Goethe House visit.

Siegfried Schocken murmured a croaky farewell and left the museum. Megan and Dee were dying to comment on the mourning band he was wearing but the guard kept too close to them for any private conversation. It can't be this easy was the mutual thought left unspoken.

The museum layout was both simple and effective. Kollwitz prints and drawings covered the two opposing side walls while casts of the artist's sculptures stood against the curtained windows opposite the entrance. All the walls were painted forest green making the black and white images by the artist stand out even more than usual. A sign at the entry presented a count of Kollwitz's graphic work: 42 woodcuts, 99 etchings, 133 lithographs, and some 30 drawings. It also showed ten different photographs of the artist taken at different periods of her life. All of them testified to the artist's dark eyebrows and generous space between her nose and long upper lip. Megan and Dee began with the right-hand wall. Kollwitz self-portraits ranged from her earliest years to the final ones. They were not displayed chronologically, however, nor thematically, but in groups of various media—etchings, intaglio, aquatints, lithographs, woodcuts, drawings. In her six-decades of work Kollwitz had created over one hundred self-portraits. Megan could not help but think not only of Ensor, but also of Rembrandt and Schiele, both of whom were also frequently drawn to representing themselves.

But Kollwitz's self-portrayals were different. So often the always recognizable likenesses showed her as universal absorber of grief, of sorrow, of agony. A powerful vessel.

"Look how often she holds her hand to her head," murmured Dee.

"Yes. It's especially strong in this woodcut. Unpretentious always. Barely aging; already old somehow."

"Oh! But look at those two—she's actually smiling."

"Occasionally she did show herself that way. Especially around the time of her marriage to Karl. And although she usually showed mothers worried or in distress, she did sometimes show them lifting up their children in happiness."

"Ah ha! This is the self-portrait lithograph *you* have at your house," Dee said with satisfaction as she pointed to a 1933 image in which Kollwitz showed herself in profile at work. Her arm and hand were extended toward a drawing surface indicated by a single upright diagonal line. Her fingers were pressed together on a piece of black chalk and some dozen broad downward strokes along her arm radiated pure energy.

After thoroughly taking in the potent self-portrait images, the friends turned to the opposite wall. It displayed the artist's second major cycle of works, *Peasants War*. It had taken her several years to complete the series to her satisfaction, from 1902 to 1908. Some of her discarded drawings and etchings for the series had been acquired by Schocken's granduncle and were hung near the corresponding final seven images.

"Oh, they are larger than the print you showed me by her in the Ensor House."

"Yes, that was from *A Weavers Revolt*, her first print cycle. But she was bolder now and required more space while at the same time considerably compacting her images. And she took advantage of the rough aspects of etching to press home her messages."

"Was there a *real* peasant war to which these prints refer, Megan?"

"Oh, yes. It was a sudden outbreak, a revolution really, that occurred in southern Germany in the early sixteenth century. It probably held special appeal for Kollwitz because legend has it that a woman called Black Anna was a main instigator."

Megan pointed to one of the images in the middle of the wall.

"There she is, her back to us, arms raised above her head, urging on the surging wedge of peasants that races across the paper. It's obvious that Kollwitz identified with Black Anna, both urging people to resist and right social wrongs, whether of the feudal system or of modern societal subjugation."

"What's the print called?"

"The German is *Losbruch*, so you could translate either 'Breakout' or 'Charge.'"

"And what is the sequence of these seven prints? Are they and the discarded preparatory drawings displayed in order?"

"I'm sure they must be. Let's start over here on the left. Yes. First we have *Plowing* with a harnessed man straining almost to the ground to pull his primitive plow. Shows the terrible conditions under which the serfs worked. Then here is *Raped*—look, there's the violated woman in a field. left sprawled on her back with her legs forced wide apart. And see Kollwitz's irony in showing sunflowers blooming around her."

"Why that's horrifying."

"And then here's *Sharpening the Scythe*, with the face, hands, and blade seen extremely close up."

"Is that a *woman* whetting the scythe?"

"It is. Look at those two curving lines just above the waist indicating the weight of her breasts. Having the scythe sharpener be a woman would fit right in with the artist's beliefs. When they were children she and her brother would play at defending noble causes behind makeshift barricades."

"What's this one called, with its swirl of peasants grabbing weapons and exiting from what looks like a cave?"

"It's called *Arming in a Vault*, and yes, the peasants are robbing their overlord's vault. Only now comes *Outbreak* with Black Anna."

"Ah, it means even more when we look at the images in sequence."

"Absolutely. Sorry I headed for it first. Couldn't resist. And here are the last two, both signifying the defeat of the rebels. This almost all black one is called *Battlefield*, and you can just see a woman bending over the corpses on the battlefield."

"So powerful."

"Certainly is. And here, finally, *The Prisoners*—see the peasants all crowded together with their hands tied behind their backs."

"And just a single length of rope tying off the whole group—they must be three deep."

Dee turned back to the sixth image, *Battlefield*, which was so dark she had barely been able to make it out. She said so to Megan.

"Ah, but you must come up really close to it. There's a reason for this darkness and this is, for me, the most poignant scene of the whole series. The stooped-over woman in the middle of a field of corpses at night is searching for her son by the light of an oil lantern and this is the moment she holds it up to a young boy's face. Gives one the shivers."

"Oh, lord, yes. And when you think that in another few years Kollwitz would lose a son on the battlefield. Whew."

The women were silent for a few minutes, then Megan spoke.

"Let's cheer ourselves up by taking a look at the sculpture casts before we call up to Schocken's house, okay?"

"Definitely."

The women walked slowly around the six casts of Kollwitz's work. In addition there was a 1937 self-portrait bust in bronze. Its likeness to photographs of the artist was extraordinary. The themes of the other sculptures centered on protective mothers with small children.

"This one of a mother with two babies in her arms you're going to see when we visit the Kollwitz Museum in Berlin. It sits outside the front of the building."

"I'm looking forward to that."

Their spirits lifted, they walked back out to the foyer. Megan nodded to the guard and he immediately phoned Herr Schocken.

"The ladies have finished their museum visit, Herr Schocken." A moment passed.

"Herr Schocken says please to walk right up to the house. He and Frau Schocken are ready to receive you."

"I suppose you want me to break away now and reconnoiter the grounds for a family cemetery," Dee giggled.

"We've lost our chance for that, I'm afraid."

They had not yet reached the house when the great doors were swung open by Siegfried Schocken, his beaming wife at his side. A petite woman with dyed red hair, she too was wearing a black arm band over the sleeve of her right arm.

After introductions had been made, Sandra Schocken led her guests through the living room and into a pleasant all-glass solarium. Its doors were open to a magnificent garden and an expanse of low hills beyond.

Megan and Dee were waved to seats around a circular table upon which all the settings for tea were laid, and within minutes a maid brought in a tray of sandwiches and cookies.

The talk naturally centered upon Kollwitz and how Siegfried's granduncle had come to have such success collecting her works.

"Did he ever meet her?" Dee asked.

"No. And that was one of the big disappointments of his life, since they both lived in Berlin until he fled Hitler for Israel.

"And like Kollwitz, Granduncle Salman was a social democrat," Sandra added helpfully. "They would have had much to talk about."

"So that must be why you have Kollwitz's memorial print to Karl Liebknecht hanging in the living room?" asked Megan, looking at Siegfried.

"Quite so," Siegfried answered. "It was one of the first prints my grand-uncle acquired. The woodcut is amazing, I think, with its lamenting crowd of workers above the laid-out body, and how crowd and corpse are connected by the man who stoops to place his hand on the sheet covering the dead man. And then, look here, the mother who has brought her baby to see the martyred man."

"I am beginning to find it a constant in Kollwitz's work that she prefers to show the *effect* of a tragedy, rather than the tragedy itself," Dee observed. Her hosts nodded in approving assent.

Now that they were talking about a sad event—the 1919 murder of Karl Liebknecht by Berlin police—Megan worked up courage to ask the couple for whom they were wearing mourning bands. Could she have hit detective gold with this very first visit to one of the suspects on Laura's list? No, it just wasn't possible, she told herself. A pause in the conversation provided the opportunity.

"Herr and Frau Schocken. I can't help but ask for whom you are in mourning."

"Our older son Johann," Sandra answered before Siegfried could speak. "He was killed two months ago in a freak automobile accident. A car ran into him and his wife at a busy pedestrian crossing. The driver claimed she hadn't seen them. Johann was killed instantly. His wife Wendy is still in the hospital with a broken pelvis and a concussion."

She stopped suddenly as emotion overcame her. Siegfried took over.

"These have been the worst months in our lives. Johann is buried in our family cemetery right here on the estate and we took some comfort in the unusual gravestone we were able to create for him. It was just delivered yesterday, as a matter of fact."

Megan and Dee both strove not to show their excitement and a second later they were rewarded.

"We visit it every day. Would you like to see the gravestone? I believe you might appreciate the connection it makes with the living."

Now the two American visitors had to mask their eagerness.

"Why, yes," Megan answered for them both. "If it is not too upsetting for you. It would be an honor." She worried, however, as to whether Dee would be up for what must be quite a walk.

"Then I'll send for transportation," Siegfried replied, ringing a bell on the table. He murmured something to the maid who instantly appeared, and in another few minutes a golf cart pulled up in front of the solarium. The driver jumped out and nodded respectfully at his employer.

"This is how we go there. We're not much for walking these days. Do climb in. There's plenty of room for four." Siegfried shepherded the three women toward the cart, then took the wheel. Some minutes later they came to a tall circular hedge and drove through a leafy arcade into a small graveyard. Some very old tombstones were at the far side of the cemetery while newer ones faced them at the entry. Johann Schocken's fresh grave was immediately recognizable.

Megan's jaw dropped.

There, set into the granite tombstone, was the Kollwitz sculpture of clasping hands created for the Levy grave in Cologne.

31

Iliana had made her decision. She would visit her patient Mahdi Kartal at his home in Knieper Nord that very evening. She would give him the bad news that he had asbestosis as gently as possible and recommend treatments to prolong his life. But she would not urge him to sue Dorotek. The danger, if her suspicions about their employer were correct, was just too great for him and his family.

She had no telephone number for the man, only his address. When she arrived back on the mainland she hailed a taxi. To her astonishment, then suspicion, the apartment was in the same complex where the two lethal "gas leaks" had taken place. Looking at the general poverty of the neighborhood, she made an appointment with the taxi driver to return for her in an hour. No taxi stations here.

Mahdi Kartal answered the door at her knock and his eyes opened wide at seeing the physician from Dorotek. His expression of surprise gave way to one of concern.

"Please, come inside Doktor Frankel. What honor." He led her into the front room of what had to be a very small apartment. Two teenaged children who had been watching television disappeared as soon as they saw their father with a guest. Sounds and smells of cooking drifted in from the nearby kitchen.

"Herr Kartal. I think you know why I have come. I wanted to communicate to you in person the results of your tests, and I thought it would be best to tell you in your own home rather than at work."

Kartal paled.

"Please tell me worst."

"Well, the news is not good. You do have asbestosis. The good news is that it has not yet migrated from the lower lung lobes. You do have plaques in the parietal pleura, but about fifty percent of people with your condition do. I'm talking about the space between your chest wall and your lungs."

"I see." As soon as Kartal had uttered those words he was overtaken by a severe fit of coughing, gasping for breath, his lungs rattling audibly. Finally his cough subsided and he was quiet for several seconds, composing himself for the question he needed to ask. He looked directly at his physician.

"Is anything you do for me?"

"Yes, yes, there are several things we can do." Iliana was happy to move on to the palliative treatments available. Without appearing to stare, she was gauging the clubbing of her patient's fingers. The fingernail beds were soft, bulging at the end of the fingers due to the decrease of oxygenated blood flow.

"I will prescribe two medications for you which will relieve most of your pain and will help to thin the secretions when you cough. Also we can give you oxygen therapy to help with your shortness of breath."

"This encouraging, Doktor."

"There is something else you should think about. We don't want you to be exposed to any more asbestos than you already have been. So I recommend you consider getting employment elsewhere as soon as you can."

"But, Doktor, Dorotek *is* my employment! I not trained for anything else. I have only job in family."

"Nevertheless, I urge you to look for another job here on the mainland."

"I tell you what I do," Kartal said, his voice rising in anger and his whole body shaking.

"I make lawsuit against Dorotek!"

"No, no, Mahdi, you would lose. It would take a battery of high-priced lawyers to initiate a legal battle against such a large company. You do not have the funds."

"I try."

"Mahdi, Mahdi. Listen to me. Think, just think for a minute. Our employer Reinhold Fromm is a very powerful man. His company Dorotek is very powerful. Remember what happened just yesterday near your own apartment. Two Muslim families blown up! And *both were suing Dorotek*. Do you think the two explosions were a coincidence?"

An expression of horror and disbelief crossed Mahdi Kartal's face. For some time he was speechless, staring straight ahead. Finally he spoke.

"Now I sue for sure. For them, for me."

Iliana heard herself saying, "You do not want to spend your remaining time in a bitter battle which you cannot win."

"'Remaining time'?"

"Yes. I am sorry, Mahdi. There is no cure for asbestos poisoning."

Again the man was silent. Then he began coughing again, violently. He forced himself onto his feet, then screamed at the top of his voice.

"*Then I kill Fromm!*"

32

Monika looked at her husband with affection. After dinner that evening he had taken a box of sugar cubes and was laying them out on the kitchen table in the shape of a ziggurat. Akram had not returned to his trashed studio over the weekend. He simply could not bring himself to do so. Monika had hired a cleaning service to put things right, including saving any intact parts of his models. And the report was encouraging: a number of the Palmyra modules were intact.

Akram took in the encouraging news with a seeming lack of emotion. Watching him constructing a sugar cube ziggurat made Monika eager to find something uplifting that would engage him. And then she thought of it. She had seen an interesting notice in the day's paper.

"Darling, I noticed there's going to be a lecture at the Kollwitz Museum tomorrow evening at seven. It's by an American scholar and the title is 'The Unknown Kollwitz.' Sounds interesting."

The suggestion worked. Akram looked up at her with a smile.

"Why, yes, my love, what a nice idea. I should like that very much."

"And we could go early. After all, we only looked at her sculptures when we were there before. We could study her prints and drawings this time."

"Yes. Let's do it."

Monika was thrilled to see such a swift change of mood in her Akram. It did not occur to her to wonder why.

33

Jarir Uthman had not returned the rented boom truck the morning he and Kadeem arrived back in Berlin from Nordhausen with their damaged cargo. Nor had he forgotten that Kadeem had held a stiletto to his throat while accusing him of having stolen his lost misbaha.

Although his reading command of German was only fair, Jarir had absorbed the main points of a front-page newspaper article that appeared the day after his abrupt dismissal by that bully Kadeem. It was about the robbery of a second set of life-size kneeling figures. This time not from a remote cemetery in Belgium but from one of Germany's major cities, Cologne. Both sets of granite figures were connected with an apparently famous artist by the name of Käthe Kollwitz. Now Jarir realized his Belgian cemetery heist with Kadeem was part of the news story.

Reasoning that Kadeem would probably be bringing the second set of sculptures to the same Nordhausen address as he had the first, Jarir was struck by the idea that there must be some aspect of the double thefts from which he could benefit. He researched the name Kollwitz on the web and opened every pertinent URL until he had seen an image of every sculpture the woman had ever created. One item fit the bill for relatively easy removal and transportation. A plan sprang to mind.

What if he were to offer that petulant Arab prince at Nordhausen yet another cemetery trophy?

He called a trusted colleague and acted on the idea immediately.

34

"Ah, yes. I see you are quite surprised," Siegfried Schocken said, smiling ruefully and looking at Megan Crespi's face. They had pulled up to his son Johann's grave with its new headstone embellished by Kollwitz's clasping hands relief.

"We commissioned a local sculptor to create a copy of the four clasping hands part of the Franz Levy tombstone in Cologne and this is the gratifying result. Extraordinary similitude, is it not?"

"So similar I thought it was the real thing for a moment," Megan had to admit.

"You have both no doubt heard of the recent theft of the original?" inquired Sandra.

"Yes, and it happened so soon after the double theft of Kollwitz's *Grieving Parents* and their replicas in Cologne," Megan said.

"It's as if there were some greedy collector out there wanting to grab all the Kollwitz sculptures that exist," added Dee.

"You know, Frau Whally," Siegfried rasped through his trach, shaking his head morosely, "you just might be correct. My theory is that they are being stolen for a mysterious, fanatic Asian collector and that they will never be seen again in the Western hemisphere,"

"What an interesting theory," said Megan, making a mental note to pass this idea on to Laura and Detective Schauen back in Cologne.

After an appropriate amount of time at the cemetery the group returned to the house.

"Goodness, how time has passed," said Megan. "We still have a long drive ahead of us if we want to get to Berlin and check into our hotel before dark."

"And tomorrow you have a lecture," smiled Siegfried.

"Ha! Yes. How do you know that?"

"Because we plan to attend. To hear you, Frau Professor Doktor, and on our beloved Kollwitz, is an occasion not to be missed."

"Then I look forward to seeing you there and I thank you for today's visit. Your Kollwitz collection is exceptional. What a treat to see it."

As they walked to the front door Siegfried turned to a table near it and opened a drawer. He drew out a slim book and handed it to Megan.

"May I present you ladies with this catalogue to our museum?"

More thanks were uttered, friendly farewells made, and finally Megan and Dee were back in their car.

"Well, there goes the Goethe House," moaned Dee dramatically.

"Afraid so. But I'll drive us by it at least."

Megan headed for the Frauenplan which the three-story long yellow house overlooked, and they drove slowly and reverently by.

"See, how all eight windows on the second story give out onto the square. Oh, and in the back is a garden where his wife grew fruits and vegetables for their meals," Megan explained.

She decided to drive by one more intriguing Weimar icon before they left the city. It stood in front of the court theater in the center of town. That was all she would tell Dee until they came to a stop within sight of it.

"So that's what you wanted to show me. A larger-than-life double statue. I guess the bronze man on the left, the one holding a laurel wreath is Goethe, right, Megan?"

"Right. Although he is shown a bit taller than he really was. Now who do you think the fellow on the right is?"

"You got me there. Could it be his patron?"

"Nope. It's his fellow poet, Friedrich Schiller. They were quite close—an unusual literary friendship. In fact Goethe staged a number of Schiller's plays at the court theater there behind the statue."

"Well, it's a great theme. Both of them look quite inspired."

"Guess who else thought it was a great theme?"

"Don't know. You tell me."

"German societies in San Francisco, Cleveland, Milwaukee, and Syracuse. There are replicas of the monument in all those cities—in parks, actually."

"Megan, you come up with the darndest pieces of information."

"Somehow peripheral facts like that stick in my mind. Or the beginning lines of a few poems. For instance, when I first visited this double statue there was a group of young school children milling around it. I asked them if they knew who the two figures were. They all shook their heads no. I was just flabbergasted. Didn't the Communists teach children about Germany's greatest poet? I decided on the spot to 'educate' them and recited his most famous poem. I'll say it in German first:

Über allen Gipfeln
Ist Ruh,
In allen Wipfeln
Spürest du
Kaum einen Hauch;
Die Vögelein schweigen im Walde.
Warte nur, balde
Ruhest du auch.

Above all summits
it is calm.
In all the tree-tops
you feel
hardly a breath;
The little birds in the forest are silent,
just wait, soon
you will rest too.

"Very, very nice. But rather sad."

"Yes, as they say, a whole universe is invoked in those brief lines, from nature, large and small, to our imitation of nature in eventually finding eternal rest."

"Gives me goose bumps."

"Oh, and one more thing while we're here in the *Hoftheater* square."

"As long as it's not another quiz."

"No, no, I'll tell you outright. Franz Liszt conducted the premier of *Lohengrin* here in, I think, eighteen-fifty."

"Oh, well now I love that little fact. And I love the opera."

"Me too. And now I'll get us back on the highway. But at least you've seen two Weimar sights other than Nussweg 3 and its private Kollwitz Museum."

"Yes, and I really liked Siegfried and Sandra Schocken."

Heading east they joined the A 9 some twenty miles outside the city and began the northern drive that would take them past Leipzig and Halle right up to Berlin, entering through Potsdam. They should get there in a little under three hours, Dee calculated.

"Haven't you told me you've lectured in Leipzig several times, Megan?"

"Yes, And they were exciting times. It was during the early eighties when the city was still part of East Germany."

"How did you get invited there? Was it because you were teaching at Columbia University then?"

"Oh, no, not at all. I was already teaching at SMU. It was because, just by chance, the conductor Kurt Masur heard me lecture for the Dallas Symphony after conducting the Brahms Fourth there. Shortly afterward, I received a letter from his secretary asking me to speak at the biennial Gewandhaus music symposium. The subject for that fall was Brahms and I was only too happy to oblige because I had just finished writing an article on pictures and objects in the composer's possession. I worked with photographs taken in Brahms's apartment shortly after his death and titled the article 'The Visual Brahms: Idols and Images.'"

"Is that what you addressed at the symposium?"

"Yes. And I was the only art historian there. All the other speakers were musicologists."

"And you gave the speech in English?"

"No. Masur had it translated before the event and I was handed it the evening before I was to speak. I got the translator to read the speech out loud while I recorded it. Then in my hotel room I listened and listened until I got the phrasing and pronunciations just right. I was very scared."

"How did the lecture go?"

"Very well, apparently. And when one of the slide projector lamps blew and they brought me a cup of coffee while a new bulb was being installed, I was actually able to do a little funny ad-libbing about what we'd just been looking at—Brahms' special Kaffee set."

"And you lectured there again?"

"Yes, for a symposium on Anton Bruckner. Again, I was the only art historian. And a really funny thing happened when we speakers were sitting at a long table facing the audience for questions afterwards. A musicologist from Budapest was hogging the mike and Masur finally stopped her, saying 'Ich unterbreche nur ungern—I interrupt only unwillingly'—but I mistakenly thought he'd said he only interrupted Ungaren—Hungarians, so I began laughing hysterically. He realized what I thought and began laughing too. Tears were coming to our eyes we laughed so hard."

"And you continued to keep in touch?"

"Oh, yes. In fact I have a congratulatory telegram from him sent on the occasion of a fancy event at SMU in nineteen-ninety when I was presented with the Austrian medal of honor for my work. The ambassador almost pierced my breast as he pinned it on."

"I've seen you wear that."

"Not very often. I have it as a neck band, but the sharp edges of the decoration tend to puncture my throat."

"And your mother got a similar medal from the Italian government you told me."

"Yup. For founding the Italian Department at SMU. I used to show the photo I took of her receiving it as a lesson in body language."

"What do you mean?"

"Well, in the photo my father is standing with arms crossed proudly against his chest. That's an easy read. But my mother is steepling and at waist level."

"What is steepling?"

"People tend to touch the tips of their fingers together when they are in possession of information or are trying to communicate it, or wishing to appear calm."

"I see politicians do that on television all the time."

"Yes. it's a standard taught gesture for politicos. But do you remember the chess champion Bobby Fisher? He used to steeple so high when facing opponents that he looked at them through his fingers. It really unnerved them."

"You said your mother steepled at waist level."

"As a feminist I'm sorry to say that women in general tend to steeple at waist level while men steeple at chest level or above."

"And this is the sort of thing you taught your classes?"

"In a lateral way, sure. Art history is full of gestures."

Their conversation had brought them to turnoffs for Leipzig.

"Oh, there's one more thing I want to tell you, Dee, about my days with Kurt Masur in Leipzig. He hated the Communist system and the way he showed it was by wearing a bolo tie he had bought in Texas. Not when he was conducting, of course, but for everyday things."

"That's marvelous. Didn't he die recently?"

"Yes. I wrote his widow, Tomiko, a condolence letter in which I described the 'Hungarian' incident.'"

"Good for you. I've always thought a condolence letter that includes a joyous memory is better than one just sending condolences."

"*Watch out!*" Dee suddenly screamed. A large delivery van traveling in the opposite direction had just crossed the median and was hurtling directly at them, the bearded driver braking desperately. Megan swerved and the van came to a shrieking halt just behind them.

"God! That was close!" Megan could feel her blood racing. Dee's face had gone white.

They drove in silence, slowly recovering from the shock of a terrible accident narrowly averted. Megan found herself wondering who would care for little Button if she had been killed. Probably her sister, but she already had four Japanese Spaniels and two cats. Better not to engage in such gloomy thoughts. But it was part of her character and she had a name for it: ANT—automatic negative thought. Her mother had been that way too, whereas her father was an eternal optimist with his Italian high spirits.

Passing the turnoff for Halle reminded Megan that Handel was born there. She had once visited the Handel House with a dear former student, Ehrengard von Gemmingen, who was a cellist. Afterward they dropped in at the Marienkirche where the young woman reverently tried out the acoustics by playing an homage to Handel on her cello. The beautiful vibrato waves of sound floated high above them and it was a magical experience. One shared by several astonished tourists. Now to calm their spirits Megan recounted the experience to Dee. Then she posed a question occasioned by passing the composer's birthplace.

"Dee, do you realize that Handel and Bach were born in the exact same year? Sixteen-eighty-five?"

"Nope, I certainly do not. How do you remember all these dates? Hm. Which one lived longer?"

"Handel, by almost ten years, I think."

"I associate him with England. In fact I remember seeing his grave slab in Westminster Abbey," Dee reminisced.

"Me too. He did spend the greater part of his career in London after all."

"I've read that he wrote lots of *operas*. Wonder why we don't see them performed much."

"We will, I'm sure. There seems to be a revival of Handel scholarship right now."

They began singing bits of *Messiah* as the drive continued. Traffic was light and they were making good time.

"Oh, I have a funny, true story about the *for unto us a child is born* section, Dee."

"Funny?"

"Yes. At least is was for me. When I was a student in Vienna in nine-teen-fifty-six-and-seven, I joined the Vienna choir association. Well, we were scheduled to sing *Messiah*, in German of course, and guess who came to conduct us? Herbert von Karajan. When we came to this part: 'For unto us a child is born,' which in the German version is '*Uns ist ein Kind zum Heil geboren,*' Karajan suddenly stopped us, yelling '*Heil, heil! Nicht HEUL!*'

Seemed it was the Viennese accent making the word '*Heil*' sound as though it were like a baby *howl*—'*zum heulen*.' I was so very proud of being bawled out for having a Viennese accent in my then almost nonexistent German."

"That's a lovely story."

"How about some of that wonderful music right now?" Megan requested. As they got closer to Berlin, traffic had picked up. Dee reached over for her iPad and activated her iTunes. Immediately the sounds of *Messiah* pealed forth and they listened in contented silence.

After a while, as they neared Potsdam, Dee turned off the music.

"Gene and I visited Sanssouci once years, no, decades ago, anyway before he began to show signs of Alzheimer's. We loved it with its Rococo interior."

Megan thought about the seventeen years brave, loyal, and sometimes desperate Dee had nursed her husband at home through the worsening stages of his disease. After he died, she described herself to friends as being "between grief and relief." She had gone through so much and Megan was extremely pleased for her that their trip to Germany was proving to be so interesting.

"I knew what the wood floor paneling at Sanssouci looks like *before* I went there," she bragged.

"How could you know that? Did someone tell you?" Dee had just invited another Crespi story.

"No. I was familiar with it from a painting by Berlin's much-loved Adolph von Menzel, who depicted just about everything, but especially history. The painting I'm thinking of shows Frederick the Great playing his flute in Sanssouci's music room. Probably playing one of his own compositions—he wrote over a hundred-and-twenty flute sonatas and four flute concertos. Well, the checkered wood floor is very prominent in the painting. Frederick is standing on it under the light of a huge chandelier. He's before his music stand, which is lit by two candles, and performing in front of a circle of admirers. And he's facing the court musicians, who have paused in their accompaniment, indicating that Old Fritz is at the cadenza point. The man in profile at the keyboard is Bach's son, C. P. E. Bach. Pretty exciting, huh?"

"For you as a flutist, yes, I can see. Have you ever played any of the king's works?"

"Read through a few of them. Not particularly inspiring but certainly accomplished. Well, when I finally saw Menzel's painting in the flesh I was thrilled because one could clearly see the black wooden flute Frederick was playing. And that's what inspired me to add a wooden Haynes flute to my flute collection. When I play Baroque period music I use it. Although I find it harder to play than my regular silver one."

"So you were musically influenced by a painting."

"Never thought of it that way, but yes, you're quite right."

Megan was now maneuvering the streets of the outskirts of Berlin, heading for the Kempinski hotel downtown. By eight o'clock they had checked into their room and were eating a well-deserved dinner at the quiet Kempinski Grill.

At another, far humbler grill by a gas station on the highway to Nord-hausen, a still shaken Jarir Uthman was rehearsing his plan for the next day.

35

"And as of now one of the two remaining Muslim families has decided to call off its lawsuit against Dorotek."

"Excellent, truly excellent." Reinhold Fromm was talking to the agent responsible for the "gas leaks" that had caused the deadly explosion of two apartments in the Muslim district of Knieper Nord on the mainland.

"So now we have only one family to contend with," Fromm continued, sipping his morning coffee. What have you in mind for them?"

"We have infiltrated the local Muslim Brotherhood and expect positive results within the week."

"I presume the means you will use differ from the previous strategy?"

"Definitely. The police will have no evidence pointing to a connection.

Only the target will. We expect full acquiescence. Annihilation may not be necessary."

"I am pleased with your work so far. Contact me when it is completed."

Fromm replaced the receiver on his phone and smiled. One professional can certainly appreciate another professional. He picked up the day's *Berliner Zeitung* he had been reading when the call came in. Among the cultural events for the week an interesting lecture was announced for the next evening, "The Unknown Kollwitz." That, coupled with another interesting item in the paper—the acquisition of a rare Kollwitz Secreta drawing by Berlin's renowned Galerie Zamann—was enough to bring him back to Berlin. It would be quite a surprise for his wife and children, who only saw him rarely and even then only on weekends. He would leave for the city early tomorrow morning. And he would take his own Kollwitz Secreta drawing with him to show the Galerie Zamann people and, perhaps, even the evening lecturer. It would be most interesting to have an idea of the commercial value of his dominatrix drawing.

36

Although it would be on a week night, Abraham had agreed to attend an upcoming lecture in Berlin with Iliana. Her desire to learn more about "his" Käthe had increased enormously after finishing the biography he had lent her on the artist.

"I have a real *hunger* to know more about her and her works," she told him on the phone after getting back to Berlin from her dramatic visit with Mahdi Kartal. She had tried to calm the man down, telling him that what he needed to concentrate on now was his health. By the time she left he did appear to be seeing reason.

"You know, Iliana, if I perceive that the speaker we'll be hearing tomorrow evening has a true command of Kollwitz and seems like an honorable person, I'm tempted to tell her about the journals, or at least a few of them."

"What? You would reveal that they exist? But you've kept this a secret for so long."

"But you see an American scholar like Professor Crespi would be removed from the art politics that go on here. And I would like to speak to someone knowledgeable about what should be done with the journals after my death. I do not feel I can part with them in my lifetime. They mean too much to me. But I would like to be sure the right thing is done with them after I die."

"Oh, dear, I think I've caught you in a very morbid mood, Abraham."

"No, no, not at all. I just looked up the speaker online and like her credentials."

"That's funny. I did the same. On the train back to Berlin. You do realize she must be in her late seventies or early eighties."

"I don't see that as a minus. She should have the wisdom of a person of her years and she could give an unbiased suggestion as to what to do with the journals."

"But how could you get her alone to tell her such a private thing."

"Oh, of course that's not something to undertake at a lecture event. I would ask that we meet as soon as might be convenient for her, depending on how long she may be staying in Berlin."

"Has she written books on Käthe?"

"I don't know. But there is a long and interesting essay by her called 'Kollwitz in Context' that I found online. And I also found a YouTube interview with her after receiving an award from something called 'Veteran Feminists of America' in which she speaks animatedly of her travel all the way to Königsberg in search of Kollwitz."

"Oh, that's very good. I'll look both up on the train back to Prora tomorrow."

They turned to another subject, Abraham's clinic.

"I'm rather concerned, Iliana. The complexion of my patient makeup is changing radically. Arab migrants are appearing at the clinic not for foreskin restoration, but to be treated for AIDS, or tuberculosis, or syphilis. If I tell them I do not handle those illnesses they become noisy, rude, and storm out. One man actually spit at me."

"Why that's awful! I suppose they are new arrivals from Turkey?"

"Yes, well, via Turkey at least. Many of them are from Syria, as best I could make out."

"Our open border system for these refugees has been strained to the breaking point. At least, for now, Germany has closed its borders."

"But a million new refugees are already here. I just don't know how we physicians are going to cope with the health care so many of them need."

"For heaven's sake, Abraham, I had no idea your clinic was being affected. After all, your sign doesn't even say 'Clinic' on it, just 'WGI.'"

"That makes no difference. Word gets around that it's a medical institution. They come in demanding to be seen. And they scare my regular patients."

"What is our country coming to?"

"I don't know, but something has to be done. Where are all those greeters who used to show up at the railroad stations, welcoming refugees? Why aren't they helping now?"

"And I hear there was an anti-Muslim demonstration in Cologne yesterday in which shots were fired by some Muslim counterdemonstrators. I think one person died."

"Yes, yes, I read about that. Several protesters were wounded as well."

That night after they had said goodbye, both Iliana and Abraham went to bed feeling depressed. So much to worry about.

But both looked forward to what should be an uplifting Kollwitz lecture the next evening.

37

"And on the way to Kollwitz's grave, I want to show you another famous woman's burial site."

Megan and Dee had just exited the taxi they had taken to Berlin's Lichtenberg district early that morning to visit what was often referred to as the "socialist" cemetery of Friedrichsfelde. Their SUV would stay in a parking garage for the duration of their stay in Berlin, as they did not want to mess with trying to find parking places on the city's crowded streets.

First they headed for the only Totebusch grave Dee had been able to find for the Friedrichsfelde cemetery on the Internet while doing cyber research back in Dallas. A helpful man in the cemetery administration office had given them a map, circling the section where the Totebusch grave could be found. And soon they came across what they were looking for. In a long row of headstones, there was indeed a well-identified Totebusch one. It gave the names and dates of four family members. The father's name was Karl Ernst Totebusch and his death date was 1957. The wife had died twelve years later and the youngest child of the four children in the family burial plot had a death date of 2006.

"I never heard of this branch. Don't think they are in our direct family line," said Dee, photographing the graves nevertheless.

"The Totebusches I'm looking for are from further east in Prussia, from Greifswald, where we're going. We might as well walk on over to your Kollwitz gravesite." Megan could tell that Dee was disappointed.

"Okay, but, as I said, I first want to show you the grave of another woman buried here."

They walked toward a tall stone obelisk that stood in the center of a circle of ten flat gravestones. Tooled prominently in white on the gray obelisk were the words: *Die Toten mahnen uns*"—"The dead remind us."

"Look here. She is the *only* woman buried in this honor circle. See? 'Rosa Luxemburg murdered nineteen January, nineteen-nineteen.'"

"Oh, wait a minute. I know that name. From *Downton Abbey*. Robert Crawley says something about having to invite 'this tin-pot Rosa Luxemburg' every time they entertain. I think that's what he said."

"Now that you mention it, I do remember that wry comment. Well now look over here. This is the grave of her colleague, see: 'Karl Liebknecht murdered nineteen January nineteen-nineteen.'"

"How horrible! But who *were* they? I know we just saw Kollwitz's memorial woodcut to him at Schocken's villa."

"Luxemburg was an idealist Polish Jewish woman who had come to Berlin and found her far-left ideology matched that of Liebknecht. He was a Berlin lawyer who wrote against militarism and was active in parliament. And he was sent to prison several times. During World War I he and Luxemburg were cofounders of the antiwar Spartacist League which then became the Communist Party of Germany."

"I didn't realize Communism spread to Germany so early."

"Oh, yes. And as party leaders they were both tortured and killed by government-sponsored armed bands during a left-wing uprising on the streets of Berlin. Her body was thrown into a canal and wasn't recovered until several months later. Their murders inspired further uprisings across Germany in those terrible postwar years when people were literally starving."

"Did Kollwitz have Communist leanings?"

"No, she was sympathetic to the social problems they highlighted but not to the party itself, even though later she and her husband traveled to Russia and she was greatly moved by seeing Lenin's tomb."

"I guess her 'proletariat' themes were well received in Russia."

"You bet. Anyhow, Dee, the reason I wanted you to see these two graves is because of the Kollwitz connection. It was at the request of Liebknecht's family that she created the woodcut. You remember how black prevails and how, Kollwitz being Kollwitz, a *woman* brings her child to witness the solemn moment."

"Yes, I certainly did notice that."

"We didn't have time really to study it at Schocken's, so I'll show it to you when we get back to my laptop. You'll see a banner running along the bottom of the print that reads: '*Die Lebenden den Toten*' which means 'The Living to the Dead.'"

"Oh, that's good, very potent."

"And even more potent if you know Kollwitz was *reversing* the title of a poem she had loved as a girl: 'From the Dead to the Living.'"

Dee looked around her at the green cemetery grounds.

"So the fact that Kollwitz and, you said, her husband are buried here in this 'socialist' cemetery is particularly meaningful. Echoes her convictions."

"That's right. Let's walk over to the Kollwitz family tombstone now. It's over there."

Megan kept her pace to Dee's slower one as she told her about the site and the image she would see on the tombstone.

"Three other family members are buried there. Her brother, Konrad, his wife, Anna, and her brother-in-law, Georg Stern. Their dates are given but under her husband Karl's name, Kollwitz had the word '*ARZT*'—'physician' added. The most touching thing about the simple gravestone is that the bronze bas-relief you'll see on it above the names had been created expressly for that setting by the artist ten years *before* she died."

"So she planned even that."

"Yes, even that. We're almost there, you'll see. It shows the face of a sleeping woman, eyes closed, totally peaceful. And the features are very much Kollwitz's own. One small hand hangs onto the sleeve of an unseen entity whose arms and hands cradle her. These are the hands of god and..."

Suddenly Megan gasped and started to run ahead, leaving a surprised Dee behind.

Megan reached the Kollwitz tombstone and stopped, staring at it and panting heavily. She looked back at her mystified friend rushing to catch up with her and shouted.

"*It's gone! It's gone! The Kollwitz relief! It's been pried off the tombstone!*"

38

In his modest motel bedroom off the highway outside Nordhausen, Jarir awoke before the sun rose. During the night he had experienced second thoughts about offering to sell the unique item in his delivery van to the querulous initiator of his and Kadeem's rejected first delivery. Might the strange man refuse *his* offering? What if paying his bachelor friend Nadeem Naji to follow his van in Kadeem's rented boom truck last night to that deserted Jewish cemetery in Cologne had been in vain? It had been easy enough to dig up the ground around the Levy tombstone, attach wire roping, and crane-lift it up for transfer to his van.

But what if that filthy rich Iranian prince, or whatever the hell he was, turned him down? Or what if he didn't care for the tombstone's theme of clasping hands? Or was offended by the Jewish name below? That, after all, could always be ground down and obliterated.

Oh, well, Jarir finally reasoned to himself, he had taken the trouble to acquire the heavy thing from the Cologne cemetery, had driven all this way, and the piece *was* after all by the same artist who had done the kneeling figures he and Kadeem had removed from the Belgian cemetery. It was worth a try.

After a small breakfast and a cup of very hot coffee which they insisted upon pouring in small doses into the second empty cups they had asked for, Jarir and Nadeem walked to their respective vehicles, discreetly parked off the highway and in back of the motel, and began the short five-mile drive to Nordhausen. They would be there by nine o'clock. It would take another eighteen minutes or so to drive slowly, very slowly, up the steep ascent leading to the Iranian's mansion. No road damage to the sculpture this time. Jarir calculated he would simply appear at the man's entry gates. He would then announce himself and his "extraordinary" load.

A muscular, bald-headed, clean-shaven gatekeeper who looked rather like a bulldog walked over to Jarir's window when he pulled up with a boom truck right behind him. Jarir observed that a pistol was tucked in the un-smiling man's belt. Next to it hung a misbaha. A fellow Arab?

"I have sculpture delivery for His Eminence."

"Oh? I have no such notification."

"Delivery delayed."

"And that crane truck behind you?"

"That maneuver sculpture."

The bulldog man looked at Jarir suspiciously and with obvious dislike for him.

"Stay here. I'll inform the house."

"The house? His Eminence not here?"

"Yes. But it is his secretary I am to call."

The gatekeeper walked out of hearing distance and made the call. An expression of irritation crossed his jowly face. He returned to Jarir, phone in hand.

"I am to ask what sculpture?"

"Kollwitz."

"Koll Vitz?"

"Yes. That is only thing His Eminence need know. He will understand."

The bulldog, whose name was Wafiyy, scowled, then went back out of earshot before conveying the information.

The scowl did not leave his face when he turned, opened the gates, and abruptly waved the two vehicles through.

As he got to the front of the palace where he and Kadeem had pulled up previously, a man appeared at the door. Jarir recognized him. It was Pahlavi himself.

"I know you from before," the prince said evenly.

"Yes. I aid with first two sculptures, ones we took back."

Jarir wondered if the prince would reveal more. Had Kadeem returned with the second set reported stolen? His wish was granted.

"I did not ask for any more Kollwitz than what your colleague delivered."

"Indeed. But I have inside van *genuine* Kollwitz." He paused, then said bravely "And what you have is copies."

Pahlavi looked at him with penetrating eyes. Jarir worried he had overstepped. Indeed it was unusual for him to be so daring. Especially with a man of such station and wealth. But after all, they were equal before Allah. His courage returned.

"If you come back of van I honored to show you what could be yours."

"Lead on."

Jarir jumped into the driver's seat and touched the button controlling the vehicle's rear door. He raised it while Pahlavi walked to the back and waited. Jarir climbed into the open van and rolled forward the steel dolly onto which the strapped Levy tombstone sat. He pulled off the blanket draped over it. In the daylight the clasping hands stood out dramatically.

"I see," Pahlavi said slowly. "Four clasped hands. A spectacular idea."

Jarir drew a sigh of relief. Pahlavi continued.

"You have shown great ingenuity, young man. What is your name?"

"Jarir. Jarir Uthman."

"Ah. Jarir—'one who can pull'—how appropriate," Pahlavi mused, looking him up and down.

"Now let us settle on the price," he said. "What is Kadeem Tawfeek asking?"

Jarir flushed, then decided to tell the truth.

"Kadeem not involved in transaction."

"Yes. I know."

Then why did he ask, Jarir wondered.

There was a long pause. Again Pahlavi looked him up and down. Finally he spoke.

"And what are *you* asking?"

"Thirty thousand euros. This fair price. For you, is *original* work of art, and for me, because I need rent boom truck and hire driver to come here, help with transfer of tombstone to site you want it."

"All right. I will pay your price. But there must be absolutely no damage in transferring and placing the cargo. In addition, I want you to obliterate the name and dates carved below the Kollwitz hands."

"Yes, I do that immediately." Jarir grinned, hardly believing his bold plan had succeeded so well.

"Then walk down the side road with me and I will show you where to bring the vehicles. Your crane should be able to place the tombstone within a centimeter of where I want it placed. This will involve lowering it into an open courtyard. Keep up with me."

Jarir had to jump to stay in step with the brisk pace of his new employer. The road followed the side of the complex and apparently ran around to the back as well. About two thirds of the way down Pahlavi came to a halt and pointed to the wall. It was some seven feet high and the lush branches of several tall shade trees could be seen above it. The prince marked a large X on the wall with his pen.

"This is the point where your crane should lower its load. I will have my man bring a ladder so you can have visual contact with the site. In the meantime, I shall lay out four planks to outline exactly where to place the tombstone in the courtyard. I want it in the far front corner. Understood?"

"Understood."

"Then let us walk back to your vehicles."

The two men walked in silence. Then the prince spoke again.

"After your work is complete, you are never to mention my name or refer to the actual identity of the cargo. The same applies to your helper in the boom truck." Jarir nodded vigorously in assent.

"And that inscription must go."

"Inscription I take care of immediately."

Pahlavi smiled for the first time.

The prince left Jarir by his van and walked past the boom truck to the front of the complex. He signaled his gatekeeper to approach and gave him instructions.

Jarir conferred with Nadeem, then climbed into the back of his van. Because of a recent job requiring etching on a glass door, he still had the handheld sandblaster he had used, along with a hopper of extra-fine, ninety-mesh-grade sand. Donning his visor and hood, he slipped on heavy gloves and aimed the hose nozzle of the sandblaster gun at the inscription on the Kollwitz gravestone. With a psi of 300 the procedure was more than effective. The noise was deafening and sand streamed everywhere, but the task was accomplished within twenty minutes. Jarir then applied some closely matching gray patch material he had on hand. When it dried one would hardly be able to notice the alteration. Lowering the rear door he walked back to the boom truck to instruct Nadeem, passing the prince and the unsmiling gatekeeper on the way.

"And *after* the placement?" the bulldog asked his master.

"You will proceed as you did with Kadeem and his men."

The gatekeeper smiled.

39

"I tell you they've taken the Kollwitz relief!"

Dee had caught up with Megan and was staring at the vandalized upright slab. The names were there but the bas-relief Megan had described to her was not. Deep gashes of a power tool were evidence of how the sculpture had been pried away from its bronze backing. What an outrage!

"This must have just happened," Megan cried indignantly. "I'll call the police." She grabbed her iPhone from her purse and dialed 112. A male voice answered. Megan gave her section location in the cemetery and described what had happened. The man said tersely he would send officers there immediately.

"I've got to let Laura know in Cologne," Megan told Dee. "How odd: *she* told me about the theft of the second set of grieving parents and the Levy gravestone; now *I* inform her about *this* robbery."

After telling an incredulous Laura about the theft, Megan looked up the cemetery office number and informed the helpful man they had met of what had happened in his own cemetery. Within minutes two very worried looking men ran up to them—the cemetery administrator and a young employee.

"I don't *believe* it," the younger man yelled as they caught sight of the defaced tombstone. The men stood catching their breath and looking around them. The young man looked at his employer beseechingly.

"This must have happened during the early morning hours. I made the usual check last night and everything was fine."

"Is there a morning check?" Megan wanted to know.

"No. There's never been any reason to have a morning check," the administrator answered.

An approaching siren sounded and a police car soon pulled to a stop in front of them.

After the situation had been explained to the officers, the two cemetery employees and the American visitors were asked to regroup in the cemetery office while the police began a thorough search of the grounds around the Kollwitz burial site.

As they waited to give their accounts to the police, Megan, who had been pensive since they arrived in the office, pulled Dee aside and whispered to her.

"Our thief has to be someone who is fascinated not only by Kollwitz but obsessed with death. Just think of it. Four figures in mourning taken, two, from a remote cemetery, and the other two, stolen from the ruins of a bombed-out church memorial to the war dead. And now two further images on tombstones. It's becoming downright spooky. Like dealing with a necrophiliac."

"You are right. And from your list of suspects we can now exclude the Siegfried Schocken family. At least it certainly seems so."

"Yes, I think so too. Well, that still leaves us our suspect list: there's that grandson of Kollwitz's best friend, Julius Bonus who lives in Hamburg."

"Now hold on, Megan. I am definitely *not* going to Hamburg."

"No, no, not to worry. Detective Schauen said he would handle that. I'm just going down the list. Remember, we did think he seemed unlikely. And I certainly wouldn't tab that gadabout as a man obsessed by the dead."

"Then there's Ernst Nehmen of Cologne. Detective Schauen is investigating him as well, of course. That leaves the mysterious 'Marie Schmidt,' whatever her real name is, and industrialist Reinhold Fromm of Rügen Island."

"How convenient it is that one of our travel goals is already Rügen," Dee said, relieved that Megan was not once again amending their travel itinerary.

"But how are you going to make contact with the multimillionaire head of a busy factory?" she asked.

"I haven't figured that out yet."

"And do we even know where 'Marie Schmidt' lives?"

"Nope. Not yet. But with all this activity something's bound to happen. Someone's certain to make a foolish move."

"You talk as if it were a chess game."

"In a sense it is. And we have to figure out the pattern of the plays as well as who the players are."

Just then one of the policemen entered the cemetery office and began taking down their statements.

Afterward, with police permission, Megan took photographs of the vandalized Kollwitz tombstone to e-mail Laura. She even conducted a quick search of the grounds on her own, wondering, foolishly, she told herself, if she might somehow find another misbaha in the grass nearby. Nothing.

It was time to go. Especially if they wanted to fit in the one museum visit they had planned before resting and eating an early dinner with the Kollwitz Museum director before that evening's event. And, as always,

Megan wanted to practice her lecture one final time. During the forty-one years of her teaching career at Columbia and SMU she had followed the same routine: practicing with the images the night before class, and then running through the lecture again just before giving it the next morning.

They walked to a nearby taxi rank and gave the driver instructions to take them to the Museum Island and drop them off at the Bodestrasse. Megan wanted to show her friend two just-restored famous works by her nineteenth-century idol, Caspar David Friedrich, to whose hometown, Greifswald, they would be driving. The large oils were *Abbey in the Oak Forest* and *Monk by the Sea*. Both had just gone through a three-year restoration. Megan was eager to see the results and the Alte Nationalgalerie owned the greatest collection of Friedrich's works.

Megan had been worried that the double set of steps leading up to the venerable museum might be too daunting for Dee, but she soldiered on gamely, pausing on the first level to admire the bronze equestrian statue of Friedrich Wilhelm IV fronting the center of the building on the top level.

"Now you've got a real treat waiting for you inside. A wonderful two-figure statue of the two Prussian princesses, Luise and Friederike."

They could see it as soon as they entered the building, and Dee gasped with pleasure. The two sisters, carved in pristine white marble, stood frontally, side by side, their bodies pressed lightly against each other. The older Luise, destined to be queen, had her left arm protectively around the shoulders of the younger Friederike, who confirmed the hug by gently placing her left hand on her sister's draped fingers. Her face was dreamy, fixed on an inner vision, while Luise seemed to be gazing resolutely ahead at her future.

"I *love* them!" Dee exclaimed, drawing closer to the marble pair. "Who'd you say did these figures?"

"I haven't yet," laughed Megan. "He was Gottfried Schadow and the double statue was completed in seventeen-ninety-five. You might be surprised to know that it was considered 'too erotic' and temporarily banned from public exhibition."

"Too erotic? But wasn't that the style of dress then, clingy frocks accentuating the breasts?"

"Yes, and in marble it becomes a sort of wet drapery and very form-revealing. You can also see, encapsulated right here in the two figures, how, over the centuries, sculpture evolved from archaic flatness to classical three-dimensionality."

"I can?"

"You can. Look at the flatness of Luise's garment and the greater rotundity of Friederike's garb. Can you see how those impressions are conveyed?"

Dee studied the statues up and down.

"Oh, yes. I see what you mean. Luise's dress is indicated by long vertical folds and Friederike's skirt falls in curving horizontal bands. I can see that it has a greater three-dimensionality."

Megan smiled and pointed to the right where a dense crowd of visitors was forming.

"Oh, oh, looks as though we may have to stand in line to see those two Friedrichs."

While they waited for the line to move forward into the Friedrich room Megan told Dee a bit more about Queen Luise, one of her favorite historical personalities. Especially because she died so young, at only thirty-four, after giving birth to nine, some say ten, children.

"Ah, well, nine or ten children was standard for those days, wasn't it?" Dee, mother of two sons, sighed.

"Did you know that Luise pleaded in person with Napoleon to spare Prussia?"

"Where? Did she go to France?"

"No, no. The meeting took place at Tilsit up in East Prussia after the Germans' disastrous losses to the emperor."

"And was she successful"

"Unfortunately, no. But her people loved her for that act of courage and, after she died, Napoleon is supposed to have said that the king had lost his 'best minister.'"

"Hm. I'd like to read a biography of her when we get back to America."

"I'm delighted to have piqued your interest." Megan paused, thinking about the word she had just used. Then she made a confession.

"You know, Dee, I've always liked the word 'piqued,' as in pique interest, but I'm never quite sure how to spell it. Is it peek, peak, or pique."

"I had trouble too until I learned a neat phrase. It goes: 'I wasn't going to look at the beautiful mountain, but the peak piqued a peek.'"

"Marvelous! Now I'll always remember the distinctions." They continued to study the Luise and Friederike images in silence while waiting for the line to move forward into the Friedrich room. Then Megan spoke.

"I just want to tell you one more thing I've always remembered about Queen Luise. You know how I'm always afraid of drafts and that I might lose my voice or come down with a cold just before giving a lecture. Well, she too was worried about drafts and created the fashion of wearing a neckerchief at all times."

"I can certainly see why that important historical fact would stick in your mind, Megan." Dee looked at her hypochondriac friend fondly.

The line finally moved inside the room with the two Friedrich paintings. Each had a wall to itself along with didactics and photographs of the restoration process.

"They're both so large," said Dee, surprised by their size. The glimpses she got of the paintings through the crowd showed they measured nearly six feet wide and four feet high.

"Large in size, yes, and grandiose in meaning. And the reason they're here in Berlin is that just a few months after Queen Luise's death, the king bought them for his private collection. So he must have had a sense of their deeper significance."

Megan looked to her left and saw an opening in the crowd.

" Let's go over to *The Abbey in the Oakwood* first. There're fewer people there."

They stood in front of the painting, taking in the eerie scene depicted. At first it seemed as if it were a painting about light: the upper two thirds of the canvas were illuminated by an almost blinding setting sun. Puncturing the silver-yellow light were the leafless branches of gnarled black oak trees and, in the center, the single remaining arch of what had once been a monastery. Only after taking in the lifeless silhouettes above did Dee's attention shift to the abysmally dark lower third of the painting and its small, black-clothed figures. There, amid tombstones and crosses, a ragged procession of monks bore a coffin to an open grave yawning in the snow.

"I take it this sad display is more than just a burial scene in front of an abandoned abbey ruin," said Dee after a long silence.

"Yes, you're so right. With his beloved silver-gray mists Friedrich always intoned multiple meanings. For instance, here we could have raw nature taking over what had once been man's cultivation of it. On another level the gothic abbey ruin could stand for the decline of faith as the painter sensed it. But the most searing meaning is, of course, death and decay. The trees and bushes are lifeless, as is the roofless abbey ruin."

"It's very, very powerful," Dee said earnestly.

"Yes. And the interesting thing is that when it and the other painting in this room, *Monk by the Sea*, were completed and Friedrich showed them together in Berlin in eighteen-ten, he specified that the *Abbey* picture be hung *beneath* the *Monk* painting."

"And do we know why?"

"I have a theory, but no one really knows why for sure. Let's go look at it."

The crowd had thinned and they were able to stand quite close to the *Monk* painting.

"Oh, my gosh, he is so small compared to the rest of the picture," Dee commented. "He's almost lost within those bands of sky and sea and beach."

"That's true. And notice that there is no depth, no perspective in this painting. Everything is forced to the front. And another thing contributing to the monk's miniature status within the painting is that his head is *below* the horizon of the ocean."

"You know, the S shape of his body looks almost like a question mark. Is it?"

"That's a possible reading," Megan smiled, now in her element. She continued.

"Certainly as companion piece to the *Abbey*, every element—monk, beach, ocean, sky—is open to multiple understandings and interpretations. Friedrich originally had the monk looking to the right, and his feet are still facing that direction, hence the swayback that looks like a question mark. But thinking of it that way is good because it's clear the monk is contemplating the elements. You can just make out that his chin rests on one hand as he looks out at the vast churning sea and brightening sky above it."

"The monk seems to be a redheaded monk."

"Right. That's what makes scholars think it must be a self-portrait. Friedrich was in fact a redhead, as his frontal self-portraits show. And he seems to be dressed as a Capuchin monk, which signals a longing for the faith and simplicity of earlier times."

"The painting is so effective with its horizontal bands of raw sand, ocean, and sky. And the monk—the only vertical in the entire painting—hasn't even made it to the center of the composition yet. He's still far to the left," Dee pondered out loud.

"Guess where scholars have located the beach site," commanded Megan.

"Let's see. It can't be Greifswald because that city is inland, on a river, and not directly on the Baltic coast."

"Right and..."

"...Oh, I know! It must be Rügen."

"Right again. Friedrich escaped to his beloved island whenever he could. And he took his bride there on their honeymoon."

"Wow. We can reenact the picture when we get there. What do you think those white flecks on the water are? Whitecaps or birds?"

"Perhaps both? Most of them do look like swallows with their wings extended, but I think Friedrich also wanted to suggest the surging power of the sea, just as he wanted to invoke the vastness of the sky above. See how only at the top does the blue sky triumph over the storm clouds below. And you can easily see Friedrich's scumbling technique there in the transition to that celestial blue."

"What the heck is 'scumbling'?"

"It's just a term for applying, in this case, multiple thin layers of blue gray over an underlying white. The restorer had to be especially careful not to disturb the brushwork there."

"Now I see it."

"Another thing the restoration revealed is that Friedrich originally planned to have a few boats offshore, but then deleted them in favor of the powerful economy his bands of sand, sea, and sky broadcast. In fact you could almost say that there is a direct line from this swelling painting of bands to the abstract bulging shapes of a Mark Rothko."

"And yet, because of the monk, Friedrich's image is not abstract," Dee objected. "We contemplate what *he* contemplates."

"Quite right. It is the monk, with his back to us the viewers, that produces the empathy we feel. What Friedrich did in this picture is use what's called in German a *Rückenfigur*, a figure seen from the back so that we look over his shoulder, experience the same vastness of nature he feels. And the word for empathy in German is also a good one: *Einfühlen*."

"Nice. So tell me, Megan, why do you think Friedrich wanted his *Monk* picture hung *above* his *Abbey*?"

"I think that it's because his *Abbey* painting deals with death, including the ostensible death of religion, and so it is irredeemably pessimistic. But the *Monk* picture ultimately throbs with life. Nature, even if at times it seems threatening and overwhelming, is a vibrant force. It is life itself. And after all, there is optimistic blue sky at the very top of the picture."

"So you think Friedrich wanted the viewer to read from bottom to top?"

"I think so. Perhaps from death to eternity, something like that."

"It's nice that they were sold as a pair then."

"Yes."

"It's funny. I can get my fill of the *Abbey* picture after looking at all the details—the monks, the crosses, the two candles, the freshly dug grave—but it seems to me that I could look at the *Monk* picture forever."

"Ha! You are echoing the sentiment published by a friend of Friedrich. He wrote that in looking at the *Monk* he felt as though his eyelids had been cut off, that he could never *stop* looking."

"Interesting. Now you've made *my* eyes hurt."

"Sorry. Here's one more fact that will make you hurt. Guess who, in later times, adored these two paintings?"

"I give up. Who?"

"Hitler. Friedrich was prized by the Nazi Party as supremely German since he was painting at a time when his homeland—Pomerania—was still a dominion of Sweden. Ah, you're surprised. It's true. Sweden had owned Pomerania on the Baltic coast since the early seventeenth century. Then, briefly but dramatically, Napoleon's troops occupied it, including Friedrich's hometown of Greifswald. Pomerania was only ceded to Prussia in eighteen-fifteen, at the Congress of Vienna when they parceled out all the lands Napoleon had conquered."

"So the Nazis considered it a statement of independence, of longing for German identity."

"That's a nifty way to sum it up."

The crowd had thinned and the women were able to walk back and forth between the two works, reading the didactics and studying the restoration photographs. They returned to the irresistible *Monk* image and stared at it anew.

Megan finally spoke: "On a happier note, Dee, both paintings had an influence on Wagner's opera set designers."

"That does make me happier. Now I'm going to, with great effort, tear my lidless eyes away from the *Monk* and suggest we have a little lunch before going back to the hotel to rest and for you to practice."

"Lord, how the time has flown. You're so right. We need to leave. There's a quiet café on the first floor of the Neues Museum, just next door, so we can get something simple right here on Museum Island before we take a taxi back to the hotel."

"The less walking the better."

"And I promise you I'll show you only one thing in that museum."

Dee looked worried. Her friend was unstoppable once in a museum.

"Oh, dear, what's that? It better be worth the walk."

"It's just the bust of Nefertiti."

"I'm running, I'm running!"

40

The elders of the Muslim Brotherhood of Berlin in the district of Wedding were worried. A demonstration in front of the main railroad station in Cologne two days earlier had turned ugly. In the face of a strike by unemployed German truck drivers protesting the continued emigration of refugees from Syria and the resulting loss of jobs in the trucking business, some local Muslim youths had fired shots at the protestors, wounding four and actually killing one. So far they had eluded the police and anti-Muslim sentiments were growing. This was the last thing Muslim Brotherhood organizations in German cities needed.

And now four different Muslim women had come forward to report their husbands were missing. The leader of the group was Zaeemah Tawfeek, wife of a Kadeem Tawfeek. Her story was that of the other women: the husband had left on a "two-day job" but had not returned home on the third day. The elders were at a loss. From the wives they had been able to establish that all four men knew each other. As for professions, two of the men were experts at explosives, and in addition one of them was a professional welder. A third was a crane operator. Zaeemah Tawfeek described her husband Kadeem as proficient in transport. But none of the men had returned from what seemed to have been a collective out-of-town assignment.

Should the Brotherhood elders inform the Berlin police? In the face of such animosity toward Muslims right now it was doubtful whether the police would place much importance on a report of four missing Muslim men. The elders decided it would be prudent to wait one more day. Surely at least one of the husbands would show up by then. Now was not the time to make waves.

41

Reinhold Fromm's morning in Berlin had been productive. He had, incognito, visited the city's famous Galerie Zamann and studied the new Kollwitz Secreta drawing on display. It showed a pair of lovers with features very like the man and woman of his own Secreta drawing. Only this just-discovered example showed them lying down in a mutual embrace, their lips touching, their nude bodies entwined, with the man gently bending over the acquiescing woman. The gallery was full of gawking potential buyers.

Fromm did not inform the personnel that he himself had a Kollwitz Secreta drawing in his briefcase, but he was more than pleased to note that the asking price for their version was 85,000 euros.

Now, as he sipped champagne and ate fresh oysters for lunch at Fasanenstrasse's new Mediterranean restaurant, suitably named Inizio, he speculated on what the "unknown Kollwitz" of the evening's lecture might be. Could there exist, as he hoped, more of the artist's Secreta drawings? And would he find the American professor knowledgeable enough to inspire sharing his own Secreta drawing with her?

Time would tell. So far no one, not even his wife, or should he say *especially* not his wife, knew he had a collection of erotica drawings in which a Kollwitz dominatrix image figured. And he would most probably keep it that way. Still it was stimulating to consider sharing his secret. He glanced at his watch. Another six hours to go. He could return to the Galerie Zamann, give a false identity, ask to speak to the owner, and have him evaluate what *his* Kollwitz would fetch on the open market. It might make for an interesting afternoon.

Hm. "Zamann." That was not a German surname he was familiar with. He looked it up on his smartphone. It only gave the name with one "n" at the end and as a given name, not a surname. And it wasn't German, it was Arabic. Meantime, the passage of time, or age, or destiny. The fellow, if he looked Arabic, must have changed the spelling of his name to appear more German. Well, perhaps destiny had something in store for him today. He glanced down. The briefcase at his feet held, literally, a secret. Fromm decided to return to the Galerie Zamann.

42

Iliana left Prora early that afternoon. She wanted to get back to Berlin in time for a relaxed dinner with Abraham before they attended the Kollwitz lecture. Hot-headed Mahdi Kartal had visited her office that morning. He was still fuming about the explosions in his neighborhood that had killed two former workers at Dorotek and he was still threatening to kill the company's CEO. Iliana had used all her persuasive powers to calm her patient down, to reason with him, and she believed it had worked. At least he no longer spoke of killing Fromm.

On the train she read the latest news about the Cologne protest and the frightening rise of anti-Muslim sentiments in its wake. An amazing verbatim account by a female Czech physician who had worked in Munich for years was given. It ran in part:

Yesterday, at the hospital, we had a meeting about how the situation here and at the other Munich hospitals is unsustainable. Clinics cannot handle the number of migrant medical emergencies, so they are starting to send everything to the main hospitals.

Many Muslims are refusing treatment by female staff and we women are now refusing to go among those migrants! Relations between the staff and migrants are going from bad to worse. Since last weekend, migrants going to the hospitals must be accompanied by police with K-9 units.

Many migrants have AIDS, syphilis, open TB and exotic diseases that we in Europe do not know how to treat. If they receive a prescription to the pharmacy, they suddenly learn they have to pay cash. This leads to unbelievable outbursts, especially when it is about drugs for the children. They abandon the children with pharmacy staff with the words: So, cure them here yourselves! So the police are not just guarding the clinics and hospitals, but also the large pharmacies.

We ask openly 'where are all those who welcomed the migrants in front of TV cameras with signs at train stations?' Yes, for now, the border has been closed, but a million of them are already here and we will definitely not be able to get rid of them.

Until now, the number of unemployed in Germany was 2.2 million. Now it will be at least 3.5 million. Most of these people are completely unemployable. Only a small minimum of them have any education.

What is more, their women usually do not work at all. I estimate that one in ten is pregnant. Hundreds of thousands of them have brought along infants and little kids under six, many emaciated and very needy. If this continues and Germany re-opens its borders, I am going home to the Czech Republic. Nobody can keep me here in this situation, not even for double the salary back home. I came to Germany to work, not to Africa or the Middle East!

Iliana was nonplussed to read such a frank and damning account. The physicians in her circle, with the exception of Abraham, had all been too politically correct to complain openly. And here was this brave Czech physician down in Munich detailing the truth. Why hadn't the news channels given greater coverage to the situation? What was the matter in Germany that the only people who really spoke out were displaced truck drivers?

When Iliana got to her apartment she stood in front of her Kollwitz picture of laborers returning home and stared at it as though to receive fresh energy, fresh strength from the artist's vigor. She thought of Abraham's recent complaints about the refugees crowding his clinic and how they frightened the other patients. She thought about her own patients at Dorotek. And in what poorer health the Turkish migrants and their families were than their German coworkers.

It was six-thirty. She must shake off this morose mood and be in good spirits for Abraham at dinner. Perhaps the evening's lecture would be uplifting. Käthe! You who were so strong, give me some of your strength.

43

Akram got home early from his vandalized sculpture studio in order to fix dinner for Monika and himself before attending the lecture at the Kollwitz Museum that evening. The studio was now cleared of the trashed objects, and he was slightly heartened by how many of the ziggurat and Palmyra sculpture fragments were salvageable. That is, should he ever return to his two projects. They had both been intended to win back his father's approval. At the moment he did not have the heart to continue with the miniature replicas. And a daring idea had taken hold of him.

What if he were to obtain—temporarily, of course—an original Kollwitz statue from which to make a further cast? Yes, it would be a surmoulage and unauthorized, but still it would be a Kollwitz. He would present it to Monika in celebration of the gift they were expecting. His darling wife was now almost four months pregnant. They could keep the new Kollwitz at their Rügen *Trosthaus* hideaway. No one would ever know.

Their visit to the Kollwitz Museum this evening would give him the opportunity to slip up to the top floor and reconnoiter. Take a look not only at how firmly the small sculptures were affixed to their pedestals, but also discover where exactly the exit door led. Was there a fire ladder or stairway down to the ground from above?

All this was going through Akram's mind when he heard the sound of a door opening. Monika was home early. He jumped up and ran to embrace her. They smiled into each other's eyes. Then Akram fell to his knees, placed his hands lightly on his wife's belly, throbbing with life, and declared as he had so often: "Under the skies of Berlin, I pledge my everlasting love to you and our child."

He did not tell her of his plan for later that evening.

44

With Dee as the only audience, Megan had practiced her PowerPoint lecture in plenty of time for a slow walk over from their hotel to the Kollwitz Museum on the nearby Fasanenstrasse. In addition to her small sling purse, Megan was carrying a light portfolio with her and she thought with amusement about the intricate loads she used to carry to her class and public lectures.

"Dee, do you realize that just fifteen years ago I would be carrying two slide carousels instead of a tiny thumb drive. What a miracle."

"I keep telling you, we live in incredible times. And I'm so happy we both are still here to witness and enjoy them."

"You know, when I began teaching, the department of art history at Columbia still had four-by-four-inch glass-bound slides in its collection. We had four slide projectors in each classroom: two for the regular 'modern' two-by-two-inch glass slides, and two for the almost obsolete but seemingly irreplaceable larger slides. And probably someday PowerPoint will seem old-fashioned."

"Well, certainly all things are possible."

"I was stopped by the US customs once when returning from giving a lecture on Schiele at the Courtauld in London. They examined one of my slide carousels with suspicion and instructed me to take out a few slides and hand them over. Unfortunately, the ones they held up to the light pictured some of Schiele's most erotic works. You can imagine the disapproving looks I received."

"I can indeed. The life of an art historian can be fraught with danger," Dee joked.

As they turned to mount the steps to the museum a smiling woman with gray hair opened the door, and waved a welcome. She was the new director, Dr. Grete Bulliet. Megan had not yet met her in person although they had had an active e-mail correspondence. They shook hands heartily and Dee was introduced.

"Would you first like to check out the room where you'll be speaking, and download your flash drive into our computer? We are eating a light meal right next door so we have plenty of time."

Bulliet gestured in the direction of the famous Literaturhaus with its Café Wintergarten, and Megan's face flushed with delight.

"Oh, I love that café. How perfect. And yes, let's make a tech check first. And if I may, I'd like to leave this portfolio inside the podium, if the room is secure." Grete nodded a reassuring yes.

Dee waited at the admissions desk while her friend followed the director up the stairs to one of the first-floor rooms. The download was swift without complications and the room, lined with Kollwitz graphics, had been outfitted with folding chairs. A large screen with a simple podium to the audience's right were at the far side of the room.

Megan and the director returned downstairs and steered Dee to the connecting café's garden.

"Would it be all right with you if we sat outdoors?" Bulliet asked solicitously.

"We'd love that, wouldn't we, Megan?"

Megan nodded enthusiastically and the women sat down at a corner table. Their conversation centered naturally on the recent Kollwitz sculpture robberies. Bulliet's theory was that an Arab gang was behind them, probably selling the stolen goods abroad.

"I can tell you that the police in Cologne are investigating this very aspect," said Megan.

The talk turned to Kollwitz collectors in Germany. Megan described their visit to Siegfried Schocken and his Kollwitz collection.

"Oh, yes, it's one of the finest private collections in existence. Of course he bills it as a 'museum' for tax reasons, but I suppose that's within his rights."

"I was so sorry about their son's recent death," Dee said

"Yes, a *terrible* car accident," Bulliet responded, then added: "The Schockens are attending your lecture this evening."

"Ah, ha, they did mention that they'd be here. A bit of a drive from Weimar. I hope they're going to stay here overnight."

The director leaned forward conspiratorially. "And another very unusual guest—she's practically a hermit—is also coming."

"Who?"

"She calls herself 'Marie Schmidt.'" Bulliet lowered her voice.

"*But I know her true identity.*"

Just then a dignified, white-haired woman in her seventies approached them. She was in a wheelchair and a male attendant stood behind her.

"Frau Doktor Bulliet, good evening."

"*Ach, Gott,* I was just telling my guests here that you were coming to our event this evening. Frau Schmidt, may I introduce tonight's lecturer, Frau Professor Doktor Crespi, and her friend Frau Whally."

Marie Schmidt looked up at Megan, eyeing her keenly.

"I look forward to your presentation, as you are American," she said crisply without smiling.

"Thank you. It's always such a privilege to speak about Käthe Kollwitz. More and more people in America are beginning to appreciate her work."

"Won't you join us if you've come here for dinner?" Grete Bulliet asked.

"No. I am meeting someone here." Schmidt looked around the garden.

"Ah, there he is." A portly man with dark hair and beard was standing to one side of the garden looking at them. Marie Schmidt waved him over.

"Ladies, I present Lukas Zamann of the famous Galerie Zamann here in Berlin."

After introductions were made the pair, accompanied by Schmidt's caregiver, slowly moved off to a nearby table of their own. Megan overheard a terse remark the wheelchair-bound woman hissed to Zamann as they left: "It is time you delivered what you assured me you could procure." Megan was not able to hear Zamann's answer but saw him nod his head vigorously.

"I can't tell you what I was going to tell you now," Grete Bulliet whispered to Megan, "but perhaps after your speech."

"You are so mysterious, Grete. I'll rush through my lecture so you can tell me who she really is."

Grete looked worried until she realized Megan was only joking.

The sun was beginning to set and a gentle breeze could be felt in the garden. The women eagerly attacked their light meal. Megan declined the offer, but her companions happily ordered the slightly sour, cloudy beer called *Berliner Weisse* along with their meal. Megan's refreshment was the knowledge that her "unknown Kollwitz" speech would truly be revelatory for a German audience.

45

At his suggestion, Akram and Monika arrived at the Kollwitz Museum forty-five minutes before the evening lecture was scheduled to begin. She was pleased to study the graphics displayed on the second and third floors, whereas Akram expressed a desire to revisit the sculptures on the top floor. Monika was happy not to climb the extra steps.

Admiring the artist's sculptures, aside from Akram, was a young couple with two children. When would they leave? They were grouped in front of Kollwitz's ten-figured *Soldiers Wives Waving* and the children were excitedly pointing up at the two standing children in the group.

"That's *me*, that's *me*," insisted the little girl. She looked to be about ten. Her older brother was no less enthusiastic.

"And that boy is *me*," he proclaimed.

The parents smiled in approval and then herded the children toward the staircase up which they had come. Akram stood at the far side of the room impatiently waiting.

Once he heard the clatter of the group's descent echoing on the stairs, he walked quickly to the heavy white exit door. He had spotted it on his first visit. It was to the left of Seitz's effigy of Kollwitz. Gingerly he pressed on the door. It moved outward from the mansard roof slightly. Would an alarm go off? He pressed again. No alarm sounded. Then Akram pushed a bit harder and the metal door swung slowly out and onto the upper deck of a fire escape. Moving out onto the deck, Akram looked up and could just see the clearstory rise of small windows framing the large room below. He looked down. Five flights of stationary metal stairs with hand railings led to a small inner parking area running along the side of an adjacent tall building. Three cars were pulled up next to it.

Ah, perfect. Akram could park his van in the same place, say around two that morning, mount the fire escape stairs, open the exit door, and enter the sculpture room within a couple of minutes. One sculpture under his left arm shouldn't hinder his descent. He would leave the back of his cargo van open so he could load the sculpture securely. The whole procedure should take under fifteen minutes at the most.

What he needed to be sure of was whether he would be able to open the exit door from the outside. An inconspicuous wedge of some sort was what was needed. Akram had just the thing. The laces of one of his white tennis shoes. The left one. Going back inside the sculpture room he inserted the white lace at the bottom between the door and its frame. Unless you were looking for it you would never know a wedge was there. And if Monika noticed that he had only one shoe lace on, he would say he'd slipped it off in the van because it pinched his foot while driving.

Now the only thing to do was decide which sculpture to borrow. Akram looked at his watch. Still twenty minutes before the lecture began. He studied each sculpture on its own white pedestal, but in his heart he already knew the answer. The one most suitable for Monika, the expectant mother, was the small 1915 mother with a child in her lap. As he had remarked upon first seeing the work, it was monumental in feeling if not in size. And the fact that the heads were generalized rather than specific was attractive as well. His decision made, Akram ran quietly down the three flights of stairs to the lecture room.

He would borrow the statue tonight.

46

Laura Forelle's flight from Cologne to Berlin-Tegel had arrived eighteen minutes early and she was inside the Kollwitz Museum and in her seat a good fifteen minutes before that evening's lecture was scheduled to begin. She hoped to surprise Megan by her unexpected presence. It was a last-minute decision to come, since, when Megan was in Cologne, she had told her regretfully that she didn't think she'd be able to get away. But the lure of an "unknown Kollwitz" was too strong to ignore. She had tried to get Megan to tell her what the speech was going to be about, but Megan had just smiled enigmatically and murmured something to the effect that Americans can sometimes bring surprises to Germans.

Laura looked around at the rapidly filling room. Ah! Sandra and Siegfried Schocken were just entering. Laura rose from her seat, beckoning them to join her in the front row. They came forward and exchanged embraces, all talking at once.

Another couple entered the room but Laura did not recognize them.

The man looked Arabic with heavy eyebrows and full beard; the woman looked German and might be pregnant from the way her long blue blouse fell over her stomach. They took seats in the very back of the room. Laura switched her attention to the Schockens.

The physicians Iliana Frankel and Abraham Rückgabe entered next. He led the way to seats on the inside of the narrow center aisle and advised his companion to take a quick look at the Kollwitz works on the walls before the speaker appeared. He would save her seat for her. Iliana crossed over to the near wall and hastily took in an assemblage of the artist's depictions of mothers—mothers alone and mothers with children. The images covered forty decades in the artist's life and were riveting.

While Iliana was absorbing the powerful images, a small slender woman wearing a hijab entered the room and took a seat in the very back on the far aisle. Ignoring the Kollwitz works on the wall, she sat somewhat sideways in her chair, keeping an eye on who was entering the room.

A distinguished-looking woman in a wheelchair was gently maneuvered to the near side of the front row by her male attendant. Walking alongside her was the city's well known art dealer and gallery owner, Lukas Zamann. He was greeted by a man who was already seated, Reinhold Fromm, CEO of Dorotek.

Monika stood at the foot of the stairs looking up worriedly. Where was Akram? The lecture would soon begin.

But just then Akram came bounding down the stairs, a reassuring smile on his face. He looked happy and Monika was relieved. They took their seats in the very back of the room and whispered to each other animatedly until suddenly there was a hush.

The museum director had entered with the guest speaker at her side. Briskly they walked to the front of the room and Megan stood to the side of the podium, smiling modestly, she hoped, as Dr. Bulliet gave a short introduction.

"Ladies and gentlemen, good evening and thank you for coming to Berlin's Kollwitz Museum. Our speaker, Frau Professor Doktor Megan Crespi, is well known as a scholar to Kollwitz lovers in Germany. She comes to us this evening from Dallas, Texas, where as a professor she taught two generations of students to appreciate Kollwitz's art and life. Tonight she will present a lecture for which we have been waiting with great suspense: 'The Unknown Kollwitz.' Ladies and gentlemen, I am honored to present Megan Crespi."

Megan greeted the applauding audience with a wide smile and deep nod of the head, made sure her small Spiderman thermos of water was reachable and not knock-over-able, then slipped on her rimless glasses as she looked down at the text she had already placed on the podium during the tech check. All was in order.

She beamed up her first PowerPoint image. It showed two black and white photographs of Kollwitz, one taken when she was in her twenties, the other when she was in her sixties. The images were set against an 1890 color map of Germany in which the cities of Königsberg, Berlin, and Munich were circled. Megan began with a quick review of Kollwitz's career and of recent lucky acquisitions by the Cologne Kollwitz Museum. She mentioned the new Secreta drawing that had just turned up at the Galerie Zamann. Then she turned to the announced subject.

"'The Unknown Kollwitz.' *Can there be such a thing*? Don't we, some three quarters of a century after her death, collectively know all there is to know about the great artist?

"Well, there is fresh news on this front. You have, I am sure, all heard of that turn-of-the-last-century American dancer Loïe Fuller?"

An image of the dancer doing her famous *Serpentine Dance*, with her dates underneath, came onto the screen and many in the audience nodded audible assent.

"The incarnation of Art nouveau's mellifluous movement, she was born in Chicago, Illinois but made her home in a wildly receptive Paris between several tours of Europe."

The next image came up on the screen showing still pictures of Loïe in movement, arms raised gracefully, waves of silk rippling outward. Megan continued.

"Loïe choreographed her own dances and performed them in volumi-nous folds of silk, which she manipulated like large flapping butterflies under changing colored lights. The unusual stage lighting was her own as well, and she used chemical salts for some of the luminous color effects she achieved. Indeed she consulted with Pierre and Marie Curie as to whether their new discovery of radium could perhaps be used for her lighting effects. The answer was a friendly no, but she and Marie maintained a lifelong friendship, as did Loïe with the Queen of Romania."

Megan could see that the audience was interested but puzzled. She came quickly to her point.

"In the early spring of eighteen-ninety Loïe was booked for a long engagement in Munich, where she introduced her 'natural dance' techniques in nightly performances. During the day she often visited different art schools to talk to the instructors there, as she was interested in improving her drawing skills to communicate her choreography ideas. At one of the schools, the Women's Academy, she sat in on a drawing class given by a certain Ludwig Herterich."

Megan paused as she heard several listeners give a gasp of recognition. Grete Bulliet's was the loudest. Megan continued, slowly emphasizing her first sentence.

"Ludwig Herterich was also the teacher of Käthe Kollwitz, at that time Käthe Schmidt." Several people nodded knowingly and Grete Bulliet found herself voicing a loud "Ah ha!" Megan smiled at her, nodding her head knowingly, and continued.

"Käthe's father, recognizing his daughter's talent, had sent her from Königsberg to Munich for two years of classes at the Women's Academy." The room was silent with attentive suspense.

"Twenty-eight-year-old Loïe and twenty-two-year-old Käthe were in the same drawing class one morning when the professional model didn't show up. Sensing the situation, Loïe offered to pose for the class. The teacher saw no objection, not even when Loïe asked to borrow two unused smocks hanging on pegs on the classroom wall. She then announced, in English of course, that she could not hold a stationary pose. She would have to be in movement—slow but fluid. The two smocks would serve as extensions of her arms.

"And no, Professor Herterich did not object. In fact, he liked the idea, saying that yes, it would be good for his students to try to capture the human body in motion. To aim for conveying the *intensity* involved."

Megan beamed up a photograph of a much older Kollwitz, supporting her chin and cheek with her right hand, and posed a question to her listeners.

"Do you remember the words Kollwitz wrote much later about her first experiences drawing the dock workers in her hometown?" Without waiting for an answer she continued.

"She wrote that to her their movements were 'beautiful.' 'Beautiful to me were the Königsberg dock workers; beautiful was the bold outline of the movements of ordinary folk.'"

Every audience member sat up straight, attention totally fixed on the next images Megan showed.

They were six drawings the world had never seen before. Megan continued.

"The class and Loïe's dances lasted two hours. All the students were enthusiastic and Loïe demonstrated genuine interest in their drawing results. One girl shyly showed Loïe her drawings. *They were these drawings. And they were by Käthe Schmidt.*"

A few exclamations of disbelief could be heard.

"Yes, I know. But here's what happened next. Loïe asked if she could have the drawings, she found them so interesting. Käthe acquiesced and Loïe asked her to sign one of the drawings, this one with the two smocks suspended in air. Now if you look closely down at the lower right, you'll see a signature. It reads 'Käthe Schmidt.' Here's a blowup of that signature."

The audience studied the cursive signature that spelled out the artist's given and maiden name. Then Megan brought up a second image next to it—one of the artist's signatures with her married name. The similarity in script was indeed convincing—regular and readable. A new image came to the screen. It showed an older Loïe Fuller teaching a dance class.

"When Loïe could dance no more she taught, in both France and America. Her students were called the 'Fullerets.' She died in Paris of pneumonia at the age of sixty-five on the first of January, nineteen-twenty-eight and her ashes are at the Père Lachaise Cemetery. Her sister, Mollie Fuller, who had a long career as a vaudeville actress, was with Loïe in her final days and she was the one responsible for distributing her belongings."

A black and white image of Mollie Fuller, her husband, fellow actor Frederick Hallen, and their daughter Iris appeared on the screen.

"Mollie ended up in Hollywood, California, and when she died in nineteen-thirty-three, Iris kept the drawings her mother had said were of her famous aunt Loïe. Iris in turn married and had a son, Joseph, and it was this man, Joseph Magil, who approached me after a lecture I gave on Kollwitz at the Los Angeles County Museum last month."

The image on the screen changed to a color photograph of a smiling man of middle age holding a briefcase and shaking hands with Megan in front of the museum.

"He showed me what was in the briefcase—the Käthe Schmidt signed drawing and the other five—and asked if I could recommend a museum to which he could give the six drawings. He said he knew they were not typical Kollwitz works but that perhaps some museum would like them. His mother had told him that his aunt acquired them from a young student who later became known as a graphic artist and sculptor in Germany.

"'But don't you want to keep them, or *sell* them?' I asked. He answered that he didn't want that sort of bother. He would, however, be willing to give them as a gift to a suitable museum. I told him that I was leaving for Germany in two weeks and that did it."

Megan smiled, then showed the six drawings again along with a photograph of the very museum in which they were all gathered. She turned to Grete Bulliet, picked up the portfolio at her feet under the podium, and held it out to her.

"I thought that, as an encouragement and a welcome, the new director of the Berlin Kollwitz Museum might like her museum to be the recipient of the drawings. An American's gift to Germany. 'The Unknown Kollwitz.'"

Bulliet gasped in sheer disbelief as the audience jumped to its feet and began applauding.

Laura Forelle stood up as well, but her feelings were a wee bit hurt. Why hadn't Megan offered the drawings to *her* museum? And then she remembered something Megan had said during their recent visit just before all hell broke loose with the news of the other Kollwitz thefts. Laura had been boasting of how extensive the Cologne Museum's Kollwitz collection had become and Megan had answered thoughtfully, "Perhaps it's time to give the Berlin one some encouragement." They both knew the museum had been going through hard times lately and that the new hire of the knowledgeable Grete Bulliet was pretty much a last ditch effort to get the museum back on its feet. So Laura forgave her friend and joined the crowd of people lining up to speak to her.

"Laura!" Megan cried out in surprise when she spotted her friend. "Oh, dear, I didn't expect you to be *here*. Now I feel like a traitor."

"Don't, dear, don't. I understand why and what you've done. And you've brought young Käthe back to her homeland after all." She nodded understandingly as they both eyed the line of people waiting to talk to Megan, and gestured that she would slip out. They had had their talk in Cologne, after all.

"You were marvelous, as always," she said, blowing her a kiss and exiting the room.

***

Hardly noticed by the crowd, another woman, wearing a hijab, left the Kollwitz Museum at the same time as Laura Forelle. Her name was Aisha Saqqaf and she had been shadowing Akram al-Aljamie and his woman for several weeks. She had already carried out her first order from Akram's father, Dief al-Aljamie. But the destruction of his son's studio contents did not seem to have served as the warning Dief al-Aljamie intended. Akram had not repented his infidel status nor had he forsaken the German woman he blasphemously called his wife.

As soon as she reached the Kurfürstendamm and a café with good Wi-Fi, Aisha placed her call. It was only an hour later in Baghdad and her employer answered immediately.

"Your news?" he asked.

"The woman. She is pregnant with his child." There was a long silence.

"Are you certain?"

"I saw her this evening. Her belly protrudes. It is unmistakable."

"*Carry out my other order immediately.*"

***

Finally the room was clearing, but Megan could see that there were still a number of people waiting to speak to her. Dee was used to this and sat patiently in her chair at the back, checking e-mail on her iPhone.

Sandra and Siegfried Schocken were next in line.

"Marvelous!" Siegfried began, pressing his finger to his trach.

"Really worth the trip to Berlin. We are honored that you visited us in Weimar and we certainly learned a lot this evening."

They exchanged a few more pleasantries and Megan was happy she had taken a look at the catalogue Siegfried had given her so that she could talk about it. Sensitive to the fact that other people were waiting to speak to her, the Schockens soon moved on.

A young student, tall and thin with beautiful blonde hair in a bun and compelling amber eyes, moved forward and held out her hand to shake Megan's. It looked as though she had been crying, in fact that is what she admitted.

"Your lecture, Professor Crespi, moved me to tears. I have one question for you, if I may. Do you believe, had Kollwitz lived now, during our modern times with the influx of so many Muslims into our country, do you believe that she would have been sympathetic or unsympathetic?"

Megan did not even have to consider her answer. It came straight out.

"I think she would have been extraordinarily sympathetic, especially to the women and children. And I think she would have approved of the females shedding their hijabs or burkas when they were outside the home. I am sure Kollwitz would have wanted them to have the same opportunities to engage with the outside world and to have the same educational opportunities as the men."

Megan was surprised by the passion of her response. Especially to someone she did not know. But talking about the artist whom history recognized as a universal mother had quickened her empathic impulses.

"I am Lisa Strauss, and I thank you, Professor Crespi, for your rich answer." Overwhelmed, she gripped Megan's hand again, then turned on her heel and left the room, wiping her eyes.

The woman in the wheelchair Megan had met briefly at Café Wintergarten was the next person waiting to talk to her. Her attendant wheeled her forward.

"A most instructive and surprising presentation, Doktor Crespi. Many aspects and questions come to mind. Kollwitz is a passion of mine. How much longer do you plan to be in Germany?"

"Oh, another week."

Without hesitation Marie Schmidt slipped an envelope into Megan's hand.

"Then I insist you visit me. You select the date within that week. Look inside the envelope later. An enclosure will tell you how and where to reach me."

Schmidt signaled to her attendant and was wheeled out of the room. She did not look back nor did she see the bewildered expression on Megan's face.

Lukas Zamann interrupted her questioning thoughts.

"Frau Professor Doktor, a most stimulating lecture indeed. And thank you for publicizing my gallery's recent acquisition of one of Kollwitz's Secreta drawings."

"Well, I do follow your gallery's news online, and just had time to add it to my talk, thanks to the fact that you reproduced it online. I hope you didn't mind."

"Mind? No. The more exposure, the better. 'Exposure'—what a choice word when applied to the Secreta drawing, eh?"

Megan began hoping the unfunny man would move on. Two couples behind him seemed most intent on talking to her and were waiting patiently. But Zamann continued talking.

"I hope that while you are in Berlin you will take the opportunity to visit my gallery. Our present exhibition features Ernst Barlach, Kollwitz's great colleague, as you must know."

"Yes, indeed I do know. Once, on my way to Greifswald from Berlin, I made a point of driving to see his studio preserved at Güstrow."

"Oh." Zamann's voice fell in disappointment. "I have not yet had a chance to do that, but of course I intend to."

"Hum, well I do hope we'll have a chance to drop by your gallery before we leave Berlin."

Megan gave what she hoped was a smile of pleasant dismissal and looked beyond her chatty interlocutor to the first of the two waiting couples beyond. The woman looked German; the man was heavily bearded with thick eyebrows and could have been from the Middle East. Zamann finally moved on.

"We so enjoyed your speech, Frau Doktor Crespi," said the woman. "I am Monika, formerly von Putbus, but now happily Frau al-Aljamie, and this is my husband Akram. We have both been students of hands-on sculpture at the Universität der Künste here, and we would like to ask you a question relevant to your theme of the 'unknown Kollwitz.'"

"Please go ahead. I only hope I can answer your question."

"Might you have a lead on where one might search for the lost limestone version of Kollwitz's *Crouching Mother with Two Children*?"

Megan laughed. "Well, that is the million euro question, isn't it? I wish I could give you a tip but if I had one, you can be assured I would have passed it on to the Kollwitz museums by now. The only thought I would have on the subject is that the sculpture could be somewhere right here in Berlin." She smiled sympathetically at the couple, so obviously in love with one another. And it looked as though Monika was expecting.

"There is that wonderful photograph you showed of the older Kollwitz standing next to what I presume must be that limestone sculpture," Akram said almost wistfully.

"I suppose it will continue to remain a mystery, unfortunately," conceded Monika. Quite conscious that other people wanted to talk with the speaker, she tugged at Akram's sleeve and they graciously took their leave.

A short, gray-haired man of middle age with a very low forehead stepped forward, ahead of the other waiting couple.

"Professor Crespi, I took an art history course on Romanticism with you at Columbia. But because I didn't show up for the final exam, I got an F. Is there any way we could correct that now?"

Equally nonplussed and irritated, Megan, who had been standing for well over an hour, blurted out: "No. Certainly not. What a crazy question!" The man scowled and immediately turned away.

Megan smiled encouragingly and with relief at the couple waiting to speak to her. But before they could step forward a short, overweight man cut in ahead of them. His black eyes were fixed judgmentally on her.

"Yes?" Megan was vexed by the man.

"Interesting talk. You mentioned the new Secreta drawing at the Galerie Zamann. Well, I own a Secreta drawing by the artist that is totally unknown to Kollwitz scholarship. I should like to show it to you in private. I have it here in my briefcase."

Megan squirmed inside. How many times had people approached her in order to show her a "just-discovered," or "just- inherited" Kollwitz Secreta drawing? And how many times had she been shown a forgery? She had lost count. She had a whole collection of the images that had been e-mailed to her. And now she was feeling an extreme dislike for the pushy man.

"I am afraid that I am meeting with friends now and cannot linger."

"Well, how about tomorrow morning?"

"My whole day is filled," Megan lied expertly, managing to affect a look of regret.

"But I must return to Rügen tomorrow afternoon."

"Rügen?"

"Yes, Rügen. I am Reinhold Fromm of Dorotek. My factory is located at Prora."

Megan's curiosity overtook her.

"It just so happens that I am driving to Rügen in a few days," she admitted. Immediately she was sorry that she had done so.

"*Ach*! Then you can see my drawing there. Here is my business card. You call me when you arrive on the island. We will set up a time and place. And by the way, I have a formidable collection of erotic art. Not just Kollwitz. I think you will be impressed." He looked at Megan with the hint of a lascivious smirk on his face.

Why do I always get myself into these situations, Megan scolded herself. Unwillingly she took the card and turned purposefully to the patiently waiting couple behind Fromm. They were the last of those in line.

The man introduced himself and his companion.

"Good evening, Frau Professor. Certainly a stimulating lecture. May I introduce the two of us. I am Doktor Abraham Rückgabe and this is my colleague, Doktor Iliana Frankel. There are two unusual things we thought you might like to know concerning Kollwitz. First, Iliana? May I?" Iliana nodded assent.

"My colleague here has a unique connection to Kollwitz. She is the granddaughter of Hugo Heller."

"Oh, my goodness!" Megan was entranced. "How extraordinary. That is indeed a unique connection. May I tell the Berlin and Cologne Kollwitz Museum directors about this?"

"No, no, I would rather you did not," Iliana answered hastily. "It is because we judge you to be a person of integrity and discretion that we tell you. And Abraham has something even more fascinating to tell you, to share with you, but it must be totally confidential."

Megan surveyed the room. Dee was still seated, occupied by her e-mail, and Grete Bulliet was in animated conversation with two men on the opposite side of the room.

"I should be honored to hear what you have to say, Doktor Rückgabe."

"Well, I too am the grandchild of someone having a connection with the artist. My grandmother Lina was live-in housekeeper to the Kollwitz family for several decades. A few days after the bombing of Kollwitz's Weissenburger Strasse, Lina went searching through the ruins looking for any personal items that might be recovered. What she found was a metal trunk. Inside it were thirty-six black oilcloth journals in her employer's handwriting. She did not know how to contact her, as her family had convinced the artist to leave Berlin shortly before the bombing..."

"...but this is amazing," Megan whispered, bending in closer to hear the physician's story.

"Lina kept the journals all her life, and when I received my medical degree she gave them to me. I have since *lived* with the diaries. They cover the years nineteen-eight to nineteen-forty-three. I have never revealed the fact of their existence before. Only to my dear colleague Iliana here. Now, if you have the time, I should like to show them to you."

Megan was stunned.

"I will *make* the time. And I feel so privileged that you are willing to allow me to see them."

"Would as soon as tomorrow evening be possible for you?"

"Definitely. What time would you like this to be?"

"If you could possibly have dinner with us at a restaurant near my home, I will give you a rough idea of what is covered in the journals. Then we could proceed to my place and I could show you entries from the years that interest you. I have almost memorized what she has written."

The trio conferred about time and restaurant location and exchanged e-mail addresses. Megan promised them complete confidentiality. Her heart was pounding with excitement.

Dare she wear her Google Glass to the meeting?

47

The bulldog smiled at his master.

Prince Pahlavi was actually complimenting him on a job well done.

It had not been as easy as the first task, even though there were only two men to eliminate this time instead of four. But Wafiyy had made the mistake of allowing Jarir and his helper to get back into their vehicles after the art object—a gravestone of some sort with the image of clasped hands—had been installed in the master's inner garden.

Now, not able to dispatch both men at once, Wafiyy first ran to the delivery van parked behind the boom truck. It was already starting to back down the side road. He yanked open the driver's door and shot Jarir once directly in the heart.

The man in the boom truck in front opened his cab door to see what the noise was and Wafiyy shot him twice from a distance of eighteen feet. Both bullets found their mark although it took some five minutes for the second man's convulsions to subside.

The bulldog loaded the still jerking corpse onto a wheelbarrow and pushed it further down the narrow side road that led to the back of the complex. He dumped it beyond four graves covered with vigorous new growth. Then Wafiyy rolled his empty wheelbarrow back up the road past the boom truck to the delivery van and collected the limp body he had shot first. He heaved it into the wheelbarrow. As he rolled the corpse back toward the impromptu graveyard, he cursed himself. When he was moving the small ditch digger into position to finish scooping out two new graves, he had missed the fact that both new victims-to-be had completed their work and were already in their vehicles and ready to leave as soon as they had been paid by the prince.

But soon all was well. The graves were dug, the two men were buried, and a layer of top soil covered the fresh graves. All that was left was to drive both vehicles into the large warehouse at the back of the complex.

Wafiyy surveyed his work with some satisfaction, then returned to his post at the front gate. It was there that the prince had praised his labor. A compliment to remember and cherish.

And so the bulldog smiled.

48

Soon he would have to stop working at Dorotek altogether. Violent coughing spasms and convulsive gasping for air had sapped Mahdi Kartal's strength. How could he follow the advice of that nice woman physician who visited him at his home and had urged him to leave work and concentrate on his health? He was the only breadwinner in the family. His resentment against Dorotek's CEO was now a simmering rage. If asbestos poisoning was to take his life, he would take the life of the man responsible.

How to do it? He knew exactly how. He would buy a twenty-centi-meter switchblade and stab the man in the throat multiple times. It would do no good to attack the man in the office halls of Dorotek. Too many people around. Not possible to make a quick escape. But the factory parking lots were a different situation altogether. Dr. Frankel saw her patients in the modern annex facing the old factory headquarters. And the old factory was where criminal Reinhold Fromm had his lavish top-floor office. Mahdi knew what the CEO's car looked like and exactly where he parked it. The spot, the one nearest the employee entry, was reserved for Herr Reinhold Fromm. His automobile was a gray Mercedes Benz sedan.

This much was easy. But even so, too many people around. What he could do, Mahdi reasoned, was pry open the car trunk by engaging the latch's pull-switch cable with a flat-head screwdriver or even with his knife blade. He would slip inside the popped trunk toward the middle of the afternoon when people were not likely to be about, taking care not to let the latch reengage. Then wherever Fromm drove, Mahdi would be with him. And if it was to his house, as he presumed it would be, then he would bide his time and proceed after Fromm left the car. It would be most convenient, killing the man in his own home.

The only question with his plan, Mahdi realized, was: would he be able to suppress his wheezing cough while in the trunk?

49

It had been a long evening. But a rich one, Dee and Megan assured each other as they walked back to the Kempinski Hotel from the Kollwitz Museum. Once in their room they changed to comfortable pajamas and sat facing each other on their beds, discussing Megan's lecture and its prodigious aftermath.

"I'm sorry I can't include you in the dinner tomorrow night, Dee, but I promised the two physicians complete confidentiality."

"Of course, I understand. No apologies or explanations necessary."

"But the whole morning, tomorrow, I promise, will be devoted to visiting the other cemetery where you discovered some Totebusch people were buried."

"Yes, the family tree I have shows them as distant cousins by marriage. How far from our hotel is the cemetery, anyway?"

"Not too far. We can take the U-Bahn to Berlin-Kreuzberg. Or a taxi for what's called a *Kurzstrecke*—a short haul for four euros. Unless the distance exceeds two kilometers, which it might."

"Let's take a taxi regardless. Beats walking anytime."

Megan showed Dee the exact location of the old Dreifaltigkeitsfriedhof I on her iPhone, and how they would have to enter by way of Mehringdamm and the newer Cemetery III.

"That is so helpful. I'll say it again. What an era we've been lucky enough to live into, long enough to witness and partake in all this cyberspace connectivity."

"Oh, yes. Gone are the days of desperately hoping a specific library book with the information you need will not be out on loan. Now you can just look up the information, *any* information, on the Internet, and on a gadget as small as this iPhone. And usually you get more than you imagined or even needed. Of course, you always have to check to be sure the information is correct. In its early days, Wikipedia made some real booboos, for example."

"By the way," said Dee, "what did that interesting looking woman in the wheelchair have to say to you? Marie Schmidt, wasn't that her name?"

"Oh my god! I totally forgot about the envelope she pressed into my hands after the lecture. Let's hope I thought to slip it into my purse."

Megan lifted up her capacious shoulder bag from a counter underneath the TV and felt around inside it. Sure enough, there was the envelope. Very high-grade quality.

"Let's see what we have here." She took a metal fingernail file out of her cosmetics bag and carefully slit open the envelope. A large embossed card was inside. It read in italics:

Baronin Marie von und zu Falschfingen, Kusine dreimal entfernt von Käthe Schmidt Kollwitz, Kastell Königfeis, Moritzburg, Deutschland, 49-35207-82717 / BVFKK@Freenet.de.

"Good lord! How fancy-schmancy. A 'cousin of Kollwitz,' 'three times removed'? Hm. What an ego. And she expects me to come to *her*. At her castle, no less. And at Moritzburg."

"Where is that? Near here?" asked Dee.

"No, not near here. It's down south by Dresden. It's where Kollwitz moved when things got too dangerous because of the air raids over Nordhausen. Moritzburg is where she died. And her simple lodgings there are now a *Gedenkstätte*—a memorial. A long silence ensued. Megan was thinking and Dee was watching her.

"Okay, Megan, I *know* what you're going to say next. So just tell me: do we drive there *before* or *after* Rügen and Greifswald?"

Megan's eyes danced with pleasure. Her friend knew her only too well. She thought for a moment, then gave her answer.

"I think *after* our Pomeranian tour. That way, we'll get the cemeteries investigated and I'll get brash Herr Fromm out of the way at his Dorotek factory. We can consider the 'Third Cousin Thrice Removed' visit as our reward, our dessert."

"It's bound to be weird."

"That's for sure."

"So are you going to e-mail her the date we will be coming?"

"Why not? We should have the most bizarre adventure at the end of our trip. I'll e-mail her right now, make it for next Saturday."

The two friends turned out the lights and after a bit of give and take fantasizing about what might happen at alliterative Kastell Königfeis, both fell soundly asleep.

"Just *what* does 'Dreifaltigkeitsfriedhof' mean anyway?" Dee asked as their taxi neared the old Berlin graveyard the next morning.

"It means Trinity Cemetery."

Dee counted the letters in German out loud.

"Golly, twenty-three letters for *that*?"

"Believe me, there are many longer words than that in German. And English too, come to think of it. How about antidisestablishmentarianism?"

"Good point," said Dee. Let me see, yes, it has twenty-eight letters. We used to be told in school it was the longest word in the English language, but recently I learned there are six much longer ones."

"Really? Can you recall any of them?" Megan asked.

"Let's see...one of them is easy to remember because it means 'fear of long words.' It's, are you ready? Hippopotomonstrosesquippedaliophobia."

"Good grief!"

"Well, it uses the word sesquipedalian, which is an adjective meaning having many syllables, which this railroad-car word certainly has. And then the word phobia at the end, plus the word monstrous in the middle and the hippopoto word at the beginning, so it all knits together quite nicely. Means fear of monstrously multisyllabic words and adds up to thirty-six letters versus only twenty-eight letters in that old diehard antidisestablishmentarianism."

"Dee! How on earth can you remember such things?"

"I just wish I could remember more *useful* things."

"Well, now that we're into long words in English, I remember a funny duet in the film Mary Poppins. It was called Supercalifragilisticexpialido-cious. I don't recall who sang it, however."

"I'd forgotten that but, sure, I remember that duet. It was sung by Julie Andrews and Dick Van Dyke."

They had reached their cemetery destination and Megan paid the taxi driver a bit more than the *Kurzstrecke* fare she had praised the night before. They sat down on an inviting bench under a mulberry tree while Megan consulted her iPhone.

"It would have been too much to hope that the graves list would include Totebusch, but just guess who *is* buried here." Megan was highly excited.

"Tell me."

"Both Felix *and* Fanny Mendelssohn."

"Who was Fanny?"

"She was his sister and just as talented a composer as her brother. But their father discouraged her from continuing to play and compose. In fact he wrote her a famous—for feminists—letter in which he said something like 'music will perhaps be Felix's profession, whereas for you it can and must be only an ornament.'"

"Ouch! How terribly painful."

"Right. But Felix was very supportive of Fanny in private. She continued to compose even after she'd married their painter friend Wilhelm Hensel. And when Felix published some early songs, he included, under his name, of course, six by Fanny."

"How do you know all this?"

"I know because it resulted in a very embarrassing moment for Felix when he went to England and was received by Queen Victoria at Buckingham Palace. She hummed her favorite of his songs and it turned out to be one of Fanny's. Poor Felix had to confess that his sister had written it. I've always loved that story."

"It's quite a story. So both sister and brother are buried here."

"Yes, and not very far away. Shall we go take a look?"

"Oh, sure," a patient Dee agreed.

It turned out that brother and sister were buried side by side. Felix's grave was marked by a large white marble cross and read "Jakob Ludwig Felix Mendelssohn Bartholdy." Fanny's grave, to the right, was marked not by a cross but by a tall headstone that read "Fanny Cæcillie Hensel born Mendelssohn Bartholdy." In addition, below her dates, 1805-1847, the concluding bars and words of a song she had completed the day before her death were engraved: "Thoughts and songs pass until they reach the heavenly kingdom."

Dee was very moved by the tombstones and she studied them for a long time while Megan documented them with her iPhone.

"Fanny died so young, only forty-one. Do we know how she died?"

"From the same thing that killed Felix six months later and both their parents and their famous grandfather, the Jewish philosopher Moses Mendelssohn. A stroke."

"A stroke? So it ran in the family."

"Yes. In her case she was actually rehearsing one of her brother's cantatas on the piano and paused to say that her fingers had suddenly gone numb. Then she collapsed and died from a massive stroke that same evening."

"How awful."

"Yes, it's so sad. But things are looking up in recent scholarship about her. She wrote over four hundred and fifty compositions—songs, piano works, chamber music, choral works. It's really amazing, and finally she's getting the attention she deserves."

Megan took a few more photos of the two graves and finally turned to Dee.

"Shall we look for the Totebusch graves now?"

"Yes. But where to begin? There are so many tombstones here."

"We'd better go to the cemetery office and ask if they have a register of graves."

"By all means let's do that, rather than just wandering around."

A few minutes later they were talking with a gregarious, lean, gray-haired man who they first took to be a grave-digger, but who proudly informed them he was in charge of all three Trinity cemeteries. He spoke excellent English. Dee explained they had come from America to search out Totebusch burial sites.

"Yes, we do have a list of everyone buried here. It goes back to the early eighteenth century and into the nineteenth century. Because of our cemetery's closeness to central Berlin, and the fact that it was open to many different religions, it became popular to be buried here in Cemetery I."

The helpful man, one Erich Hubner, flipped the pages of an old record book and paused at one.

"Here, here is a Totebusch entry. Let's see. Husband and wife. Manfred and Charlotte Totebusch. Both born in Greifswald in the late eighteenth-century—see here, he in seventeen-eighty-four, she in seventeen-ninety-three. Both died in the year eighteen-forty-two and were buried here."

"Can you tell us where their graves might be?"

"Sz!" Erich Hubner hissed loudly, raising his hands as if to ward off something unpleasant.

"Let me explain something to you American ladies. Eternal rest here is not like eternal rest in your country. We, like all German cemeteries, exhume remains every fifteen to thirty years. Families rent a grave for usually twenty years, then renewal payments are required to keep the grave. When, however, graves are recycled and new occupants are buried, the old tombstones are removed at that time. So it is very likely that the remains of these two Totebusch persons are no longer available or even discoverable."

"So there wouldn't even be a gravestone?"

"I am sorry, but that is most likely. No Totebusch gravestones because they were buried too long ago."

Hubner looked at the two women, then leaned toward them and whispered conspiratorially.

"Nowadays our problem is rot. Or rather, the fact that corpses do *not* rot. They do not putrefy as they should after a certain period. And the reason is we just do not have good soil. Our ancestors who laid out the three cemeteries here bought the soil from local farmers. The soil had a very high clay content that formed compact layers. That makes a terrible substratum for burial. There is poor drainage and because of the fact that air cannot permeate through the clay, normal decomposition of the corpses doesn't take place. Instead, as time goes by, the remains coagulate and form a hard, waxy buildup. I can tell you that when you knock them with a shovel the waxy bodies give off a hollow sound."

Dee found she had to sit down in order to fend off the horror story she was hearing.

"So how are you and other German cemeteries dealing with this terrible problem?" Megan asked, who like her mother, had always been attracted to morbid matters.

"It's not so much what we cemeteries do," Hubner continued, gratified to have an interested listener.

"It's what the *funeral* industry is doing. They're making millions creating watertight concrete coffins—individual burial chambers that are vaulted. Why, Cologne just ordered some five thousand of them! They are supposed to produce an environment conducive to what we call in the profession, rapid rot. And the idea is catching on fast."

"But would there be room for all these large new coffins in the cemeteries?"

"Not really, because..." Hubner looked around to make sure no one else was around, "the *Muslims* are taking over the choice ground. A lot of them ship bodies back to Turkey or Lebanon, but a sizeable number are being buried here in what they call 'virgin' soil—where no one else has been buried. They believe in eternal rest and in order to achieve that, the deceased, wrapped in only a shroud after prayers and ritual washing, has to be buried immediately. Now this is contrary to our German law that stipulates relatives must wait forty-eight hours before burying their dead. Not only do the Muslims insist on *immediate* burial but the body must be placed sideways in the grave—no coffin, mind you—with its head facing Mecca."

"That's fascinating," said Megan, fully entranced.

"So what we cemetery people are seeing is an increasing number of Islamic grave fields being created within our German cemeteries. But, you see, a body buried in a winding sheet will not decay in damp soil and for that reason shroud burial is illegal in most of Germany. There are lots of law suits about this. On both sides—the government versus individual Muslims, Muslims versus the government. The biggest one was in Cologne some years back when some Muslims discovered that two hundred and seventy-seven Muslim graves were due to be exhumed according to German law."

"Who won that?" Megan asked, quite captivated by the subject.

"They did. The Muslims got a stay."

"So there is nothing commemorating my ancestors to be found here, not even their remains?" Dee asked querulously, impatient to get back to the reason she was there.

"No, no chance at all."

"So why are the gravestones of the *Mendelssohn* family still here?" Dee was indignant.

"Ah, but they were famous *and* rich. And with our cemetery's location, in the central part of Berlin, our Dreifaltigkeitsfriedhof became a popular location for the rich and famous. And the city pays for the upkeep of celebrity graves."

"Well, then I think we have concluded our business with you," Dee said, standing up abruptly. It was clear to see she was very upset.

Megan thanked Herr Hubner over-enthusiastically in order to make up for her friend's brusqueness. They walked silently back the way they had come under the overhang of silent sycamores.

50

The director of Berlin's Kollwitz Museum had been looking for Megan Crespi's telephone number in vain. Finally she Googled her and came to her homepage, www.megancrespi.com. A number was given and Grete hoped it would be the professor's cellphone number.

She dialed it and got an instant pickup on the other end.

"Hello?"

"Megan? This is Grete."

"Oh, hi Grete. You've caught me at the Dreifaltigkeitsfriedhof of all places. What's up?"

"I wanted to continue the conversation about Marie Schmidt we had at dinner last night. You got away so fast after your fan club left that I didn't have a chance to catch you."

"Oh, yes, sorry about that. To tell you the truth I was so tired of standing I just had to get out of there and back to my hotel."

"I empathize, believe me. Anyway I wanted to tell you who Marie Schmidt really is."

"Grete, she actually beat you to the punch. She's invited, rather, *commanded* me to visit her. She slipped an envelope into my hands while we were briefly conversing at the museum last night. When I opened it at the hotel everything was revealed. I can quote it to you word for word: '*Baronin Marie von und zu Falschfingen, Kusine dreimal entfernt von Käthe Schmidt Kollwitz, Kastell Königfeis, Moritzburg.*' Following that mouthful were her telephone number and e-mail address."

"I am flabbergasted that she allowed you to know her true identity. The woman is notoriously secretive."

"How did *you* find out who she is?"

"Pure serendipity. My brother-in-law's daughter lives in Moritzburg and her maid Trude is friends with Marie Schmidt's maid, who told her that her employer at Castle Königfeis was addressed as Baroness by young Prince Nicolae of Romania when he visited her last month. Seems his grand-father, King Michael, had just cut him off from the line of succession to his throne—not that there is any Romanian throne these days. Hasn't been since nineteen-forty-seven. Anyhow, Trude described him as alternating between fits of weeping and cursing. She overheard him telling the baroness that he hated being back at the family castle because he couldn't get pizza delivered there."

"What a remarkable story."

"And *you* have been invited to the castle! Are you going to go?"

"Yes, how can I resist? I sent her an e-mail saying I would come to Morizburg next Saturday."

"Did you hear back?"

"Yes. Five words. '*Dinner at seven. Come alone.*'"

"Well, I do hope you'll let me know what happens, Megan."

"Of course, but by phone, not by e-mail. I must be discreet."

"What about Laura Forelle? Are you going to tell her who Marie Schmidt is?"

"Naturally. I will keep you both abreast, but I think we should keep it to the three of us for now."

"Agreed."

Megan and Grete said goodbye just as Dee collapsed on the bench under the mulberry tree where she and Megan had sat before.

"You didn't tell me you'd gotten an e-mail from that Marie Schmidt person saying you should come *alone* for dinner next Saturday," good-na-tured Dee, already in a bad mood, actually pouted.

"I'm sorry. I was so angry at her imperial tone that I just blocked it from my mind. Decided to deal with it later."

"Oh, I don't really mind, Megan. I'm just depressed that there are no Totebusch tombstones to be found here. And because of the German burial laws, I'm beginning to realize there may not be any in Greifswald either."

"Well, just remember what Churchill used to say: 'Never, never, never give up.' And we won't either, I promise you."

51

"You have waited too long!" the woman in the burka shouted. "You said one more day. Now it is *two* more days. And our husbands have not returned."

Hudun, wife of Kadeem Tawfeek was speaking for the wives of the missing men. All four had disobeyed their husbands' mandate that they swear the men had never left Berlin. Desperate, the women had returned to the mosque and were confronting the elders of the Muslim Brotherhood again.

The most senior man raised his hand for silence.

"You are right, my daughters. You have been more than patient. We shall report the missing men to the Berlin police and we shall do so now. Give your husbands' names and your home addresses to Abdul-Hakim here and he will take the information to the police.

52

Reinhold Fromm had just left the Galerie Zamann after looking at its Kollwitz Secreta once again. Although he had his own drawing by the artist in his briefcase, he decided, on second thought, not to show it to Lukas Zamann. There was something too pushy about the man. And how could he trust him to keep silent about there being yet another Secreta in the Kollwitz art world?

Had Fromm remained ten minutes longer he would have run into Professor Crespi. After a lunch that included delicious Viennese Apfelstrudel at the Café Einstein on Unter den Linden, Megan had sent her exhausted travel companion back via taxi to the Kempinski. She herself would take advantage of the opportunity to visit Zamann's gallery well before that evening's dinner with the two Berlin physicians who had such interesting and unique ties with Kollwitz.

Once inside the gallery door Megan spotted and went straight to the Kollwitz drawing. It was hung on its own wall, with facsimiles of the other known Secreta drawings. Much the same as some of the artist's other depictions, this one showed a couple lying in a tender, mutual embrace. Kollwitz's face was recognizable even with just a few definitive strokes of the pencil. Yes, it was the genuine article. Unlike one of the facsimiles on the wall next to it. It showed just the reverse, with the woman lying on the man, but the pencil stroke was definitely not that of the artist. It was much too tenuous.

Should she alert Herr Zamann of the forgery? Megan had no sooner thought that when the man came racing over to her.

"*Ach*, Frau Professor Doktor Crespi! So super that you could drop by. And how do you like the Secreta?" Zamann practically pushed his face into Megan's as he asked the question.

"It is indeed a fine one. Radiates the same mutual love and passion represented by the other drawings in the series."

"*Sehr gut!*" Zamann's face lit up with pride and pleasure. "I should quote you."

Megan stepped back, realizing she somehow did not care to discuss the facsimile of the forged Kollwitz with the man. She turned to go, but the gallery owner blocked her move and hunched in even closer to her face.

"Now that you are here, Frau Professor, I beg you to sign a statement to that effect. And that this Secreta is genuine. A testimonial from you would greatly benefit the asking price."

Megan was furious, but did not show it. Instead she murmured her answer.

"I am sure written testimonials help the price you are asking, but we American art historians do not furnish such opinions to commercial galleries."

"But you are a Kollwitz *expert*!"

"I'm sorry, Herr Zamann, but I cannot aid you there."

"But if I *pay* you?"

That was it. Megan drew herself up to all her five-foot, four-inch height and faced the importuning man.

"I consider that an insult. Good day." She turned on her heel and walked out of the gallery. Zamann raised his hands and sputtered in dismay. A few gallery visitors looked at him with curiosity, then gathered to gaze at the drawing that had ignited such a loud, if incomprehensible exchange.

53

Officer Anton Reininger of the Berlin police force, Wedding district, was conscientiously taking notes on what the tall, bearded man in front of him at the desk was telling him.

It seemed that four Muslim residents of the district had disappeared off the face of the earth. No one had seen them for several days and their wives had heard nothing from them. It was known that they had left Berlin on an assignment and that a rented boom truck was involved. This latter fact was known because the rental company had lodged a complaint against the man who had rented it: Kadeem Tawfeek, one of the missing men.

Officer Reininger, aware of that complaint, was listening intently to the Muslim man's report and recognized the name Kadeem Tawfeek when it was mentioned. He looked up from writing his report.

"Oh? You have word of him?" asked Abdul-Hakim hopefully.

"Um, no, not directly. But I recently ran across a citation for a Kadeem Tawfeek for running a red light at an intersection in Wedding. And then his name came up again just yesterday when I talked to my colleague Detective Herbert Schauen in Cologne. An overhead street camera surveys Quartermarkt street there and on the night of a recent terrible fire in that neighborhood, a delivery van established as belonging to Tawfeek, was sighted parked there at two-thirty in the morning. The camera also showed a boom truck was parked behind it on the street."

"So are you saying that the men might have been in *Cologne*?"

"Yes. It looks that way. That's why my colleague called me after he learned that the delivery van belonged to a Berlin resident."

Abdul-Hakim looked baffled.

Officer Reininger shuffled his papers, then looked at his visitor.

"You say that as much as you could gather from the wives, all four of the men were out on the same job?"

"Yes, the wives all agree on that. Knew their husbands were part of a team of four. But they did not know their destination."

"So if the three other men were on a job with Kadeem, then they must all have been in Cologne at the time of the fire."

"Surely you do not think they could have anything to do with that?"

"Yes, I do. During the bedlam of the fire two famous statues were stolen from a nearby church."

"Oh? I did not know that. So you think that would explain the delivery van in front of Kadeem's rented boom truck."

"Yes, it would. But what did they do with the statues, if my theory is correct? And why didn't the men return home?"

"That is what their wives are so worried about. This is why I came to you."

"Tell you what. I will take up this case with our local detectives right away. Thank you for coming in. You know what a high priority we give to good relations between Muslims and Germans."

Abdul-Hakim did not say what he was really thinking. He merely thanked the police officer and left.

Something was definitely wrong. Why would Kadeem steal some famous statues from Cologne? Just after an identical set of statues had been stolen from a Belgian cemetery? And how could *four* members of the Muslim Brotherhood all have disappeared at the same time?

Officer Reininger decided he needed to talk to his Cologne colleague Herbert Schauen again. Between the two of them they should be able to determine why so many calamities pertaining to large works by the sculptor Käthe Kollwitz were taking place. Even two tombstones with her artwork had been stolen.

And why were the thieves in at least two of the heists Muslim Turks?

54

It was four in the afternoon in Berlin and nine in the morning in Dallas. Stretched out on her comfortable Hotel Kempinski bed, Megan was watching the antics of little Button back in Dallas on the Amcrest App installed on her iPhone. He had just been served breakfast, and was trotting a zero line to the bowl set in the far corner of her sister's dining room. Megan decided not to call out his name and divert his interest from eating. Just seeing him was enough.

"If you're meeting those physicians as early as six, I think I'll have dinner in the hotel at that time as well." Dee was sitting at the desk in their room catching up on e-mail.

"Good. We'll go down together. Do you want to see what little Button's doing before I close down?"

"Oh, sure." Dee got up from the desk and walked over to look at the image Megan was holding up to her.

"Just precious. What a brave little blind boy."

Megan sighed. "Gosh, I do miss him."

"Steady, girl, steady." Dee loved to use that admonition and it always cheered her friend up because she delivered the command in such a low, serious voice. It was enough to make them both laugh.

After depositing Dee at Reinhards restaurant inside the hotel, Megan checked the map on her iPhone showing the Wedding restaurant where she was to meet Abraham Rückgabe and Iliana Frankel. Called Fünf & Sechzig, it was at Torfstrasse 9. Dr. Rückgabe had e-mailed her inquiring what sort of restaurant she liked, and her answer had been any place she could eat a really good schnitzel. Up to the last minute Megan had argued with herself as to whether she should wear her Google Glass. She had decided against it finally and treated herself to a taxi rather than brave the U-Bahn at the dinner hour. The taxi dropped her off at a corner building sporting the logo of the restaurant.

The physicians were already seated at a corner table against a colorful wall and Abraham rose to greet her.

"Our restaurant has a craft beer you might like with your Wiener-schnitzel," Iliana told Megan after she had ordered.

"Lovely. I enjoy craft beer."

The talk over dinner, during which they switched to first names, centered on the mysterious multiple thefts of Kollwitz sculptures, and they traded theories on why they were stolen. Abraham thought it must be an international art theft ring looking to sell abroad, perhaps to China. Iliana agreed with Megan that it could be a collector obsessed somehow with death. Megan told them about her visit to the Schockens and the momentary jolt she experienced when taken to their son's burial site. They all had a laugh over the incident. Then they became serious as coffee was served.

Abraham gave Megan a brief description of what each of the thirty-six journals addressed.

"I want to show you the year or those years of Käthe's journals in which you are most interested. Just tell me what subjects you would like to read about."

"What a banquet you are offering! I suppose I'm most interested in her thoughts on the creative process while she was working, and also, Iliana, how she felt about her affair with your grandfather. Which ultimately leads to how she felt about her husband."

"Can do. Shall we go to my house now?"

Abraham signaled discreetly to the waiter and insisted on paying the bill despite the protestations of Iliana and Megan. They walked to his building and entered his large apartment.

Megan was thrilled to see Kollwitz's *Weavers Revolt* cycle on one of the living room walls and said so as she headed straight to them.

"If you give me a few minutes I shall bring in the journals pertinent to your interests. In the meantime, Iliana, would you like to serve Megan and yourself some after-dinner liqueur?"

"Delighted to. Megan, what's your choice? I see Abraham has brandy, Cointreau, ouzo, crème de menthe, Baileys Irish Cream..."

"Stop right there!," Megan smiled enthusiastically. "I absolutely love Baileys Irish Cream. Haven't had it for a while now."

"Perfect. I too like it."

Iliana poured them both a generous amount.

"Iliana, while we're waiting for Abraham to bring in the journals, might you tell me a bit more about your grandfather, Hugo Heller?"

"What I do know about him I only learned from friends of his, colleagues to whom I went after learning he was my grandfather. They talked about the fascinating people who spoke for monthly meetings held at his bookstore/gallery: Arnold Schönberg, Peter Altenberg, Arthur Schnitzler, Reiner Maria Rilke, Ernst Mach, Thomas Mann, and of course Freud."

"That is exciting. Surely your grandfather must have left an extraordinary trove of writings, publications, and letters."

"He did, and they are in an archive at the Vienna National Library, I've been told. Unfortunately, I never had the time to examine the archive as I was already deep into my medical studies here in Berlin as well as going through a difficult divorce back home in Vienna."

"Here we are, ladies," Abraham came into the room rolling a tea cart with two stacks of black oilcloth journals. He was beaming with pleasure. At last, a scholar to show them to, and a neutral one who was not mired in the intrigues of the German art world. She could very likely also recommend without bias to which of the three Kollwitz Museums the diaries should be left—Cologne, Berlin, or perhaps even the Moritzburg Kollwiz Memorial House.

"Shall we begin with her thoughts on her own creative progress?"

"By all means."

Abraham reached for the top volume on the right and opened it to the year 1912. It was headed "New Year's Day."

"This entry addresses two of your interests, Megan. May I read it aloud to you and Iliana?"

"Yes, please."

Abraham sat down in his reading chair opposite the couch on which the two women were seated and began. The inflections of his voice revealed his intimate familiarity with the words.

What about myself? Summing up of nineteen-eleven? Progress? No progress in my relationship with Karl. What he always speaks of, what seems to him still the sole worthwhile goal of our long living together, that we should grow together in the deepest intimacy, I still do not feel and probably never will learn to feel.

"How long had she and Karl been married by this time?" Iliana interrupted. Abraham and Megan gave the answer at the same time.

"Twenty-one years."

They all laughed. Abraham continued his reading, and Megan realized that he was purposefully invoking the lilting cantilena of what would have been Kollwitz's Königsberg accent. She interrupted to tell him so and he smiled broadly.

"Yes, and in order to hear Käthe's native accent for myself, I actually visited Königsberg a few years ago. What a pity that, ever since World War II, it's been Kaliningrad in Russia."

"Gosh! I've also been in Königsberg—twice—and partly for the same reason. To hear Low-Prussian phrases like '*Flundere, frische, scheene Flundere*'—'Flounder, fresh, beautiful Flounder!' Phrases which she heard from the fishwives on the docks."

Abraham and Megan smiled at each other in mutual admiration.

"Did you know that she had a slight lisp as a girl?" Megan asked.

"Yes. But tell me, what else were you looking for in Königsberg?"

"The first time, probably the same thing you were searching for: any buildings that remained of the old German Königsberg."

"You're quite right about that. Aside from the cathedral, all I really saw was the old red brick city gate."

"Right, with traffic, even a streetcar passing right through it."

"And why did you go back a second time, if I may ask?"

"Oh, the second time was for a completely different reason. I was on the track of a long-lost Egon Schiele nineteen-ten self-portrait that had mysteriously turned up there. I did see it, but soon afterward the owner of the painting, a very nice elderly lady, was found murdered on her own doorstep."

"How terrible!" Iliana exclaimed.

"Yes, it was. But, please, let's go on with the journal reading." Abraham returned to where he had left off.

"Now here she was only forty-four on New Year's day when she wrote these words."

For the last third of life there remains only work. It alone is always stimulating, rejuvenating, exciting, and satisfying. This year I have made excellent progress in sculpture. I can see an advance between the first group of mother with child and the last finished group.

"And to think Käthe lived to be seventy-seven," said Iliana, taken with the phrase "the last third of life."

Abraham smiled and turned several pages further in the journal.

"Here we are at February eighteenth of nineteen seventeen." He read out loud.

Strength is what I need; it's the one thing which seems worthy of succeeding Peter. Strength is: to take life as it is and, unbroken by life, without complaining and overmuch weeping, to do one's work powerfully. Not to deny oneself the personality one happens to be, but to embody it.

"Goodness," Megan said, "she became the embodiment of strength. Not only in her character but also in her work. Her sculptures are realizations of intense concentration. Amazing abbreviation of form. Look how long it took her to be satisfied with her *Grieving Parents*. Almost twenty years!"

"As an artist she is profound," added Iliana.

"*That's* the word," Abraham said, looking at Iliana fondly. "Her work, her themes are profound."

"For me," said Megan, who in her eighty years had lost several relatives and close friends, "the piece that speaks to me the most is the one she created after Karl died, *Abschied—Farewell*. The palpable reluctance of the man as he gently pulls away from the embrace of the woman is heartrending. It's Kollwitz's experience, yet she makes it universal, speaks for everyone."

Iliana nodded in agreement.

"In fact," Megan continued, I love that particular sculpture so much, that when a surmoulage of it came up on EBay, I couldn't resist buying it."

"What is a surmoulage?" asked Iliana.

"It's a bronze made from another bronze. In other words, it's a copy, and not an original work of art; not taken from the artist's original model or mold. Also it will not have all the detail of the original and it will be slightly smaller than the original."

"How can that be?"

"That's what happens with bronze casting. As the metal cools it shrinks. So my sculpture, even though it is in bronze, is a surmoulage—'on' a 'cast.' A casting of a casting. Some might say even a forgery. But I don't buy that interpretation."

"Well, I wouldn't either," protested Iliana. After all, it would still have the *imprint* of the original, wouldn't it?"

"That's exactly why I bought it. Made me feel close to Kollwitz. And by the way, anatomical moulage casting was an important part of medicine. Teaching students with gelatin molds, and later wax molds taken directly from a corpse goes all the way back to the Renaissance."

The two physicians realized they had both been the beneficiaries of such anatomical moulages during their student days. As students, they had studied the wax models at the Charité Hospital's museum right there in Berlin.

After pausing to discuss this, Abraham turned a few pages in the journal he was holding and suggested they return to Kollwitz.

"When she was still conceiving her *Grieving Parents* sculpture she wrote this in December: 'I want to make these parents—simplicity in feeling, but expressing the totality of grief.'"

"Would you care to hear another of her entries on Karl and their relationship?" asked Abraham.

The women nodded eagerly and he picked up a different journal, that of 1916.

"Here is the most moving one. It's headed 'For our silver wedding anniversary.'"

> Dear husband: when we married, we took a leap in the dark. We were not building upon a firm foundation, or at least one firmly believed in. There were grave contradictions in my own feelings. In the end I acted on this impulse: jump in—you'll manage to swim. Mother, who realized all that, and was often worried, once said to me: "You will never be without Karl's love."
>
> That has been true. I have never been without your love, and because of it we are now so firmly linked after twenty-five years. Karl, my dear, thank you. I have so rarely told you in words what you have been and are to me. Today I want to do so, this once.... The tree of our marriage has grown slowly, somewhat crookedly, often with difficulty. But it has not perished. The slender seedling has become a tree after all, and it is healthy at the core. It bore two lovely, supremely beautiful fruits.

Megan and Iliana were moved to the core and neither one of them said anything for a full minute. Finally Iliana spoke.

"Oh, Abraham, that is so moving. What a beautiful image about the tree of their marriage."

"And her candor with him," Megan added. "The fact that she worried whether her envisioned life as an artist would conflict with the life of a wife and possibly even motherhood. But she did it all."

Time passed rapidly as Abraham read aloud pithy or poignant entries from various years having to do with what Megan had enunciated was of particular interest to her. Suddenly Iliana remembered that Abraham had not shown her what he called Käthe's "coded" references to her grandfather.

She begged him to do so now.

"I didn't lay out those volumes, but here is one brief reference, not coded because she mentions him by name. And you'll like this, Megan, because it also refers to Käthe's work." Abraham opened a diary from 1910 and began reading an entry from April.

I am gradually approaching the period in my life when my work comes first. When both boys went away for Easter, I hardly did anything but work. Worked, slept, ate, and went for short walks. But above all I worked. And yet I wonder whether the "blessing" is not missing from such work. No longer diverted by other emotions, I work the way a cow grazes; but Heller once said that such calm is death....Yet formerly, in my so wretchedly limited working time I was more productive because I was more sensual; I lived as a human being must live, passionately interested in everything.

"Fascinating," Iliana murmured. "So she did mention my grandfather by name."

Megan glanced at her watch and gave a start.

"Oh my goodness! Do you realize it is past eleven?"

Abraham and Iliana checked their watches. It was true. They had all been so intent on the journals that no one had noticed how quickly the time had flown by.

"I wish we could go on forever," said Megan wistfully.

"I realize you must go, and I'll call an Uber for you both, but Megan before you do go, might I ask your advice on where—what institution—the Käthe journals should go after my death?"

Megan thought carefully about her answer.

"Well, Abraham, you could, of course, donate them to the German National Library in Leipzig where they would eventually get digitalized for all the world to read. And probably the Kollwitz Museum in Cologne would be the depository that would garner the most public attention. They have the space there to dedicate at least a window, if not an entire display table for select journal pages on a changing exhibition schedule."

Abraham looked a trifle unconvinced.

Megan continued to ponder the situation, then said what was in her heart.

"Were it up to me to choose, however, I would have no hesitation. Berlin was Kollwitz's adopted city for fifty-two years. It was where she spent her married life, where she gave birth not only to her two boys, but also to her most significant art. I would leave the journals to the Berlin Kollwitz Museum."

"I *like* your advice, Megan. It's such a deserving institution. And along with the journals I could leave funds for an addition to the museum—there is space in the parking lot behind the building—an addition that could be *totally* devoted to the journals. Where future Kollwitz scholars could come and work. Thank you, Megan. You have helped me make my decision."

"Good," Iliana added, "I think leaving the journals to the Berlin Kollwitz Museum is a grand and proper solution."

"Let's drink to that," said Abraham. He called Uber and gave the address, then filled three liqueur glasses with Remy Martin VSOP cognac.

"*To Käthe!*"

55

Later that same evening, or rather, at three in the morning, Akram slipped out of their bed where Monika was sleeping soundly. In her fourth month of pregnancy she had been having trouble sleeping and occasionally took sleeping tablets. The previous night, after hearing Dr. Crespi's lecture on Kollwitz, she had not been able to sleep at all, she was so revved up. Tonight Akram had urged her to take a sleeping pill.

Slipping soundlessly out of their apartment, Akram drove his van over to Fasanenstrasse—a matter of just a few minutes—and, with his lights off, drove slowly into the back courtyard shared by the Berlin Kollwitz Museum and another building. He backed in and parked right by the fire escape, then opened the van's back. Mounting the five flights of stairs with no difficulty, Akram reached the exit door on the top floor. Was his tennis shoe lace still wedged in it after a full day had gone by? Wouldn't the museum guard have found it? Such a pity he could not return there the same evening as the Crespi lecture. But a sleepless Monika would have known if he left their apartment in the early hours of the morning. But now he was here. After inserting a knife blade in the crack of the door he gave it a gentle pull. The door swung outward without a sound and his tennis lace fell to the ground.

The next moment Akram was inside and heading for the sculpture he had decided upon earlier, the mother and child ensemble of 1915. He had brought the right tools to disengage it from its white pedestal and within three minutes he was out of the museum and running back down the fire escape, the priceless treasure against his chest. Carefully wrapping it in a felt blanket he placed it inside a wheeled carrier he had in the back of the van. He covered the carrier with a blanket, and drove quietly out of the courtyard.

Back at the apartment he slipped onto his side of the bed, drawing his part of the sheet over him. Monika was sleeping soundly and never heard her husband's heart pounding loudly.

56

Berlin police officer Anton Reininger's curiosity was roused. Abdul-Hakim's urgent report about four missing Muslim men presented evidence furnished by their wives that they had definitely not been in Berlin the night of the Cologne Kollwitz robbery. This substantiated the police surveillance camera photos that showed two vehicles associated with the missing men parked in front of the city's Alt St. Alban church.

Reininger phoned his colleague in Cologne, Herbert Schauen, to update him on the new data provided by the Muslim man who had visited him. The so-called initial fact that the men were at home the night of the Cologne fire and robbery was now definitely proven untrue. The question had expanded beyond the strange disappearance of the four men, to the fact that their two vehicles—a boom truck and a delivery van—seemed to have vanished off the face of the earth.

Both officers promised to step up investigation and vowed to share any new findings immediately.

Almost instantly Officer Reininger had another piece of information to impart to his Cologne colleague. A woman wearing a hijab had timidly entered the station and was waiting to talk to him. She was there, she said, to report that her husband was missing. His name was Jarir Uthman and he had left Wedding on a delivery job two days ago. She had not heard from him since, although they were usually in frequent phone contact during his work days. No, she did not know what vehicle he was driving for the out-of-town mission. His old Volkswagen was parked near the Wedding housing complex where they lived. Yesterday had been their son's eighteenth birthday and it was unthinkable that Jarir would not have contacted the family. But he had not. Could the police help?

Reininger reassured her as best he could and tried to hold out hope. He noted down the distressed woman's name—Maryam Uthman—telephone number, and address and solicitously saw her to the door.

As soon as she was out of sight he called Cologne.

"We now have a fifth missing Muslim," he announced to his marveling colleague. "One apparently not involved in your Alt St. Alban robbery, but one who, two days later, also left Berlin on a delivery job. *I think we have just been handed a missing link.*"

57

On their last day in Berlin Dee proposed that they visit the square named after Kollwitz. Megan could not have been more pleased. Although she had been to the Kollwitzplatz recently in pursuit of a major missing painting by Oskar Kokoschka, she was happy to return. It would be fun to show Dee the park's magnificent effigy of Kollwitz seated—a bronze version of Gustav Seitz's sculpture in the Kollwitz Museum. And usually there were excited children competing to climb up onto Kollwitz's lap. Dee would be charmed.

As they were driving to the park in the Prenzlauer Berg district of Berlin, Megan's iPhone rang. The car audio system announced Laura Forelle. Her voice sounded agitated.

"Megan, has Grete Bulliet gotten through to you yet?"

"No. What's up?"

"There has been another Kollwitz robbery. At Grete's museum. It happened last night. Wasn't discovered until this morning."

"Oh, no, I can't *believe* it! What was taken?"

"Another sculpture. The mother and child from nineteen-fifteen. Pried loose from its pedestal. Entry and exit through the fire escape on the top floor. No witnesses."

"Oh that's just awful. Poor Grete."

"She's beside herself."

"Considering the history of all these recent robberies, there's now a deviation with this latest theft," mused Megan.

"What do you mean?"

"All the previous robberies concerned Kollwitz works associated with death. This one concerns the living and life."

"Oh, god! Are you saying there could be yet another thief involved? Perhaps a copycat thief?"

"That remains to be seen. It's just interesting that a different *theme* has been the target of this burglar's attention."

"An excellent point. I'll call Grete and tell her to bring police attention to this 'deviation,' as you called it."

"It's also interesting that so far none of the thefts have been concerned with Kollwitz's graphic work. Not even those with the theme of death."

"Well, let's hope they don't get stolen next. Grete has already hired a night guard."

"Good! All right, Laura. Let's stay in touch and I'll call you if I see any more 'patterns' in the thefts."

Dee was horrified by the news and agreed with Megan that it was indeed exceptional that this new robbery was different from the others.

"I had half expected them to try and take the huge Pietà at the Neue Wache next," she said.

"Listen. That's no joking matter. I wouldn't put it past these incredibly bold characters."

Megan called Grete and commiserated with her about the daring robbery in her museum. When Megan brought up the fact that, thematically, this theft was unlike the previous six thefts, the museum director was fascinated. She begged Megan to call the helpful policeman, Officer Anton Reininger, who was handling the case and tell him her theory.

"All right, if you think it might help."

"Oh, yes, please do."

Grete gave Megan the policeman's phone number and after they hung up Megan called Reininger. He was extremely interested in her theory and thanked her.

"I will also tell my colleague in Cologne about your observation."

"Detective Schauen?"

"Yes, do you know him?"

"We met in Cologne after the first robberies and went over a suspect list that the director of the Kollwitz Museum there had prepared for us."

"Excellent. Let's keep in touch and if anything else turns up, please do call me again."

"I certainly will. We are glad you are on the case. I know Grete Bulliet is most appreciative."

Megan and Dee drove on to Prenzlauer Berg in companionable silence, each wondering to herself what sort of fanatical person or persons could covet Kollwitz so insanely. And, again, always the question, why?

58

Eleven hours had passed before Jarir Uthman awoke to find himself lying on his left side in a shallow ditch. He was scarcely breathing and he had lost a great deal of blood. Its flow had been staunched by the gravel, dirt, leaves, and grass with which his body had been packed and covered.

"*Ma*—I lie in my own grave!"

Eyes closed, he began clawing at the suffocating layers on top of his face. He was too weak to use much force but despair gave him stubbornness and he continued to claw. His breathing became heavier and suddenly he was aware that he was drawing in air untainted by dirt. Cautiously he opened his eyes in narrow slits. He could see the sky. It was night. The moon was bright and directly overhead.

He pushed enough dirt off himself to see the entry wound where he had been shot. A large knot of congealed blood had sealed it. The bullet had only grazed his heart, throwing it into ventricular fibrillation. That was what had made him appear to be dead to the gatekeeper who shot him. He now remembered that in the moment his heart had returned to its normal rhythm he had, despite the pain, resolved to play dead. He was too weak to fight off the bulldog of a man who had dumped him into a wheelbarrow. Then he had passed out. He had no memory of being thrown into the ditch where he now found himself.

Jarir realized that he must move very slowly even though he was yearning to heave himself out of the trough of dirt, leaves, and grass into which he had been thrown. His exertions were beginning to make him feel dizzy. Gingerly he touched his wound. It was not bleeding, Allah be praised.

He lay still for some minutes, breathing deeply until he felt stronger. Finally, he was able to raise himself and force his right shoulder and hip through the dirt and grass. After resting again, he made a final effort and was able to rise to his knees. Again he tentatively touched his wound. The bandage of coagulated blood had held fast. Could he stand? Better not chance it.

He began to crawl slowly away from the shallow trench that had so recently been his grave. Suddenly he stopped. The ground beneath him gave way and he fell downward some eight inches. It was another trough and he found himself *on top of a cadaver*! It was his friend Nadeem Naji.

For several minutes Jarir vomited without letup, all his newfound strength leaving him as he sobbed and threw up in turns. Finally he calmed down and furtively looked around in all directions. He saw mounds of grass over what looked like four more graves!

He must get away from this horrible graveyard. Away from the building where the prince lived. He must somehow get down the winding mountain road and reach the town of Nordhausen. Thank Allah it was night and no one would see him crawl away from the palace grounds.

But would he have the strength?

59

"After that intriguing lecture last night I think a perfect thing for us to do today would be visiting the Kollwitzplatz," Monika said to Akram over breakfast.

"That's right, darling. We haven't been there since we found out who Kollwitz was and fell in love with her work," Abraham looked up from his coffee, smiling tenderly at his wife.

"Good. I'll get ready. And I'll prepare a picnic lunch. Shall we take my car or yours?"

"Um, let's leave the van here. I've got work tools in the back."

Monika put on her pale blue short-sleeved maternity dress. She had bought three of them in different hues of blue, hoping that fate would allow her to present Akram with a son.

Half an hour later, with Monika driving her car, they were at the Kollwitzplatz. It was crowded, as usual, and they had to park far down Weissenburger Strasse, the street on which the artist had lived for five decades. As they approached the square the high-pitched sound of children happily shouting became almost overwhelming.

Monika grinned and looked up at her smiling husband.

"There will come a time when we bring our own wee one here."

They joined hands and slowly walked toward the statue of Kollwitz. A crowd of children were all over the great bronze lady—pushing each other to sit in her lap, scrambling at her feet, climbing up or jumping from the large pedestal.

"How truly wonderful. Such a different feeling from the sad Neue Wache sculpture we used to meet by," Akram mused, putting his arm around Monika's shoulders. They continued to stand there, enchanted by the children's antics. The sun was out and the chirping of birds filled the air.

"Let's sit down at the picnic table over there, by the hedge," Monika said finally. It was the only table still free, as picnickers were beginning to gather. They sat for a long time there not saying anything, just holding hands. It was a halcyon moment.

All of a sudden Akram straightened up and pointed toward the statue of Kollwitz.

"Look! Isn't that Professor Crespi?"

"Oh? Yes, yes, it *is*."

"You stay here and I'll go speak to her. Perhaps she and her companion will join us at the table."

Dee had indeed been charmed by the animated spectacle taking place around the Kollwitz statue. But she was ready now to sit down and said so to Megan, who was taking countless photos of the children with her iPhone.

"All right. Just one more photo."

"Professor Crespi?"

Megan wheeled around at the sound of her name.

"Professor Crespi!"

"Yes?"

"I'm Akram al-Aljamie. My wife and I spoke to you last night after your lecture."

"Ah, yes, of course. I remember. Your wife, Monika, isn't it?"

"Yes, and she's sitting right over there at that picnic table. Won't you and your friend join us for a bit?"

"That sounds delightful. Only we haven't brought any food with us."

"We have plenty. Do come sit with us."

"Herr al-Aljamie, this is my friend Mrs. Dee Whally. Dee, this is Akram al-Aljamie. He and his wife Monika are graduates of the Universität der Künste here in Berlin and were at the Kollwitz lecture last night. They would like us to come join them at that picnic table over there. See? Right in front of the hedge."

"Ah, ha. How nice."

Seeing that her husband and the two women were looking her way, Monika began waving vigorously.

As they began to walk toward her she jumped to her feet in welcome.

At that exact same moment, and in front of the horrified eyes of the approaching trio, a woman wearing a hijab dashed out from behind the hedge and stabbed Monika repeatedly in the stomach.

"Die, you German whore, die! And your cursed child with you!"

60

Reinhold Fromm sat in his Rügen house den. He was examining the Secreta drawing he owned by Kollwitz. Certainly it was superior to the one he had seen at Galerie Zamann. One of the facsimiles he had seen at the gallery of other Secretas was similar to his own. It showed a man lying down with a woman on her knees and elbows above him. Another version of his own *sexuelle Hörigkeit* Kollwitz. How he adored this drawing of sexual bondage.

His wife back in Berlin must never know about his private collection of erotica. He had taken measures to ensure that should he predecease her, his executor would immediately go to his Rügen home and remove the portfolio.

Fromm's thoughts turned to the American he had heard lecture on Kollwitz so recently. Would she use the business card he had pressed upon her and give him a call when she got to the island? How could he make sure? Perhaps she was reachable online. Turning to his laptop on the desk behind him, he typed her name into Google. Ha! There she was, Megancrespi.com. He went to the website and there on the upper right hand side was her e-mail address and phone number. What time was it? He glanced at his watch. Noon. Perhaps too early. He would try later in the day. Surely Crespi would want to see one of the few extant Secreta drawings. The Munich gallery dealer who sold it to him had informed him that the drawing was from the trove her son Hans had retrieved after her death in 1945. What a distinguished provenance, what a perfect pedigree!

61

A gaping crowd had quickly collected around the woman who had fallen to the ground and was bleeding from a horrific knife attack. The blood-soaked blade glistened in the grass next to her. Monika's husband was on his knees beside her, his arms under her head, talking desperately to her.

"Monika, Monika, my darling, stay with me. Help is coming, Don't leave me, darling, don't *leave* me."

Dee was standing by them, muttering words of comfort to both husband and wife. Megan had immediately called the police and now she was searching the hedge behind them—the hedge from which the murderer had sprung. She had been wearing a hijab and should be easy to spot as she ran from the scene. But, even though Megan was in pursuit of the woman right after calling the police, Megan realized she might be too far behind by now. She began shouting to startled passersby.

"Stop her! Stop the woman in the hijab! She's just tried to kill someone! Fan out. Help me find her!"

A few hearty souls began to run in different directions. Surely the woman must be somewhere nearby.

And now two policemen arrived. One questioned the despairing husband in vain, as the other called for an ambulance. A panting Megan ran back to them.

"Please look for the woman who stabbed her," she urged. "She was my height, and wearing a hijab."

One officer ran off in the direction Megan indicated. The other stayed at the crime scene hoping he could obtain some information from the man bending over the woman who had been attacked. But the man was hysterical and did not respond to, or perhaps even hear, his questions.

Dief al-Aljamie's operative, Aisha Saqqaf, had ripped off her hijab the moment she reached the safety of the hedge again. She had concealed a baby carriage behind it. Wearing beige slacks and a simple long-sleeved white blouse, Aisha looked for all the world like any of the other mothers strolling in the Kollwitzplatz with their babies. A few minutes later she had reached her car, loaded the perambulator in the backseat, and was off.

When she reached the first red traffic light she called al-Aljamie and reported in.

"*All has been carried out according to your command. Both whore and child.*"

Monika looked at her weeping husband with glazed eyes. She was in exquisite pain from the deep slashes in her stomach. Not only was she bleeding profusely, but the fetus had been penetrated and a new life was flooding out with her own blood.

Aware that she was dying, she made an enormous effort. Her eyes cleared for a second and she moved her lips ever so slightly. Akram bent closer, desperate to hear what she was trying to say.

"Rügen," she mouthed. "Rügen. Our *Trosthaus*. Akram! Protect it always. For us, for our..."

These were her last words.

Akram, Megan, Dee, and the curious bystanders saw her convulse once, then fall back with staring wide eyes and slacked jaw. In sad irony, the ambulance now arrived and two men were running toward them with a stretcher.

Akram was frozen. He could not speak. Megan turned to the policeman and spoke for him.

"He is her husband. We three saw the stabbing. I, my friend, and Akram here."

She described the attacker, a woman wearing a hijab, and how she had suddenly appeared from behind the hedge, repeatedly stabbed the victim in the stomach, and then fled.

"She seems to have completely disappeared, yet she *must* be somewhere in the park," Megan concluded desperately.

The ambulance roared off toward Prenzlauer Berg's local hospital with Monika in it, leaving an uncomprehending Akram standing behind. He had not answered the driver's question as to whether he wanted to accompany the body. Megan saw his state and stayed with him, muttering comforting words and gently massaging his back. Finally he seemed to comprehend.

"I must get to the hospital! I must be with her. I must see her again."

"He's in no condition to drive," Dee whispered to Megan.

"We can take you there, Akram. Come, let us take you."

Still dazed, Akram obediently followed the women out of the park and up to where they had parked. With Dee giving directions from her iPhone map, Megan drove them to the local hospital.

They stood on either side of Akram as he identified himself to the receptionist at the front desk and asked where his Monika was. The clerk called Dr. Friedman, the ER physician who had received Monika's body. He appeared within minutes and immediately extended his hands to Akram.

"My sincere condolences, Sir. Your wife passed away while still in the ambulance."

"No, no, no! It can't be true. Don't tell me that!" Akram pleaded with the doctor.

"I am so very sorry. You may see your wife now, if you wish, but we will have to perform an autopsy, since this is a case of murder. After that we can release her body to a funeral home of your choosing."

This seemed to have convinced Akram that his wife was gone.

"I want my wife to have a Catholic service and burial. When can she be transferred to a mortuary?"

"Not for at least three days, I should think."

"Three days or even later? And you said I may see her now."

"Yes, now. I will take you to her if you wish."

The women waited for Akram while he went to say his farewell to his wife. When he returned he looked so dazed that Dee proposed they see him home. Almost incomprehensibly, Akram muttered his address and Megan was surprised to learn it was so close to their hotel. The afternoon traffic was building up but they reached Akram's building in good time. Like a zombie, however, he just sat in the car, silent, staring straight ahead.

"Perhaps we should get out with him and ask him to lead us to the apartment," whispered Dee. Megan nodded.

"Akram," Dee said kindly. "Akram, won't you kindly take us up to your apartment?"

The question triggered something in the poor man's mind. He stepped out of the car, and now the women had to hurry after him as he walked to the building's front door and unlocked it. They went up one flight of steps and a few seconds later they were following Akram into his dwelling. Megan was surprised to see a small replica of Kollwitz's Pietà piece in the Neue Wache on the dining room table, but said nothing. After all, this was the former art student who had asked whether she might know of any leads to finding Kollwitz's limestone sculpture of the *Crouching Mother with Two Children*. It made sense that someone as interested as that would have a Kollwitz piece in the house. It was bronze, or bronzed, either a cast of a cast, or a ceramic copy to which bronze-colored paint had been applied. But it explained why Akram and his wife had been so interested in pursuing further Kollwitz sculptures.

Once in his own home, Akram became a completely different person. He thanked the women profusely for their help. When he saw Megan eyeing the Pietà he spoke in the most normal voice to her about it.

"Ah, you have spotted our Kollwitz. Monika and I used to meet by the large one at the Neue Wache, and so I made a clay copy, fired it in my studio kiln, and painted it to look bronze. It was my wedding present to..." He choked up, broke into tears, and was unable to speak further.

The women tried to comfort him and after a while he regained his composure. He even asked where they were going to next, after they left Berlin.

"We're both lovers of the painter Caspar David Friedrich so we're driving to the island of Rügen next, tomorrow in fact."

Megan could not understand why what she had said would set Akram to crying again. She and Dee stood in silence as he apologetically tried to dry his tears. Finally he was able to speak.

"My darling wife was *from* Rügen. Our second home is there, *Trosthaus*. It is a hunting lodge that was handed down from generation to generation in the Putbus family. Monika's last words to me were about our home there. I shall go there tomorrow and then come back for her transfer to the mortuary. Please, oh please, as you are going to Rügen tomorrow, won't you consider being my guests while you are on the island? It would be so terrible to be in *Trosthaus* for the first time alone."

Dee looked at Megan who nodded assent.

"If you have room, we would be honored to stay there," she said.

"Yes," Megan seconded, "if you give us the directions, we could arrive tomorrow afternoon." They both were feeling extreme pity for the man.

"You are too kind. I feel as if we have been friends a long time. As though you are my mothers, if I may be so bold. I will write out the directions for you. But first I must offer you some tea. Please sit down. Where are my manners?"

Without pausing for their answer Akram went to the kitchen. Megan and Dee sat down at the large dining table, half of which obviously served as a desk. Behind it on the wall above the Pietà copy was a framed text. It had been hand embroidered in white onto a piece of black linen. Dee, who was closer to it, studied it, surprised to see it was in English.

"Goodness, that's by Matthew Arnold. It's from his *Empedocles on Etna*."

"I know of the author and I have climbed halfway up to Etna, but I'm not familiar with the work. What's the quote?"

"Golly, Megan. I'm surprised you don't know it. It used to be quite famous *in my day*," she chided in a low voice.

The ribbing spurred her younger friend to action and Megan walked over to read the verses. She spoke them out loud.

> Is it so small a thing
> To have enjoy'd the sun
> To have lived light in the spring
> To have loved, to have thought,
> to have done...?

"Hm. I do like that sentiment. Wonder what Akram and his wife found in it?"

"I couldn't even begin to explain. The poem supposedly quotes two friends of the philosopher who are trying to dissuade him from committing suicide. But they are not successful. Empedocles was a real, historical person who became disillusioned in philosophy and politics and threw himself into the crater of Mt. Etna."

"Dee, you do know the most astonishing things."

"No. I just know a few things."

Akram appeared with a tray loaded with the paraphernalia of a true tea connoisseur. The women could tell how settling it was for him to pour out the steaming hot liquid from a heavy iron pot into their individual iron cups. Megan could not help rephrase the first line of the poem she had just read. She turned to Akram and said gently: "Is it so small a thing to have drunk deep of tea..."

The bereaved man instantly understood the spirit in which Megan offered the paraphrase. They talked of the legends concerning the Greek philosopher's death.

"And why did Monika and you so especially prize these particular lines you have on your wall?" Megan dared to ask Akram.

"We thought they applied to the life we have, *had* chosen for ourselves—to take comfort in the small joys around us despite the terrible condemnation of our marriage by both our families."

Akram looked as though he might weep again and Dee quickly changed the subject to Rügen.

"Oh, yes, let me draw you a map and give you directions how to reach *Trosthaus*."

It was quite a document Akram handed over by the time he had finished drawing not only a detailed map but also a view of the zigguratlike lodge.

And now it was time to go. Megan and Dee looked at each other and nodded in silent agreement. Akram insisted upon walking them out to the street where their car was parked. He leaned down and lightly embraced them both, then stood watching them as they drove off.

"Monika, my darling. *You have sent me these two angels from America.* I thank you, I thank you!"

62

Police officer Reininger had come up with some fascinating information after talking to his Cologne counterpart about the mysterious disappearance of four Turkish Muslims from their Wedding neighborhood. Redoubling his efforts, he concentrated on lost person reports filed in nearby German states. So far, no Turkish Muslims had been reported as missing. Not satisfied, he tried another search, this time of Muslims who had been murdered in Berlin, which was both city and state. None in Berlin. But when Reininger looked up murder statistics in nearby states and came to Mecklenburg-Vorpommern, one police report originating in Stralsund caught his attention.

It concerned two unexplained explosions in the impoverished Knieper Nord district of the city. Unexplained explosions that had killed the inhabitants of two apartments in a dense housing complex. All the dead were Turkish Muslims. And the heads of both households were former employees of the famous Dorotek manufacturing complex at Prora on Rügen. But the most interesting thing about the report was an anonymous note addressed to the Stralsund police. Quite short, it read: "For Your Information. Both families killed by recent explosions at Knieper Nord were in the process of suing their employer Dorotek on charges of asbestos poisoning."

Officer Reininger lifted up his phone and dialed his Cologne colleague. He muttered to himself while waiting for the call to go through: "*Now we're getting somewhere.*"

63

To reach the ancient island of Rügen on his honeymoon trip there in 1818, Caspar David Friedrich drove his large four-wheel, hooded carriage onto an open barge ferrying passengers to and fro. While on the island he painted the riveting image that would fascinate generations: *Chalk Cliffs on Rügen*. From the height of the great white cliffs, framed by two trees, three figures—a woman and two men—gaze at the blue sea so far below. A painted treatise on the transience of life and the abyss of death.

Two centuries later, in the early morning hours of a halcyon day in July, another mode of transportation—a Nissan cargo van—brought an anxious young man to the refuge of Rügen. He too was aware of the transience of life, and painfully so, as his own precious wife had just been murdered. Her last words to him had been "protect *Trosthaus*."

Akram knew only too well to what she was referring. Her rapacious cousin Rolf von Putbus. Just a week ago Monika had shown him a letter from Rolf's lawyer announcing the commencement of a suit against her questioning the legality of her ownership of *Trosthaus*.

Without stopping at Putbus—site of the selfie he and Monika had once so gleefully taken of themselves—Akram sped on southwards toward the beech forests above Lauterbach. Only one vehicle passed him, a small black truck. In his rear view mirror Akram saw the driver toss a bundle onto the side of the road. Typical, he thought. No appreciation for the sanctity of the forest. He turned off at the narrow dirt road that led through several hills and valleys to the lodge. Finally pulling up in front of the zigguratlike building with its three-step base, he noticed something odd. Something certainly not there when he and Monika had visited *Trosthaus* only eight days earlier. The entry door had been boarded up by two four-by-four panels of wood. It effectively blocked entry into the house.

As Akram got closer he saw that a large hand-printed sign had been placed on the upper panel. It read: "Closed due to litigation proceedings."

The colossal nerve of that hateful man Rolf! There was no one else who could have done such a thing. Certainly it was not a police sign.

A horrifying thought overcame Akram. *Was it possible that Monika's scheming cousin had commissioned her murder in order to appropriate Trosthaus?* How else to explain the speed with which the lodge had been boarded up? And the sign! Did Rolf presume that Akram would not be returning to the hunting lodge anytime soon?

As far as he knew, no litigation had been instigated. Monika had told him about Rolf's threat, but she did not believe he would really try to contest what was the unassailable legitimacy of her ownership.

Abruptly, Akram was overtaken by an urgent desire to enter the house that was now so holy, so sacred to him. Surely Monika's spirit was almost palpable inside her beloved parental home. He needed to be with her.

Returning to the van he picked up a large claw hammer and crossbar and walked back to the boarded-up door. The wooden panels were large but they separated easily under the twisting of Akram's hammer and crossbar. It took only fifteen minutes to completely dismantle the thing. Obviously, it had been hastily assembled and by an amateur at that.

Akram gingerly slid his key into the door. Good. It was still locked. No one had attempted to open it. Still, he entered the house cautiously. He checked every room. No sign of anyone's having been inside. He returned to the room where he and Monika had shared so many nights of love and tenderness and lay down on the bed. Sobs shook his body. He did not try to suppress them and lay like that for a long time.

Sitting up at last, he noticed Monika's favorite scarf on the top of her side of the chest of drawers. She had forgotten to put it away. Was it a sign? Akram walked over, picked it up, drew in its fragrance, then slipped the light blue and white scarf into his shirt pocket. She *was* with him still. He would carry the scarf with him always.

A new energy filled Akram. He checked the guest bedrooms again, this time with an eye to making sure everything was in order for his American guests. Everything was in order. So were things in the great room, dominated as it was by the Bresser telescope. In the kitchen, however, an empty refrigerator commanded his attention. The makings for breakfast were needed. He would drive back to Putbus and pick up eggs, bread, butter, jam, fruit, and coffee well before his American guests arrived late that afternoon. And the makings for dinner too, so they would not have to drive to town again in the evening.

A high whining sound interrupted his thoughts. Finding nothing in the house, Akram went cautiously down the corridor to the door and opened it. A very small kitten stood looking up at him. Its green eyes were large and its honey orange and white fur was caked with mud and leafs. An open wound on its right shoulder oozed blood.

Without hesitation Akram picked the kitten up and gently rocked it in his arms. This was the bundle he had seen that passing truck driver throw out onto the side of the road.

"You are safe now, you sweet thing. Monika sent you and I will take care of you always."

64

"You said WHO wants to see me?"

Reinhold Fromm was furious. He had jumped to his feet upon being told by his secretary that he had a visitor who identified himself as being a government inspector.

"Herr Emil Schnüffler of the Department of Labor."

"Have him wait out there and get Schlau in here damn quick."

What the hell was going on, Fromm demanded of himself. First lawsuits, now *government* interference? The wait for his lawyer seemed interminable.

There was a single knock on his office door and Wilhelm Schlau entered. His face was expressionless as he closed the door behind him.

"Did you see the man waiting out there?" Fromm asked, sitting down at his desk.

"I did."

"Do you realize who he is?"

"I do not. Tell me."

"He's a government agent. From the Department of Labor."

Schlau feigned surprise.

"Why the hell do you think he's here? And unannounced. Why didn't we get a letter notifying us of his arrival?"

"Let's play it close to the chest," Schlau answered. "You don't yet know why he's here."

"If it's about asbestos, *I expect you to do your job.*"

Fromm rang his secretary and told her to show the man in.

"Herr Direktor, Herr Emil Schnüffler to see you, sir."

"Sit down, Herr Schnüffler." An unsmiling Fromm indicated one of the two chairs in front of his desk with a brief flick of his forefinger.

"This is my company lawyer, Herr Schlau."

The two men nodded silently at one another as the lawyer sat down in the empty chair next to him.

Schnüffler came right to the point.

"I represent the Department of Labor. Disturbing reports have come to us recently concerning your factory here at Prora regarding the putative presence of residual asbestos. Furthermore, we understand that you are at present involved in a number of lawsuits from the families of former employees and that they all claim asbestos-related deaths. Given these circumstances, I am authorized to conduct an immediate on-site investigation for traces of asbestos and any other dangerous materials that might be present in your factory."

"That's outrageous! You can't just walk in here and expect to start a physical examination of my factory. It would be extremely disruptive, halt production, and, furthermore, it would be in vain. There is no asbestos here."

In his agitation Fromm had risen to his feet again. Realizing this he sat back down and looked urgently at his lawyer who turned to the visitor.

"We would need to see a copy of your written orders and your government identification before you proceed further."

"Yes, of course. I have them both here."

Schnüffler reached down into his briefcase and handed Fromm's lawyer a sheath of papers. To that he added an ID card from his wallet.

Schlau pretended to read the papers in detail. In truth he knew what they were all about. After all, he had been responsible for initiating this "surprise" visit. He turned to his impatiently waiting employer.

"These papers are in order, Herr Fromm, and we must comply, I'm afraid. And at once."

"This is despicable!"

Fromm jumped up again from his desk, looking from one man to the other. In his agitation he was seized by a brief fit of coughing.

"I will file a lawsuit against your department so fast your head will spin," he said finally.

Schnüffler stood up and left the office without uttering another word. He and the team waiting below in their government van had work to do.

65

"I can't believe you *did* that!"

Knowing her penchant for exaggeration, Dee did not trust Megan's account of the time she was mugged in New York. After a late lunch at their beloved Kempinski, they were on the autobahn again and headed due north for Stralsund on the coast and the bridge across to Rügen. Megan was at the wheel.

"Yes, really, it's just as I told you. Wayne Conway, my favorite colleague at Columbia, and I had been picking slides for class until very late in the evening as usual, and even though Wayne lived on the other side of campus he always walked me home. But when we got to my street, Claremont Avenue, I announced that I thought we'd seen all the muggers for that evening and I could continue on home alone. He agreed, we parted company, and just as I was unlocking the front door to my apartment house, two arms embraced me from the back. I wondered who knew me that well.

"But then a voice said: 'Give me your money, give me your money!' I was about to pull my mace out of my blue winter coat pocket when a second voice said: 'Hurry up!' I was so nervous that I stamped my foot and said: 'Just a minute! This is the first time I've been mugged and you're making me nervous!' One of them immediately said: 'Oh, I'm sorry.' True story, I kid you not. At my request, they threw my wallet with all my photos and credit cards back at me after they'd removed the cash."

"Is that why you were ready to leave Columbia when SMU invited you to teach for them?"

"Well, in a way. That and the fact that my apartment had been broken into and robbed a short time later."

"Oh, yes, you've told me about that. That they got in through the window and left by the your front door. What did they take?"

"Just some costume jewelry; nothing I couldn't replace. But the amazing thing is that my Haynes silver flute was right there on the piano in its case and they didn't bother with it. I had no alarm system then whereas, as you know, I certainly do in Dallas."

Megan was thinking about the time a thief had broken into her home while she was away on an art-theft case in Vienna. He had tried to make off with a Schiele drawing, but her alarm had been triggered and the police came immediately. Unfortunately for the robber, he was shot to death when he tried to charge the police officers. Megan was not able to get over the fact that a man had been killed in her own home and she referred to the whole ghastly event as the Schiele slaughter.

"I don't suppose there are any historic towns we'll be going through on our way up to the coast?" Dee asked.

"Not really. At least nothing of interest to us. It's just a straight shoot up to Rostock on the A 19, and then we take the A 20 northeast to Stralsund." Megan had thoroughly checked out their four-hour route on her laptop.

"And what about Rostock? Somehow that name sounds familiar."

"Maybe because it has one of the earliest universities in Europe?"

Dee shook her head.

"That's impressive, but don't think that's why I know the name."

"Well, I know that during the years leading up to World War II, Rostock was enthusiastically pro-Nazi and that the city's Jewish synagogue was burned down during Kristallnacht."

"Terrible. But still that's not why the name rings a bell. Seems as if it has something to do with factories."

"I get it, of course. Rostock was a center for aircraft manufacturing during the war and the British really bombed the hell out the city."

"That's it. I remember hearing about the bombing raids and that historic buildings were hit as well as factories."

"So are we in agreement? We head straight for Stralsund without stopping there and take the bridge right over to the island?"

"Sounds good to me. Because we want to have plenty of time to find Akram's hunting lodge paradise, even though the map he drew for us is very clear. He places the lodge as being in the middle of a beech forest." Dee was studying the makeshift map Akram had drawn for them the day before.

"I see," she continued, "there's actually a town called Putbus not far from the lodge. That's the surname he mentioned in regard to his wife's family, so they must go way back in history if there's a town named after them."

"Interesting." Megan was concentrating on driving. The two friends fell silent, enjoying the music Dee was playing on her iPad. In homage of the Mendelssohn graves they had so recently visited, she had chosen Felix's magical incidental music, *A Midsummer Night's Dream.*

66

Aisha Saqqaf had been recalled to Iraq.

Not that she hadn't done her job well, Akram's father explained. In fact she had carried out the two strikes extremely well—the ransacking of his son's studio and the elimination of his son's pregnant whore.

But the unexplained, brutal murder of a pregnant German woman by a Muslim woman had become the lead story in the Berlin tabloids. Public rage against women wearing hijabs was incendiary, and the Berlin police were carrying out an extensive investigation that, from what his contacts informed al-Aljamie, was coming dangerously close to home. The police had a clear set of prints taken from the knife used in the stabbing. They had already interrogated local Muslim Brotherhood members and their women, and had combed the neighborhoods near Kollwitzplatz. Their next sweep was scheduled to take place in the district where Aisha lived. She had to get out. And now. He would personally meet her plane when it arrived in Baghdad.

What Dief al-Aljamie did not tell Aisha was that he had already replaced her with a male agent. One commissioned to make life extremely difficult for his son. Not to harm him. At least not just yet. First, dissuade him from continuing to think of Germany as his home. Second, ensure that he is on a plane back to Iraq in a matter of days.

If Hamzah el-Hashem could not persuade Akram to repent and return to the true faith, then the ultimate punishment for being an infidel would have to take place.

67

"But the murder victim was in the audience the night of the Kollwitz lecture, I tell you." Iliana, back in Berlin after a weary day of seeing patients at Dorotek, was on the phone with Abraham. Uncharacteristically for her, she had picked up one of the evening tabloids for the train ride home. On the front page was a photograph of the woman who had been murdered in Kollwitzplatz. She was identified as Monika von Putbus.

"But surely you remember, Abraham? We were standing in line behind her and her husband, waiting to talk with Professor Crespi. I distinctly heard her introduce herself as 'Monika, formerly von Putbus, but now happily Frau' something or other, it was obviously some Arabic surname."

"I do remember now. He was a swarthy young man with a beard and seemed very much in love with his wife."

"That's the couple. We stood right behind them. I can't believe it!"

"Putbus is a very old German name, Iliana. There's a Putbus town on Rügen and there used to be a Putbus castle there before the communists tore it down."

"Oh! I didn't make the connection. Of course, I remember now there's a town on Rügen called Putbus. But my work at Dorotek takes up whatever tourist travel I might like to do around the island."

"Ah, you Viennese, you are so ignorant of our German history," Abraham joshed his friend.

"Unfair! But what I'm getting at, my dear, is that we ought to contact the police about the people who were there along with Monika Putbus at the Kollwitz lecture."

"And why so? Do you think someone in the *audience* was the murderer? That's a laugh."

"No, listen, I'm quite serious. Don't you remember that sitting in the back row of the lecture room when we came in was a lone woman wearing a hijab?"

"Oh, my god, that's right!"

"There has to be some *connection*: a woman with a hijab at a lecture on Kollwitz and a murder the very next day in the Kollwitzplatz by a woman wearing a hijab."

"Your argument is most compelling, Iliana. What are you going to do?"

"I'm going to call the police as soon as you and I hang up."

68

At Dorotek, Fromm called in his chief engineer, Ferdinand Fehler. The man was informed of what had just happened and that even now a government inspector and his team were preparing to examine the Dorotek factory buildings for signs of asbestos presence. Could anything be done to block or neutralize their findings? And how long would it take for laboratory tests to confirm whether there was asbestos present?

Fromm asked these urgent questions of his engineer in front of his lawyer, whom he had enjoined to remain present after the Department of Labor man had left so abruptly. Schlau could only shake his head at what he realized was going to be a judgment against Dorotek.

Engineer Fehler was obviously overwhelmed, receiving the rapid fire questions from his plump employer in silence. Finally he spoke.

"Unfortunately, Herr Fromm, there is no way to conceal the toxic mineral from detection. We have it, as I told you a few days ago, in our electrical wiring, in the lining of the heating pipes, and in the cement foundations."

"Why, that would tear my factory apart! Surely we can stop them from doing that?" Fromm looked at his lawyer.

" It would take several days, perhaps weeks, to get an injunction, and that is only *if* we could get one. Destruction of property in this case is not a strong argument. The whole purpose of a surprise visit is specifically to prevent any efforts at a cover up, which in the case of asbestos is not possible anyway."

What if I have Doktor Frankel testify that she has seen absolutely no cases of asbestosis, or mesothelioma, or whatever the god damn hell you call it?"

Before either man could answer, Fromm put his words into action and rang his secretary telling her to get the company physician into his office and fast.

69

Prince Yusri Pahlavi stood in one of the courtyards of his newly completed complex overlooking Nordhausen and hugged himself with joy. Mother would adore *Jamshad*. And the two large Kollwitz images of grieving parents he had positioned facing what was to be her suite of rooms would be such a comfort to her. He took one last proud look around, then joined his waiting chauffeur for the trip down to the Frankfurt airport where his mother would be arriving in a few hours. He had been looking forward to this moment for well over three years.

70

It was twelve noon. Rostock behind them, Megan and Dee were playing a music quiz on their last lap to Rügen.

"I'm going to hum the first two notes of a popular song and you identify it, okay?" Megan had challenged Dee. Her friend accepted the challenge, as her excellent memory for songs and their texts went back at least eight decades.

"Okay. Hum away."

Megan hummed an upward fourth from middle C to F, both notes held for equal lengths of time.

Dee identified the song immediately.

"That's *All the Things You Are!*"

She sang the opening lines: "You are the promised kiss of springtime that makes the lonely winter seem long."

"I love that song" Megan said, "but I hate the last line."

"What do you mean?"

"You remember the ending goes 'when all the things you are, are mine.'"

"Oh, come on Megan. You can't take umbrage at that."

"But I do. If I were the object of that song I'd want all the things I was still to be mine."

"Honest to god, Megan. Sometimes your feminism really gets in the way. It's just a song lyric and its intentions are really very sweet."

Megan sulked. "Nevertheless, I still would like whatever I've worked hard to become to be mine."

"You truly are missing the spirit of the song. But never mind. Now hum me two notes again."

"Okay. Here they are." Megan hummed a D above middle C, then dropped down to the D below middle C.

"Now, really, how do you expect me to identify an octave?"

"Think about it. Hum it yourself. Both notes the same length."

Dee did so.

"I'm not getting anywhere."

"And if I were to tell you that the first two words are the same ones as the song I just gave you to identify?"

"Ah ha! 'You are my lucky star...'"

"Yep, you got it."

"All right, Megan. Take that same octave but hum it upward. What do you get?"

Megan obliged and immediately recognized what song Dee had backed her into.

"That's 'Somewhere Over the Rainbow.'" They sang the song lustily. Then Megan thought of another challenge.

"Okay, Dee. I'm now going to apply that same upward octave to classical music."

"You're kidding. Just two notes and I'm supposed to identify the piece?"

"Try it. You'll like it."

Dee hummed several times to herself, then exclaimed in triumph, "I've got it!" She hummed the beginning notes of Mozart's Haffner Symphony.

"Brava, Dee!"

The two friends continued to play their amusing game until they reached Stralsund and came within sight of the embankment and its two bridges to Rügen.

"Which shall we take? The new one or the old one?" Megan looked at her friend inquiringly.

"How about crossing over on the new one and coming back on the old one? That way we can hit two bridges with one Volkswagen."

"Ouch. That was really awful. The new bridge is bound to be the faster," conceded Megan. "But let's check them both out online before we cross."

Dee opened her iPad and after several tries found a helpful URL with a detailed map as well as text.

"Okay. The map shows both bridges crossing over a small island called Dänholm before they reach the much larger Rügen island. And the text says that the new one-tower suspension bridge was completed in two thousand and seven to replace the aging original bridge, called the Rügendamm. It provides the only access to Dänholm. So we could take the old bridge back to the mainland, that is, if we want to check out the little island."

"Neat. We might just do that if we still have the energy."

"Oh!" Dee was still reading the text she had pulled up on the two bridges. "Guess who opened the new bridge? Chancellor Agata Merle. Now that's really great. I think she's wonderful."

"Me too. All right, here we go." Megan turned onto the sleek new bridge.

"Says here it's almost two miles long. Oh, wow, look! We're passing right over the Dänholm island. It's like being in a low- flying helicopter. Look down there. See that houseboat? I've read about the houseboats up here. Some of them are little private hotels, each with a bedroom, kitchen, living room, and bathroom."

Just then Megan's iPhone rang. The car's audio system announced only a set of letters and numbers.

"Hello?" Megan said tentatively.

"*Ach!* Frau Doktor Crespi. I am so glad to reach you. Here is Reinhold Fromm of Dorotek. We met at your glorious Kollwitz lecture and you told me you would be coming to Rügen. Is this still so?"

Megan rolled her eyes heavenward and reluctantly answered Fromm's question in the affirmative.

"Wonderful. I gave you my business card, but perhaps you have been too busy to call me. I went online and found your contact information, so here I am. When do you expect to arrive?"

"Um. Probably very late this evening." Prevaricating came easily to Megan when speaking to this pushy man.

"Excellent, excellent! So we could meet tomorrow morning?"

Megan did not want to clutter the next day with an impending appointment when they would be touring the island, so she set what for her would be a very early time.

"Um, say around nine-thirty?" Better to get the business meeting out of the way as early as possible.

"Perfect. I e-mail you directions to my factory at Prora immediately. We meet there and then we go to my home very nearby where you will see my Kollwitz Secreta drawing. Is this to your liking?"

"All right. But I won't be able to stay very long. I have a lunch reservation in Sassnitz with my travel companions." The fib came to her naturally. And after all, it wasn't a complete lie: they *would* probably be having lunch with Akram the next day—somewhere. So there! Megan soothed her conscience.

"For you I clear parking space right next to mine, with my name on it. And perhaps you be so kind as to call me when you park there? I shall come down immediately."

"Thank you. I shall do that."

"Then we say goodbye for now, Frau Professor." Fromm hung up before Megan could. They had just exited the bridge on the Rügen side. Dee conferred with her paper map.

"If we stay on this main road we can drive to a town called Bergen and from there drop down to a town called Putbus, which isn't far from Akram's place. 'Putbus.' Isn't that the surname of poor Akram's murdered wife?"

"Yes. I remember her exact words to me after the lecture. She said: 'I am Monika, formerly von Putbus, but now happily Frau al-Aljamie.'"

"How very sad. Well, then by all means let's drive to Putbus. We could have lunch there. Akram isn't expecting us until around three at *Trosthaus*."

"While you have your iPad open, Dee, try looking up Akram's surname, would you? It's two words linked by a hyphen: al-Aljamie." Megan spelled out the two words. Dee typed out the entry and a few seconds later came up with some information.

"Dief al-Aljamie. Important Iraqi archaeologist and excavator whose name is linked to the discovery of carvings and secret chambers in Iraq's best known ziggurat, Aqar-Quf." Dee tried several tentative pronunciations of the ziggurat then looked at Megan helplessly.

"Don't ask *me*," Megan laughed. "Does it give his dates?"

Dee found only the date of his birth. But the entry showed he had three daughters and one son, Akram.

"Bingo! Now we know a bit more about our host. And why he was interested in sculpture. Let's talk to him more about Kollwitz when we're with him."

"But, wouldn't that make him sad? After all it was by her Pietà in the Neue Wache that they used to meet." Dee paused. An awful thought had come to her. She voiced it.

"Don't tell me you could possibly suspect *Akram* as the Kollwitz robber?"

"No, no, very unlikely. But one must keep one's mind open to all possibilities."

"Oh, come on, Megan, how cold-hearted can you be."

To take her mind off what they had just discussed, Dee began to study the brochure that had come with their rental car. It touted something called VW Car-Net and claimed that, in addition to GPS, it could beam up maps, music, URLs, and all sorts of things on the Volkswagen dashboard screen. Something to try out when we make the drive to Greifswald, she decided. I'll do the driving and techie Megan can put it into operation.

She replaced the brochure in the glove compartment, switched back to her iPad, and began looking up restaurants in Putbus. Almost all of them seemed to be attached to hotels. She found one she knew would lift the gloomy mood that had descended upon them.

"Okay, Megan. I've found the perfect restaurant for us, seeing that we're on an island. It's called Nautilus, and the interior is decorated to look like an old submarine. There are two tanks: one is a large aquarium and the other has two turtles. Feel like turtle soup?"

"No, but how can we resist such an unusual restaurant. Let's try it."

"The only critique I find here is that the portions are overlarge."

"Fine. We can split one dessert."

Thirty minutes later they had parked next to the Hotel Nautilus on Dorfstrasse and were studying the appetizing fish menu of the Nautilus restaurant. Asparagus and chips accompanied each order and the variety of chips was legion, from onion to blue cheese to honey.

After they had ordered—trout almandine for both, no chips, thank you—Megan began discussing the famous chalk cliffs of Rügen painted so magnificently by Friedrich. At Dee's request she picked the painter's most famous view to describe.

"The jagged white cliffs look out from a great height directly onto the Baltic Sea below and the span of water seems endless. The leafy branches of two trees form an oval frame that makes us think we are seeing the scene through a telescope. There are three people at the edge of the cliffs with their backs to us, so we see what they see. We identify with them. A woman dressed in red is on the left and she bends and points to something on the ground. To the right of center a man on his hands and knees, his hat on the ground, is edging toward something—perhaps a flower that has attracted the woman's attention. Then to their right, a man stands, his hat on, and his arms folded across his chest. His gaze is directed toward the endless sea, but it's hard not to think that he is contemplating not only immensity but also his comparative insignificance. The permanence of the elements, the brevity of human life."

"I can almost *see* the painting from your description. Sounds as deeply philosophical as the two Friedrich paintings we saw in Berlin."

"Yes. He truly was a philosopher-painter. And he was never popular in his own time. Very few people understood his gloomy pictures."

Megan took out her iPhone and a few seconds later showed Dee the image they had been discussing. Then she swiped to a second image of the chalk cliffs painted by Friedrich. It was similar to the first one but this time the onlookers were two men. Again their backs were to the viewer. An essay on friendship and sharing.

"I always showed the first version on the final exam I used to give my students. But one time, I had an outed gay student in class who always sat in the front row, took copious notes, and made straight As. So, especially for him, I showed this version, and after he instantly wrote down the name of the artist, he looked straight up at me and we exchanged a conspiratorial nod unnoticed by the hundred other students."

"Oh, that's a sweet story. By the way, did Friedrich ever marry?"

"Yes, and he spent his honeymoon on Rügen. He wrote a charming letter about being married. It ran something like this: 'Now that I am no longer one but two, everything is needed: coffee beans, coffee grinder, coffee pot, coffee cups, coffee spoons...'"

"That's really sweet. Love the alliteration."

"That's why I've never forgotten the letter, I guess."

Dessert was offered—cookies in the shape of fish—but, full of the "overly large" dinner, they actually declined. They were eager to press on to *Trosthaus*.

"And I sure hope you don't expect me to *climb* those chalk cliffs tomorrow," joked Dee.

71

Police officer Anton Reininger was on the phone with a Dr. Iliana Frankel. She was a resident of Prenzlauer Berg and had something to tell him that might be of interest concerning the recent murder at Kollwitzplatz.

"And what is that?"

"Well, what I know from the newspapers is that the murder occurred near the large effigy of Kollwitz and that the fatal stabbing was committed by a woman in a hijab. Correct?"

"Correct."

"This is what I have to tell you. Two evenings ago there was a lecture at the Kollwitz Museum here in Berlin. I was in attendance and I noticed that a slender woman wearing a hijab was sitting in the back row. She left the moment the lecture was over. Now I find it beyond coincidence that, within two days, a woman with a hijab was present at two different locations having to do with Kollwitz."

"Hm. I certainly see what you mean. I shall call the museum director immediately to see if there was an invitation list. Thank you so much, Frau Doktor Frankel, for bringing this to police attention."

"Well, I just hope it helps somehow."

"It does indeed. We can extend our questioning of the Muslim populations to *three* districts now: Wedding, Prenzlauer Berg, and the Mitte."

A minute later Iliana was back on the phone, this time with Abraham, happily reporting her success with the police. His voice sounded strange, however, when he responded to her news.

"That is very good, Iliana. But my clinic just called to report a malicious smashing in of the front windows. The axe used was left at the entry door, along with a sign saying 'Betrayer of Muslims.' I was just about to call the police, so give me the name of the officer with whom you spoke."

Within moments Abraham Rückgabe was talking to a concerned Officer Reininger.

72

Pinning down Professor Crespi to come see his Kollwitz Secreta was the only bright point of an otherwise wretched day in the life of Reinhold Fromm. He had called her while waiting for his company physician to come to his office, ignoring the presence of his lawyer and engineer.

Damn the woman! How long could it take to walk over from the annex? And would she cooperate? He needed company loyalty. A woman's calm, soft voice interrupted his gloomy thoughts.

"You wanted to see me, Herr Direktor Fromm?" Iliana entered the office. Schlau and Fehler stood up in acknowledgement of her presence. Fromm remained seated. For a moment he was distracted, imagining he could detect the woman's scent. Certainly he had absorbed the sexiness of her low voice. He could feel a stirring sensation in his loins. But not now. He needed to concentrate and find his voice.

"Yes. We have an urgent problem, Doktor Frankel. A team from the Department of Labor is here—without warning—preparing to conduct an investigation to see if asbestos is present in our factory."

"And they will find it, according to the construction date of this complex and the findings of Herr Fehler," answered the physician, coolly holding her employer's eyes with hers. Undeterred, she continued.

"We had this conversation about the presence of asbestos in your factory just a few days ago."

"Never mind *when* we discussed it. The point is they're looking for it *now*."

"This must be quite concerning to you," said Iliana, enjoying what was quickly turning into a cat and mouse game.

"The point is I want you to tell the team director that as the company physician you have encountered no cases of illness caused by asbestos." He looked at her beseechingly.

"And you know I cannot do that. We also discussed this a few days ago."

"I am your *employer*."

"And I am your company physician. Devoted to the health of your employees."

Fromm stared at the physician, his cheeks suddenly taking on a ruddy complexion. Iliana continued.

"In fact I feel obligated to tell you that I have just confirmed the presence of asbestos poisoning in one of your workers." She looked at her employer challengingly.

"*Who? Who?* You will tell me the name of the individual immediately and I shall take it from there." Fromm's whole face was now red as a beet.

"I am sorry, Herr Fromm, but I cannot and will not do that. All of my patients have a right to privacy."

"This is true," intervened the company lawyer.

"I want all of you out of my office immediately," Fromm yelled. "And you, Fräulein Iliana of the holier-than-thou attitude, your employment at Dorotek is severed immediately." Iliana turned on her heel and faced her irate former employer calmly.

"Thank you, Herr Fromm. I was just about to hand in my resignation."

"And I do so as well," echoed his lawyer Schlau.

Engineer Fehler was the only one who kept silent. But the look on his face spoke volumes.

After the ingrates had left his office, Fromm sat desperately trying to figure out how he could save his Dorotek. Suddenly a brilliant thought occurred to him.

He placed a call.

73

Frankfurt airport was unbearably crowded, as usual. Parking was almost impossible at Terminal 1, so Yusri Pahlavi left his chauffeur to hover near the main exit as best he could while he went inside to meet his mother's Lufthansa flight from the United States. He stood by the baggage claim on the ground floor and watched for her to appear. His heart was full of happiness as he imagined his mother's wonderment at what he had created at *Jamshad*. She would love having her own multiroom living quarters. Quarters which faced the courtyard and the two Kollwitz grieving parents. What a solace they would be for her. And the gravestone with interlocking hands she would read as symbolizing their unbreakable mother-son bond.

Some eleven minutes later he spotted his mother's elegant figure coming through the sliding doors of the baggage area. Carrying a white shoulder bag, she was dressed in a white jacket, striped black-and-white blouse, white slacks, and white shoes. How distinguished she looked with the dyed blonde highlights in her short white hair.

Yusri ran to meet her and their happy embrace was hard and long. They had not seen one another for almost four years.

"Ah, Mother, you look exactly the same. You haven't aged at all."

"That's kind of you, my darling boy, but I know and *feel* otherwise."

She spotted her large suitcase and her son sprinted to get it. A few minutes later they were in Yusri's black Audi A6 limousine heading toward Nordhausen. Their cheerful chatter knew no pauses.

74

"This has to be the road. Akram's map is very clear." Dee was reading their new friend's instructions out loud while Megan slowed the car down to a snail's pace, as there were several turnoffs from the main road. The one Dee indicated was almost hidden by deciduous beech trees and it was extremely narrow. They turned there and drove about half a mile before they saw a clearing ahead. In front of them was the strangest "hunting lodge" either one of them had ever seen. It looked more like a miniature ziggurat with its stepped base and peaked roof. But this building was only one story high. No pyramid here.

They also saw what had to be Akram's mode of transportation—a white Nissan cargo van.

Akram must have heard their car approaching because before Megan had turned the engine off he appeared at the door of *Trosthaus*. He was holding something cradled in his arms.

"Welcome, ladies, welcome," he said, smiling as he walked toward them. He held up his furry bundle.

"And please meet little Lana."

"Oh, how sweet," cooed Dee. Lover of cats, she instinctively reached out for the tangerine and white little kitten with its large green eyes.

"'Lana.' Does the name Lana mean something in Arabic?" Megan asked.

"Yes it does. It means to be soft, as indeed she is, to be tender, to be gentle."

"What a perfect name for her," said Dee, rocking the purring little creature in her arms.

"Ah, but what you do not know about her is her history," Akram pronounced mysteriously. Come inside and I shall show you the lodge, then get you something cool to drink, and tell you about Lana."

Megan and Dee were fascinated by the various rooms of the house, the comfortable guest bedrooms, and most especially the living room, dominated as it was by its enormous black Bresser telescope. A circular retractable skylight in the ceiling furnished its access to the stars beyond. Akram pointed to the Bresser.

"Tonight after dinner I am going to give you ladies a telescopic treat. In July we can see a bright red Mars, we can see Saturn with its rings, and of, course, giant Jupiter."

Motioning his guests to comfortable leather armchairs, he disappeared into the kitchen for a few minutes, and returned bearing tall glasses of iced lemonade decorated with mint.

"Now let me tell you the story of Lana."

"Please do. We didn't see her at your Berlin apartment. Surely she doesn't stay out here alone?"

"Lana has only been with me one day, today. She appeared at the door late this morning whining, her fur full of mud, and bleeding from a shoulder wound."

"Oh, no, how terribly sad," said Dee.

"Yes, that part, yes. But, don't you see the *significance* of Lana's appearing when she did?"

"I think I do," Megan said quietly. "This was your first day at *Trosthaus* since Monika died, and here was new life to greet you in the form of a kitten."

"So true, so true. But don't you see? *It was Monika who sent her to me!*"

75

Although it was nine o'clock in the evening, Officer Reininger had been the concerned officer to meet Abraham at his vandalized clinic.

"Considering the note they left on the axe, this is vandalism with a very specific purpose," Reininger confirmed. He thought for a moment, then turned to the physician.

"And what do the initials WGI of your clinic stand for, Herr Doktor Rückgabe?"

"They stand for *Wiederherstellung Genitaler Integrität.*"

"Hm, Restoration of genital integrity. Very interesting. And whom do you treat?"

"Jews, of course. However, most of my patients are from the Middle East, especially Turkey. As you know, Officer Reininger, Muslim Turks make up the greater part of Wedding. That is exactly why I located my clinic here. To help circumcised Arabs and Turks."

"Excuse me, but aren't Muslim Turks Arabs?"

"Oh, no! That's a common error. The only thing they share is religion, if they are religious."

"I'm sorry, but I don't understand."

"Well, it's complicated. Racially, Turks are Indo-European while Arabs are Semitic. And Turks speak a totally different language from Arabic."

Reininger shook his head.

"So this sign that was left at your clinic could have been made by either a Muslim Turk or a Muslim Arab."

"Quite right."

"Then do you have any Muslim suspects, whether they be Turk or Arab, who you think might have done this?"

"The big trouble is, Officer Reininger, that a number of my patients could fall into that category. Especially if the operations I conduct on them don't seem immediately to have the results they expected. Post-ops can be impatient, whereas the procedure needs *time* to be effective, as I am always careful to explain before operating."

"Have any of these disaffected patients ever made complaints in person?"

"Yes. Two that I remember. Tomorrow morning my secretary will call you with the particulars. But that can quickly be narrowed down, as only one of them was Muslim, Turkish, I might add. The other was Israeli. He would hardly accuse me of being a 'betrayer of Muslims.'"

Abraham paused, then decided to give the policeman an insight into the recent influx of would-be patients at his clinic.

"Also, there are those who are not patients at all, but recent Muslim Turkish emigrants who line the corridors not only of our hospitals but periodically crowd the waiting room of my clinic. They do not believe in paying for my services and they are very vocal in their demand for them."

"Sounds as if that is where we should be looking. Does your secretary have their names and addresses?"

"She does and she doesn't. By that I mean that the registration forms they fill out are largely incomplete and the names and addresses given are frequently *identical*."

"What a morass. But if you give me the list I'll get on it immediately. We'll begin locally with Muslim Turks in Wedding. It just so happens we have another reason to be clamping down on them as well."

"The sooner the better."

"May I ask you a personal question, Herr Doktor Rückgabe?"

"You may."

"You are Jewish, correct?"

"That I am."

"Do *you*, as a Jew, have a prejudice against Muslims?" Abraham looked at the officer with disbelief. Had he heard correctly?

"Officer, it has been my lifework to provide men who have been circumcised at birth the restoration of their genital integrity. When I set up practice here in Berlin I purposefully chose Wedding, primarily because of its high Muslim population. Over the years my clinic has aided hundreds upon hundreds of men, the majority of them Muslim. Our referrals are mostly from Muslims. I can say without qualification, I have no prejudice against Muslims."

"Thank you, sir, and I do apologize for the question."

The two men clasped hands and a shaken Abraham turned to go home. Reininger remained, watching his men investigate the grounds and clinic interior. The axe and its vile sign were already on their way to the lab.

Could fingerprint analysis help solve this strange hate crime when there were so many suspects? Reininger was pessimistic.

76

It was the last of a day that could have ended terribly for Reinhold Fromm. Neither his lawyer nor his chief engineer could prevent the unannounced government search of Dorotek for signs of asbestos. He had had to fire his surly company physician when she refused to back him up. And his disloyal lawyer had peevishly resigned. Only his engineer remained on the job. Things could have ended badly, badly indeed.

But he had made that call. And his contact, always ingenious, always willing to take on difficult tasks for a price, had agreed to Fromm's idea to intervene. It would be physical. Herr Fromm should watch the evening news.

Gratefully the CEO of Dorotek replaced his phone and strode briskly over to his small office bar. He poured himself a shot of his favorite whiskey, Canadian Crown Royal. He returned with it to the swivel chair behind his desk, placed the glass on his desk, raised his arms over his head, and slowly stretched to his full body length. He visualized Iliana Frankel naked, bending over him with dangling breasts, a short whip in her hand. He swallowed hard and gulped down his whiskey.

Almost immediately he was seized by a cough so violent that it shook his whole body, leaving him shaking and gasping for air.

Damn acid reflux! It seemed to be coming on more often now. But no way was he going to give up his evening whiskey. In defiance he stood up and poured himself another shot. This time it went down smoothly.

77

The body of a bearded man on the side of the road leading into the outskirts of Nordhausen had been found by a passing motorcyclist in the early hours of the morning. He was barely alive. A deep wound in his chest had opened up and new blood had coagulated over old blood. An ambulance was called and the man, identified as Jarir Uthman of the Berlin district Wedding, was rushed to the ER of Nordhausen's local hospital. He was in a coma and it was a tossup as to whether or not he would recover.

One of the overworked nurses, Brenda Gerhardt, resolved to try to contact the man's family when she went on break. She had been shocked by the casual way in which the doctors had treated their patient when they realized he was Muslim.

78

The conversation between reunited mother and son ranged widely as they were driven back from the Frankfurt airport to Yusri's compound at Nordhausen. Farah spoke of her charity work in and around Washington, DC, and Yusri talked about the palatial building he had created on a hill overlooking a river.

"I simply cannot wait for you to see it, Mother."

He did not tell Farah that part of the complex was dedicated to living quarters for her. They, along with the Kollwitz grieving parent sculptures, would be the colossal surprise he had waiting for her. He had an unforeseen chance to prepare the way when his mother began to speak of mutual friends who were now deceased.

"It is good that I do have my charity work in Washington. Otherwise I should find life quite lonely. So many of my contemporaries have passed away recently."

"Remember, Mother, you do not have to be alone. You will always have me."

"Yes my dear, I have you via telephone and e-mail, but not in the flesh. We should never have allowed so many years to pass by without our seeing one another."

"Mother, have you ever thought of relocating now that so many of your friends are gone?"

"I do think of it from time to time. But what would I do elsewhere? My personal connections are in Washington; my charity work is there."

Yusri pressed his point.

"When you say 'personal connections,' whom are you speaking of?"

"Well, I mean my physicians primarily. My maid has been with me for years. And then there are your cousins whom I see from time to time."

"I think you are lacking a son."

"And whose fault is that?" Farah looked at Yusri and smiled sadly.

"Perhaps that could change."

"Do you mean you might be coming back to the States?"

Yusri did not answer. He merely smiled at his mother. Their talk turned to other distant relatives, their locations, and their activities.

Farah opened her large purse to pull out some photographs to show her son and the newspaper she had been reading on the plane fell out.

"Oh, yes. I saved this because I wanted to show you an article about the terrible spate of art robberies that has been going on for the past week or so here in Germany. Have you heard about them?"

"Um. I don't think so." Yusri felt his blood run cold.

"Well it's outrageous. A terrible crime. I hope the criminals are caught. They ought to have their hands cut off. Just look here at the photos. Aren't the statues beautiful? So noble, so eloquent. Look: these are bereaved parents who have lost a son in senseless war."

Silence greeted her words. Her indignant outburst continued unabated.

"And the amazing thing is the thieves seem to be interested in only one artist's work. And it's a woman, a sculptor. Have you heard the name Käthe Kollwitz? She was very famous in the last century. Her work often concerns death and its effect on the living. And these are the very works that have been stolen. Surely you've heard her name?"

"Tell me more about her," her son said, dodging the question. He could feel perspiration collecting on the back of his neck.

As his mother responded, Yusri could think of only one thing. *Cover up the statues. Cover up the gravestone.*

They were still about an hour away from Nordhausen. Yusri told his chauffeur to stop by the side of the road. His mother looked at him questioningly.

"Sorry, Mother, but I suddenly have to relieve myself; I cannot wait until we get home."

He leapt out of the car and ran to a tree. Standing out of sight behind it he grabbed his smartphone and hastily called his gatekeeper. The call was answered right away.

"Wafiyy. I want you to go to the courtyard and cover up the two statues there. The gravestone with clasped hands also. Be sure they are all fully concealed. From top to bottom. *Do this immediately.*"

79

"*Tafathalo*—do me the honor," a smiling Akram said, indicating where Megan and Dee were to sit in the small dining room at *Trosthaus*. He had prepared an aromatic Arabic dinner of baby lamb stuffed with spiced rice. Two stewed vegetables, okra and green beans, complemented the meat. Tall glasses of cold tea were at each place.

They were all hungry and the delicious meal was consumed with gusto and multiple compliments from Akram's guests. Dessert consisted of stuffed dates with "secret" ingredients that their host would not reveal, although Dee suspected an almond paste of some sort with orange and cinnamon.

"And now we travel through the night sky by way of the Bresser, my ladies."

They adjourned to the big room and watched as Akram adjusted the settings on the large scope. He invited Dee to step up onto the low platform first.

Now look to the west. That very bright star-like object you see is Jupiter. Do you see it?"

"Oh, yes, I see it, I see it."

"Good. Now look south and you'll see Mars. With an ordinary telescope it looks red but you can see through our Bresser that it is actually a pale orange."

"Ah, yes, it is rather orange."

"And now if you look to the left of Mars you will see Saturn with its many rings. Do you see them?"

"Oh, I do. How thrilling. How close this Bresser brings things."

"Hey, it's my turn," Megan reminded them.

She and Dee exchanged places and Megan stared through the lens, repeating the eye movement directions Akram had given.

"This *is* exciting. I can see all three planets. And wait a second. I see something bright just under Saturn."

"That's correct. It's the star Antares. And you can see it makes a triangle with Saturn and Mars. And now I think it's late enough for you to make out on the southern horizon a constellation pattern that is called Scorpius arcing across the sky near the horizon. It won't be there very long since we are at a mid-northern altitude here. But I'm hoping you can get a glimpse of it."

"Yes, yes, I see it, I think. Does it have a hook-like shape just below Antares?"

"You've got it. The famous fishhook pattern."

"Well, that's funny. The hook seems to have multiple blurry ends and they are getting larger, darker. Now I can't see the Scorpius constellation at all. And Antares is almost out of sight."

"What? That's not right. Let me see."

Just then Akram's cellphone rang. He did not recognize the caller ID but switched the phone on anyway. He heard a voice that could have been male or female, so distorted was it. The echoing voice sounded as though it were blowing through a clasped fist tube. The separate syllables of words were propelled outward in a bizarre manner. They were enunciated in English.

"*You De-fec-tor A-kram. Pre-pare to leave god-less Ger-ma-ny and re-turn re-pen-i-tent to your home land im-me-di-ate-ly or else.*"

"Or else *what*?" Akram answered defiantly. The distorted voice must have been that of Monika's cousin Rolf, stupidly disguised in this infantile manner. Obviously Rolf was trying to frighten him. Frighten him away from *Trosthaus*.

"*You have been war-ned, In-fi-del. Con-si-der this. Have you seen your small cat late-ly?*"

80

In the den of his Rügen house Fromm turned on his TV set. His contact had advised him to watch the evening news for "something physical" in regard to the government inspection of Dorotek. It was the first story. Live feed showed the site of a terrible accident that had just occurred on the old Rügendamm bridge. Apparently in order to avoid commuter traffic on the new bridge, a government van crossing over to the mainland had been rear-ended by a large vehicle, causing it to spin to the right, crash through the bridge's guard rail, and plunge some 300 feet into the water. So far there were no survivors, but police boats were searching the water. One American witness to the scene identified the fleeing vehicle as a white Dodge Ram 5500. A search of all connecting highways as well as the city of Stralsund was in progress, but so far without success. Viewers were urged to report any sightings of the powerful truck.

Yes indeed, that certainly was "something physical," Fromm congratulated himself. The lamentable accident would delay asbestos findings at

Dorotek for a period. Long enough to have his engineers engage 24/7 in a massive removal and masking job.

81

At Nordhausen Hospital the man known as Jarir Uthman had, against all odds, made a miraculous recovery. His heart rate was close to normal and although he was very weak, he was able to whisper. The nurse on duty, Brenda Gerhardt, was now able to learn his family's whereabouts and how to contact them by phone.

Armed with the information, she devoted her next break to contacting the man's wife. She was successful and was gratified to hear such joy at the other end of the line.

"I had been so terribly worried," Jarir's wife told her. We had not heard from him for two days. And he always calls. Especially as it's our son's birthday."

"You need not worry now. We don't yet know his story, or why he was found wounded and passed out on the road into Nordhausen, but all this will come out soon and I'll be able to inform you. In fact, as Herr Uthman becomes stronger, I hope he will be able to tell you himself what happened."

"But Nordhausen? I don't even know where that is."

Nurse Gerhardt named some neighboring cities, including Leipzig, and assured Frau Uthman that she would keep her updated on her husband's progress. Again, she stressed how miraculous it was that he was over the worst and on his way to recovery.

The moment their call was ended Maryam Uthman dialed the Wedding police number of Officer Reininger and told him that her husband had been located. He had been injured and was in a coma, but thanks to Allah, he was rushed to the Nordhausen hospital where he had revived and now seemed to be making a recovery.

"Do you think I could speak to him, Frau Uthman?"

"I am told he can only whisper right now and that he slips in and out of long periods of unconsciousness."

"I see. Well, I am so happy for you and your son, Frau Uthman. Thank you for letting us know we no longer have a missing man from Wedding."

He made a quick call to Cologne to update detective Herbert Schauen on the latest event. They both agreed he should get himself to Nordhausen Hospital as quickly as possible. There was much to be learned from this just-found missing Muslim.

With the approval of his superior officer, Reininger left the office and within minutes was on the highway driving south to Nordhausen. Barring any slowdowns, it should take just under three hours to reach the hospital. He ought to arrive by five-thirty p.m. A thousand questions crowded into his mind as he drove. How he hoped that the man's testimony would help solve the case of the other four missing Muslims from Wedding. Instinct told him it would.

82

"You have created a veritable palace here," Yusri's mother pronounced, looking at *Jamshad's* entrance.

"It reminds me of our homeland," she continued, looking at the facade with its bulging balconies, horseshoe arches, abstract tile designs, and roof garden where the tips of imported palm trees could be seen.

"Just wait till you see the interior," Yusri said, hiding his nervousness. Had his man managed to cover the three Kollwitz sculptures? To seal them from view?

They walked inside the enormous building and Farah had to adjust to the light. If it had been almost too bright outside it was the essence of darkness inside. Slowly she perceived what the darkness was made of. A huge reception room with ceilings painted black and hung with multiple chandeliers, dark wooden walls supporting tapestries, large Persian carpets everywhere, and black leather chairs grouped around low tables on top of which were small oriental rugs of silk.

"How marvelously comfortable, my dear. Again, it's like being in a palace. Our old palace at home." The memory of former times choked her up momentarily.

"And just for you, I have a palatial music room." Yusri beckoned his mother to follow him into the next room, which was almost as dark as the first. Here on the walls and in display shelves was a variety of drums, string, and wind instruments. Several santurs—trapezoidal box zithers with walnut bodies and ninety-two steel strings—stood with their wooden mallets on dedicated tables. On the walls hung different sized long-necked spike fiddles—jozas—with their small, membrane-covered circular bodies and their curved bows.

But what caught Farah's eye was the sight of a pear-shaped, short-necked wooden instrument with twelve strings just waiting to be plucked—an oud. Farah was an oudist of considerable ability, and tired as she was from her trans-Atlantic flight, she picked up the lute and played an ancient melody Yusri had loved when he was a child. It was a magical moment for both mother and son.

Yusri then gave her a tour of the ground-floor rooms beyond, including his cozy study, his large contemporary bedroom and an equally modern, smaller guestroom, an inviting dining room, and finally the modern, brightly lit kitchen where a smiling cook indicated with pride the makings of the meal they were to enjoy this evening.

"And now I show you what I have built for *you*."

"For *me*? What do you mean? Am I not to stay in your guestroom?"

"No. You are to stay in your own...residence. Follow me."

Mystified, Farah obeyed as they crossed though several interconnected courtyards and then into an open one surrounded by lush shade trees. In one corner a very large Persian rug had been wrapped around two items and a smaller rug covered an object on the opposite side. But Farah scarcely noticed them as her son stopped and pointed to the imposing residence beyond. Its façade was a duplicate of the entrance façade writ small.

"This, Mother, I have built for you. As with my part of the complex, it has seven rooms and four bathrooms."

"Why, this is a royal residence!"

"A residence I fervently hope you will soon call your home."

Yusri stared deep into his mother's brown eyes, and repeated the words "your home" again and again.

Farah silently took in the enormity of what her son was suggesting. But she was suddenly very, very tired and said so.

"Let me have a nap and then we shall have dinner and talk, my dearest."

Yusri readily agreed. It would give him time to investigate the job Wafiyy had done at his behest. Perhaps he could improve on it.

After he was sure his mother had gone to her bedroom and retired, he walked over to the two Kollwitz statues. Yes, the enormous rug covered them nicely, but some weights on the bottom edges would be helpful. The same for the Kollwitz tombstone in the other corner.

He picked up his cellphone and instructed Wafiyy to enact the improvements right away. And to be quiet, as his mother was sleeping.

Yusri could only hope that with the passage of time and sharing *Jamshad* with her only surviving child, Farah might understand his noble motive for procuring the comforting Kollwitz effigies for her. It would be their secret and, ultimately, it would bring them even closer together.

83

Fromm's chief engineer had also seen that evening's local news channel. He was horrified. The government van that had left the factory at five p.m. with evidence of the presence of asbestos was the victim of an accident that resulted in its being hurled into the water from Rügen's old bridge. It was all much, much too convenient for Dorotek's CEO. This "accident" had given Herr Fromm exactly the time he needed to essay a cover up.

Well, he would have no part in trying to deceive the government. In fact he now intended to visit the government Department of Labor in person.

Tomorrow, like his friend Iliana, he would hand in his resignation. Reinhold Fromm be damned!

84

"Have you seen your small cat late-ly?"

The stranger's question shook Akram to the core. He looked around wildly, shouting to his two guests.

"Where is Lana? Have you seen Lana?"

Megan and Dee looked around. There was no kitten to be seen. Akram began running to the various rooms of the lodge while the women started looking under the furniture, all calling Lana's name.

They regrouped in the living room and looked at each other in desperation, panting from their efforts.

"She's gone! Oh, Monika! They've taken her!" sobbed Akram.

Dee and Megan sat down next to him, holding his hand, lightly massaging his back. The distraught man was inconsolable.

As the trio sat in silence they suddenly heard the intermittent sound of a high whine. It became louder and more insistent.

"But that's Lana! She's here, she's here! But where could she be?" Akram jumped up, wheeling round and round, trying to locate the direction of the sound.

"It's the *telescope*," Dee exclaimed suddenly. "She's somewhere on the telescope."

Megan, who was closer, ran around to the front of the Bresser. Then she saw Lana. She was crouched on the outer rim of the great lens and whining loudly. *She* had been the bulging black shape that had blocked Megan's view of Scorpius and Antares.

Akram was right behind Megan. He scooped the frightened kitty up off the lens with one hand and held her close to his face. The yowling subsided, Lana licked his face with her rough little tongue.

"Ah, Monika, you have returned Lana to me. Thank you, thank you."

Then the thought came to him: how could the man who called even know he had a kitten? His veiled threat was empty, but how did he know about Lana? There was only one conclusion.

Trosthaus was being watched.

85

Officer Anton Reininger hurried down the hospital corridor toward the room in which, along with several other patients, Jarir was. Nurse Gerhardt led him over to the man, instructing the officer in a low voice that he should speak quietly and slowly, as any excitement might set her patient back.

Reininger introduced himself and said he was sorry for what Jarir had gone through and that he would like to catch the man or men who had shot him.

Jarir seemed to understand, nodding his head weakly. Reininger waited while Jarir collected himself, heaving deep breaths and grimacing at the pain. Finally he spoke in short bursts.

"Gatekeeper of man I deliver gravestone to, shoot me. He name Wafiyy."

"To whom were you making your delivery?"

There was a pause. Jarir was breathing heavily. But animated by a sense of purpose, he began gasping out words.

"Fellow Arab. He prince. He live high on hill in palace. I sell him art gravestone I take from cemetery Cologne. I place it in courtyard, then Wafiyy shoot me, think he kill me. I think so too. Then I play dead. Then I pass out long time. He do kill my partner Nadeem."

"So you had a partner?"

"Yes. He in grave next to me."

Jarir fell silent. Pain was written on his face. Then he held up four fingers on his right hand and waved them in front of Reininger's face.

"What does he mean, do you think?" the officer asked nurse Gerhardt. "Does he want us to go away?"

"Is he trying to tell us a number?"

Jarir nodded vigorously, then found his voice. He trembled as he spoke.

"*Four* more graves back of palace. I think they deliver large man and woman art statues before I come."

Reininger was stunned. Jarir began to shiver from his effort.

"We *must* let him rest now," nurse Gerhardt commanded.

"Just one last question. Do you know who made the art piece you delivered?"

But Jarir could no longer mouth any words. With one last effort he laid his right index finger on the bed and creased the sheet with all his might, drawing one letter.

He had pressed the letter K.

86

Awakening in the beautiful bedroom Yusri had built and furnished for her, Farah felt refreshed. She had slept long and well. Glancing at her watch she saw that it was almost eight in the evening. Her son would be waiting to dine with her. She changed clothes and, foregoing a look around the residence rooms till later, she walked outdoors and into the open courtyard. There her glance fell upon the curious carpeting that covered something large underneath. She looked at a smaller rug cloaking a smaller object on the other side of the courtyard.

Curiosity overcame her. She walked over to the larger object, pushed an anchoring stone to one side, and slowly pulled up the carpet. What she saw was a sculpted pair of knees. Life-size. A kneeling man. With difficulty Farah raised the carpet higher. Then she gasped. It was the same image she had seen in the newspaper on the plane! It was the stolen Kollwitz. The grieving father figure that had been taken by thieves. Next to it was another similar size figure, also kneeling on the ground. In growing horror Farah rolled the carpet back. It was the grieving mother figure! Kollwitz's two mourning parents, carved in granite. Here in her son's home!

Farah ran over to the other covered object, pushed away the stones and lifted the rug. It was a tombstone showing clasped hands. The same image she had seen in the newspaper.

What had her son been thinking? How could he have betrayed the family honor by becoming a thief? By stealing such valuable and famous artworks? Tears of shame sprang to her eyes.

There was only one thing to do.

Angrily she marched toward Yusri's quarters. She knew exactly what she was going to say to him, to the contemptible criminal who had once been her son.

87

That Lana was not missing, but just an enthusiastic stargazer, had brightened the mood at *Trosthaus*. The two women relaxed again and Akram masked his concern over the threat issued to him by the mysterious caller. Two more days until Monika's body would be released to the mortuary. He had to divert his mind. He did not want to be morose in front of his two angel guests.

"Tomorrow, after Frau Megan has concluded her appointment with Dorotek's CEO, I shall take you ladies on a tour of the island and little Lana shall come with us."

"What a nice treat," Dee answered. "To have a tour and a kitten along with us."

"Might it not be too hot, leaving Lana in your van?" ventured Megan.

"It will not be too hot if I leave the motor running with the AC on, and lock my van." Akram pulled out an illustrated map of Rügen and pointed out the route they would take, describing each stop. We'll have lunch here, in Sassnitz, and after lunch we shall drive on to what will be the climax of our tour, the white cliffs of Rügen."

"Wonderful. What a finale!" Dee was now totally in the Rügen spirit.

"We had just been discussing Caspar David Friedrich's extraordinary paintings of the cliffs. Do you know his work?"

"Unfortunately I do not know the works of this artist. Is he contemporary?"

"Not contemporary. He worked during the first half of the nineteenth century and actually he was from Greifswald, where Dee and I go next. But Friedrich loved going to Rügen and painting those famous cliffs."

"Here, Akram," Dee said handing him her iPad, "I've gone to the Friedrich site online. Now you can see what his works look like."

Akram studied the images closely.

"I like him very much. Thank you both for the education."

It was getting late. After the women were shown to their bedrooms and Akram settled in his, he began once again to ponder who the threatening caller might have been, if not Rolf. And how could the caller have known about Lana? It was not beneath Rolf to address him as an infidel, knowing how hurtful that would be for any Arab of faith.

But what if the sexless voice were that of a woman? If so, then Akram knew exactly whose voice it must be. That of the woman in the hijab who had murdered his beloved Monika. That made sense. Except, why would she have spoken to him in English, and not Arabic or German?

On the other hand, he was almost one hundred percent sure that it was Rolf. After all, it had to have been he who boarded up *Trosthaus*. Only he would know that the lodge might be the subject of a litigation suit. If Rolf were secretly watching the comings and goings at *Trosthaus*, it would be he who saw him come out with Lana to greet the American ladies. And he might have spoken in English to throw Akram off the scent.

Yes, that was it. It was Rolf.

Akram got out of bed and went quietly outdoors to his van. He came back to the house with a surveillance camera and mounted it on a tree facing the lodge door. Then he connected it to an app on his smartphone. Now Akram could keep tabs on whoever might be visiting *Trosthaus*. He went to bed feeling somewhat safer.

And pressing gently against his back was his little feline companion, sleeping without a care in the world.

Sometime during the night a black truck came to a stop just before the final bend in the forest road that led to *Trosthaus*. A man dressed in a hoodie stealthily made his way toward the open space where the lodge stood. Opposite the building on the other side of the clearing two vehicles were parked. A Volkswagen SUV and a Nissan cargo van. Without hesitation the man made a beeline for the van and slipped underneath it. Within seconds he had attached a GPS car tracker in a thirty pound magnetic mount case to the underside of the vehicle.

88

Anton Reininger left Nordhausen Hospital and drove immediately to the city police station. After conferring with the highest ranking officer there, he initiated a conference call with him and his Cologne colleague, Detective Herbert Schauen.

"Hallo Schauen. I'm talking to you from Nordhausen and am here with the local police chief. We've had a tremendous break in our Kollwitz robberies case and also regarding the five missing Muslims. Plus a sixth we didn't even know was missing."

"Fantastic. A break at last. What are the details?"

"Well, it's not absolutely clear yet whether all six men had something to do with the Kollwitz thefts, but all except one of them were killed and buried in makeshift graves. Graves behind the recently completed complex of an Arab prince named..." Reininger paused and looked down at his notes, "Yusri Pahlavi. Now, one of the Muslim men, Jarir Uthman, was not mortally wounded by the shot he received to his heart, but he played dead before passing out. When he came to he managed during the night—last night—to dig out of his shallow grave. It was then that he found, in a narrow grave next to his, the body of his helper, Nadeem. After that he spotted four more graves and his only thought was to escape. To crawl down the road toward Nordhausen. He was found unconscious on the city outskirts early this morning and rushed to the ER here where it was expected he wouldn't last. But a few hours later he rallied, and just now he was able to tell me his story. At least the basics."

"Incredible! And what are they?"

"Well, Jarir admits to stealing a tombstone with an image by Kollwitz."

"Which one? The Levy stone here in Cologne or the Kollwitz family gravestone in Berlin?"

"The Levy one."

"And you think the four other men reported to be missing, and whose vehicles we have documented as being in Cologne the night of the Kollwitz robbery, are all buried in the back of the prince's compound or castle or whatever it is?"

"Yes. I think it is highly likely. The chief here tells me the building and grounds are enormous."

"That would explain the missing boom truck and delivery van as well. The original four men reported missing used both types of vehicles for the Cologne theft."

"Those trucks are probably up at the complex, possibly in the warehouse at the very back of the property," volunteered the Nordhausen police chief. "We've done aerial recognizance of the site a number of times. It has a helicopter landing pad, a hangar, and a large warehouse."

"So, colleagues," Schauen continued, "the chronology seems to be that first, four Muslim men from Wedding—I'll spare you their surnames—a Rashad, a Hashim, and an Amin, headed by a man named Kadeem, drove from Cologne to Nordhausen to make a delivery of Kollwitz sculpture to this Arab prince's mansion, right?"

"Correct."

"And since a boom truck *and* a delivery van were involved we can presume the art pieces were either the Belgian set of grieving parents or the two in Cologne."

"Or *both*," interjected Reininger.

"God, what a thought! But why would anybody want identical sets of the same two statues? Anyway, to continue our theoretical chronology. Step two: your Jarir man in the hospital and his dead helper Nadeem. They also made a delivery to the prince, just two days later. And their delivery was a small piece—just a tombstone. Yet they too needed a boom truck and a delivery truck. Now that's an awful lot of large vehicles."

The Nordhausen police chief broke in.

"Believe me, Detective Schauen, that so-called prince's warehouse is large enough to hold two jumbo jets. It would be quite possible to hide all four of those vehicles inside."

"All right. Understood. So how many Kollwitz sculptures do you think are up there, Reininger?"

"If we include the ones stolen from the Belgian cemetery, the ones taken from Cologne, and the Levy tombstone, there could be five. Six, if you count the Kollwitz family gravestone stolen in Berlin. Hard to believe."

"Sounds like a museum up there," said Schauen sarcastically. His Berlin colleague still had more to tell him and the local police chief, who was listening intently to the conversation.

"Did you two know that there has just been a *seventh* Kollwitz statue stolen?"

"You've got to be kidding."

"No, I am not. From our Berlin Kollwitz Museum. I met with the director right afterward and she wants to keep the theft hush-hush for now. She doesn't want to release it to the newspapers or television yet."

Schauen sounded exhausted by all the information he was receiving.

"So what are you going to do, Reininger?"

"The chief here is getting a search warrant, but it's six o'clock and the judges are out of their offices. So as soon as it's signed tomorrow morning we are going up to that palace in force. Helicopter and squad cars. We don't want that prince to get away. God knows what other stolen art we might find there."

"Please keep me informed. As you said, this is a tremendous break and it may resolve all our Kollwitz calamities with one blow." The conference call ended on a high note and Nordhausen police chief Karl Schneider was thrilled to think he might be in on solving one of the biggest art and murder crimes in Germany.

89

"Ah, Mother! I was just coming to wake you. Dinner is ready to be served." Yusri was delighted to see his mother.

"*You, you are no longer my son. You are never to speak to me again.*"

"What?"

"You have brought shame to our family. You are a criminal. You are the thief who stole the Kollwitz statues. I have *seen* them in the courtyard."

"But Mother, Mother, I can explain."

"I want only one thing from you. Send your chauffeur for my luggage. He shall drive me back to the Frankfurt airport immediately."

"Please, please listen to me, Mother. There is a *reason* I acquired those sculptures. They are for *you*. To comfort you who are, like Kollwitz, a grieving parent."

"Call the chauffeur."

Yusri looked at his mother. Her face was set in stone. She refused to return his gaze. Arms crossed over her chest, she turned her back on the wretched man and waited for her command to be obeyed.

On the three-hour drive back to Frankfurt, alone with only the silent chauffeur, Farah went over the disaster that had just been visited upon her. She had severed her son from her life. Should she now denounce him to the police? The family name would forever be tarnished if she did so. No. She could not do that. She could only hope that Yusri would turn himself in. That he was still capable of feeling guilt.

90

Iliana had not been home in Berlin during a weekday for years. She liked it. Her gentle cat Uli liked it too. He was not used to receiving so much attention.

But she was worried about dear Abraham. His clinic had been vandalized last night and, although the police were pursuing the case, there was not much hope the criminal or criminals would be caught. Not in the closed, protective Muslim community that crowded the bleak tenement houses of Wedding.

And why would the sign left behind call Abraham a betrayer of Muslims? God knows he had treated many of them in his clinic, all with successful results to her knowledge. Abraham had explained to her when they talked this morning about how newly arrived Turkish Muslims were now appearing at his clinic, treating it as a hospital for all sorts of needs, requesting free medication. It seemed entirely likely that the culprit was one of these recent arrivals.

As she sat on her couch gently massaging a purring Uli, her thoughts turned to Dorotek and the bombastic scene of yesterday when she severed her relationship with the company. That corrupt Fromm was in a pickle and all because of his refusal years ago to take his engineer's advice and get rid of the asbestos in his factory buildings. Asbestos that had caused the death of former employees and fatally sickened her patient Mahdi Kartal for whom she could hold out no hope. Of course, his threat to kill Fromm was empty, but still it, along with the slew of lawsuits against Dorotek, showed how much anger had built up toward its CEO. She wondered how the man could live with himself.

Over the grapevine she had heard about the robbery of the mother and child sculpture at the Berlin Kollwitz Museum. Just two nights after she and Abraham had attended the Crespi lecture there. She looked up a reproduction of the work in the oeuvre catalogue she had acquired of Kollwitz's sculptural work. It was a truly moving concept of mother and child. How odd that the robber or robbers of this artwork had deviated from the death motif of the six works previously stolen. That could be important.

She would ask Abraham what he thought about the intriguing deviation at dinner tomorrow evening. He had invited her to join him and his mother, since she was no longer limited to dinner with him only on weekends. He had heartily approved of her resignation from Dorotek, or as she referred to it, her "fireignation."

As for Abraham, an idea with great appeal was forming in his mind. It would be marvelous to have such a dear and dedicated person as Iliana as his partner at the clinic. He was overwhelmed with work and, except for the surgery, much of it could be handled by an expert general practitioner. And certainly Iliana had been that for the past twelve years, despite the fact that at medical school she had been drawn to obstetrics and gynecology.

But there was a problem with having Iliana join him and it was a difficult one. Most of the Muslim immigrants he treated would never ever allow a woman physician to come near them. On the other hand, migrant *women* turned up every day at his clinic, not realizing the special purpose to which Abraham's practice was committed. He would broach the subject to Iliana at dinner tomorrow evening. He knew his mother would enthusiastically approve. She was very fond of Iliana and had long wished her son would marry her.

91

Akram was up long before his two guests and he had had a chance to check his surveillance video. No one had approached the entry door. Nothing had triggered the camera. Good. He brewed a generous amount of coffee and the aroma brought Megan and Dee to the kitchen in their bathrobes. It was seven o'clock.

"Would you dear ladies like an omelet with green peppers and cheese, perhaps?"

"Wonderful idea." Dee spoke for them both. She gulped down her senior pills with the generous amount of fresh orange juice her host had supplied.

After they had finished breakfast and were sipping a second cup of coffee, Megan asked Akram what route he recommended for driving to Prora for her 9:30 morning appointment at Dorotek.

"Here, I'll draw you a map. It's really not far from here. You go back the way you came, through Putbus..." Akram's voice broke for a moment at the mention of his wife's family name.

"Then north to the Karow intersection and east to Prora on the shore. If you leave at nine you'll get to Dorotek in plenty of time for your appointment. You can't miss the factory. It's housed in a series of ugly, contiguous buildings facing the beach on one side."

"Oh, yes. I have read that Fromm's factory is housed in a building complex erected by Hitler. It's supposed to be three miles long."

"Hm. Let me convert that in my mind, um, let's see, that would be a little under five kilometers, so, yes, that's right."

"And you told us he'll be taking you to his house to see the Secreta drawing," Dee confirmed.

"Well, I'm not going to go with him in *his* car. I'll just follow in mine so I can get out of there as fast as possible and..."

"Listen," Akram interrupted, "I don't mean to be pushy, but I think I have a better idea than your driving out to Prora alone. Why don't we all go in my van, you connect with Fromm at the factory, and then we simply follow you two to his house and wait outside."

"Ah, I *like* that," Megan said, realizing that she had not really been very happy about going to Prora alone.

"And the fact that you need to join your waiting friends for our tour of the island might help make your visit shorter," added Akram.

"Love it."

"Ditto to that," said Dee.

"And," said Akram, looking at the kitten bidding for his attention, "we shall bring little Lana along."

"That would be so nice." Dee glanced happily at the little kitten who already seemed to know her name.

Megan went to her bedroom for a minute, brushed her teeth and put on her Google Glass. She was ready. She wondered if Fromm could possibly be as pious as his surname indicated. Hardly likely for the boastful owner of a Kollwitz Secreta drawing.

With Lana in Dee's lap, Megan taking photos of scenic spots with her iPhone, and Akram driving his handsome white van they drove via Putbus and Karow to Prora.

"There it is," announced Akram. "The three-mile-long, six-story Dorotek factory."

"Mm. Is it ever gloomy," said Megan, eying what looked like a colossal comb in concrete with prongs every thirty feet.

"There's no view of the water from this side," Akram said. "But on the other side of the complex every unit had a view of the sea. That was Hitler's bright idea—a seaside resort reward for being obedient German workers."

"And now the factory has replaced the housing units?"

"Correct. Okay, I'm going to pull in here—looks like the main parking lot."

They drove directly to the row of cars nearest the main factory entrance. Facing the entry door was an empty parking space. A red cone had been placed in the center. Next to it was a gray Mercedes sedan. It faced the curb on which was printed "*Reserviert für Herr Reinhold Fromm, Geschäftsführer.*"

"I guess 'Geschäftsführer' is our equivalent of chief executive officer," said Dee, looking at the large lettering. "Sounds scary to me."

Akram got out of the van and placed the red cone on the sidewalk. After he pulled the van into the parking space he looked at Megan.

"We'll be right here, waiting for you to emerge. Take as long as you like."

"Oh, gwad, I forgot Fromm said to call him when I got near Prora." Megan dialed the number she had added to her contacts and the call was answered immediately.

"We're here, Herr Fromm."

"'We?'"

"Yes. I mentioned to you that I'd be having lunch with my travel companions today. We have reservations in Sassnitz."

"In that case I come right down." The man sounded definitely irritated.

And indeed he was. He did not return Megan's smile when emerging from his building, but instead looked disapprovingly at the van parked in the place he had reserved for the Frau Professor. Nor did he show any interest in meeting her friends.

"I drive you to my house immediately," said Fromm, indicating his car.

"Fine. My friends will follow us, to be ready to continue our tour when you and I are finished."

"I certainly hope your friends do not expect to look at the Secreta with us."

"Oh, no, not at all."

Fromm seemed to relax a bit. His route took them south a bit and up a hilly road. Within minutes they arrived at a small house surrounded by low heather and set back from the road. It had an unhindered view of the beach. Akram parked unobtrusively some distance away from Fromm's car which had pulled up to the front door.

"Please to follow me inside." Fromm tried to hide his irritation. He had looked forward to showing the American not only Kollwitz's Secreta but also his entire collection of dominatrix images.

Megan followed her hostile host into his den. Laid out on a low table opposite a desk was a leather portfolio. Next to it was what looked like an old-fashioned dictionary stand with two pairs of white gloves on the narrow shelf below. While Megan stood at his side—there had been no invitation to sit down—Fromm pulled on two of the white gloves, then carefully opened the portfolio and placed the matted sheet within on the tall stand.

Megan smiled. For some inexplicable reason the man had positioned the drawing at a quarter turn to the left from its central axis. That made it horizontal rather than vertical. Before she had a chance to ask why, she was eagerly interrogated.

"Do you not agree Frau Doktor, that even though it is not signed, this is an original Kollwitz?"

"Yes, absolutely. There can be no doubt. It is a magnificent drawing. But..."

"Observe, please, how the woman crouches masterfully over the man, her arms on either side of him, pinning him down. She seems about to bite his ear, her mouth is so close to it. See how near her naked body is to his naked body."

"Megan looked obediently at the superb drawing and absorbed the rhythm and strength of its caressing lines. But she could no longer suppress her irritation and wonder at the fact that Fromm had placed the drawing horizontally rather than vertically. And the matting, wider at the "bottom" of the drawing repeated the mistaken orientation.

"It is one of the best Secreta drawings I have seen, Herr Fromm."

Fromm beamed with pride and pleasure.

"But I must ask: why do you place it turned this way? As though it were a quarter to twelve, rather than twelve noon."

Fromm's face instantly turned red.

"*Quarter to twelve? Twelve noon?*' What the hell are you talking about?"

"I mean, just a moment while I get these," Megan said, slipping on the other pair of gloves. Gingerly she turned the mat with its precious drawing one quarter turn to the right to its correct orientation.

"The subjects were drawn like this, Herr Fromm. Vertical, not horizontal. It is a mutual *embrace*, desired by both partners. See how the woman hugs the man close, how he starts to raise his right leg to encompass her, and see the closed eyes of the woman in this moment of mutual bliss."

"Are you telling me this is *not* a dominatrix drawing?" Fromm's eyes blazed with indignation.

"Yes. It has nothing to do with sexual bondage. But surely you understood this?"

Megan could not believe how blinded the man had been, so urgently did he need the drawing to be one of *sexuelle Hörigkeit*.

"I understand only that I want you out of my house, and immediately. It was a mistake to invite you to see my precious Secreta. *And now you have ruined it for me!*"

Megan was only too happy to make for the door, unaccompanied by her sulking host. Even better. She already had her Google Glass shots of the drawing with its bizarre orientation. What a story she had to tell Dee and Akram.

92

Prince Yusri Pahlavi was devastated. What had he done? His mother was right. He had brought dishonor to the family. How could he have thought that having the Kollwitz statues brought to *Jamshad* to comfort his mother in her grief could be justified? No matter how noble his motive, it was true that he had engaged in an unforgiveable crime. He was nothing but a thief, hiring others to commit crimes that were his and his alone.

Oh, why had he not seen this? That there would be only one way for his mother to react. Nobly and with horror. She had told him he was no longer her son. She had left him last night without even uttering a farewell.

Early the next morning, after a sleepless night, Yusri dismissed his staff. He sent the cook home. Even loyal Wafiyy was told to take the day off, go into town.

He went into the music room and picked up the beautiful wooden oud his mother had played so recently. For a long time he hugged it to his chest, sobbing.

"Forgive me, Mother, forgive me. I am not worthy to hold this instrument made holy by your touch."

He held it out at arm's length. He had sullied it merely by picking it up.

Suddenly he threw the instrument down onto the floor and stamped on it with all his might. Fragments of wood scuttled across the floor.

"There! Now I have destroyed everything, everyone that was holy. Now I shall obliterate the unholy!"

Filled with purpose, Yusri strode to the open courtyard and the Kollwitz sculptures.

93

"The search warrant has finally been signed. We're ready to go when you are."

It was almost noon. Nordhausen police chief Karl Schneider was on the phone with visiting Berlin police officer Anton Reininger.

"I'll be there in five minutes."

94

Dee and Akram could not stop laughing even though the Kollwitz drawing scene Megan described to them had been deadly serious.

"I guess it's a case of sex being in the askew eye of the beholder," summed up Dee giggling.

"Pardon me, I do not know the word 'askew'," confessed Akram, still giggling.

"Askew means off center or misaligned," Megan answered.

"You told Herr 'Unfromm'—I guess we should call him that now, 'Unpious'—you told him that we had lunch reservations in Sassnitz. Well, in fact we do," said Akram, as he drove them northward up the coast on highway 96.

"We're going to my favorite restaurant there, the König Gustav right on the main street of town. They have all sorts of fish and a great variety of fresh vegetables, all very tasty and beautifully presented. But although theirs are very good we won't have our desserts there. Instead we'll go down to a charming harbor café, the Gumpfer, and have our coffee with a slice of their divine cheesecake. That is, if you two ladies like cheesecake."

A chorus of yeses answered his question. The three of them were sitting together on the front seat of the capacious van. Dee was holding Lana. When they arrived at Sassnitz, Akram was able to park right on the Hauptstrasse. He rolled up a bath towel and made a little bed for Lana, who seemed quite content to stay under the driver's seat. A sea breeze was blowing and with the windows cracked, the van interior was nice and cool.

Megan and Akram were so occupied with helping fragile Dee out of the van that no one noticed the small black truck that pulled into an empty parking space two car lengths behind them. With Dee leaning heavily on her cane, they slowly walked down a block to the Restaurant König Gustav. It was a white standalone three-story house with a cheerful red tile roof.

"I didn't know Germany had a King Gustav," commented Dee after they had studied the menu and ordered the dish Akram recommended—ginger sea bass over rice and wilted greens.

"I wouldn't know that, but I think the Gustav of this restaurant probably refers to one of the Swedish kings," said Megan.

"A lot of them were named Gustav and Rügen shared the history of Swedish Pomerania for more than a century-and-a- half, when it was taken by Prussia. And the island's remained German ever since, right Akram?"

Akram, who had been intently studying an image of *Trosthaus* on his smartphone, threw up a hand apologetically.

"Don't ask me. I'm not much on German history, I'm afraid."

Their fish arrived and conversation was suspended while the trio devoured an exquisite meal.

"You were so right to bring us to this wonderful restaurant," Megan pronounced happily. She also liked the coziness of the interior, with its white walls and brown trim.

"Good. I'm so glad. Now I hope you will like the Café Gumpfer as well."

"We're not going to *walk* there, are we?" Dee asked. Akram laughed reassuringly.

"No, no, we are going to drive there. Not to worry. In fact if you wait here, I'll go get the van for us.

While they waited on the sidewalk, Megan spotted a small pet supply store across the street.

"You know what, Dee? I bet that store would have a cat carrier. That's just what Lana needs. I'm going to run over and see."

A few minutes later Akram pulled up and was surprised to see only

Dee waiting on the sidewalk. She explained where Megan had gone and he helped her into the van. Lana meowed in greeting and leapt onto Dee's lap. A few minutes later a triumphant Megan appeared waving a blue mesh cat carrier and a small litter box. She crossed the street and handed the items to Akram who tenderly placed the kitten into the carrier along with the towel he had used to make her a bed on the floor. Instantly Lana curled up and began purring in contentment.

"That was a brilliant idea, Megan. Thank you so much."

It was a short drive to the foot of the main pier. At the water's edge, the yellow and white Café Gumpfer looked like the top of a lighthouse sliced off and set on the ground. Its superb coffee was outmatched only by the cheesecake, something Megan had not allowed herself to eat for several decades.

"The only thing missing is little Lana," sighed Dee contentedly.

"Ah, but I wouldn't dare let her out of the carrier here." Akram had not told his guests the real reason he had brought the kitten along. To leave her alone at *Trosthaus*, should Rolf von Putbus attempt another of his dirty tricks, would be unthinkable. The few times Akram had checked his smartphone app, the surveillance camera had so far not been triggered. The lodge entry was undisturbed and unvisited.

"It is time now to show you Rügen's amazing chalk cliffs," he announced as they rose to return to the van.

"Do you think it will involve much walking?" Dee whispered to Megan.

"I have no idea. Let's wait and find out."

"We shall not take time to see the ones around here. I am going to drive you up north beyond Sassnitz to the most famous one, the *Königsstuhl*—the King's Chair."

Megan was excited and even Dee felt pleasure at the prospect of seeing the mighty chalk cliffs.

"*Caspar David Friedrich, here we come!*"

95

Nordhausen police chief Karl Schneider had assembled a formidable force of squad cars. The police helicopter was already in the air over the Arab complex and had reported no visible activity below.

Reininger was in the lead car with the police chief, and the caravan silently sped up the curving mountain road that led to the remarkable complex built on a promontory overlooking the Zorge River.

A set of great iron gates confronted them. They were closed and no one was in the adjacent guard house. Thanks to aerial recognizance, Schneider had come prepared for just such a situation and within minutes his officers had melted down the locks and opened the gates. Silently the squad cars parked in front of what looked like a palace entrance. One police vehicle drove down the road that led along the side of the complex to the back of the property to cut off any attempt to escape.

Oddly enough the front door was not locked and Schneider's crew quickly entered the building, pistols drawn. Not a person was in sight. No staff, no prince. The men ran though what seemed to be a large reception room leading to a music room filled with strange instruments. The two bedrooms were empty, as were the dining room and kitchen. Reininger noticed that the music room opened onto a covered courtyard.

"This way!" he commanded, running toward the courtyard. Nothing. The courtyard was empty, as was the one beyond it. But this second one gave onto an open courtyard above which the helicopter was now hovering.

"Something peculiar down below," the pilot reported. "Looks like a man lying on his back."

Schneider and Reininger ran into the open courtyard and stopped abruptly. There, in one corner at the foot of a granite tombstone, lay a man dressed in a long white kurta, his head covered by a once white kufi. He had shot himself in the head. A pistol lay next to his outstretched right arm and dried blood covered his face. Fragments of his brain were spattered over the ground.

"Horrible. Looks as if he knew we were coming," surmised Schneider.

"Look here!" Reininger squatted down next to the tombstone.

"He's attached a cardboard to it and there's a text printed in Arabic and German."

Schneider bent down and read the inscription in German out loud.

"By this act of self-obliteration I, Prince Yusri Pahlavi, formerly of Iran, do hereby attempt to right the wrongs I have committed: theft and murder. May Allah forgive me and restore the glory of my family name."

"Murder? He's confessed to *murder*," Reininger said grimly. "Let's see where that makeshift graveyard is that Jarir mentioned."

"Start taking photos and dust the pistol for prints," Schneider commanded his men as he and Reininger hurried back to the front door and outside.

"Quick! Drive us down that side road to the back," the police chief ordered the waiting officer at the wheel of the lead car.

They piled in and roared down the road, reaching the back of the complex in fewer than three minutes. Two officers were standing next to their squad car pointing and taking photographs. They had already lifted prints off the wheelbarrow as well as a shovel propped up against a small ditch digger by the graves.

"We've found the graves!" yelled one of the men. "There are six in all. One of them is empty. Another is partially pulled apart."

That matched the information Jarir had given Reininger.

"Start uncovering the graves," the police chief commanded.

Ten minutes later Schneider and his Berlin colleague were staring at the result.

Five cadavers lay in five shallow graves.

96

"I follow them now," Hamzah el-Hashem was reporting to his employer Dief al-Almamie, as he drove behind Akram's van at a discreet distance.

"And you say he shows no sign of remorse, of renouncing godless Germany and returning to the homeland?"

"No. I have given him the two warnings. He cares not. You will not believe! Today he is out showing *tourists* around Rügen!"

"Then I consult with my imam and call you back."

"And I continue to keep him in sight."

Ten minutes later Akram's father called el-Hashem back. He gave him a final command.

97

Jarir had suddenly taken a turn for the worse. He was suffering convulsions. Realizing that his end was near and that Allah would judge him, he beckoned nurse Gerhardt to bend in closer to him so he could whisper in her ear. She had been very kind to him, contacting his wife Maryam and transmitting messages back and forth between them.

Now he had a final message. But it was not for Maryam. It was for Officer Reininger.

"Tell him I know where are Belgian statues."

"Belgian statues?"

"Yes. He know what I mean. They in Berlin. Warehouse of Kadeem Tawfeek."

Those were Jarir's final words.

98

Akram's guests were in awe. The car park entrance to the Königsstuhl stood in an ancient woodland. The birch trees were so thick they seemed impenetrable. But several paths had been cut through them. One could either take a look at the small museum inside the visitor center or take the major path right away to the edge of the cliffs that stood almost 400 feet above the shore.

"Why are they called 'King's Chair'? Megan asked.

"Legend has it that whoever climbs to the top of the highest cliff will rule the island," Akram answered.

"How long a walk do you think it might be?" Dee whispered to Megan trepidatiously.

"Not to worry," said Akram, overhearing her question. "It's just a bit of a walk from here through the forest to the three platforms. And platform number two has the best viewpoint, Monika and I discovered."

"Gosh, I didn't realize it would be this windy," said Megan, buttoning up the neck of her blouse and sorely wishing she had a scarf with her. Akram locked up the van with a questioning Lana in her carrier. He then went around to the back of the van and locked a padlock on the rear doors.

"Now look here," he commanded his guests. "See how I hide the keys deep in the exhaust pipe. I do not want to carry them with me to the cliffs. Just in case I fall off," he grinned.

They set out on their hike. Soon there were several other people on the trail behind them, including some young men wearing identical soccer shirts and a few tourists with noisy children.

Following Akram's suggestion, however, they skipped walking out to the first platform, whereas most of the tourists, including the children, turned off the path to do so. When they arrived at the turnoff for platform number two only one other person was behind them.

"Now it's not too far for you to walk, Frau Dee, if you just take it slowly."

"That's the only way I *can* take it, is slowly," laughed Dee.

They came within sight of the high viewpoint from which the jagged cliffs dropped dramatically.

A welcome bench stood some forty feet from the drop-off and Dee sank down upon it with a sigh of relief.

"We'll go on ahead, if you don't mind," Megan said.

"Of course, dear, I'll join you just as soon as I catch my breath." Chin propped on her cane handle, Dee concentrated on breathing deeply.

Both Megan and Akram became silent as they stood at the railing at the edge of the great precipice. The sea was the bluest, the cliffs were the whitest, and the forest was the greenest one could ever hope to see. It was magical, and Megan felt she was in the middle of a Friedrich painting.

"This was my Monika's favorite view. Here I feel serene and so very close to her," murmured Akram, turning to Megan with a wistful smile.

At that very moment, from out of nowhere, a man wearing a hoodie lunged with both arms extended toward Akram. The force of the impact knocked Akram forward over the guardrail and off the precipice. He fell some 400 feet, his body banging time and again against the jagged face of the cliff.

Horrified, and rooted to the spot, Megan desperately shouted Akram's name over and over again as he fell. It seemed like an eternity. Then, sobbing, she wheeled to scream at the man who had committed such a horrendous act. But he was on the run and she saw only his back.

From her bench Dee heard the commotion, heard Megan shouting Akram's name, then saw a man in blue jeans and a hoodie running toward her. He would pass just by where she was sitting.

"Stop him, stop him!" Megan yelled, running after the bolting man.

Instinctively, using all her strength, Dee thrust the head of her cane straight into the man's path. He tripped over it just as the group of tourists from the first platform appeared.

"Stop him, stop him!" Dee shouted.

"*He just killed a man,*" yelled Megan, running toward them.

Several members of the soccer team ran toward the fleeing man and tackled him to the ground. One of the team members yanked his hood back revealing the face of the man who was shouting in a foreign language. He had dark skin, a shock of black hair, and a black beard. Megan realized he was sputtering in Arabic.

99

"Where do you think the servants could be?" Reininger asked Nord-hausen's police chief after they had gone back to the house.

"Perhaps they're in cahoots with their master and have fled the scene?"

"It's very strange that no one is here and that the front door was unlocked."

Schneider's cellphone rang and he answered it, listened to the caller for a few minutes, then hung up. He turned to Reininger.

"Speak of the devil. One of our squad cars just intercepted a man on a bicycle approaching the complex. When asked why he was coming up here he said he worked for the prince. Said his name is Wafiyy."

"Wafiyy? That's the name Jarir gave me at the hospital yesterday. He said it was Wafiyy who shot him and his assistant Nadeem."

Schneider immediately dialed back the officer who had called him.

"Hold that Wafiyy man and place him under arrest. Take him back to the station and get his fingerprints. I think we have a matching set here."

100

The park guards took over the job of subduing the struggling man who had been accused of murder. Of pushing a tourist off the Königsstuhl in plain sight of a fellow tourist. A little while later the Sassnitz police arrived, attentively took down Megan's eyewitness account, and procured a statement from Dee as well. They also questioned the soccer players who had tackled the fleeing culprit, then prepared to cart the surly man off to jail. They had to read him his rights in English as the man did not speak German, only Arabic and English. A deserted black truck down at the car park was identified as having been rented by the Arab.

Overwhelmed by the events Megan and Dee sat in the visitor center collecting their thoughts and waiting for their heart beats to return to normal.

"What do we do now?" asked Dee finally.

"First I need to call Officer Reininger of the Berlin police with the news of Akram's murder."

"Of course. You should give him a first-hand account of what's happened."

"Then we can return to *Trosthaus* I think, collect our things, pick up our own car, and drive back to the mainland. The police didn't say we needed to stay here on the island. They said that our statements were good enough to secure a murder indictment against the man. One of them told me that, if needed, they could interview me further on closed circuit TV."

"Well at least we have poor Akram's van as transportation. And...oh my god, we also have Lana! What will become of her?"

"One thing at a time, I guess. We can try to find an animal shelter on the mainland."

"Or perhaps take her back to America with us," conjectured Dee, who had been a cat owner all her adult life. Her latest cat, Toby, had died just recently.

"Well, perhaps," Megan said, picturing to herself possible problems with the hotels they would be staying in at Greifswald and Moritzburg, to say nothing of the Frankfurt airport on their way back to the States.

They finally felt recovered enough to return to Akram's van. Megan retrieved the keys from the exhaust pipe and opened up the front. Lana was sound asleep in her carrier on the floor and only barely acknowledged their appearance.

"Oh, this is so sad. Entering Akram's van without his being with us. Such a tragedy," said Megan.

Lana must have heard the agitation in her voice. She began pacing the carrier and meowing loudly.

"I think she needs some water," said Dee.

They looked in the side compartments of the two-door van and under the dashboard. There was nothing.

"Maybe there are some water bottles in the back," Megan said, getting out of the driver's seat and walking around to the rear of the van. She unlocked the padlock and raised up the hinged lift gate. No bottles. She reached back as far as she could toward what looked like a large ice chest with wheels, partially covered by a blanket. Yes, of course. That would be the place to keep water bottles. She could not quite reach it so she climbed inside the van. Yes, it was a large plastic cooler and the top opened easily. Megan gasped.

Inside was the mother and child sculpture that had been stolen from the Berlin Kollwitz Museum.

101

Perhaps he could work off his anger in the gym, Fromm told himself. A letter of resignation signed by his company's chief engineer had greeted him that morning when he returned to Dorotek after the Megan Crespi debacle. The nerve of that damned, so-called art "scholar"! Questioning his orientation of the Kollwitz drawing. Of course it was a dominatrix scene! That Crespi woman was a puritanical, dried up bitch.

And now this Ferdinand Fehler blow. Imagine! Leaving Dorotek when he, Fromm, needed him most. And without a word of explanation. Just one short legalistic sentence "tendering" his resignation, effective immediately.

He would have to assemble a new team and do so quickly. New lawyer, new chief engineer, new company physician.

Tomorrow he would instruct his chief of staff to begin assembling the credentials of possible candidates. Right now he needed to take out his frustration in the gym. Throwing Fehler's letter across the room—a violent action that triggered a brief coughing spell—he rose from his desk and strode through his wondering secretary's office without a word.

Dorotek's gymnasium was on the ground floor of the building that housed the company cafeteria. As Fromm passed in front of the cafeteria entrance one of his employees emerged and bumped right into him. It was Iliana's patient, Mahdi Kartal.

"Watch where you're going, you idiot!"

A furious Fromm gave the man a violent shove and strode on to the gym.

Coughing violently and still shaking from the unexpected encounter, Mahdi stared after the retreating figure of Dorotek's CEO.

Today will be the day, he vowed to himself. I will get into the back of his auto now. It doesn't matter if I have to wait for hours. Today will be his last day.

Mahdi made the long trek through the factory complex to his locker and took out the Hycodan that Dr. Frankel had given him for cough suppression. It had hydrocodone in it and was extremely effective. He could be concealed in the trunk of Fromm's Mercedes and not have to worry about any telltale coughing. He needed only one more item. His new switchblade was on the floor at the very back of the locker.

The gym workout had done nothing to improve Fromm's foul mood. He found himself actually hating Dorotek and the factory's asbestos problems—that cursed legacy from Hitler times. There was no point in staying at the office any longer today. Back at his Rügen home, and online, he might find the peace of mind to begin the arduous process of researching likely candidates to replace his three disloyal employees. In order of importance, he needed first, an experienced engineer, then a capable lawyer, and finally, a physician who did not diagnose asbestosis in every patient who had a slight cough. These were the instructions he would give his chief of staff tomorrow, but he could get a start on it at home. He was in no mood to speak to anyone at present.

He tied up a few loose ends on his desk, walked to his car, and roared down the road to his house. It was a small two-story beach house punctured with windows on the attic floor and painted blue with white trim. The house had a pitched roof, and a little balcony over the front door led out from the attic double doors facing the sea. Fromm had converted the attic into his den and it was there that he headed after parking his car to the side of the house on the low growth of heather that ran down to the beach.

From his hiding place in the trunk of Fromm's car, Mahdi felt the vehicle come to a halt and heard the driver's car door slam shut. He would wait a good five minutes before easing open the trunk lid mechanism to peer around. Just to be prepared for all emergencies, he took another sip of his cough suppressant. So far he had not coughed once. Allah was with him.

After five minutes had passed, he slowly raised the trunk lid. The car was parked to the side of a wooden beach house. No one was about. Mahdi slipped out of the trunk and quietly lowered the lid again. He crept toward the back of the house and saw a door with a window on either side. A possible entry point. Mahdi then slipped to the front of the house and peeked around the corner. Two small windows framed the front door. Above the door was a single French door that gave out onto a white wooden balcony. The July evening was still too bright to indicate whether lights were on in any particular area of the house.

Accessing the balcony would be impossible without a ladder. The ground floor windows were too small to crawl through. The only way into the house was either through the front door or the back door.

Which part of the house was Fromm in? Mahdi decided to try the back door to what was obviously a kitchen. He pushed it gingerly but it was locked. He went around to the front door and gave it a tentative push. Soundlessly it swung open. In a mini-second Mahdi was inside, switchblade in his right hand. No one on the ground floor. Silently he mounted the narrow stairway that led to the attic. At the top of the stairs he saw Fromm sitting at a desk in front of an open laptop. The obese man's back was to him.

Mahdi sprinted toward Fromm, switchblade out and open. He stabbed the startled man repeatedly in the neck and in the back. Instead of collapsing, Fromm managed to turn around and face his attacker. Deftly, despite his bulk, he grabbed Mahdi's upraised arm and wrestled him to the floor. Then he lifted the man's head with both hands and banged it on the floor repeatedly until the invader passed out.

Fromm staggered down to the kitchen, found some duct tape, and returned to his den. He bound the man's hands and feet and placed tape over his mouth as well. Straining to regain his breath, Fromm called the Prora police. It was only then he realized he was bleeding profusely. He called for an ambulance.

The police arrived first. They searched the ground floor then ran to the attic where they found two men lying on the floor. One of them was dead; the other unconscious.

102

"I cannot believe Akram would be involved in stealing Kollwitz!"

"I can't either, but here it is. Straight out of the Berlin museum," Megan answered Dee sadly.

"What should we do?"

"Let's get back in the van and sit down, first. When I get my breath back, I want to call Grete Bulliet with the good news. She'll be thrilled to learn that at least *one* stolen Kollwitz is accounted for now.

"Yes. One. That leaves six still to be accounted for. Do you think Akram could be behind all of the thefts?"

"I don't. But I now have to reconsider something his wife said to me when they came up to talk to me after my lecture at the museum."

"Oh? What's that?"

"Well, she introduced herself and Akram as former sculpture students and then, apropos my theme, the 'Unknown Kollwitz,' she asked if I had any idea where the limestone version of *Crouching Mother with Two Children* was. Now in retrospect, and considering what we've just found, that seems like a red flag to me."

"Didn't the TV accounts of her murder mention that she was pregnant?"

"Gosh, you're right. So maybe that's why they were interested in locating it and that's why the Berlin mother with a child in her lap was stolen. A way to match the big event in their own lives."

"But even so, what a terrible thing to do."

"Certainly misguided. But I better not wait any longer to call Grete with the good news."

Megan dialed the Berlin Kollwitz Museum and got through to the director immediately. She told her the strange story of the sculpture's discovery after the murder of Akram. At first Grete was incredulous, then concerned about the sculpture's condition, and finally she wanted to know how soon the museum could have it back.

"Unfortunately we're not returning to Berlin or we could bring it with us," said Megan. "Our flight back home leaves from Frankfurt."

"Then I shall drive up myself to get it. Will you still be at Rügen?"

"No, Grete, our next destination is Greifswald for two nights, and after that we descend upon Moritzburg for my command performance at Marie Schmidt's castle. And from there on to the Frankfurt airport."

"Well, it would certainly be more convenient for me to drive south to Moritzburg rather than up to Greifswald. Have you booked a hotel there?"

"Yes. And since I have been *enjoined* by her highness, the baroness, to come alone to her castle, it would actually be nice for Dee to have some company there. I'll obviously have quite a tale to tell after I see Käthe Schmidt's 'cousin.'"

"Perfect. And which hotel?"

"It's the Hotel Landhaus Moritzburg."

"'Hotel Landhaus? Sounds nice and countryish. Okay, I'll drive down in the museum cargo van and make an overnight reservation there, but for which night, Megan?"

"We're down for two nights in Greifswald, beginning tonight, so day after tomorrow."

"I shall be there. This is such joyous news, Megan. But I'll keep it from the press until the piece is safely back in the museum."

"Right. I didn't want to tell the local police here at Rügen anything about my discovery until I'd spoken with you."

"Oh, *please* do not tell them a thing. God knows, they might sequester the Kollwitz as having something to do with the murder."

"Perhaps it does. Don't worry. I won't tell them a thing."

"You know what, Megan, I think I'll call Laura Forelle. She might like to take a break from Cologne affairs and join me for this happy drive down to Moritzburg.

"Oh, that would be terrific. And she could call her Detective Schauen with the good news. It would be grand to include Laura in this recovery mission. By now we all need some happy Kollwitz news."

"Now, listen, I have to ask you," Grete said. "How *safe* do you think the statue will be just left in your car for two days and nights?"

"At the moment, as I told you, it's still in Akram's van. I haven't had a chance to transfer it to our SUV yet. Haven't even lifted it yet to see how heavy it might be."

"Oh, *please don't*! Do keep it in its cooler container. The sculpture is shellacked plaster, so if the container it's in is plastic you should be able to lift the whole thing without too much trouble. But perhaps you could get someone to help you. Without letting them know what's inside?"

"All right. I'll see what can be done and I promise you, I will be extremely careful. As for leaving it in our vehicle, there's that pull flap in the back; it hides everything. And I think our Greifswald hotel has a garage or at least secure private parking."

"This Kollwitz recovery is a miracle! And leave it to an American to solve the crime."

"That was pure happenstance. And I'm still having trouble thinking of Akram as a criminal. There is so much still to find out. Remember, we were with him right after his wife was murdered. We even *stayed* with the poor man here at Rügen."

"I understand, Megan. But now I want to call Laura and let her know that our missing Kollwitz has been found and ask whether she'd like to join us for the great retrieval."

The two women hung up jovially, promising to meet in two days.

Megan needed to recover. Akram's murder and the discovery of a stolen Kollwitz in his van were too much to absorb emotionally. She took several long sips from the treasured Spiderman thermos she had brought with her from America. It was just the right size for most car cup holders. And the water was doctored, as always, with Dasani drops, the strawberry kiwi flavor.

103

The damage to Fromm's body was extensive. He had been put on IV fluids for shock and bleeding, but along with multiple stab wounds around the shoulders and lower neck his trachea and cervical esophagus had been severely injured. To make sure the lungs had not been compromised the ER doctor at Prora Central Hospital ordered an MRI be performed at once. The results were at once reassuring and sobering.

When the injured man regained consciousness, the physician in charge of his case instructed the waiting policemen to remain outside in the hall while he entered the man's room. He approached his patient, MRI results in hand.

"Herr Fromm. You have suffered multiple stab wounds to your neck and back. Your trachea and upper esophagus are injured. With time and treatment, however, they will heal."

"*Ach*, this is good. I guess being slightly overweight was a good thing in this circumstance."

"You might say so." The doctor did not smile.

"Do the police have the man who attacked me in custody?"

"He is dead of multiple concussions."

"Oh. Well. Serves him right."

"Now, Herr Fromm, these MRI results show something else."

Um?"

"Follow my finger. These large white bulges are pleural plaques. They are bilateral and diffuse. We are looking at an irreversible interstitial fibrosis of your lungs."

"What the hell are you telling me?"

"*You have asbestosis.*"

104

Clear prints had been obtained from both the shovel and the wheelbarrow at *Jamshad*. Schneider had already returned to the Nordhausen police station and Reininger was about to drive back to Berlin when his cellphone rang.

His Cologne colleague's voice was vibrant with excitement.

"Reininger! I've been trying to reach you. They finally gave me your cellphone number. Aren't you in Berlin?"

"No, as a matter of fact, I'm not. I'm down at Nordhausen in Thuringia, just finishing up a big case. In fact I was about to call *you*. I've got some fantastic news."

"So do I."

"Okay, tell me yours, Schauen. Then I'll tell you mine."

"We've just learned that the Kollwitz statue stolen from your Berlin museum has been recovered."

"What?"

"The director of the Kollwitz museum here in Cologne called me with the good news a few minutes ago. Grete Bulliet of the Berlin Kollwitz had just called her. An American scholar I met a few days ago in Cologne concerning the Belgian Kollwitz theft, Megan Crespi, had discovered Kollwitz's stolen mother and child statue in the back of a friend's van. It was hidden in an ice cooler."

"Did the friend have an explanation?"

"That's the other thing. He had been murdered just an hour earlier; pushed off the Königsstuhl cliffs at Rügen. The killer was caught and detained. And, get this. Both men were Arabs."

"Wow. You are not going to believe my news now."

"Tell me."

"Well, you have one Kollwitz statue. But I have six Kollwitz *thieves*!"

Reininger described the cascading series of events at Nordhausen— Jarir's deathbed confession, the incidence of an Arab prince's suicide beside the Levy gravestone inside his palatial home, the finding of not only the Levy gravestone there, but also the two Cologne grieving parents sculptures. And then the discovery of five bodies buried in the back of the complex, all of them Muslim men from Berlin, all of them implicated by the dying Jarir as being involved in both the Belgian and the Cologne Kollwitz thefts. Jarir had also revealed the whereabouts of the Belgian statues as being in a Berlin warehouse.

After he got over his astonishment, Schauen summed things up succinctly.

"So we have six recovered statues out of seven stolen and six identified thieves."

"Whew!" Reininger said. "Identifying the last thief should be easy."

"Maybe not," said the more experienced Schauen. "Maybe not."

105

Prora police were in active cooperation with their colleagues at Stralsund. The death of a Dorotek employee, Mahdi Kartal, at the hands of Dorotek CEO Reinhold Fromm in "self defense" had raised red flags on both Rügen and the mainland. Now a total of *three* Turkish Muslims with a connection to Dorotek were dead. Substantiating this was the anonymous note received by Stralsund police concerning the families killed in the Knieper Nord explosions. It claimed that the two family heads, both former employees of Dorotek, were in the process of lawsuits against the company.

Things were less clear about the Arab man who had been pushed off the Königsstuhl cliffs by another Arab. Neither one had any connection with Dorotek as far as the Stralsund *Kripo*—police involved in major crimes— could tell. The murdered man, Akram al-Aljamie, an Iraqi, was a resident of Berlin according to an American friend who witnessed the crime. No information was yet forthcoming concerning the Arab man who had pushed al-Aljamie over the cliff. Not even his nationality. He had no identification on him. The rental firm from which he had leased a truck had him down as Hamzah el-Hashem with an unverifiable Berlin address.

Although Dorotek's CEO was still in the hospital, Prora police had managed to obtain a warrant allowing them to examine calls made to and from his office. One of the recurring calls over the past few days was from a single caller: a male who left the same message each time he called. "Where is my payment for latest services rendered? You saw confirmation of their outcome on television. Now I want my fee."

That was enough to initiate a criminal investigation of Herr Reinhold Fromm.

106

"I'm glad you didn't tell the Prora police about having found the Kollwitz sculpture in Akram's van." Dee was thinking about Megan's animated conversation with the director of the Berlin Kollwitz Museum.

"Yes. It could definitely have delayed our getting back to the mainland, and maybe even just returning to *Trosthaus* to pick up our belongings. Anyway, Grete will tell the Berlin police and they'll contact the Prora officers. Complicated, but we've got to get out of here and on to Greifswald."

Megan drove them back to *Trosthaus* the way they had come. Akram's key chain had the keys to the car and house. It took the two friends fewer than fifteen minutes to pack up their belongings.

"What do you think we should do about the things in the refrigerator?" Dee asked.

"Just leave them. We have more important things to worry about," said Megan almost crossly. She was hoping they would not have to ask for help in moving the Kollwitz from Akram's van to their SUV.

It was as though Dee read her thoughts.

"Thank goodness you rented an SUV and not a sedan."

They walked over to the two vehicles. When she had parked at *Trosthaus*, Megan had positioned the van so that its back faced the rear of the SUV. Now she raised both lids, then pulled the cooler with the Kollwitz sculpture to the edge of the van. Bending her knees, she slowly picked up the precious cargo. It wasn't easy but it was doable. After the transfer had been made Megan sat down, panting but relieved. She couldn't help thinking about how the house that was supposed to represent consolation—*Trosthaus*—had been deprived of living up to its name.

They locked the door, placed Lana on the floor in her carrier behind the driver's seat and took off in silence. Neither one of them looked back at the lodge as they drove away. When they reached the two bridges to the mainland they opted for the new one again. No taste or time for loitering now. They wanted to get to Greifswald. Dee deserved this delayed reward. And, for her sake, Megan so hoped they might find traces of the Totebusch family there.

Once on the highway their glum mood began to lift. After all, they were on the way not only to Totebusch territory, but also to Caspar David Friedrich's hometown.

" I could have reserved us a picturesque hotel down by the fishing piers, Dee, but I thought we'd get enough of picturesqueness just by being in the ancient red-brick town. So I reserved a modern one near the University. It's called Europa Hotel Greifswald and, drum roll please, it has its own parking area."

"What good luck, considering we want to park in a place where the Kollwitz will be safe."

"Let's hope so. I'm certainly not going to cart it up to our room."

"The blanket you put over the cooler totally hides it from view, so that's good."

"By the way, another advantage of staying in this hotel is that it's near the Caspar-David-Friedrich-Zentrum. That center wasn't here when I was in Greifswald before, so I'm very eager to see it."

"Does the name 'Greifswald' mean anything, Megan?"

"Yes. Kind of scary. It means 'Hawks Wood.'"

For the rest of the short drive to Greifswald, which was only twenty-two miles from Stralsund, Dee and Megan played their competitive music identification game. As they crossed over the River Ryck bridge to the old town, they spotted an ancient draw bridge on their right. It was closed to cars.

"That's quite a river," said Dee, looking at the rippling water beneath them.

"You can see why Greifswald became an important commerce town. The open sea is only about three miles downriver and the river flows right into the sea, so there's easy access to all the Baltic ports. In fact, along with

Stralsund, Greifswald became important enough to belong to the Hanseatic League."

They were now on the Domgasse looking for the turnoff to their hotel.

"There it is." Dee pointed to a cross street named Hans-Belmier-Strasse.

It was six o'clock and after they had parked in the hotel's private lot, checked in, and put out the litter box for patient little Lana, they collapsed on their beds for awhile.

"Are you beginning to feel hungry?" Megan asked finally.

"I was just about to ask you the same thing."

"I'll look at our restaurant choices."

Megan opened her laptop and ran down a long list. None of them spoke to her except for one. And it was not a very Greifswald sort of restaurant.

"Hey, Dee, feel like having a pizza for a change?"

"That's a great idea. I'm a bit tired of fish, I have to confess."

"Then let's try this one. It's called La Piazza and has good ratings—number eleven of sixty-nine restaurants listed here. And it's very near. Right on the Market Square."

After a very satisfying four-cheese and spinach pizza with some König Pilsener to go with it, they walked around the square a bit, admiring the ancient red brick buildings so typical of this part of Germany, and inspecting the modern cafés. On the way back to the hotel Megan checked the rear of their SUV. Kollwitz was safe and sound.

Now all they needed was a good night's sleep and they would be ready for ancestry research and Friedrich masterpieces tomorrow.

107

Grete Bulliet had called Officer Reininger immediately after receiving Megan's good news. On his way back to Berlin from Nordhausen and the shocking series of discoveries there, he was only too happy to hear Bulliet's report that the missing Levy tombstone had been found. He filled her in on the stunning finds at Nordhausen.

When Bulliet mentioned she would be driving to Moritzburg in two days to pick up the Kollwitz statue and that there was a small memorial house there with some of the artist's works on loan, Reininger was struck by a thought. Interesting that no thefts from there had been reported. He wondered, in the light of six Kollwitz thefts having to do with death motifs, whether the Moritzburg Kollwitz Haus might be a sitting target for theft if it also contained any death-related images. At any rate it could prove most interesting to drive down there and have a look around. Instinct told him that somehow it would be.

108

Rahel Rückgabe looked fondly at her son Abraham and his dear friend Iliana Frankel as they sat drinking wine outdoors at their favorite restaurant, the Taverna Hellas in Wedding. The slim, dignified woman with short swirls of gray hair and warm brown eyes sat facing busy Utrechter Strasse and her adorable, talented son. He was trying to convince Iliana to join him as his partner at the clinic. Rahel felt great affection for the woman and she loved to hear her Viennese accent when she talked. Right now the young physician was not talking but listening to Abraham's earnest arguments as to why she should come work with him now that she no longer spent "half her life" commuting to and from Rügen.

Finally Iliana spoke and her considered answer was pretty much what Abraham had thought it would be.

"Listen, Abraham, dearest. I've been a practicing GP for the past dozen years in spite of the fact that my specialty at med school was ob/gyn, as you well know. Your Muslim men would never accept me, nor am I qualified to do the surgery you do."

"I pretty much thought you would give me those arguments," Abraham smiled. He had a surprise in store for her and for his mother.

"And what would you say if I told you that I intend to *change* the focus of my clinic—our clinic, I hope—to one of general practice? No more restoration surgery."

Both women's eyes opened large in astonishment. Then they understood. The vandalism of Abraham's clinic and the malicious sign calling him a betrayer of Muslims had changed his thinking. He wanted to serve, but serve a different clientele.

"I still want to help the Muslim community here in Wedding, but from now on attend to the general health of both the men *and* the women. What better combination could there be than the two of us, Iliana? And of course I would change the name of the clinic to reflect our services: OB/GYN and General Surgery."

"That puts an entirely different light on things," admitted Iliana.

"I love the idea! The two of you working together." Frau Rückgabe was beaming.

There was a poignant silence. Then Abraham heard himself saying out loud what he had been thinking for months.

"I want you to be my partner in medicine and also in life."

"You mean, move from Prenzlauer Berg to Wedding?"

"I mean I would like you to *marry* me."

Rahel clapped her hands.

"Yes, yes! And it's about time!"

Iliana looked at Abraham.

"And I would like to marry you."

She raised her wine glass.

"Here's to the woman who brought us together Käthe!"

109

By noon the next day Megan and Dee had visited the major churches of Greifswald. They began with the enormous city cathedral of St. Nicholas, built in the red brick gothic style so characteristic of the region. Someone was practicing the organ when they entered and the music provided a nice background for scanning the faded walls and looking at some of the tomb inscriptions. Megan almost paid the three Euros to climb up to the observation terrace with its panoramic view of the city, but thought better of it as they had three local churches to check out, including the castle-like Marienkirche, also called by the locals "dicke Marie"—"fat Mary."

But all three of the churches turned out to be disappointing as there were only interior tombs and wall plaques honoring various local dignitaries. No outdoor cemeteries to explore. But they had not wanted to take any chances by not exploring the churches.

Dee was disappointed but not surprised. In the crowded Old Town there was hardly room for outdoor cemeteries. However, they had a plan B that seemed more promising. Outside the city was the very large Alte Friedhof—the Old Cemetery. After lunch at a café on the Market Square and a quick check on Lana, they picked up their vehicle—Kollwitz still undisturbed, thankfully—and drove out of town to the cemetery. They entered the main entrance and parked. A small office stood to their left.

When they entered, a pleasant looking woman stood up from her desk and greeted them.

"Good afternoon. Can I help you?"

"Good afternoon. Yes. We have come from America in search of my friend's ancestor. May I give you the surname we are searching for and see if it might be in your records?"

"You can give me the name, but we haven't had any grave records since the Russian and Communist takeover after the war. When East Germany rejoined the West there was an effort to find them but without success."

"No records at all?"

"Not really. Just area and lot dimensions of the different sections of the cemetery. What name are you searching for?"

"Totebusch." Dee had understood enough to realize what the woman was asking.

"Totebusch. Yes, a good north German name. But I don't have any records that could help us, unfortunately."

"We're certainly willing to try to find any possible Totebusch graves, but could you at least give us an idea of what section we should begin searching?"

"Do you have any death dates available?"

Megan translated for Dee.

"Tell her we're looking for anything between eighteen-fifty and nineteen-hundred."

After taking in this information, the helpful woman gave them a small map of the cemetery and circled an area to the northwest not far from where they were standing.

"Can you believe how ragged these lines of gravestones are?" Dee asked after they had been walking up and down long, irregular rows of graves for some thirty minutes. The markers on most of them were no longer erect but sagging forward.

"This is an impossible task, Dee."

The area was over a half mile in diameter and they had only covered the first five rows.

"I know, I know." Dee was limping badly now, leaning on her cane.

"Why don't you rest awhile and I'll go on ahead."

"No. I have a better idea."

"Oh?"

"We give up."

"Aw, that's not good."

"But this is madness, Megan. No grave records and it's even hard to read the years on these neglected gravestones, much less the names."

Discouraged, they gave up and hiked slowly back to the car.

"How about a little lie-down?" Megan's suggestion was gratefully received and they drove back to the hotel. Dee went sound asleep immediately. Megan looked up the new Friedrich Center online. She was dying to visit it. It had some of the artist's greatest paintings, including one of his famous views of the cloister ruins at Eldena, outside Greifswald on the road toward the beaches. Would it be insensitive, when Dee awoke, to suggest they visit the

Center? It was near enough to walk to and perhaps the artworks would take Dee's mind off their failed mission. Or was Megan just being selfish?

Before she could answer her own question, her friend woke up. She looked rested.

"It's too early for dinner. So what would you like to do now?" she asked.

Megan suggested they visit the new Friedrich Center and Dee welcomed the idea.

Twenty minutes later they were in the modern complex, absorbing the great Romantic artist's nature philosophy in paint. A large picture held Dee's attention. It was Friedrich's commanding view of the gothic ruins at Eldena. She said nothing but Megan could see the painting seemed to hold meaning for her.

After they had gotten their fill of Friedrich, the question of dinner came up.

"Would you like to eat down by the old harbor? The whole thing has been preserved as an outdoor museum with lots of old ships at anchor."

"Hm. That means a fish dinner doesn't it?"

Megan nodded assent.

"You know what? After that pizza last night and after so many fish dinners, I feel like having a *steak*."

"Ha! Good. I'll look up restaurants when we're back at the hotel."

True to her word, Megan did some research and finally found one steakhouse in the area. Jack and Richies Steakhouse. But it was outside Greifswald. The accompanying map showed it was on the road to the Baltic shoreline. Then Megan spotted something else on the same road, quite near the steakhouse. The ruins of Eldena.

"Dee, I know you particularly liked the Eldena ruins painting we just saw. How would you like to see the real thing? It's on our way to the steakhouse."

"Yes. That would be intriguing. Perhaps we could even *feel* what Friedrich was feeling when he painted them."

Somewhat buoyed in spirit by the idea, they fed Lana, got in the SUV and drove to Eldena. The ruins were clearly marked and it was fascinating to walk around the remains of what had once been part of the cloister church. Eager to photograph the ensemble from a different angle, Megan walked to the far north edge of the ruins bordered by a dense forest. There something caught her attention. It was another ruin, that of a small church, neo-gothic in style and abandoned. All around it were small gravestones—it was what Germans would have called a Waldfriedhof—a forest cemetery. She walked over to examine the headstones and could not believe what she saw.

There, on the largest one, was engraved the name Jacob Totebusch.

An inscription below the name gave his dates, 1823–1876, and his identification: "Beloved founder and first minister of the New Lutheran Church of Eldena."

"Dee!" Megan shouted. "Come here to where I'm standing. *I've found you a Totebusch!*"

As she elatedly watched her friend hobble toward her, Megan could not help but think of the extraordinary analogy: Kollwitz's grandfather Julius Rupp had also founded a small Protestant sect, the first Free Evangelical Congregation of Königsberg.

110

Dorotek's former lawyer Wilhelm Schlau had come to a major decision. Ferdinand Fehler, the company's chief engineer, had called him that morning concerning TV coverage of the terrible accident to the government van which fell some 300 feet into the water from Rügen's old bridge. An accident? Really?

Yes, Schlau had also seen it. And he had been sorely tempted to express his opinion to the local police that it was no accident. Now Fehler was telling him that he had just contacted the Department of Labor to testify that asbestos was indeed present in Fromm's factory. They would be sending out a second team to gather evidence immediately. His next calls had been to both the Stralsund and Rügen police concerning his suspicions about the bridge "accident."

Vitalized by the engineer's bold actions, lawyer Schlau decided to contact the Labor Department as well. He would give them the names of all Dorotek employees, former and present, with asbestosis-related lawsuits pending against the company.

CEO Fromm's days were numbered, he told himself. He could not have known how right he was.

111

Dee was still euphoric over the Totebusch gravestone discovery as she and Megan left Greifswald the next morning for the 250-mile drive via the A 10 and A 13 down to Moritzburg, their final stop. To pass time, she suggested a new musical identification game of tapping out the first-line rhythms of songs, but just as they began, Megan's iPhone rang.

It was Grete Bulliet, bursting with news of police discoveries at Nordhausen. Officer Reininger had just phoned to tell her they'd found Cologne's *Grieving Parents* and the Levy tombstone, plus information that the Belgian *Grieving Parents* were hidden in a Berlin warehouse. In addition, the man responsible for the thefts—an Arab prince who had furnished his palatial Nordhausen residence with three of the sculptures—had committed suicide.

"So we'll never even know his motive," Grete concluded angrily.

"Never mind that. This is absolutely marvelous news," said Megan. "Counting the one I found in Akarm's van, we now have *six* of the seven missing Kollwitz sculptures. And all within the space of forty-eight hours."

After Grete hung up, Dee and Megan excitedly discussed the new events and found themselves trying to figure out what on earth the reason for the robberies could have been. It was only at the midway rest stop near Lübben that they gave up wondering what had motivated the bizarre, what Megan called the granite necrophiliac.

112

"And I've squeezed in a honeymoon trip for us while the clinic is being refitted and our new sign installed," said Abraham. He and Iliana had married quietly that morning in a civil service and were ready to go to work as soon as the clinic was ready.

"Oh, I really don't think we should leave the country right now, dear. Not with all the things our moving to a new apartment entails. It's a good thing you like cats, by the way."

"Yes, I like cats, especially your brave little Uli. *And*, we can take him with us on our honeymoon if you like."

"How can that be?'

"I checked. The hotel I've booked for tonight accepts pets."

"And just where might that be?"

"Right here in Germany. Moritzburg. Our Käthe's final dwelling place."

"Oh, what a marvelous idea, Abraham."

"And we can visit the little Kollwitz Museum there. I've wanted to see it forever. Just never had the time."

"A first for both of us. And to see her final home. What a wonderful honeymoon, Abraham. Uli, did you hear that? We're going on a trip today."

113

Officer Reininger pulled into Moritzburg at five in the afternoon that day. Too late to visit the Kollwitz Museum there, he would treat himself to a nice hotel and be at the museum when it opened the next morning. On the Schlossallee he passed an atmospheric building surrounded by trees and greenery, the Hotel Landhaus Moritzburg. Perfect. He checked in and enjoyed an excellent dinner in the hotel restaurant. It was packed with diners but the atmosphere was cozy and quiet. He had brought a biography of Kollwitz with him to dinner and planned to spend the evening reading it. Especially thought-provoking for him was a dictum she had written concerning her art: "All my work hides within it *life itself*, and it is with life that I contend through my work."

Had Officer Reininger been less engrossed in his Kollwitz biography and more attentive to the presence of fellow diners, he might have noticed the three women seated a few tables away. He had recently made the acquaintance of one of them in Berlin.

Dee, Grete Bulliet, director of the Berlin Kollwitz Museum, and Laura Forelle, director of the Cologne Kollwitz Museum, were discussing the adventure Megan Crespi must be having that very moment up at the baroness's castle.

"'Dinner at seven. *Come alone*,' she'd commanded," giggled Dee.

"She does have a superb Kollwitz graphic collection, I've heard," said Grete.

"Does she have any of the artist's sculptural work?" Dee wanted to know.

"Don't think so," answered Laura. "I have heard nothing to indicate that. She is only interested in the graphics, I do believe."

"What about the Kollwitz Memorial Haus here in Moritzburg. Is it very large?"

"No, it is quite small," Laura answered. "There is an entry hall downstairs and a couple of rooms where some of her prints are exhibited. She lived one flight up, had a modest living room with a little balcony and a small bedroom. There she found comfort in rereading Goethe time and again."

"I guess she preferred literature to music, then?"

"Don't get me wrong. She did love certain musical classics, but reading was her preference." Laura assured Dee.

Dee was thinking she would never be able to choose between the two.

"Isn't it funny," Grete said, "here I thought the Kollwitz statue was going to be really difficult to transfer from your SUV to our museum van, but Megan and I were able to lift it easily enough."

"We're just happy it's no longer our responsibility. And that it will be going back to its rightful home," smiled Dee.

In the capacious dining room yet another conversation concerning Kollwitz was taking place. Sitting at the far end of the room by a large window overlooking the verdant lawn, Abraham and Iliana were planning their day tomorrow.

"First thing, of course, we'll go to the Kollwitz Museum. And then in the afternoon we shall tour the magnificent castle of the prince who offered the artist lodgings in town."

Abraham had their itinerary all plotted out, including visiting some of the nearby lakes where the Brücke artists from Berlin such as Ernst Ludwig Kirchner and Erich Heckel, painted during the summers. Their jarring Expressionist colors and jagged motifs were contemporaneous with Kollwitz's work in the first two decades of the twentieth-century and, although very different in purpose and subject matter, they had one thing in common: reduction of form. Abraham thought that viewing the sites where they painted might be refreshing for Iliana after the gravitas of Kollwitz and the bulging baroque brawn of the Moritzburg castle.

114

When are we ever going to eat dinner, Megan was wondering to herself. Her hostess, "Käthe Kollwitz's cousin thrice removed," Marie Schmidt, locally known as the baroness, had sent her butler Ingelbert out to meet Megan's Uber when she arrived at Kastell Königfeis promptly at seven. But now it was after eight and the baroness was still pointing out her esoteric readings of the enormous array of Kollwitz prints hung on the walls of an endless corridor in her castle. With a well-practiced motion she rolled her wheelchair from one print to the next.

They came to the cycle *A Weavers Revolt*. The baroness owned a first edition of the series, all of them signed by the artist. As she held forth concerning the initial image, Megan's eyes wandered along the cycle sequence and came to a startled stop at *March of the Weavers*.

This was the identical signed print Megan had seen at the Ensor House Museum in Belgium! The one which had subsequently been stolen by an unknown thief, possibly working for the shady Berlin gallery owner Lukas Zamann. Megan recognized the uniqueness of this specific signature she was now gazing at because she had noticed, when the print was still at the Ensor museum, the peculiar placement of the dot above the "i" in the name Kollwitz. Uncharacteristically, it blended with the "t" next to it rather than standing alone as it did in the prints to either side.

The missing Kollwitz print was in the Baroness's collection.

Trying to mask her agitation, Megan merely murmured in the affirmative when the Baroness abruptly interrupted her own endless commentary with the question "Are you hungry?"

"Where is that butler?" the baroness asked impatiently, looking around.

"I'll have to go find that lazy man. Please, you go ahead, Frau Professor. The dining room is straight ahead. I shall join you there."

As soon as the baroness's wheelchair was out of sight Megan pulled her iPhone out of her jacket pocket and dialed Dee. She had time for only five words when Dee answered.

"*Kollwitz from Ensor's house here!*"

"Dinner is served," announced the chastised butler who appeared at the far end of the hall wheeling his irritated employer toward Megan.

Back at the Hotel Landhaus another dinner was over and as Reininger stood up from his meal, Kollwitz biography tucked under his arm, he noticed and recognized the woman at a nearby table. It was Grete Bulliet of the Berlin Kollwitz Museum. She was listening intently to what one of her tablemates was telling her. He walked over to their table.

"I see that two of us Kollwitz fans are here in Moritzburg this evening," he said to her, smiling.

"*Ach, wunderbar!* It is you, Officer Reininger. You could not have appeared at a more timely moment. My friends here, excuse me, this is Frau Whally, and this is Doktor Laura Forelle, director of the Cologne Kollwitz Museum, and this, ladies, is Officer Reininger of the Berlin police. Frau Wally has just received a call from her friend Professor Crespi. She phoned from Kastell Königfeis here in Moritzburg where she is having dinner with the baroness of the castle. She only had time for a few words but it was enough. A stolen Kollwitz print is in the castle."

At that moment Reininger knew his spontaneous sortie to Moritzburg had not been in vain. Now to find legal cause to show up at the castle door.

Once they were seated at the long dining table, the baroness stopped talking about her Kollwitz graphics and asked Megan to enlarge upon the subjects she had covered in her lecture on the "unknown Kollwitz." In between bites of pork, peas, and twice baked potatoes, Megan obliged. But her heart was pounding. All she could do was hope Dee would convey her brief message to Grete Bulliet.

As a peach compote was being served, a noise was heard coming from the corridor. The voices of two men were accelerating in volume. The butler burst into the dining room.

"I tried to stop him," he apologized. He was followed into the room by a prepossessing-looking man with dark hair and beard.

"Frau Baronin, it is here! I am unpacking it in the hall," cried Luka Zamann. "I knew you would want to see it immediately."

Livid, the baroness wheeled back from the table and toward him.

"This is the worst possible time you could have chosen to deliver my object," she hissed.

She looked at Megan.

"You will excuse me for a minute. You will remain seated, I ask you."

With tremendous force the angry woman rolled her wheelchair out of the dining room and into the hall, a chastised Zamann close behind.

There in front of her, in its just opened crate, was the Kollwitz family tombstone.

Far from obeying her hostess's injunction, Megan slipped out of her chair and peeked down the corridor. She saw what the baroness saw and gasped out loud. Both Zamann and the baroness heard the sound and turned toward her.

"Get that woman back into the dining room and hold her down," the baroness commanded her butler.

Eager to get back into his irate employer's good graces, the butler pushed Megan through the door and attempted to force her onto a chair. He stood above her and pushed down on her shoulders with his hands. Megan lowered her chin deep into her chest, then with all her might suddenly jerked her head upward, knocking the man's chin up, and dislocating his jaw. He fell backward to the floor, writhing in pain.

Megan just had time to grab her iPhone and call Dee again.

"*Help! Send police!*"

115

Dee's iPhone had rung again and, seeing it was Megan, she put the phone on speaker and held it up so Grete, Laura, and the policeman could hear. Only three words were uttered, but they were enough to galvanize Reininger.

Ignoring the woman with the cane, he turned to the museum directors.

"Quick!" he commanded. "Follow me to my car. Show me where Kastell Königfeis is! We've got to get there fast!"

Grateful not to be a hindrance to the running trio, but fearful for her friend's safety, Dee looked wildly around the dining room. Seated at a window table across the room she saw a man and a woman she recognized. They had been in line waiting to talk to Megan after her Berlin lecture. In fact, they were the physician couple with some Kollwitz journals Megan had visited the very next day. Now, noticing her agitation, they were gazing at her with professional concern.

Dee raised her hand and beckoned them to come to her. They did so immediately and automatically Iliana took the anxious old woman's pulse. Her heart rate was far too elevated. As they tried to soothe her, Dee gasped out to them what had happened and that a policeman and two museum directors were on their way to the baroness's castle as she spoke.

Everyone in the dining room was looking at them, wondering what had occurred to cause two dinner guests to leave so abruptly and two other dinner guests to rise abruptly and walk over to an elderly woman.

"Let's get away from these staring eyes and sit in the lounge," Iliana suggested.

With a solicitous physician on either side of her, Dee limped slowly out of the dining room. She already felt a little better, especially after she sank down onto one of the comfortable leather chairs in the hotel lounge.

"Is there anything we can do for you while we wait to hear from the policeman or Professor Crespi?" Abraham asked.

"This may sound absurd, but I would like to have my kitten with me. She's in our hotel room in her carrier."

"I understand," said Iliana. "Give me your key and I'll go get her for you."

Some minutes later Iliana appeared with not one but two cat carriers.

"We also have a cat with us. His name is Uli. I thought he might like to make your cat's acquaintance." What Iliana really wanted to do was distract and soothe the anxious woman while they waited for news.

The ploy worked. The carriers had been set side by side at Dee's feet and there had hardly been time to introduce Lana to Uli before both felines pressed up against each other through the mesh sides of their carriers and began purring loudly. It was a ménage-a-deux made in heaven, Dee pronounced with wonderment, her heart rate now almost back to normal.

Reininger's insistent banging on the castle entry door brought results. A wary butler opened the door a crack and asked who was there.

"Police," shouted Reininger, pushing the door wide open and entering. Grete Bulliet and Laura Forelle boldly followed him into the vestibule. Running off it to one side was a long corridor hung with Kollwitz prints.

"You have a Professor Megan Crespi here. We need to see her immediately."

"That name is unknown to me."

"Ingelbert! Who is there?" The baroness's voice could be heard all the way down the long hall as she vigorously rolled her wheelchair toward them.

"It is the police, madam."

A wild scuffle could be heard behind her. A man's voice commanded someone to be still. More sounds of desperate wrestling came from the dining room. A woman's muffled cry rang out.

Reininger ran down the hall past an open crate, and, pushing the baroness's cumbersome wheelchair to one side, entered the dining room. Grete and Laura were hot on his heels. There, crouched over on the floor, her hands tied to her feet with a man's leather belt, and a napkin stuffed into her mouth, was Megan Crespi. Her muffled cries came at an even more urgent rate once she saw the policeman.

"Down on the floor, hands and feet spread," Reininger commanded the man standing over her, pulling out his pistol. Whimpering, Lukas Zamann obeyed.

"And you, stay right there," Grete Bulliet warned the angry baroness. Then she ran over to Megan, pulled out the napkin from her mouth and began loosening the belt that held her hands and feet together.

"Thank god you came!" Megan gasped. "They were about to transfer me to Zamann's car trunk and you would never have found me."

"Frau Whally put your second call on speaker and so we were able to hear you whisper for help," said Laura.

"If I hadn't had my iPhone with me who knows what might have happened."

Reininger slipped out his cellphone and summoned the local Moritzburg police.

Though still shaken, Megan got down to business.

"Grete, the Kollwitz print that was stolen from the Ensor House Museum in Ostend is hanging on the corridor wall halfway down to your right. It's *March of the Weavers*, a first edition and signed."

"And the crate in the hall?" Reininger asked. Neither he nor the two museum directors had stopped to examine the contents when they rushed down the hall to Megan's aid.

"What's in it solves the last of the Kollwitz robberies," said Megan triumphantly. "*It is the Kollwitz family tombstone.*"

"Oh, good god, woman," Laura angrily addressed the baroness. "Robbing the Ensor House to complete your collection with a first edition, signed print from the *Weavers Revolt*, I can understand, reprehensible as it is. But why would you want Kollwitz's *tombstone*?"

"Because, as Käthe Schmidt's cousin, I wanted to protect it from the thieves who were stealing her sculptures right and left. I knew the tombstone would be next on their list, since all the pieces they stole were connected with death." A righteous expression colored an otherwise stonelike face.

"You actually believe you were doing the art world a service, don't you?" Megan confronted her insane hostess.

"Of course I do. And if you hadn't interferred, the tombstone would have been safely installed here, away from common thugs."

Megan drew herself up to her full height and looked straight into the deranged woman's eyes.

"It is *you*, Marie Schmidt, who are the common thug."

Back at the Hotel Landhaus an hour later, a happy group of seven was assembled in the building's cozy lounge. Drinks had been ordered all around and the conversation was spirited. The Kollwitz calamities were over. All seven stolen sculptures were now accounted for, and a signed Kollwitz print stolen from the Ensor House/Museum in Belgium had been retrieved.

Two of the women present, Iliana and Dee, were patting the cats on their laps. The loud, vibrant sound of double purring amused the group.

"How I wish Lana could be with Uli more often," Iliana murmured. "It's obvious they have fallen in love."

Dee looked at Lana, then Uli, then Megan, who read her thoughts and nodded encouragingly. Dee turned to Iliana.

"You know, we are driving to the Frankfurt airport tomorrow for our return flight to the States. It's going to be rather difficult traveling with a kitty." Megan nodded again.

"Iliana, if you agree, we would like to give you little Lana as a playmate for your Uli."

Reininger, Grete, and Laura all smiled.

"Oh yes!" cried Iliana, looking at Abraham. He smiled a yes.

"What a perfect honeymoon."

Megan lifted her glass and addressed the happy group.

"*To Kollwitz!*"

"*To Kollwitz.*"

Readers Guide

1. Two monumental granite statues by Käthe Kollwitz—the *Grieving Parents*—have been stolen from the German Soldiers Cemetery near Diksmide in Belgium. *What could the motive have been for such an unlikely theft?*

2. While retired art history professor Megan Crespi is visiting Dr. Laura Forelle, director of the Kollwitz Museum in Cologne, a call comes in that two major Kollwitz statues have been stolen. Forelle persuades Crespi, who is traveling with her old friend Dee Totebusch Whally on a Totebusch ancestor hunt in Germany, to go to the Belgian cemetery and investigate. What do the two women also discuss at length?

3. Famed surgeon Dr. Abraham Rückgabe has two passions. One is his clinic, perhaps the most successful one in private hands in Berlin. The other is an intriguing collection of thirty-six diaries he inherited from his grandmother. What is his clinic's specialty and who are its main clients? Does the physician's surname reflect this? And whose diaries are in his possession?

4. At Prora, on the island of Rügen off the Pomeranian coast in the Baltic Sea, an urgent meeting is taking place. Reinhold Fromm, CEO and founder of Dorotek, one of Germany's largest manufacturers, was in heated discussion with his company's physician, Dr. Iliana Frankel, his company lawyer, Wilhelm Schlau and his chief engineer, Ferdinand Fehler. It has come to light that the Dorotek factory buildings, originally built by Hitler as a resort for loyal German workers, contain asbestos and thirteen lawsuits have been filed against Dorotek. What is Fromm's plan to combat the legal proceedings against Dorotek?

5. As Dr. Iliana Frankel walks to her train to Berlin, the sight of tired workers shuffling into and out of the Prora train station looked just like a poignant image she had recently seen in the window of a small Berlin Antiquariat near her Prenzlauer Allee train stop. What does she decide to do?

6. In the summer of 1943, finally persuaded by her anxious family to flee the intensified bombing raids over Berlin, seventy-five year-old Käthe Kollwitz reluctantly abandoned her Wörther Platz home of fifty years and moved to Nordhausen. Did she remain there? Also in 1943, a special complex had been built there by the Nazis. What was its purpose?

Some three-quarters of a century later, Yusri Pahlavi, youngest son of the late Shah of Iran, has just finished building a vast compound outside Nordheim which he named *Jamshad*—shining river—overlooking the Zorge River. Do we know yet why an Arab prince has elected to construct a royal residence in the heart of ancient Thuringia?

7. Megan and Dee drive from Cologne to Belgium and have lunch in Ghent. For what is Ghent famous? And what holds Megan's attention when regarding it? At the cemetery where the Kollwitz statues have been stolen something catches Megan's eye. What does she find and what new light on the theft does it suggest?

8. Iliana Frankel acquires the drawing she had seen in an antique store's window in her Berlin neighborhood. When she removes it from its mat she finds a handwritten title "Workers Going Home at the Lehrter Railroad Station." There is also an illegible signature and a date, 1897. What is at the site of the former Lehrter Bahnhof now? Why does Iliana call her colleague Abraham Rückgabe?

9. Twenty-one-year-old Akram al-Aljamie, only son of the famous Iraqi archaeologist Dief al-Aljamie, has persuaded his father to let him study sculpture in Berlin. During his final year at the university he meets the mysterious, head-turning beauty, Monika von Putbus. They are instantly attracted to each other and begin meeting in the Neue Wache, not far from where they both live. There, they admire a large bronze sculpture showing a mourning mother holding her dead son in her arms. The artist, unknown to either of them, is Käthe Kollwitz. Where and why is the sculpture placed inside the Neue Wache? Months after Akram and Monika have become gentle lovers, she reveals her aristocratic family heritage to him and decides to show him the Putbus sites on Rügen island. At the family's romantic hunting lodge she reveals a secret to Akram. What is the secret and why does it prompt Akram's proposal of marriage? What is *Trosthaus* and what unusual object does it contain? What are their wedding gifts to each other? And what is Akram's one worry?

10. Kadeem Tawfeek was not enjoying the good fortune of his surname. His precious misbahah was missing. He accuses his helper Jarir of stealing it. What does he do then? After Abraham Rückgabe arrives at Iliana Frankel's apartment what happens?

11. Megan and Dee leave the Kollwitz cemetery and decide to make the thirty-minute drive to Belgian artist James Ensor's house/museum in Ostend, where they will spend the night. How does Megan characterize the intensity of Ensor's work as compared with that of Kollwitz?

12. Akram telephones his father with the news of his marriage to a German woman and his conversion to her Catholic faith. What is the father's reaction?

13. At his Dorotek office on Rügen, Reinhold Fromm is fretting over yet another lawsuit claiming asbestos poisoning caused by his company. Going over the names of the complainants he realizes suddenly that four of them are Muslim Turks. What happens next?

14. Abraham and Iliana arrive at his apartment and she is amazed by all the Kollwitz prints she sees on his walls. He explains the difference between lithography and etching and talks her through the six prints of *The Weavers Revolt*. What are the themes of the six images?

15. At his Nordhausen complex, Iranian prince Yusri Pahlavi contemplates his family's tragic past. How did a chance encounter with two works of art three years earlier affect what he has done now? How does his mother fit into his actions?

16. Megan and Dee visit the Ensor house/museum and spot a first edition Kollwitz print from *A Weavers Revolt* on the wall. What does the museum caretaker tell them about it? Why do they decide to spend one more night in Ostend?

17. "*Give me twenty-four hours and I can rectify this.*" Kadeem and Jarir have unloaded the two Kollwitz statues at *Jamshad* and Yusri Pahlavi sees the scar damage on the sides of the statues. He is furious. What is the daring plan Kadeem comes up with?

18. Akram and Monika visit the Kollwitz Museum in Berlin, heading immediately for the top floor where the sculptures are. What are the themes of the sculptures and what happens when they leave the museum?

19. Iliana is at Abraham's flat again to learn more about the life of Kollwitz. He reads aloud to her from one of the journals and shows her one of the "Secreta" drawings the artist kept to the end of her life. The intimate drawings are the result of an extramarital affair Kollwitz had had with a charismatic Jewish activist from Vienna. Why does Iliana's face go white when Abraham tells her the man's name?

20. Kaheem and three new helpers carry out a daring theft of the two Kollwitz *Grieving Parents* replicas from Cologne's Alt St. Alban Church ruins. How do they accomplish this difficult operation?

21. On the way back to Cologne, Megan learns from Laura Forelle that two more Kollwitz statues have been stolen. Megan confers with Laura and Detective Herbert Schauen. They go over a list of possible suspects, including one whom Schauen describes as a "Wagnerian Jew." Why and who are the other suspects? And what unlikely news do they learn when Schauen's cellphone rings?

22. In Stralsund on the mainland two apartments of two Muslim Turkish families suing Dorotek are simultaneously blown apart. What is the apparent cause?

23. Akram and Monika visit Akram's sculpture studio. What new project is Akram working on and why? Is there anything of which the two are unaware?

24. On their way from Cologne to Berlin Megan persuades Dee to drive by way of Weimar so they can visit the "Wagnerian Jew" suspect. Are they successful?

25. Dorotek CEO Fromm receives the call he has been waiting for. What is it?

26. Akram's studio has been ransacked. What has been destroyed? And who is Rolf von Putbus?

27. Iliana picks up a newspaper as she exits the Prora station. The headline causes her to confer with Dorotek company lawyer Wilhelm Schau. What does she learn and why does she decide to visit her patient Mahdi Kartal that evening? What terrible news does she have to give him?

28. When Megan and Dee meet Siegfried Schocken and his wife Sandra, they are both wearing mourning bands. Why and what do the Schockens show them that is such a shock?

29. What is Mahdi Kartal's reaction when Iliana gives him his medical diagnosis? And what is his diagnosis?

30. Jarir Uthman, fired by Kadeem, has not yet returned the rental boom truck. After reading about a second set of Kollwitz statues being stolen from Cologne, why does he research the artist and what daring plan springs to mind?

31. As Megan and Dee drive from Weimar to Berlin they are almost in a traffic accident. Do we have any idea who might have jumped the median?

32. After Fromm receives news concerning the lawsuits initiated against Dorotek by Muslim Turk families, he sees two items in the day's newspaper that make him decide to go to Berlin the next day. What are they and why do they hold such interest for him?

33. Abraham and Iliana are discussing how the migrant situation in Germany is changing things for physicians. What are some of the new problems? And what uplifting event do they both look forward to the following evening?

34. One Totebusch has been found by Megan and Dee in Berlin's "Socialist" cemetery. They also look at the honor graves of Rosa Luxemburg and Karl Liebknecht. Who were they? And what happens when they head for the Kollwitz family grave?

35. Jarir and his helper Nadeem sell an unusual artwork they have brought down from Berlin to Yusri Pahlavi at his palatial Nordhausen complex. What is it and why does the gatekeeper who looks like a bulldog smile when Pahlavi instructs him to proceed, after the artwork's placement, "as you did with Kadeem and his men"?

36. The Kollwitz sculptures stolen now number six. What obsession does Megan think the robber or robbers must have? And which two famous paintings by Caspar David Friedrich does she show Dee? What are their multiple meanings?

37. In Berlin, Fromm visits the Galerie Zamann. What particular drawings does he study intently? And what sort of a name is "Zamann"?

38. Instead of repairing the sculpture damage at his studio, Akram is motivated to give a new sculpture to Monika in celebration of the child they will soon have. What does he have in mind and where is the sculpture site?

39. Megan and Dee are heartily greeted by Grete Bulliet, director of the Berlin Kollwitz Museum, when they arrive for the lecture Megan will give on "The Unknown Kollwitz." What do they do before Megan speaks? Do we know the true identity of the lady in the wheelchair attending Megan's lecture, Marie Schmidt?

40. Akram and pregnant Monika arrive for Megan's lecture at the Kollwitz museum quite early. Why does he leave Monika downstairs and where does he go? Among the characters we have met so far, which ones attend Megan's lecture? And who is the woman wearing a hijab who leaves immediately afterward? A long line has formed to talk to Megan after her lecture with its great surprise. What is that surprise and who are some of the people in that line?

41. At Nordhausen, Wafiyy, the gatekeeper who looks like a bulldog, smiles at his master. Prince Pahlavi is actually complimenting him on a job well done. What is that job?

42. How is it that Megan knows the real identity of the mysterious Marie Schmidt? Will they meet?

43. Hudun, wife of Kadeem Tawfeek speaks for the wives of all four missing men to the elders of the Muslim Brotherhood. From which Berlin district are the missing men and why is that so meaningful?

44. After dinner together at a Wedding restaurant the next evening, Megan, Abraham, and Iliana retire to his apartment and he reads aloud various entries from Kollwitz's journals. What are the themes that interest Megan and what advice does she give Abraham concerning the diaries?

45. During that same night Akram carries out his bold plan to "borrow" something. What does he do and is he successful?

46. On their last day in Berlin, Megan and Dee decide to visit the Kollwitzplatz. Why? Akram, also visiting the square with Monika, recognizes Megan and invites her to join them at their picnic table. What dreadful thing happens when, just as they reach Monika, a woman wearing a hijab jumps out from the hedge behind them?

47. Megan and Dee drive a devastated Akram back to his apartment. He beseeches them to stay with him at *Trosthaus,* as they are all leaving for Rügen the next morning.

48. Arriving at *Trosthaus* the next morning, Akram discovers that someone has boarded up the entry door and placed a sign on it. What does the sign say? And who does Akram think might have left it? A high whining sound brings Akram to the door and he is faced by a little wounded kitten. What does this signify for him and what does he do?

49. Fromm receives an unannounced visit from Emil Schnüffler, a Department of Labor inspector who announces he will be conducting an immediate investigation of the Dorotek factory. Why?

50. Akram's vengeful father replaces his female agent with a male one, Hamzah el-Hashem. What are his instructions?

51. Yusri Pahlavi is blissful. He is about to join his chauffeur for the three-hour drive to the Frankfurt airport to pick up his mother—a meeting he has been looking forward to for three years. What has he planned for her?

52. Abraham's clinic has been vandalized, its front windows hacked to pieces and a sign has been left bearing a hateful accusation. What does the sign say?

53. Fromm desperately confers with Dorotek's lawyer, engineer, and physician on how to deflect government investigation of his factory. Why is the government investigating Dorotek? What happens when Iliana refuses to help Fromm? And what does Fromm do next?

54. Shot in the heart, Jarir regains consciousness. Where is he? Later he is found by a passing motorcyclist on the outskirts of Nordhausen and rushed to the ER. What are his chances for recovery.

55. The conversation between reunited mother and son ranges widely as they are driven back from the Frankfurt airport to Yusri's compound at Nordhausen. When a newspaper falls from her purse, she shows him an "outrageous" illustrated account of the spate of thefts of sculptures by a woman artist named Kollwitz. Yusri feels his blood suddenly run cold. What does he do?

56. Akram serves an Arab meal to his guests at *Trosthaus*, Megan and Dee. They look at the night sky through the Bresser telescope under his tutelage. A threatening call comes through for Akram. What is the horrifying message?

57. Jarir seems to be recovering against all odds and his wife in Berlin is notified. She in turn calls Officer Reininger. What does he resolve to do immediately and why?

58. Yusri's mother Farah is greatly impressed by the palatial complex he has built at Nordhausen. What does he propose to her? And what does she discover after taking a nap? How does she react?

59. Jarir's sickbed confession to Reininger galvanizes him to ask for help from the local Nordhausen police. What did Jarir say?

60. Akram is aghast to realize *Trosthaus* is being watched. He connects a surveillance camera to an app on his smartphone but it does not catch what occurs during the night as he and his guests sleep. What happens?

61. Yusri's mother confronts him about what she has discovered, tells him he is no longer her son, and commands that his chauffeur drive her back to the Frankfurt airport immediately. What has she discovered that would lead to such drastic actions?

62. Iliana is enjoying being home on weekdays with her cat Uli. But she is worried about Abraham and the vandalizing of his clinic. As for Abraham, an appealing idea has come to him. What is it?

64. Trying to blot Monika's murder out of his mind, Akram gives his guests a tour of Rügen after Megan's meeting with Fromm in the morning. What does the CEO of Dorotek show Megan in the privacy of his home? What does she discover about it that angers him so much, he commands her to leave?

65. Yusri, after a sleepless night, is devastated by his mother's denunciation. He dismisses his staff for the day and weeps. Then, filled with purpose, he strides to the open courtyard containing the artworks his mother discovered. Can we guess what he will do next?

66. After lunch and dessert in Sassnitz, Akram drives his two American guests—his "angels sent by Monika"—to the great white cliffs Friedrich painted at Königsstuhl. His father's agent reports that Akram is so heedless of the warnings he has been issued that he is actually showing *tourists* around Rügen! What does Akram's father instruct his agent to do?

67. The Nordhausen police, having obtained their search warrant, raid Yusri Pahlavi's complex. What do they find in the open courtyard? And what dreadful discovery do they make at the back of the complex?

68. Looking out from the Königsstuhl with Megan, Akram is suddenly rushed by a man wearing a hoodie. What happens next? And how is Dee involved? Returning to Akram's van what unbelievable discovery does Megan make?

69. In his upstairs study Fromm is stabbed in the neck and back by his revenge-seeking employee Mahdi. Why s the man seeking revenge? What happens to him? And ironically to Fromm? Is it of his own doing?

70. Cologne detective Schauen calls Berlin officer Reininger and both have stunning news to tell the other. What is the news? And how does it leave one thief and one statue still to be discovered?

71. Travelling with the little kitten Lana, Megan and Dee arrive in Greifswald to hunt down Totebusch graves the next day. They have no luck at the churches in town nor at the Old Cemetery just outside the city. But as they turn off to see the motif Friedrich painted at the cloister ruins of Eldena, Megan makes an extraordinary find. What is it?

72. Megan and Dee play musical quiz games as they drive with their adopted kitten Lana the 250 miles south from Greifswald to Moritzburg .Grete Bulliet will also drive down to Moritzburg, site of the house where Kollwitz died. Why? Laura Forelle will also come from Cologne to be in on things and Officer Reininger decides to drive to the city as well. Again, why all this convergence on tiny Moritzburg?

73. After a civil wedding, Abraham and Iliana take a honeymoon trip with her cat Uli to Moritzburg. Why?

74. At the idyllic Hotel Landhaus Moritzburg, a diverse group of people are dining. They all have connections to Kollwitz. Who are they? And where is Megan?.

75. Megan is in the middle of a delayed dinner at Marie Schmidt's castle when the owner of Galerie Zamann arrives with a delivery. He is uncrating it in her picture corridor. Marie is furious at the poor timing, and Megan catches a glimpse at what is in the crate. She manages a call to Dee. What does she say to her? What dramatic events happen next?

After the denouement, a group of seven Kollwitz fans celebrate at the Landhaus, toasting the artist. Who are they and what are they celebrating? What is the new future awaiting the furry felines, Lana and Uli?

www.ingramcontent.com/pod-product-compliance
Lightning Source LLC
Chambersburg PA
CBHW020433030726
47495CB00006B/1787